Water Signs

Water Signs

A Story of Love and Renewal

Daria Anne DiGiovanni

Cover design by Kia Heavey

Book layout by Logotecture

ISBN: 978-0996653176

To Mom and Dad, it's impossible to thank you adequately for everything you've done, from loving me unconditionally to raising me in a stable household, where you instilled traditional values and taught your children to celebrate and embrace life. I could not have asked for better parents or role models.

And to Mark, Ralph, Paul and Carolyn, thanks for all of the wonderful memories of growing up, and for your continued support and encouragement. A special thank you to Ralph, for showing me that anything is possible with faith, hard work and determination.

For all of my loved ones who've gone on to a better life, especially Aunt Marie, Uncle Merle, Aunt Em, Uncle Al, and Nanny—you are always close in heart.

For all of my wonderful friends old and new—thanks for always being there for me! And to my cousin, Annie, my very first reader and constant champion throughout the writing process, thank you for all of the feedback and the late-night IM sessions! Finally, this dedication would not be complete without a very special thank you to the men and women of the United States Military, who protect and defend our freedom all over the world. God bless you!

Five Star Reviews for Water Signs

This book is definitely a must-read.

"Water Signs was one of those rare books I had to force myself to put down because it was such an engaging, refreshing read. I enjoyed the fact that the story was set around the Jersey shore as I am a Jersey girl myself. But what truly kept me reading was that Daria put so much life into her characters! Their personalities, personal convictions, and sense of family were so palpable that every time I read a page, it was like coming home to friends. The story kept me hooked all the way through, allowing me to experience Ken and Maddy's life journeys along with them right on to the very end." – *Amazon Reviewer*

Finally, a truly great American romantic novel.

"Daria is in love with romance and thank God for it! She writes her tale of love, life's struggles, and dreams. To read such a wonderful novel in today's world of cynics, it is truly a breath of fresh air. This story is a refreshing theme in our present society. It reminds me of those great films of the 1930s with Ronald Coleman and Greer Garson or even Errol Flynn and Olivia de Havilland. We need more romance in all our lives and Daria seems to live this in her writings! If this is her very first book, she will have a wonderful career as a writer promoting good old American values that made this country great. When men were real men with honor and courage and their women were strong, and they inspired their men to greatness." – *Jack Marino, Filmmaker*

A book of love and HOPE.

"Daria is such a brilliant writer that you actually feel like you are living the story with the main character. I was so engrossed in this book, that there were times I had forgotten that I was sitting in my bedroom! This book is an excellent escape from one's daily routine. I was always a slow reader, but let me tell you, I read through this book so fast, I even surprised myself!

"Never did I ever feel like I could relate to a character as much as I could relate to this one. I could not believe how much Madeline's life paralleled mine. It kept me wanting to read on. I can count AT LEAST five similar situations that the character and myself have been through. It blew me away." – *Nancy Di Mare*

One of those rare books that makes you want to meet the characters in person.

"Yes, they are that real. It is beautifully written with passion for our country and romance. It is one of those books that is just like a good movie, where you hate to see it end. Speaking of more...please Daria, write the sequel as we are left sitting on the edge our seats wanting more. Madeline Rose and her charming husband Kenny will enrich your lives with their love for each other. Yes, a perfect romance does exist." – *Anni*

A compelling story.

"Her descriptions draw you in, creating, as a good book should, a movie in your mind. The underlying themes of family and, most importantly, love, make this a compelling story. Daria is an amazing writer and her use of music to set the time and tone really gave me the sense of being there watching these events unfold." **– author/poet Kender MacGowen**

Contents

Foreword

Almost eight years have passed since the publication of *Water Signs: A Story of Love and Renewal*. The real-life story surrounding the evolution of this contemporary romance is a novel unto itself, one I've shared in a plethora of posts on my blog, DariaDiGiovanni.com. The condensed version goes something like this:

In January of 2008, I accompanied my dear friend Theresa (on whom the character of Elyse is based) on our annual New Year's excursion to a local psychic named Ann – a woman who is as kind and funny as she is gifted – in Lantana Florida. She'd been recommended to me by a former co-worker back in 2001, and I'd been stopping in to see her at least once per year ever since. I should also mention that in spite of my previous lifelong fear of all things paranormal, a legitimate psychic had finally rid me of the menace of panic and anxiety disorder back in 1997 (an event Madeline experiences in *Water Signs*, which is nearly 100% true to life to the extent that I could fully remember and describe how it went down). That was when I realized that psychic ability was not only valid, it was also a gift which when used properly, could heal and help other people.

The mind is a powerful instrument.

With respect to Ann, having had countless readings with her before, I never expected her to drop a name I'd forced myself to forget nearly fourteen years prior to setting foot in her store that January. In fact, when she spoke his proper, baptismal name out loud I initially thought she was referring to my brother-in-law; to my shock and dismay, she quickly retorted that the name was connected to a love interest and relationship from the past, one that had made a tremendous impact on my life. When the realization of who it was sank in, it blew open floodgates of memory in my mind I thought I'd sealed forever back when it was simply too painful to process everything that had happened. The whole ride home that day I poured my heart out to Theresa, who was perplexed that in our seven years of intimate friendship (during which we'd shared a multitude of secrets), I'd never once uttered this man's name. But the fact is, I had literally forced myself to have amnesia rather than fully experience intense, overwhelming heartbreak.

From that moment on, the memories came at me with such force and ferocity that my only choice was to sit down at my computer and start typing away. Having been a journal-keeper from a young age, I understood the truth of the old axiom "writing is therapy" and figured there had to be a way to fictionalize these events into a novel. If I had to relive every last gut-wrenching detail, I might as well get a book out of it. Funny, I'd conceived the title *Water Signs* back in 1994 (based on this man's and my shared zodiac sign), just before I forced myself to forget all about him and move on with my life. I had even envisioned the cover featuring the Pisces fish swimming around in circles in clear, shallow water, with earth-toned stones adding a koi pond effect (good thing I'm a writer, not an artist!). Once I began typing I was overcome by an unrelenting stream of consciousness: the words poured out effortlessly from head and heart to fingertips and keyboard, and ultimately to computer monitor.

Not once during this four-month process did I ever think about the mechanics of writing a book, e.g. where to end one chapter and begin another; how to employ literary techniques like flashback; or how long to make each chapter. It was as if the entire effort had been divinely ordained and assisted by an angel sitting on my shoulder. Even though at the time I had a corporate job, I wrote constantly: a minimum of four hours every evening and all weekend long. In fact, I couldn't *stop* myself from writing. By the time I finished chapter four, I realized I was going the distance. That's when I recruited a small group of trusted friends and family members to read and critique each chapter as I finished it and sought out the services of a professional designer. This was my first foray into the independent publishing industry, and I had no idea what I was doing; I was just operating on instinct and intuition.

While the entire writing and publishing process had indeed been cathartic on an intensely personal level and allowed me to finally make peace with this part of my past, I had no idea that God's plan was even greater than that. Writing a book offered a credibility I'd never before experienced and opened doors to amazing opportunities. Ultimately, *Water Signs* would lead me to a career in ghostwriting and a business partnership with my amazing friend Lisa Tarves – a talented author, editor, holistic health practitioner, angel intuitive, and radio host. I'd met Lisa over the phone in late 2012 when I contacted her for a holistic health consultation during a visit to my home state of Pennsylvania that Christmas. From the start, I'd felt as if I'd known her my whole life and our friendship took off from there. That spring when I conceived of the idea to create an internet radio network devoted to a variety of topics, I knew I wanted Lisa to host a show on spirituality. When I called her to pitch the idea, she enthusiastically accepted and in March of 2013 the Writestream Radio Network (**www.writestreamradio. com**) began broadcasting with three shows: *Just Believe* with Lisa Tarves, *Military Monday* with John D. Gresham, and *Writestream Tuesday* with Daria Anne.

Our original intent was to showcase independent authors and provide them an opportunity to discuss their books in a professional, on-air setting. For Lisa and me, it also served as a vehicle to promote our individual services – in my case professional writing, ghostwriting, and editing.

By then I was working on Shlomo Attia's ground-breaking novel, *Steps To Salvation* (**www.shlomoattia.wordpress.com**), the project that ignited my ghostwriting career – one that hadn't even occurred to me until he called me up several months after attending a 2009 book signing for *Water Signs* and insisted I was the right person for the job.

Somewhere in the middle of this challenging assignment, I co-authored Lori Colombo-Dunham's memoir *Reflections on the Ring: An Ordinary Woman's Extraordinary Tale of How She Saved Her Marriage and Family*. Simultaneously, I took on a multitude of social media projects, learned how to set up blogs, edited a variety of books and articles, and contributed blog posts for a number of cultural and political sites. From 2009-2013, I also co-hosted *Conservative Republican Forum* on Blog Talk Radio with my friend and activist Steven Rosenblum. When not working, I volunteered on a variety of political campaigns and engaged in other types of citizen activism.

All of these valuable experiences set me up for the success I am experiencing today.

Two years after the birth of the Writestream Radio Network (now broadcasting seven shows per week with the addition of *Ancient Myths and Modern Mysteries* with Von Goodwin; *Love Liberty & Lip Gloss* with Donna Lyons; *Speculative Fiction Cantina* with bestselling author S. Evan Townsend; and *Get Fit Feel Fabulous* with Britt Allen) Lisa suggested we start our own independent publishing company. Thrilled by the idea of working together in a mutually beneficial partnership, I eagerly agreed and on June 1, 2015, we officially launched Writestream Publishing LLC (**www.writestreampublishing.com**).

Based on our previous adventures in independent publishing, we created all-inclusive, affordable packages designed for all indie authors, from newbies to seasoned writers. By this time our individual networking efforts both in real life and on social media had resulted in the discovery of highly creative, trustworthy people we could contract with on everything from book cover design to professional formatting. These folks include innovative designers Kia Heavey (**www.kiaheavey.com**), herself an author of three books and Matt Margolis (**www.logotecture.com**); tech savvy document formatter and author Maureen Miles Bucci (**www.maureenmilesbucci.wordpress.com**), and ghostwriter/musician/artist/author Cherry Tigris (**www.cherrytigris.blogspot.com**).

Within 12 months we'd published ten books with the Writestream Publishing LLC imprint – *The Shattering: The Lewis Chronicles Book One* by Diane Student (**www.dianverse.com**, July 2015); *The Seventh Symbol: A Modern Allegory* by Cynthia Foster (**www.cynthiafosterbooks.com**, September 2015); *Just Believe: Commonsense Spirituality for the 21ˢᵗ Century* by Lisa Tarves (**www. lisatarves.com**, September, 2015); *Miami Breast Cancer Experts: Your Indispensable Guide to Breast Health* by Cindy Papale-Hammontree and Sabrina Hernandez-Cano (**www.miamibreastcancerexperts. com** October 2015); *Un-Selfie-Ish: Not Every Selfie is Selfish* by Cherry Tigris (**www.cherrytigris.blogspot.com**, November 2015); *Honey I'm Fabulous and So Are You!* by Leo Brown with Lisa Tarves (April 2016); *Ego in a Teabag: How Greed, Corruption and Deceit Threaten a Great American Movement* by Ken Crow (April 2016); *Moments of Choice: My Path to Leadership* by Major General Linda L. Singh (May 2016); *The Bittersweet Misadventures: My Own Little Tin Box* by Cata Munoz; and this new edition of *Water Signs: A Story of Love and Renewal* (**www. dariadigiovanni.com**, June 2016). More titles will be forthcoming in late 2016 and early 2017.

It has been a wild, wonderful and sometimes exasperating ride but I wouldn't change a thing. I've grown personally and professionally in ways I never thought possible before my fateful visit to Ann's shop in Lantana Florida that January day in 2008. I cannot wait to see how much our growing company can accomplish in the next 12 months. As for this new edition of *Water Signs*, I haven't altered much from the original – just made some minor changes I felt would enhance the story with the benefit of hindsight. If you haven't read it before, I hope you enjoy it. If you're re-reading it, I hope you'll fall in love with Ken and Maddy all over again.

Blessings,
Daria Anne
www.dariadigiovanni.com
www.writestreampublishing.com
www.writestreamradio.com

Prologue

Saint Ambrose Roman Catholic Church, Deerfield Beach, Florida

Breathtaking arrangements of red and pink roses adorned the raised marble altar, creating a stunning accompaniment to the massive golden crucifix that glittered in the sunlight streaming through dramatic stained glass windows. From a distant choir loft, the stirring serenade of a professional organ filled the room with the romantic notes of Pachelbel's Canon in D Major—the bride's preferred arrangement, prompting the formally attired congregation to rise to their feet with joyful anticipation.

Ken Lockhart stood at attention at the end of a white satin runner, clad in his black tuxedo. Though a grown man of 41, he felt and looked like an exuberant 25-year-old as a permanent, radiant smile lit up his handsome face. While his sparkling blue eyes awaited the vision of his beautiful bride, he shivered with excitement as the electrifying pulses coursed through his body.

Madeline Rose exuded pure femininity and loveliness as she gracefully walked on the arm of her beaming father, a fairytale vision in a scalloped, off-the-shoulder, silk shantung white gown encrusted with iridescent crystal and heavy lace. Her satiny auburn hair was caught back at the crown with a shiny tiara, from which a lightweight, floor-length veil floated behind her. In her arms, she carried a gorgeous bouquet of crimson roses, whose sweet fragrance permeated the air and complemented the scattered petals beneath her feet.

When her deep amber eyes met those of her waiting groom, her heart, and soul flooded with an intense gratitude, borne out of profound wisdom, knowledge and experience. By the grace and mercy of God, here she was finally about to marry her one true love at the end of a long, arduous and oftentimes broken road.

Part 1

South Jersey Shore – Southeastern Pennsylvania
1992

Chapter 1

Carmen and Madeline cruised over the Walt Whitman Bridge, leaving the Philadelphia skyline in the distance as they crossed the Delaware River into New Jersey. A not particularly nice summer was already fading into the twilight of late August, and they were eager to drink up the last rays of warm sunshine and carefree hours at the Shore.

Today the sun, at last, was shining amid white puffy clouds and a clear blue sky, though by the time they'd get to Ocean City it would be too late for bathing suits and body surfing. Not that Carmen was too concerned; she was more excited about meeting up with Mary Ellen and the new guys they were planning to party with in the Atlantic City clubs.

Madeline winced as Carmen sped along the Expressway, occasionally cutting off other cars and eliciting the ire of fellow drivers, some of whom would make their displeasure known with distinctive gestures.

"Hey, Carmen, relax! My parents' house is less than an hour away. We're going to get there in plenty of time. The last thing I need is for you to get pulled over while driving my car!"

In her usual free-spirited fashion, Carmen just laughed. "Don't worry, Maddy, I know how to get out of a ticket. Besides, it's been such a long week I just want to let loose. Here, let's crank up the radio; that'll make you feel better."

She turned up the volume, and Jon Secada's recent hit *Just Another Day (Without You)* blasted through the speakers. "See, your favorite song," she enthused. "Just sit back and enjoy, and leave the driving to me."

"You're crazy!" Madeline exclaimed. Despite her misgivings she knew beyond a doubt if anyone could sweet-talk their way out of a ticket, it was her gal-pal Carmen. A striking woman of Cuban descent, she stood about 5' 9", with a slim figure, long dark hair and an angular face, that, while not textbook beautiful, was alluring and exotic. She stood in stark contrast to Madeline's girl-next-door cuteness; when Carmen strode confidently into a room, men—and women—noticed her. It was hard to believe they were even close to the same age, with Carmen, at 27, just two years older.

"How come your family isn't getting here until tomorrow?" she inquired of Madeline, trying to distract her from her highway antics.

"Oh, I don't know, I think Mom and Dad have a barbeque at some doctor's house in Wayne, and everyone else is busy with wedding plans."

She was referring to her oldest brother Greg, and her sister Lori, who would both exchange vows soon with their respective fiancées. "I'm pretty sure they are all coming down tomorrow to at least get one good beach day out of the weekend. It's been so rainy this year, everyone wants to take advantage of the good weather, even if it means driving up and back in the same day. Before we know it, we'll be dealing with winter cold and ice again. God, I wish it stayed hot here all year round. I dread having to drive around in that crap."

As an outside sales rep for an employment agency, Madeline had had many close calls on the road, thanks to Old Man Winter's nasty blizzards. Unfortunately, in the real world, there was no such thing as a "snow day"; as nice as her boss was, she didn't take kindly to such excuses as "I'm afraid to drive on icy roads." Maddy's overprotective Mom would urge her to stay home anyway as if employers gave their employees special dispensations for having anxious mothers.

"Yeah, I know," Carmen agreed. "Sometimes I think about joining my dad in Miami. Then I remember what a witch he's married to now. Suddenly, winter doesn't seem so bad by comparison."

Madeline laughed.

"I suppose everything's relative. But at least your job doesn't involve being on the road all day. Once you get there, you can stay put until it's time to go home. I don't have that luxury."

"I know," Carmen agreed. "But believe me; I miss my retail days in New York. Macy's was tough, mostly due to a Type-A personality boss, but I met a lot of cool people. Counseling clients at New You Nutrition and Weight Loss isn't exactly a dream job."

"Doesn't it feel good to help someone lose weight?"

"Only the ones who are really serious about it," Carmen replied. "But most clients just make up excuses and waste their money so they can pretend to be doing something about their figure. And the company doesn't care because they're raking in money. Not that the program isn't good, it is. But not even the best weight loss plan on earth will work for someone who isn't committed to it."

"You should tell them you owe your skinny frame to New You, and not an inherited fast metabolism!" Madeline suggested with a giggle.

"Yeah, maybe I should," Carmen agreed. "You look good, Maddy, by the way. I can tell you've lost some weight."

"Yes, I'm trying!" she patted her tummy. "All the walking and swimming I've been doing is paying off. And I'm being really careful about everything I put in my mouth. Just a few more pounds and I'll be all set."

"Now, don't go off the deep end," Carmen warned, suddenly becoming serious. "You are such a pretty girl, and you look great. So just remember that, ok? You are beautiful the way you are right now." Knowing her good friend was still reeling from a painful break-up a few months ago, Carmen wanted this to be a fun weekend for all of them.

"Apparently Jake didn't think so," Madeline noted quietly.

"Jake? Who cares what that dumbass thinks!" Carmen's fiery Latin temper flared. "Who the hell was he to criticize you? It's obvious you weren't dating him for his good looks. He should have been grateful to have a cute girl like you on his arm, instead of acting like a complete jerk and dumping you over the phone. At least be a man and face things head on. What a wuss!"

Madeline grimaced at the recent memory. Jake had been her first boyfriend, though they'd met through a mutual family friend when she was 22. During high school and   college, a lack of self- confidence brought on by a few extra pounds had hindered her from enjoying anything resembling a boyfriend, save for the son of another family friend who thankfully, rescued her from the embarrassment of missing her Senior Prom. In return, she'd done the same for him. But although the boy had been crazy about her, she hadn't returned his feelings. He was just too serious for her, and at 17, she certainly wasn't ready to commit to anything.

"Maddy, did you hear me? Don't invest any more energy in that jerk; he never deserved you in the first place. But there's someone out there who does, and it's about time you started looking for him."

"Yes, Mom!" she answered sarcastically.

"Well, while we're on the subject, I have to confess something."

Uh-oh. Knowing Carmen, it wasn't good.

"What?" she asked defensively, bracing herself for the answer.

"Mary Ellen is trying to get these guys to bring a friend along for you—"

"Aw, Carmen!" she protested.

"Look, I don't even know if the guy will make it, but you have to start somewhere. These men are successful in business, and they're really cute. We'll all just go out and have some fun. It'll be great, you'll see!"

"Do you even *know* anything about them?"

"Well, I know they have some kind of import/export business in Atlantic City. And I think they're from Iran or someplace in the Middle East."

Fabulous.

Maddy's type was definitely the masculine, clean-cut all-American guy either in uniform or out of the pages of Football Digest or GQ; while she had an appreciation for other cultures, she had no desire to date someone from another country—European, Middle Eastern or otherwise. As was her usual reaction to distressing news, she sat in silence.

"C'mon, Mad, don't hate me," Carmen pleaded after a while. "It's just a date!"

"Well, just so you know," she finally piped up, "If the guy doesn't show up, you and Mary Ellen are on your own. I'm not going to be a fifth-wheel. Ok?"

"Ok." Carmen's tone was acquiescing as they rolled along the Atlantic City Expressway.

"Here we are little house!" Madeline chirped to no one in particular as she and Carmen carried their bags into the family room from the back porch.

"I just love this place," Carmen remarked. "It's so cozy and welcoming. And your Mom has done such a great job decorating." She looked around at the nautical-themed décor. Glass lamps filled with shells, bathroom seascapes and "beachy" colors designated the home an enchanting seaside getaway.

"Yeah, she really did," Madeline agreed.

Ocean City was a lovely little family resort; from the time she was a baby, Maddy's family had taken annual vacations here. Although it was a dry town lacking in bars and dance clubs, thanks to its proximity to places like Somers Point, Sea Isle, and Atlantic City, nightlife was never far away. And the benefits of the city's no-alcohol policy were manifested in clean streets, beautiful beaches and well-maintained cottages, duplexes, and colonials. The only thing that could have made it perfect in Maddy's eyes was if somehow summer could've lasted forever here. Alas, old-fashioned appeal notwithstanding, it was still a northeastern town subject to the brutal winds of winter.

The girls headed upstairs to get ready. It was already after 6 p.m., and they were planning to go out to eat before heading to the Key Largo dance club just over the causeway in Somers Point. At the Point Diner a little while later, Madeline watched in awe as Carmen devoured a burger and fries while she carefully stuck to grilled chicken and salad. In spite of her slim figure, Carmen often ate starchy, fattening foods, none of which ever affected her thin frame. It was a luxury Maddy had never enjoyed.

But she looked adorable in a cute white summer outfit consisting of a long, sequined white top over tight leggings, cinched at the waist. She'd pulled her flowing auburn hair back into a loose ponytail, held with a rhinestone clip, and her favorite comfy silver pumps, in anticipation of dancing the night away. Carmen looked stunning in a black linen dress and high-heeled sandals, her dark hair falling straight just below her shoulders. Little did Maddy know at the time, but she would find herself sitting in the very same booth a few hours later, under very different circumstances.

Afterward, they drove around the traffic circle to the club. Although the Shore towns were bustling with late-summer weekend warriors from Philly and its surrounding areas, they'd arrived early enough to find a good parking spot. Mary Ellen was scheduled to meet up with them by nine, followed by their dates shortly thereafter.

The girlfriends entered the tropical-themed bar to upbeat rhythms and ubiquitous strobe lights. Key Largo was arranged on two levels, with staircases leading to cocktail and pool tables, while the main level boasted an ample hardwood dance floor. Already there were a few people showing off their moves to popular hits like the Fine Young Cannibals', *She Drives Me Crazy* and Donna Summer's *This Time I Know It's for Real*.

Having met and worked at a ballroom dance studio a few years prior Carmen and Madeline were familiar with just about every good dance song; they could immediately determine whether the latest American Billboard phenomenon was a "swing," "cha-cha," "hustle," "meringue" or even a "foxtrot" or "waltz" in some rare cases.

They didn't dance right away, instead opting for a drink at the bar. Carmen ordered her customary Chardonnay while Madeline sipped on cranberry juice. Something about nightlife agreed with Carmen; her entire demeanor resonated effervescence and excitement while her eyes artfully surveyed the scene.

"There are a lot of cute guys here, Mad," she happily observed. "This could be a really great night!"

"Don't let your date catch you checking out other men," Madeline playfully admonished, hoping against hope that the third guy wouldn't show up later.

Ken Lockhart patted his face dry as he looked into the mirror. "Not bad," he thought as he studied his choice of attire. At 6'2" and about 195 (give or take a few pounds), he defined the stereotype of the all-American male. His electric blue eyes were twinkly and mischievous while his perfect white smile and thick, curly blond hair were a striking complement to his well-toned muscles. He flexed his arms for a second in the mirror, admiring their rock-solid strength. Then he laughed at his own pretentiousness.

More than anything else, he was a decent guy from Ventnor, who'd overcome serious obstacles to achieve some modest success. Though he was the youngest of four brothers, he was the first to actually own his own place, a cute two-bedroom townhouse in Somers Point, which he'd impeccably furnished. And though his current job at the electric company paid well, it was only a stepping stone to something better— something he knew he'd figure out along the way. His plans also included finding a good woman for marriage, having recently broken up with his high school sweetheart Liz Anne, who ditched him for someone else upon his return from four years of service in the Navy. Well, at least after four long years, I have some good muscle tone, he thought.

He hadn't actually planned to go out to a club tonight; he'd just worked a long shift and wanted nothing more than to kick back on the patio with a cold beer. But his friends had insisted he meet them over at Key Largo to check out some of the Philly girls, and after a little prodding, he'd finally agreed. Ken wore a pair of khaki Dockers and a crisp teal shirt, both of which he'd carefully pressed, and just a hint of Polo, his favorite men's cologne. By any standard, he was a good-looking male. But he was also a deep thinker and an ambitious striver who happened to stay true to his Catholic roots. All except for the part about waiting to be with a woman until marriage. But were there any girls these days that did? He'd yet to run into one.

Ken ran down the stairs and almost crashed into his roommate, an older woman he'd met when he parked cars for the Taj Mahal Casino, just after his return from the Navy. Though he'd moved on to the power plant within a few months, he'd made quite a few friends at the Taj, thanks to his outgoing personality. Kathy was a black-jack dealer whom he'd invited to share living expenses after he closed on his home; he didn't trust a man to keep the place neat. And conveniently, Kathy's long hours kept her out most of the time anyway.

"Oops, sorry Kath!" Ken apologized, putting his arms on her shoulders to prevent a fall.

"Where are you off to in such a hurry?" she quizzed playfully. Her gravelly voice belied her failure to kick the cigarette habit though she honored Ken's rule about only smoking out on the patio.

"I'm meeting the guys over at Key Largo," he replied. "I didn't really feel like it, but they kind of talked me into it."

"Well I think it's great," she remarked. "You've been working so hard and not taking any time out for play. You have to let loose every once in a while. You're a handsome 25-year-old young man with your whole life ahead of you. Get out there and have some fun!"

"I plan to, Kath," he promised, hoping to shake off memories of Liz Anne once and for all.

"Wanna dance?" Carmen asked as she and Madeline tapped their feet to the music on two barstools. Mary Ellen still hadn't arrived, and Carmen was feeling restless. Besides, it was a shame to waste such good music.

"Sure," Maddy complied, following her out to the floor. They joined some other assorted single women in freestyle movement as the deejay kept the upbeat tunes coming. Nearby, Ken's friends offered a dare. He'd been admiring Carmen from the moment she caught his eye. A little skinny, perhaps, but quite attractive. And he was drawn to dark, exotic looks for some reason. Maybe it had something to do with contrast; being a blue-eyed blond, he wanted something different in a woman.

"Will you just go buy that gorgeous brunette a rose," his friend Tony insisted. "You gotta get back in the game here, son!"

Lost in the music, Madeline never saw it coming, but suddenly she looked up to see a hand holding a long-stemmed rose in front of Carmen; a little red devil was attached to it. Then she caught a glimpse of the rose's buyer, and her heart skipped a beat—too bad he was interested in her friend. It seemed so unfair since Carmen already had a date for the evening, unbeknownst to this handsome stranger. But despite her disappointment, Madeline laughed right along as Carmen accepted the gesture and began to dance with her new suitor.

She made her way back to the bar and ran straight into Mary Ellen, a petite blonde who looked like she could use a few good meals. Her face was heavily made up and in her hair she wore a leopard headband that matched her micro-mini skirt and tight knit top. She greeted Madeline with a look of hostility as if someone had gravely injured her.

"What's she doing with that guy?" Mary Ellen demanded.

Hello to you too.

"Oh, he just bought her a rose, and I guess she feels like she should talk to him," she replied nonchalantly.

"Did you know we already have dates coming?" she sniped.

"Yes, I am aware of that, although I'm not sure he is," Maddy joked, nodding her head towards the dance floor. Mary Ellen in a huff was quite an amusing sight.

"Come with me!" She grabbed Madeline by the arm and led her into the Ladies room before Ken and Carmen could make their way back to the bar.

Once inside the safety of the lavatory, Mary Ellen threw a hissy fit.

"You have to get her away from him! Our dates will be here any minute, and I don't want them to catch her with another man!"

"Well, what would you like me to do, *throw* myself at him?"

"Whatever it takes!" she yanked open the door and stalked back into the club. With a roll of her eyes, Madeline followed. Both girls came upon the somewhat entertaining scene of Carmen and Ken fighting as she explained her pre-arranged plans for the evening. The two Iranian guys had shown up and also seemed pleasantly intrigued by the unfolding dialogue. Mary Ellen quickly slipped her arm into her assigned date's arm and whispered something in his ear. Maddy watched as the foursome headed out to the parking lot, with an undeterred Ken close behind.

"If you had a date, you damn well should have told me!" he scolded Carmen.

"Hey, you were the one who took a chance buying me a rose," she answered unapologetically. "I didn't want to be rude, so I danced with you. What's the big deal?"

Tentatively, Maddy interrupted, wondering what was to become of her evening. "Carmen, you guys go to Atlantic City without me. I don't want to go."

"Why not, Mads?"

"I told you I wasn't going to be a fifth wheel," she reminded her. Although she feigned disappointment, she was thrilled that the third guy was MIA; even if she ended up walking the Ocean City boardwalk alone, that was a far better alternative than hanging out with long-haired hippie types from the Middle East.

"Well, it's only ten o'clock. What are you going to do? You're not gonna go *home* are you?"

For whatever reason Ken stood nearby listening to their conversation. He hadn't realized how cute Carmen's friend was, but his pride was still smarting too much to care. As Carmen and Madeline engaged in back and forth dialogue, Mary Ellen, and the guys honked the horn impatiently, while Ken opened the trunk of his car and pulled out another top. As they stared, he unbuttoned and removed his teal shirt, briefly revealing his masculine upper body before pulling the new white tee-shirt over his head.

"Wow, that's a great idea; I've never seen anyone do that!" Maddy complimented.

"Well, I love to dance and it gets hot," Ken explained with a smile and a shrug. *Wow, she's really cute. Why is she hanging out with someone like Carmen?*

"Maddy," Carmen asked again, "What are you going to do?"

Feeling strangely emboldened, she announced, "I'm not going with all of you. I'm staying here and hanging out with Ken!" Then turning to him, she asked softly, "Is that ok with you?"

"Yes, that's fine with me," he affirmed with a high-five, much to Maddy's relief and delight. *Maybe the night's not lost after all,* he surmised. *She seems truly adorable. It won't hurt to spend a few hours getting to know her.*

"Ok, but you better be nice to her," Carmen warned him as she stepped into the back seat of her entourage's Lincoln Continental.

"Bye, Carmen!" Madeline waved. "You have a key, so don't worry about what time it is when you get back."

"Bye, girl. Have fun!"

Madeline walked with Ken back into the noisy club where he immediately strolled up to the bar and ordered a drink. "Can I buy you a beer?" he asked politely.

"Nah, just bottled water, thanks."

"You sure?"

"Uh-huh," she nodded her head. "I'm more of a dancer than a drinker."

"Well I'm afraid I'm a little of both, sweetheart," he declared. He still sounded annoyed; she hoped she wasn't destined for a lonely stroll on the boardwalk after all, watching young families take their kids on rides on Gillian's Fun Deck.

"Nothing wrong with that, Kenny. Or do you prefer Ken?" She recalled that Carmen had initially introduced him with the latter.

"Doesn't matter, I answer to anything," he replied, handing her a cold bottle of Poland Spring water.

"Well, here's to a nice evening!" she offered brightly, toasting his plastic cup of Coors Lite. He looked at her with sparkling blue eyes and smiled.

"Ok, I'll drink to that." Then as if flipping a switch, he resumed his list of grievances against Carmen. "You know I have to say I really don't understand your friend. Why would she lead me on like that when she knew she had a date? And did you see those guys? I mean, I spent four years of my life defending this country from people like that and she and her anorexic friend run off with them?"

"Hey Ken, calm down! I agree with you about Iran, but that doesn't mean those guys are like their crazy government. And you have to know Carmen; she's just a free spirit. No one tells her what to do. I'm just glad they didn't bring a friend for me, 'cause long hair and grunge is definitely unappealing."

"Well she still shouldn't have accepted my rose," he stated emphatically.

Maddy had enough. Cute as he was, she had no desire to talk about Carmen all night; watching Nick-At-Nite at home was sounding better and better. Overcoming her usual hesitance around guys, she spoke up. "Look, Ken, you're here with me now. Either we're gonna dance and have a good time, or I'm outta here! What's it gonna be?"

Pleasantly surprised by her feistiness, he took her by the hand and exclaimed, "Well, let's dance!"

Beneath flashing strobe lights, they moved to the music, with Maddy impressed by his innate sense of rhythm. Despite his big size, Ken was light and agile on his feet, with a moon walk that put even Michael Jackson to shame. It was such a pleasure to come across a good-looking guy who actually liked to dance; that was such a rarity. Jake was always so self-conscious about it, despite Madeline's encouragement and coaching. It took an act of God to get him onto the dance floor. Ken, by contrast, not only went willingly but judging by the look on his face, truly enjoyed every moment of it.

Astonishingly, Maddy felt strangely comfortable and safe with this man though she didn't know why. After all, she hadn't even been his first choice. Yet as he smiled at her from his side of the floor, she was grateful she'd had the courage to speak up. That is, until the inevitable moment when the deejay decided to "slow things down," with Elton John's new hit, *The One*, another song Maddy really loved. *Ok, what to do now, she thought. God, I hope he makes a move. If he doesn't, I'm just gonna—*

But Kenny didn't miss a beat, putting his strong arms around her and swaying slowly with her in time to the beautiful ballad. In his embrace, she felt like a doll, though he definitely noticed some muscle tone on her arms and legs. He also liked the softness of her skin and the way her hair smelled like sweet perfume. Having been used to dating a much smaller man in physical stature, Maddy liked the feel of his big chest as she reached up to hold him. Maybe she was old-fashioned, but the strong, manly type had always been her first preference. Now it seemed she might finally have it.

She closed her eyes as he serenaded her along with Elton on the dance floor. If this was a dream, she hoped it would last forever.

When the song ended, he took her hand and led her outside to the club's adjoining outdoor patio, where a cool summer breeze greeted them. "Where did your friends go?" she asked, wanting to be polite but hoping to hang out with him alone. Ken had acknowledged them on the dance floor, but the overpowering volume of the music and density of the crowd had prevented any introductions.

"I don't know; I'm sure they're doing their thing. I came in my own car," he replied dismissively. Then, looking at her with soulful aquamarine eyes, he announced softly, "I want to know more about you."

But before she could respond, he suddenly took one of her hands in his. He gazed at it adoringly before lifting it to his lips for a sweet kiss. Maddy felt a rush of energy as well as a little surprise. Most guys didn't make such old-fashioned gestures these days. At least not anyone she'd ever run into.

"You have the tiniest little hands," he remarked. "You're so cute and petite!" With that, he pulled her into a big bear hug. He was nothing if not affectionate. Though she enjoyed the feel of him against her, she remained cautious; she didn't know this guy and he was well aware that she was alone. His impressive build notwithstanding, he didn't come close to looking dangerous. And with his boyish grin, all-American looks and witty sense of humor, he reminded her of some of the guys from her high school football team. Still, she wanted to be careful.

"Ken," she laughed, extracting herself as he began to plant more kisses on her cheek. "Can we just talk for a little while?"

"Sure," he smiled, releasing her, but still holding onto her hand. "Is that ok?"

"Fine," she answered. She gently squeezed his hand and realized she was enjoying the attention. After everything she'd been through with Jake, this guy was a refreshing change of pace.

"So how do you like the Jersey Shore, you know, as compared to California?"

"What?" he asked, sounding puzzled.

"Didn't you tell Carmen you were from California?"

"Wha—oh, I sort of told a fib about that. I was just stationed there when I was in the Navy. I'm not actually from California. I grew up in Ventnor, and now I have my own place in Somers Point."

"You were in the Navy!" she exclaimed. "That's pretty cool. Tell me about it." She was a bit put off that he'd lied, but figured in a guy's mind, being from California probably sounded much more impressive to a woman than claiming New Jersey as your home state.

Under the cover of magnificent moonlight enhanced by the muted sounds of music emanating from inside the club, they chatted for hours. He shared funny and sad stories of his time in the military as she eagerly listened, fascinated by his life experience. At 25, she'd never even left her hometown, let alone traveled the world. Except for a Caribbean cruise with a few college girlfriends after graduation and some assorted family trips to places like Disney World and Chicago, she'd lived a pretty uneventful life. Heck, Maddy had even commuted to a university minutes from her house because she hadn't felt quite ready to leave the nest. At the same age, Ken had enlisted to serve in foreign lands.

She also noticed something admirable and attractive in him—an inner spark, a desire to make something of himself. He was determined to rise above his roots in a sleepy Shore town and accomplish much greater things than his older brothers, all of whom seemed content to work in a local pizza shop.

And although he was currently employed at a power plant, he was making a lot more money than Maddy and owned a place of his own. One thing was certain: whatever Ken Lockhart decided to do with the rest of his life, he would be an unbridled success.

Not that she didn't have bragging rights herself, being a talented singer and dancer who sometimes sang in a band on weekends; however, her inherent modesty and constant concern over her weight were sometimes formidable obstacles to the acknowledgment of her own success.

"Hey, when's your birthday?" he suddenly asked.

"It's in March."

"March what?"

"The seventh." His jaw dropped.

"You're telling me that March 7 is your birthday? What year?" he pressed urgently.

"Now, Kenny, didn't your mom ever tell you it's not polite to ask a woman her age?" she teased coyly.

"Madeline, what year?" he was almost sounding annoyed again. "Alright, already! 1967!"

"What—you were born on March 7, 1967?"

"Uh, yeah. Would you like to see my driver's license?" she retorted. He put his hands on her shoulders, looked at her in amazement and declared, "Maddy, not only are we both Pisces, but we're exactly the same age!"

"Really, you're not just feeding me a line?" What were the odds of that? Perhaps this charming gentleman was just pulling her leg; she was secure and self-aware enough to admit her own naiveté when the situation warranted.

"*Now* who needs to see a driver's license?" he teased. He wrapped her in a bear hug and planted a few more kisses on her forehead.

"That's pretty wild," she agreed as he high-fived her again. "Not only are we both Pisces, but we came into the world at the same time. Just don't ask me what the first-hand was on when the doctor cut the umbilical cord, 'cause I couldn't tell you to save my life. I think I was born sometime after the late show, according to my mother."

He laughed and kissed her "tiny" hands again. A few minutes later the club announced last call; it was hard to believe it was 2 a.m. already. Her time with Ken had flown by.

"Well Kenny, I guess they're kicking us out," she observed wistfully. "I'll have to give you that Jitterbug lesson some other time."

This new woman sure was a refreshing departure from the usual South Jersey dating scene. Wanting to stay with her awhile longer, he invited her to his house for coffee, an offer she firmly turned down.

"C'mon Maddy, I just bought this great new pot—do you like coffee?" She nodded silently. "Well, this makes awesome coffee! And I promise I'm a total gentleman. I won't try anything, other than to kiss these delicate little hands."

She cracked up; watching him plead his case with such adorableness practically melted her heart. But the fact remained she barely knew him and it was just too soon to be alone with a stranger on his home turf.

"I'll tell you what, Kenny," she compromised. "If it is coffee you really want, I'll follow you over to the Point Diner. I'm pretty sure they sell it there, though it's probably not as good as yours."

He laughed again. This girl was cute, educated and had a great sense of humor. He liked that.

"Well, alright, but only if I drive," he bargained.

"But Ken, I'll follow right behind—"

"I'm driving!"

"Yes, sir!"

He took her by the hand, and they walked back to his black Acura.

Chapter 2

Ken opened the door for his unexpected but welcome date. Still a bit tortured as to whether or not she was making the right decision, Maddy hesitated for a moment. "Ken, let me take my own car," she pleaded, "I promise, I—" she began before he shushed her by gently placing two fingers on her soft lips.

"Madeline, I promise you, I am a perfect gentleman. I just want to drive you around the traffic circle to the diner, where all we will do is drink coffee and talk," he said in a hushed, sincere tone. She looked up into his electric blue eyes. "Please?" he whispered.

"Oh alright, I'm sorry for being so suspicious. Maybe I'm just not used to being treated like a lady."

"Well, that's too bad because I was just thinking how lucky I was to have run into a nice girl at last, one who deserves to be treated with respect even if she did refuse my hospitality three times."

He grinned at her as he spoke but the sentiment was genuine. Ken couldn't remember the last time a woman rejected the idea of going back to his place; based on that alone it was apparent to him he was dealing with an entirely different kind of female in Madeline Rose. From the few short hours he'd spent with her already that evening he sensed she was a rare find on the contemporary dating scene: a good-looking woman with old-fashioned sensibilities. Her words and actions had sent a clear message that she had too much self-respect to settle for a cheap hook-up – or even place herself in a situation where her motivations could be misunderstood. And that made her even more irresistible.

"Oh, ok!" she laughed before slipping into the comfortable leather bucket seat. She quickly clicked her seatbelt into place, then reached over to unlock his door, a simple gesture that nevertheless made quite an impression.

"Wow," he laughed.

"What now?" she asked somewhat defensively. "Nothing. You're unbelievable, that's all."

"Why because I know how to unlock a car door?"

"Because you actually *thought* of doing it," he explained as he planted another smooch on her forehead.

A few minutes later, Ken and Maddy stepped out into the salty sea air. While a pleasant breeze blew in off of the bay in the distance, the subdued lights of Ocean City mingled with the illuminations of a thousand stars overhead. It was a magical, late-summer scene, one that would soon fade into the memory of another bygone season once the biting winds of winter came along to sweep the area into a seemingly endless hibernation.

She had dutifully waited for him to open the door for her before stepping out, lest she trample unintentionally upon his feelings. Jake had always accused her of acting like a princess for expecting such traditional courtesies; as a result, she'd long ago become accustomed to exiting a vehicle the moment he'd placed it in park to avoid unwarranted criticism and accusations of snobbery. Even though Ken's old-fashioned mannerisms rated high marks in her book, it was difficult to break old, if unfairly imposed, habits.

He kissed her hand as she got out, then held it in his until they approached the double glass doors of the half-empty diner. As he followed her inside, Maddy turned to him with a look of surprise. After all, it was well past 2 a.m., and all of the area bars were now closed; there should've been a huge crowd of people indulging in the customary post-club-scene breakfast. Yet inexplicably, the only booth and counter occupants were a few older couples and a smattering of off-duty cops. Lack of patrons notwithstanding, it seemed hours before a harried waitress even acknowledged their presence.

"Maybe we don't look hungry enough?" she teased.

"*Hello!*" Ken called out when the middle-aged waitress passed them by for about the fifth time, prompting Maddy to break out into gales of laughter. Whether as a result of being overworked or just plain rude, the woman demonstrated about zero interest in serving them. When he spoke up again, she finally scowled, "Sit anywhere you like!"

"Sheesh, Kenny, I don't think she likes us too much!" she giggled. In spite of her earlier reservations she had to admit the evening was turning out much better than she'd ever anticipated.

"Nah, I don't think so!" he agreed with a chuckle. "But since you won't go back to my place, this is our only hope for coffee." He winked at her as she playfully nudged him into a booth.

"Where are you going?" he asked incredulously as he watched her slide into a cushioned red seat directly across the table.

"What? I'm sitting across from you!"

"Please, I just wanna be near you," he begged.

"Ken, please, I'm right here!"

"Please, let me sit next to you?"

"Oh, alright," she relented. "But keep your hands to yourself!"

He grinned as he slipped in next to her and placed his arm around her shoulder. The waitress slapped two large plastic menus on the table as she rushed by.

"Hungry?" Ken inquired cheerfully. He opened up one of the menus to the breakfast page and scanned its offerings.

"A little," she admitted. "But I think we'll be lucky if we even get coffee at this point, Ken. It could be a long wait for eggs."

He laughed as he pulled her close to him and kissed her forehead again. "Ken, please, I don't even know you!" she scolded, pushing him away. Her reprimand only gave him more encouragement, and he kissed her hand again.

"We'll get to know each other sweetheart, don't you worry," he assured her with another wink.

"You're impossible!" she sighed. But beneath her aloof demeanor, her heart was fluttering.

It seemed an eternity before the wayward waitress finally returned to take their order. Maddy listened in amazement as Ken rattled off about three different entrees, a side of fresh fruit, and a rasher of bacon. *Was he really going to eat a ham and cheese omelet, a stack of pancakes, French toast, hash browns, sausage, bacon, and melon?* True, he was a big, muscular guy but still. All of this food at once, at nearly quarter past three?

As if reading her mind, he explained, "I wish you could order in halves so you could try everything."

"Yeah, good point," she concurred with a smile. *Now that did make sense.*

"Don't you want anything?"

"Uh, no – not hungry. I'll just have some coffee."

The two of them shared many laughs in those early morning hours as Kenny savored a small portion of each plate and encouraged Maddy to sample some of his choices. She finally relented and allowed her taste buds to revel in the sweetness of maple syrup soaked through expertly grilled pancakes – a treat she rarely indulged in.

"You're beautiful, sweetheart; I don't know why you think otherwise," he stated forthrightly. She was struck by his sincerity as she studied his face, not fully comprehending that such an attractive man would hold that opinion of her.

Drawn to her by some powerful, unseen force Ken leaned in and kissed her on the cheek as he squeezed her shoulder, breathing in her intoxicating Trésor perfume. That this incredible girl saw herself as anything but mesmerizing was beyond his understanding. All he wanted to do was protect her, keep her safe and happy. What a fool he'd been to seek out her skinny friend first at the club. She didn't hold a candle to Madeline's beauty—or her sweetness.

As if to shake him out of his reverie, she reprimanded him again.

"Ken, come on, I don't even know you and we're in a public place. Please, stop embarrassing me!" She pushed him away once more.

Feisty, too. He *definitely* liked that in a woman.

Safely back in the Key Largo lot a little while later, Maddy thanked Kenny for a wonderful evening. Setting formality aside, she opened her door to step out after retrieving her car keys from her evening bag.

"Wait!" He stopped her by grabbing her arm. "Are you going to the beach tomorrow?"

"Yes, definitely," she replied.

"Well, what time?" he pressed.

"Not sure, depends on when I get myself to church, and since it's already so late, I doubt I'll wake up in time for early mass."

"Aw, a nice girl who goes to church," he remarked.

"Don't make fun of me Ken," she cautioned.

"Madeline, I am not making fun of you; I am truly impressed. I just want to see you again. Will you give me your number?"

She raised a skeptical eyebrow, though the thought of meeting him at the beach ignited a wave of excitement through her entire body. When neither one of them could locate a pen or paper, Maddy told him she was in the phone book.

"Not that you'll remember my name by tomorrow morning – or rather, later on this morning," she added. In spite of the enjoyable evening, they'd shared she was still smarting somewhat over the fact that her statuesque friend had been his first choice.

"Oh I'll remember your name," he answered matter-of-factly. She was not the kind of woman a man easily forgets.

"Well just in case, I'll be at the 19th Street beach sometime in late morning or early afternoon. My family is coming down for the day, and that's where we usually hang out."

"Until then," he whispered as he leaned in to place another affectionate kiss on her cheek.

"Yeah, well like I said, we'll see if you even remember my name when you wake up." She grinned at him as she exited the car.

He watched and waited until she'd closed her car door and started the engine. Then he gestured for her to go ahead of him. Having found the little red devil still attached to the rose and lying on the passenger seat where she'd left it, Maddy waved it at him as she backed out. He just looked at her with a mixture of sheepishness and exasperation, more determined than ever to find her by the water's edge in a just a few short hours.

The golden sunlight streamed through the cream-colored vertical blinds as Maddy quickly silenced an alarm clock blaring Kathy Troccoli's latest hit, *Everything Changes.*

Grudgingly, she blinked open her eyes and sank her head back down into her plush pillow. Ugh! She didn't even drink, and she felt hungover.

As she stretched her arms over her head and gazed at the whirling white ceiling fan, she recalled fondly the events of the previous night. Even if she never saw Ken Lockhart again, she would always remember their brief time together. In just a few short hours, he'd demonstrated more respect and admiration for her than Jake had in nearly two years. It was reassuring to know that good men were indeed out there. No matter what may or may not transpire with Ken, one thing was certain: Maddy was ready to release any lingering sadness and depression over a man who never deserved her in the first place. For once, she actually felt relieved to be rid of him before doing something stupid, like walking down the aisle.

She pulled her five-foot, two-inch frame out of bed and headed for the bathroom, mindful not to wake a deeply slumbering Carmen in the next bed. As she washed her face, brushed her teeth and carefully applied minimal makeup to complement her slightly sunburned cheeks, her thoughts drifted aimlessly to the handsome ex-sailor from Somers Point. Was he sincere? Would he actually show up on the beach today? Did he really feel the same attraction?

Maddy slipped a comfortable cotton sundress over her head and adjusted its aqua spaghetti straps before smoothing the white A-line embroidered skirt and stepping into a pair of cute white wedge sandals – safe for walking the 13 blocks to and from church on the boardwalk. She stole a quick glance at her watch, confirming she had just about enough time to get to 10:30 a.m. mass by foot, rather than fight for a parking space in the overcrowded St. Augustine lot. As an added bonus, it would satisfy her brisk exercise requirement for the day. After running a brush through her silky auburn hair, she raced down the stairs and out through the back patio.

Ken awoke to a bright blue sky and streaming rays of glorious sunshine filtering through the skylight above his king-sized waterbed. He placed his hands behind his head as he gazed up at a brand-new morning, still thinking of the amazing woman he'd been with only a short time before. *Madeline Rose.* Did he dream her sweet face and adorable admonitions to knock off the PDA's? Could he ever forget the exquisite feel of her in his arms as they slow danced or the way she spoke in enthusiastic bursts about topics that interested her? More importantly did he actually stand a chance with someone so bright and educated?

He rolled onto his side as he adjusted his pillow and kicked the satin sheets down to the end of the bed. Thinking of her attending Sunday mass—most likely in a feminine dress complemented by the perfect accessories—made him smile. He could picture her long, flowing hair partially caught up in a bow and her tiny hands holding the prayer book, or reaching out to offer someone the sign of peace. Though he'd been raised as a Roman Catholic himself, Ken hadn't set foot inside a church in years. For Maddy though, he'd definitely reconsider.

Whoa! He barely knew this girl and already she wielded enough power to accomplish something no one else could: get him back into the spiritual fold as well as stimulate his mind and excite his body. Thinking of her smooth, flawless skin, his mind began to wander. He imagined what she'd feel like beneath his touch as her warm lips met his for a passionate kiss while they lingered under an incandescent moon on the soft sand.

Lost in these sensual thoughts, the obnoxiously loud tones of a ringing phone startled him back to reality with its endless responsibilities and unwavering demands. Sure enough, it was his co-worker Quentin on the line, reminding him of his promise to work at the plant for him that afternoon so he could spend time with his family on his daughter's birthday.

"My shift starts at three, don't be late," Quentin urged him.

"C'mon, man you know I am the most reliable guy in the whole place. You don't have to worry, I'll be there."

Three o'clock. Perfect. He'd have plenty of time to find Madeline Rose and sweep her off of her feet before then.

Maddy entered through the sliding glass doors of the patio to find the whole gang waiting for her. Mom, as usual, was busy preparing breakfast, while her future sister-in-law, Vanessa, set the table. Her dad, brother Greg and soon-to-be brother-in-law Vince were hanging out in the family room talking Eagles football and placing bets on what the forthcoming season would portend.

"Hiya beautiful!" Dr. Joseph Rose greeted his daughter with an affectionate hug and kiss.

"Hey, Dad! Hi everyone!" Maddy embraced her father before heading into the kitchen to help out.

"Hi Mom!" she greeted her brightly with a kiss on the cheek. As the "baby" of the family, she shared an especially close bond with her mother.

"Hi hon, do you mind setting up the coffee?" Monica Rose nodded toward the percolator pot on the counter. Maddy smiled. She always loved helping her mom with the designated "female" responsibilities.

"Did you go to mass?"

"Yeah, I made it in time for the 10:30."

"Mad, did you really walk 13 blocks?" Vanessa queried. "

Yep, sure did."

Vanessa, a tall, striking woman with thick strawberry blonde hair and bright, hazel eyes, laughed out loud.

"What?"

"Nothing, you're amazing! Out at a club all night and bouncing out of bed to walk 13 blocks back and forth to church the next day! If I even made it to church in the first place, I'd definitely be driving!"

Maddy cracked up. "Well, a girl does what she has to do stay in shape, Vaness. You're lucky you're tall. Besides, I don't drink so it's no big deal."

"So Mad, tell us all about this young dude you met last night," Greg teased as he entered the room and placed his arms around her.

"Geez, you all know about that already? Carmen was practically in a coma when I left. She sure didn't waste any time."

Before Maddy could utter another word, her sister Lori bounded down the stairs, laughing hysterically. The phone had rung a few seconds earlier and Lori had answered it in the master bedroom before anyone else had even thought of it. Nearly out of breath, she could barely speak as she ran into the kitchen.

"Maddy....it's...him," she managed to croak out in between giggles. "He's been....waiting...at the beach....for you...for hours."

"Him, who?"

"Ken!"

"Well, pick up the phone!" her mother reprimanded.

"I think I'll take it upstairs," she announced with a mixture of excitement and annoyance. Nothing like having your life spread out like a proverbial open book for the amusement of your family.

Lori followed in hot pursuit as she raced up the stairs.

"Do you *mind*?" she shot back at her big sister before closing the bedroom door. That did little to deter Lori, who hovered on the other side with an ear pressed against the door.

"Hello?" Maddy uttered haltingly.

"Where've you been, I've been waiting for you for two hours!" the deep, familiar voice implored playfully. Although her heart was pounding, she did her best to remain calm.

"Well, Kenny, I did tell you I was going to church, didn't I?"

"Yes, but I thought you'd be done by now. It's a beautiful beach day, girl!"

"I know, and I'll be there soon. I—"

Sensing a presence in the room, she turned to find her sister and mother now standing next to her. She glared at them at first but softened when her mother mouthed the words, "Invite him to breakfast."

"Uh Ken, how'd you like to come over for breakfast with my family?"

"In my *bathing suit*? Are you *kidding*? I can't meet your family like that!"

"Why not? They're gonna see you in your bathing suit on the beach anyway!"

"Madeline—"

"Please, Kenny?" Her genuine appeal melted his heart.

"Ok, tell me where your house is and I'll be there," he sighed. She directed him to their three-bedroom cottage on Simpson Avenue.

"See you in a few minutes," she said sweetly. "Maddy?"

"Yes?"

"You better be the one to answer the door when I get there." Recognizing the anxiety in his tone, Maddy assured him she would.

Kenny's bright smile greeted her a few minutes later from behind the pale pink metal door of the entryway. Her heart leapt at the sight of him, looking like an ad for Coppertone in his navy and red swim trunks and white tee shirt. In the light of early afternoon, his curly hair appeared even blonder, while his broad shoulders and toned muscles exuded alpha-male masculinity. His azure eyes twinkled as he gazed back at her, a beautiful vision, still in her sexy, but tasteful sundress that set off her porcelain shoulders and emphasized her deliciously curvy figure.

"Kenny! Come on in!" she said, as she planted a kiss on his cheek and offered him a quick hug.

"Hi...I'm really embarrassed about this, being in my bathing suit and all," he reminded her as he breathed in the familiar scent of her perfume.

"Will you relax? My family's not like that." Taking him by the arm, she led him to the dining room where everyone was already assembled and pretending to be engrossed in conversation.

She made the customary introductions, before ushering Ken to a seat and helping her mother transport plates of scrambled eggs, bacon and toast to the glass-top table.

"Maddy, he's adorable!" her mother whispered approvingly.

"Isn't he, though? I don't think I realized it until just now."

As Kenny joined in the fun, he was amazed by all of the accomplishments of her impressive family, from her dad being a respected neurosurgeon to Lori and Greg's thriving legal careers. Even the soon-to-be spouses came with remarkable résumés: Vanessa was a marketing director for a publishing company while Vince worked as a CPA for a large firm in Philadelphia. And the two siblings not present? One was an anesthesiologist with Vanderbilt University in Nashville, and the other, a Down's boy who against all odds, held a good job with a local hospital in Maddy's suburban hometown of Media.

"So that leaves me," she told him. "While I work in outside sales, I am trying to build a writing career."

"Along with your singing and dancing," her dad reminded her.

"Well, I knew about her dancing talents, but singing? You've been holding out on me, Madeline," Ken teasingly poked her in the side.

"Madeline has a beautiful voice," her mother explained, "but she lacks the confidence to really sing in front of an audience. I don't know why; she's such a pretty girl!"

"*Mom*," she pleaded as her cheeks turned red.

"She sure is," Ken whispered, squeezing her hand underneath the table.

The high surf pounded the beach as everyone helped set up camp on an empty stretch of sand. Colorful umbrellas and familiar blue cabanas dotted the shoreline as vacationers and locals alike soaked up the last days of summer. After an unusually soggy season, Mother Nature was finally treating them to the kind of weather most northerners dream about all year, and they were taking full advantage. Squealing children ran back and forth hauling plastic buckets filled with salt water while others dug trenches around crudely constructed sandcastles; teenaged surfer boys gleefully challenged the tide, and sunbathers permeated the air with the unmistakable scent of coconut oil and sunscreen.

Against this backdrop, Ken chatted and laughed easily with Maddy's entire family. And as the two of them sat on beach chairs by the water, they conversed on a number of topics, delighted to discover a shared outlook on everything from pro football to music to politics. Without even realizing it, she stunned him with her in-depth knowledge of the game and stories about being in attendance at Vet Stadium on that bitterly cold day on January 11, 1981, when the Eagles miraculously defeated the Cowboys 20-7 in the NFC Championship Game.

He loved the way she gestured with her hands when she spoke and how her voice went up a few octaves when discussing a subject she felt passionate about. Completely enthralled, Ken couldn't get enough of her, although he noticed how she kept her pink neon shorts and coordinating tee shirt on over her bathing suit. In his mind, she had a great figure, but he politely refrained from questioning her about it.

Afterward, they played catch with a football. Maddy's long braid danced in the wind as she ran after his passes, most of which he kept within the realm of possibility with an occasional overthrown lob high above her head, made for the sole purpose of being a tease. She'd then shoot him a look of feigned indignation before responding with a bullet of her own. Having grown up with three brothers, she was no stranger to good-natured teasing.

"Hey, take it easy!" he laughed when one of her tosses hit him squarely in the chest with just a little too much steam.

Around this time, Carmen, now fully recovered from her big night, joined in the surfside fun. While Maddy went to retrieve some water, Kenny took her aside and inquired about her date, offering a sincere apology for the way he'd reacted.

"You just treat Maddy right," she warned. "She's a really special girl, and I don't want to see her get hurt."

"Believe me, you have nothing to worry about there," he answered with conviction.

When he rejoined her on the blanket, he glanced at his watch and regretfully informed her that he had to get to work.

"Ok," she nodded as she got up and brushed the sand off of her. Time at the beach had passed quickly just as it had at the club the night before but she couldn't fault him for being a responsible citizen.

"Oh, I'm sorry you have to leave already, Ken!" Vanessa piped up.

"Yeah, well, I had a wonderful time, and I hope to see all of you people again real soon," he responded politely. Taking the time to shake everyone's hand he added, "Thank you for your hospitality."

Maddy accompanied him back to the street, still exuberant over her surprise weekend spent in the company of a handsome former Navy guy. It had been a far cry from her earlier expectations of the same-old, same-old just 24-hours ago when she and Carmen were speeding down the A.C. Expressway.

"Well, Kenny, it was fun. So, maybe I'll hear from you again?" she asked, hopefully.

"Oh, you'll hear from me, sweetheart." He pulled her into a bear hug and kissed her on the cheek.

Maddy floated back to the beach, her heart racing in anticipation of what was to come.

Chapter 3

Maddy stood in front of her bedroom mirror, contemplating which one out of the large assortment of summer dresses strewn across her twin bed made her look the thinnest. One by one, she held them up in front of her, carefully inspecting the line, cut, and comfort of each, along with the appropriate jewelry, shoes, and bag. Should she go with the black halter dress with the flared skirt in case they ended up dancing in a casino nightclub or the cute, knit mini-dress with the scoop neck and bright blocks of color that showed off her toned legs?

As she frantically tried on one ensemble after another, she heard her mother calling to her from the bottom of the stairs.

"Maddy, it's almost six o'clock hon; Ken's going to be here any minute!"

"Don't worry, Mom, I'm almost done!" she called back. "And I'm sure you and Aunt Maria can keep him entertained even if I'm not ready when he gets here." She sighed in frustration as her long hair caught on the zipper of a blue sundress she'd been desperately attempting to wriggle out of.

Downstairs Monica Rose and her sister Maria spoke enthusiastically about her new suitor. They'd all driven down to Ocean City together after Maddy had finished work the night before, sharing a great meal on the way at one of New Jersey's famous diners. Over tuna melts and Chef's salads, Madeline's favorite aunt had listened with unbridled joy as her niece entertained her with the now-famous story of her and Ken's unexpected meeting at Key Largo.

A romantic at heart, Maria wanted nothing more than to see Maddy happily settled with the right guy. Like Monica, she'd realized long before her niece that her ex-boyfriend Jake was a complete loser. He might've earned an MBA, but it certainly hadn't endowed him with any class or courtesy. And though neither sister interfered, both breathed a huge sigh of relief when the relationship mercifully ended, though Jake could've chosen a more dignified method: Maddy deserved better than a gut-wrenching 1 a.m. phone call. Still, she was lucky to be rid of him, his nice family notwithstanding.

Since Kenny had to work a double shift in order to have Saturday evening off to take her out to dinner, she had spent a glorious Indian summer day on the beach with the two women with whom she'd shared the closest bonds. And as the ladies sat at the water's edge, feeling the ocean's tide gently trickle over their feet, she told them about Ken's wonderful attentiveness, sweetly expressed through daily phone calls— many from work—in which he would make her laugh with a funny story from the Navy, or send happy shivers down her spine with talk of her beauty and how much he missed her smiling face.

He was so warm, kind, and complimentary it threw her off- guard. Until Jake she had never had a boyfriend; after that experience, she'd come to believe that enduring constant criticism from a man was normal in spite of the honorable model set by her own father and brothers.

And while everyone around her despised Jake's treatment no one intervened; they simply gave her the space to make her own decisions and secretly prayed she'd never end up with him. Ironically, it was Jake himself who finally saw the light after experiencing extreme guilt over yet another lie he'd told her. Unwilling to keep inflicting pain on an undeserving woman, he ended the relationship in the only manner he could.

Three months later along came Ken with his upbeat personality and shared love for all of the things Maddy treasured—freedom, family, friends, music, dancing, literature, beaches, football, nice clothes, and good food. Heck, he was even willing to start attending mass again, if it made her happy. It was all so miraculous—and unbelievable. Aunt

Maria advised her niece to just enjoy every moment because she was a beautiful, vital young woman, one that any man should be proud to have on his arm.

"Thanks, Re Re," she'd sighed, eager to believe, yet still haunted by memories of a not-so-long-ago chubby adolescence, characterized by nagging insecurities and a dearth of male suitors. It was amazing that at age 25 these things still bothered her.

But here she was, stubbornly unable to acknowledge that the insecure teen had successfully transformed into a lovely, desirable vision of femininity and charm – thus the endless wardrobe changes minutes before her date's arrival.

By the time she heard the doorbell ring, Maddy had settled on the color-blocked knit mini-dress and gold hoop earrings. She'd vigorously brushed her auburn tresses upside down, and they now spilled seductively past her shoulders and nearly midway down her back. The early autumn sun had been strong enough to add a natural blush to her cheeks, so she simply added a bit of eye shadow and mascara to enhance her features, with a shiny rose lip gloss providing the finishing touch.

She laughed as she recalled her and Lori's standing joke about their mom: "Where's your lipstick!" she'd demand whenever either of them attempted to leave home without the one accessory Monica Rose deemed absolutely essential. Maddy wouldn't have to worry about that tonight; this new shade was perfect and definitely noticeable—in an understated sort of way.

"Hi, Ken!" She heard her mother's greeting just before the sound of his baritone response released a wave of exhilaration that washed over her from head to toe. She took a deep breath, grabbed her black quilted evening bag, and ran downstairs. Before she even reached the landing, she caught a glimpse of Kenny in the mirror that hung on the first floor directly in front of the staircase.

Her breathing stopped for a second as she saw him sitting in the family room easy chair, dressed to the nines in a teal suit and chatting effortlessly with her mom and aunt. She'd almost forgotten how handsome he was, how unmistakably virile and masculine. Had it actually been two weeks since she'd seen him? They'd spoken so much during that time it didn't seem possible.

"Oh, Maddy, there you are!" Monica greeted her brightly. With that, Kenny immediately stood up and turned to face her, his smile as radiant as ever. She tried to conceal her nervousness even as she silently noted the way in which his suit intensified the hue of his effervescent eyes.

"Hi Kenny," she smiled. "It's so great to see you again."

"You look beautiful," he replied, placing a soft kiss on her cheek while Monica and Maria exchanged hopeful glances.

"She certainly does," Aunt Maria agreed.

Please don't overdo it. Please don't embarrass me!

"We were just telling Ken how much we love his suit. Isn't it a beautiful color?" Mom asked.

"Yes, it really is," she concurred softly. "It looks so nice with your blue eyes."

"Thank you." He smiled at her in that easygoing way she'd come to recognize and love already. As he took in the magnificent sight of her— the cascading auburn hair, the warm, amber eyes, the shapely legs—he thought he might actually fall over. He couldn't stop staring as time stood still in that exquisite space.

"Well, I guess you guys had better get going," her mom piped up, temporarily breaking the spell. "Aunt Maria and I are headed to the casinos tonight."

"Oh, maybe we'll see you there," Ken offered, "We're having dinner in town at Frisanco's."

"Nah, you two kids just go out and have a good time. Don't worry about us." Then, looking at her daughter, Monica asked, "You're not wearing your heels, hon?"

"No, because if we walk on the boardwalk, I don't want to get stuck in the grooves," Maddy explained. She kissed them goodbye, then led him back out through the front door. As they made their way outside, they heard Aunt Maria call out breezily, "Drive nicely, Ken. You're carrying precious cargo!"

Although slightly embarrassed Maddy figured it was best to simply let Aunt Re Re's comment go rather than make a lame joke about it. Besides, it couldn't hurt for Ken to know how her family felt about her. She carefully slid into the passenger seat as he held open the door, then leaned over to unlock his side just as she'd done that fateful evening in the Key Largo lot. He smiled at her appreciatively as he started the car and switched on the radio. As they drove off, he impatiently changed stations in search of a good song. He was about to pop in an *Earth, Wind and Fire Greatest Hits* cassette when Maddy suddenly stopped him.

"You don't like them? It's great dance music!" he pleaded playfully.

"No, I do, it's just that I love this new song that just came on—can we please listen to it?"

"You like this, too?" he asked, brightening.

"Yeah, it has a great beat. Sort of reminds me of the sand and the shells and the ocean whenever I hear it," she explained.

So as the soulful sounds of Jon Secada's *Just Another Day (Without You)* emanated through the speakers Ken and Maddy cruised down Wesley Avenue and over the causeways that would lead them into Atlantic City, site of their first official date.

Frisanco's was the kind of restaurant tailor-made for two people just getting to know each other. It was upscale, but not uppity, with soft lighting and appealing background music that complemented an intimate, yet not overly contrived atmosphere. The wait staff was friendly and welcoming, and the Italian menu, familiar and delicious.

They settled into a nice corner table enhanced by the warm glow of tea lights in crystal holders and a bud vase bearing a single red rose. Ever the gentleman, he held her seat out for her just as their server discreetly made his way over to present the evening's specials. As the waiter described mouthwatering appetizer and entrée selections, Ken could barely comprehend what he was hearing he was so distracted by Maddy's genuine sweetness which seemed to resonate in everything she did, from greeting the hostess upon their arrival to listening with active interest as this guy painstakingly detailed every item in his repertoire.

"You know, that all sounds wonderful," she commented after he finished, "But I just love the veal piccata here. It's my favorite, so I think that's what I'm gonna have tonight." She turned her gaze to Ken, still lost in his own thoughts. "How 'bout you Kenny?"

"Huh? Oh, you know, that sounds good to me, too. I'll have the same thing," he told the waiter.

"And how about some wine for you and the lady?" "Oh, uh, I don't really want any Kenny. You go ahead."

"C'mon, Mad, you're not even gonna have a glass of *wine* with me?" he pleaded teasingly.

"Do you want me to stay awake for this date?" she asked, knowing that one glass could put her right to sleep. He nodded.

"Alright then, you go ahead without me. Believe me, we'll both have a much better time."

"Guess I can't argue with that," Ken he conceded, before ordering his Chardonnay.

She later toasted him with her water glass as she continued to draw him into her captivating aura. Watching her it occurred to him that she might possibly be the most beautiful girl he'd ever seen and as a well- traveled sailor, he'd been on his share of dates. But no one had come close to Maddy's remarkable combination of innocence, enthusiasm, and sincerity; that these qualities came wrapped up in a good-looking package was the icing on the cake. He marveled at the ease with which they laughed and talked, especially appreciative of her genuine interest in his Navy service.

Maddy's questions demonstrated a real desire to get to know him as a person, not simply to use him as a vehicle for free dinners, movies, and meaningless sex. Well, it had been quite obvious from the start he was dealing with a class act where that was concerned; he just hoped that someday she could reciprocate the same deeply held feelings that had taken root within his heart. All he knew in that moment was an overwhelming desire to hold her in his arms and protect her forever.

She listened to his story with rapt attention, struck by the stark differences between him and Jake. Instead of moaning about not knowing what he wanted to do with his life like her overeducated ex-boyfriend, Ken plainly stated that as the youngest son in a working-class family, he realized early on that self-discipline and hard work would be required of him if he truly wanted to rise above his sleepy Shore town roots. Without parents that possessed the financial means to send him to college or at least help with the tuition, enlisting in the Navy was the only way to avoid degenerating into a surfer bum, like so many of his high school buddies.

And while Maddy had been part of that fortunate minority whose parents did pay for college, Kenny didn't resent her for not sharing the same challenges. On the contrary, he seemed to be in awe of her accomplishments, from making Dean's List consistently every semester to writing articles for the university newspaper. She expressed gratitude for her dad's determination to spare his children from the struggles he'd faced as a medical student who as the son of immigrants, had to work three jobs to put himself through school. Unfortunately, many of her co-eds didn't view their education as a gift or as a care package for the future, but rather, as an entitlement. None of them—Maddy included—would ever understand the intensity, sacrifice, and hardship involved in Military service.

When dinner ended, he asked what she would like to do next and was blown away by her honest request to walk on the boardwalk.

"You're kidding? That's it? That's all you want to do?"

"Well, yes, it's such a beautiful night, I'd love to just stroll along, maybe walk in and out of some casinos, get a water ice, stare at the ocean..." her voice trailed off as she imagined sharing all of these simple pleasures with his strong arm securely wrapped around her. He continued to stare at her in disbelief.

"What?" she asked, suddenly a little defensive.

"Nothing, it's just that...do you have any idea what most girls would have said? They'd want to go to some fancy, expensive nightclub, or—"

"Ken, I'm not most girls. You should know that by now."

"Oh, believe me, I do, sweetheart. Just want to take you someplace nice, that's all."

"You did. You brought me here for this wonderful dinner, and now I want to walk on the boardwalk...with you," she added softly.

"Well ok, then!" He laughed and kissed her hand before escorting her out of the restaurant.

The night sky was clear and dotted with stars as Ken and Maddy strolled hand-in-hand on the bustling, high-rise, and casino populated Atlantic City boardwalk. While they passed the endless strings of pizza parlors, custard stands, and sundry shops interspersed between the taller buildings, Ken shared stories of growing up in the neighboring town of Ventnor. It seemed funny to her to actually know someone who'd been born and raised down here. Before meeting Ken, she'd mainly thought of the area as a popular vacation spot. A narrow view for sure, but one widely held by the people of her home state of Pennsylvania.

Suddenly, a thickly accented voice rudely interrupted their flow of conversation. "Excuse me—how can you make this lovely lady walk so far?" a man who appeared to be of Middle Eastern descent demanded of Ken.

He was dressed in jeans and a tee-shirt, and standing next to a rolling chair, a ubiquitous presence for which the seaside resort was well known. Ken glanced at her, and her eyes quickly conveyed the answer he sought.

"Look, buddy," he joked, "She's the one making me walk!"

"That's right, I *love* to walk," she chimed in as she gave Ken's hand a squeeze. She never did like rolling chairs; they made her think of all of the people who, by circumstance of birth, accident, or illness had no choice but to ride in wheelchairs. If she was fortunate enough to be able to walk, then that was exactly what she was going to do.

"No thanks, then. You heard the lady," Ken repeated, prompting the man to stride away in a huff, much to their amusement. It was one of the evening's many unscripted, lighthearted moments.

After the rolling chair incident, they headed into the lobby of the Taj Majal, where Ken had briefly worked as a parking valet upon his return from the Navy. The tallest and most ornate edifice on the entire boardwalk, it greeted them with a dazzling montage of neon lights and purple and gold décor, from the loud carpet patterns to the infinite parade of gaudy chandeliers that hung from cut-out ceilings.

Ken spoke to her over the ringing clamor of slot machines. "So what would you like to do sweetheart?"

"Do you think we can go to the top? I bet the view is great from up there!"

"Sure, let's go see if I can find one of my old buddies who still work here."

He held her hand as they set off in search of the friend who could sneak them onto the special elevator that would transport them to an exclusive club. Upon finding him, Ken had to do a little negotiating before he and his date finally found themselves riding a golden car up to the special place reserved for high rollers. When the doors opened they stepped into a breathtaking world of panoramic picture windows, Indian- inspired tapestries and crystal light fixtures. Two enormous, shining doors marked the entrance into the lounge.

As he began to lead her in that direction, Maddy suddenly stopped him.

"Oh look, Kenny! Can we just stay here for a minute?" She ran over to one of the massive windows that showcased a magical, panoramic view of the ocean, lights and boardwalk below; its wide ledge was topped with a plush, purple cushion. Madeline stood transfixed as she soaked in the scene.

"That's pretty nice, huh?" he remarked softly, as he came up closely behind her, enfolding his arms around her waist and silently breathing in the enticing fragrance of her silky hair. His heart pounded in his chest; she felt so warm and perfect in his embrace, just as he'd imagined she would every night since meeting her—only somehow the real thing exceeded even the most detailed visualizations of his love-struck heart and soul.

Madeline felt a shiver of excitement as she leaned her head back against him and covered his hands with hers. Such a simple gesture, yet one that instantly created strange and wonderful sensations within her, longings she'd never experienced during her two-year relationship with Jake. It was all so exhilarating—and frightening.

"I'd be happy to just stay here awhile, Kenny," she whispered.

"Me, too," he mumbled hoarsely, as he kissed her on the temple. He moved around her then and turning to face her, sat down on the cushion. Taking her arms in his, he gently drew her near to him. Their eyes met meaningfully and the moment seemed frozen in time. She placed her petite hands on his broad, strong shoulders, trying to etch the sight of him—in all of his bold masculinity—forever in her mind.

He caressed her sweet face as he studied her, searching for signs. As much as he desperately wanted to give in to the overwhelming desire to kiss her, the last thing he wanted was to mess things up with the first girl for whom he felt so much more than just an intense physical attraction.

"So, why don't we just stay here?" he finally murmured. Ken closed his eyes and, leaning in close, placed his lips on hers. Their first kiss began as a gentle, somewhat tentative experiment, gradually increasing in passion and fervor as pent-up emotion mingled with real affection. He ran his hands through her auburn waves, tracing the curve of her back down to her waist and back up to her shoulders.

Swept away in a tide of unprecedented feeling, Madeline lost herself in the scent of his aftershave and the warmth of his body, blown away by her inability to wrap her arms entirely around him, try as she might. In his strong embrace, she felt completely safe and secure. It was as if all of the pain of the last few months had finally dissolved into nothingness as this new and wonderful man shattered every misconception she'd held about herself since childhood. Not even those who loved her most had been able to accomplish that feat; now here was this handsome ex-sailor, effortlessly knocking down the walls she'd so carefully constructed around her heart.

"You feel so good," he murmured finally, nuzzling her neck.

"You, too," she whispered, "Like a big teddy bear," as he then carefully situated her on his lap. She was now sitting on his leg, still holding one arm around his shoulder while he intertwined the fingers of her other hand with his.

"You're amazing Madeline Rose, do you know that?" He stared deeply into her brown eyes as he spoke. Maddy was speechless; all she could do was lose herself in the pools of aquamarine and the seductive feel of the toned muscles that protruded from beneath the fabric of his suit jacket. He smiled at her adoringly, and she actually felt faint for one fleeting, ephemeral moment.

Then, like a splash of cold water, a cacophony of loud voices and shrill laughter punctuated the air as in the near distance, the elevator doors opened to reveal a formally attired group of high-rolling men and women clad in black tuxedos and skin-tight gowns with plunging necklines and garish sequins. Ken and Maddy watched as they made their way into the club; for a brief second, the harmonious sounds of a live jazz band filtered into the room, only to be silenced once again when the golden doors gracefully closed behind them.

"Want to go in, sweetheart?"

As much as he'd have preferred to continue their romantic interlude he'd been abruptly awakened by this dose of reality, a harsh reminder that he and Maddy weren't truly alone.

"Sure," she whispered, sharing the same sentiment. She stood up then and adjusted the hem of her dress. Glancing at his face, she prevented him from rising to his feet.

"Wait!" she cautioned and reached out to wipe the stain of her lipstick from his mouth, gently but firmly removing every trace of it with her fingers. "I don't think it's your color," she laughed. Although she was completely unaware of it, this simple gesture had intensified his attraction.

"You know, my old boyfriend would get so mad when my lipstick rubbed off on him," she further explained. With that, he assertively took her hands in his and looked directly into her eyes.

"Madeline, I would be proud to wear your lipstick," he declared. While he appeared to be quite serious, she couldn't quite figure out what to make of that statement, which presented yet another striking contrast to Jake. She smiled as he leaned forward to kiss her forehead before taking her hand and leading her into the smoky club.

Ken and Maddy snuggled close together in their plush, clam-shell shaped booth as they listened to the sensual rhythms of a professional saxophone, each uplifted by the recent memory of their passionate embrace more than 20 stories high above the boardwalk. When the cocktail waitress came by to take their order, he smiled when he heard her ask for cranberry juice. She was truly unique. And for the first time since his return to civilian life visions of white lace, diamond rings, and picket fences floated through his mind and lingered in his heart.

"Wanna come in?" she asked as he threw the car in park. It was somewhere between 1 and 2 a.m., and they'd just arrived back at the house after driving through the darkened, tranquil streets of Ocean City.

"I'd love to sweetheart, but it's awfully late. What about your mom and your aunt?"

He wanted nothing more than to curl up with her on the couch, to hold her body close to his and smother her with kisses all over again. But she was no ordinary girl, and this was definitely no ordinary family. He still couldn't get over the way they'd all related to each other so easily over breakfast that morning. It was unlike anything he'd ever experienced. She looked up at him with a mixture of disappointment and admiration.

"You know, when you look at me like that, you make it awfully hard to do the honorable thing," he laughed, kissing her briefly on the lips.

"It's ok, I understand." She sighed as she leaned her head on his chest.

"I had such a wonderful time, Kenny. "Thank you." Maddy stood up on her toes to reach him as he pulled her into another divine embrace, leaving them both breathless. They were standing on the steps by the front door, reluctant to face the inevitable end of a perfect evening. As if suddenly remembering where they were, he quickly broke away and gazed into her eyes.

"Baby, I gotta go." He traced her cheekbone with his thumb, then settled his hands on her waist. "Believe me, I don't want to," he added, bringing their foreheads together. She smiled as she placed her hands on his chest. "And just so you know, the pleasure was all mine," he whispered. "Thank you for going out with me."

And after extracting another sweet kiss and permission to call her again, Ken drove away in his sporty black Acura, leaving them both to replay the night's exquisite events in their dreams.

Chapter 4

Maddy quietly climbed the stairs after grabbing a bottle of water from the fridge. Lingering at the top, she peered through the slightly ajar double doors of the master bedroom directly to her left, listening closely for the sounds of deep slumber.

Although it was dark, the muted glow of a seashell nightlight in the hallway revealed two covered figures fast asleep in bed. She smiled silently to herself as she noted the glaring differences between her slender mother and her obviously much larger Aunt Maria, who often jokingly described herself as "pleasantly plump."

But though there were physical contrasts between the two sisters, each shared common traits of warmth, generosity, sociability, unselfishness and—oh yes—an almost irrational love and overprotectiveness of their children. As Maddy gingerly closed the door and entered her bedroom, she nearly burst out in laughter imagining Mom staying awake just long enough to hear Ken's car pull up, followed by her key turning in the lock. Although at times annoying, it was mostly a wonderful feeling to be so loved and cared for.

She pulled her dress over her head and patted her tummy, hoping that this evening's indulgence in pasta wouldn't set her back a pound or two. Thank goodness, Kenny had been willing to walk on the boardwalk; not only had it been romantic, it might have helped her burn a few calories. She laughed at the memory of the rolling chair guy and how he'd stormed away angrily when neither one of them accepted his offer.

Maddy opened a drawer and pulled out her favorite *Victoria's Secret* pajama set—pink shorts with a matching tank top—one of many presents she'd received for her birthday. That was one great thing about being born in March, it meant getting lots of nice spring and summer clothes. Funny she and Ken had come into the world on the exact same day and year, on opposite sides of the Delaware River. Did that mean anything significant or was she just reading too much into a cool coincidence?

As she patted her face dry and applied moisturizer in front of the bathroom mirror, she paused as images of her handsome new suitor flooded the theater of her mind—his dazzling smile, the incredible feel of his muscular physique as she tried to encircle him with her arms, the way he would gaze at her longingly, then laugh with slight embarrassment when she caught him doing it—it was all such a refreshing departure, a welcome surprise, possibly even a gift from above.

And yet he scared her in many ways, too. Here he was a former Navy sailor who'd undoubtedly encountered many exotic women in ports all around the world. Would he really have the patience to date someone like her?

Maddy hugged her pillow as she settled into bed. And what to make of all these strange sensations? Sure, when she and Jake were dating, one thing usually led to another until someone put the brakes on. Once they'd even gone a bit further than was comfortable for either one of them. Still, Jake had never elicited this kind of desire.

Right from the moment she saw him, dangling that silly rose in front of Carmen, she could tell he was different. And his kiss was the kind she thought existed only in Harlequin Romance or Danielle Steele novels. Was her life really about to change dramatically? Whatever changes were on the horizon she fervently hoped they involved Ken Lockhart as she closed her eyes and finally drifted off to sleep.

A bare-chested Kenny stumbled into his most cherished possession after his townhouse and car—his waterbed—after filling Kathy in briefly about his date. Though he'd hoped to avoid it, he'd literally bumped into her as he came through the front door, on her way to go work the blackjack tables.

"Don't you look nice!" she'd complimented him. "Did yiz have a good time tonight?" Her South Philly accent often intensified when she was genuinely excited about something. Though she'd never had children of her own, she had looked upon as a surrogate son even since they worked together at the Taj. After having a front-row seat to Ken's heartache with previous relationships her fondest wish was for him to find the right girl—preferably a nice Italian girl, not that sleazy Roseanne chick or that neurotic little princess, Liz Anne. He'd pined away for her all those years in the Navy, and for what? To return home and find her engaged to his best friend? It was such a disgrace.

He truly appreciated her genuine interest and concern, although at times he found it suffocating. That was one reason why he'd tried to conceal his budding romance; he didn't want to invite any unsolicited advice or worse, disapproval if for some reason Kathy didn't like her. And even though it was hard to fathom anyone disliking a girl as sweet as Maddy, it was way too early to risk anything.

"Yes, we had a great time, Kath." Try as he might, he couldn't suppress a telltale grin.

"Aw, I'm so glad sweetheart!" she exclaimed gleefully, squeezing his cheeks. "You deserve a nice girl! Would love to chat more about it but I'm already late for work as it is. You just make sure she treats you right!" Kathy called out as she ran down the driveway.

Ken stretched out his six-foot, two-inch frame as he gazed up at the skylight. Thoughts of Madeline filtered through his mind, awakening his senses and tugging at his heart. Her big brown eyes earnestly looking into his as she asked what it was like to be on an aircraft carrier; the way he felt so at ease about sharing his dreams for the future with her; the cute habit she had of crinkling her nose when she wasn't sure if he was pulling her leg or telling the truth; and the bolt of energy that shot through his body whenever he touched her face, held her in his arms or gently explored her soft mouth with his tongue.

He rolled over on his side and looked at the clock. *Ugh.* His shift started in less than six hours. No problem, he'd just use the phone at work to give Maddy a call. With any luck, it would be a slow day, and he could listen to her sweet voice until, at last, he was free to see her again. She had mentioned that she could stay in Ocean City until Monday morning when he'd asked her about it the week before.

Uncertain of work obligations, he hadn't been able to make definite plans then. Hell, it took an act of God and two very long, back-to-back shifts just to take her to dinner last night. But she had been so very much worth the effort. And as he fell into a blissful sleep, something told him the best was yet to come.

"Morning, ladies!" Maddy called brightly, jumping on the queen-sized bed to snuggle in between her aunt and her mother. She'd awakened as soon as the sun had peeked through the vertical blinds of her bedroom. When she'd heard the two of them talking and laughing about their casino adventures the night before, she couldn't help but join them. Besides, she knew they were probably dying with curiosity, wanting to know all about her date with Ken. She'd give them just enough information to make them happy. But the way he made her feel when he looked at her, the raw passion yet exquisite gentleness of his kiss, the feel of his big, strong arms around her—those were private matters reserved for the deep confines of her heart.

"There she is!" Aunt Maria laughed in her inimitable, melodious style.

"Hey, Mad, that guy is so adorable! How was your date?"

"Wonderful!" she replied, giving each of them a peck on the cheek. "Did you notice the first thing Kenny said to you was how beautiful you looked?" Mom asked. "He's nothing like that ass, Jake. You don't know—when I would overhear some of the things he'd say to you, I had to bite my tongue. I wanted to tell him so badly to go look in a mirror; it was obvious you weren't dating him for his looks!"

"Ma—calm down. That's over," Maddy reminded her. "And you're absolutely right; this guy is nothing like Jake. I had no idea how gentlemanly and sweet a guy could be. In fact, it almost made me uncomfortable at times."

"He does look at you adoringly," her mother noted, with a smile.

"When you came down those stairs, I thought his eyes would pop out of his head. And the way he stood up right away; very respectful."

"Guess it's all that good Navy training," Maddy offered. She thought of their unstoppable kiss by the window overlooking the ocean and how his hands ran through her hair. Her heart skipped a beat.

"Well, you just enjoy it Mad, because you deserve it," Aunt Maria observed. "I'll tell you, I could've gone for him myself, he looked so handsome in that teal suit!" She gave them one of her trademark snorts, a sure sign of approval, as all three of them cracked up.

"So what did you guys have to eat?" Aunt Maria asked.

"Oh, Maria, is that all you worry about?" Mom scolded, with equal parts scorn and playfulness.

"I just want to know, that's all! I hear that Frisanco's place is really good. Carmella and Frank go there all the time when they're here in the summer." She was referring to a "snowbird" couple they'd grown up with in Germantown, who now divided their time between Pompano Beach Florida and Margate New Jersey.

"Yes, Joe wants to go there sometime," Mom concurred. "Maybe some weekend when he doesn't have surgery, you and Earl can come down with us, and we'll all have dinner there."

The sudden ringing of the phone halted any further social plans as Mom leaned over to the nightstand to answer. Maddy listened to her greet the caller in the formal tone she always used when trying to hide her excitement; she and Aunt Maria exchanged knowing glances. It's for you," Mom whispered, cupping the receiver with her hand as she turned to look at Maddy. "It's Kenny!"

Aunt Maria stifled a giggle as Maddy took the phone while Mom abruptly got out of bed. "C'mon, Maria, let's go make some coffee," she ordered. Once they'd closed the bedroom door safely behind them, Maddy answered the call.

"Hello?" She tried to exude a sort of calm enthusiasm.

"Hiya, sweetheart!" he greeted her in his deep, sexy voice. "I just had to call and thank you for a wonderful evening last night."

"Aw, Kenny, I should be thanking you. I had such a nice time." She couldn't shake the image of him smiling at her from across the table. "Where are you? I hear a lot of noise in the background."

"Oh, I'm at the power plant, had to work a morning shift today," he explained. "But I just wanted to call and tell you what a great time I had— and to ask if I could see you later. You're not driving back tonight, are you?"

Uh, no," she responded, "I can drive back in the morning, drop off Mom and Aunt Maria, and then head to work. Actually, I can just do some sales calls first, and then go into the office later on."

"Great! Can I pick you up at five?"

"Sure."

After she hung up the phone, she let out a happy squeal before flinging herself back on the bed. Then with a sudden panicked thought, she abruptly jumped up and ran into her room, in search of the perfect outfit.

Ken counted the hours until he could see her again. Time seemed to drag on, and it didn't help that things were slow at the plant today. Making matters worse, his buddy Quentin—normally one of his biggest supporters—kept riding him about Madeline, and how a girl like that would never stay for long with a blue-collar guy like him.

"You don't know anything about her!" Ken had snapped back defensively.

"Oh, I know all I need to," Quentin brusquely retorted. "Doctor's daughter, big house in the Philly suburbs, vacation home at the Jersey Shore—she may like you now, man, but she's way out of your league. I mean, really, what do you have to offer her? Do you think she really wants to end up with a working-class Joe doing graveyard shifts at Atlantic Electric? Get real!"

"Hey Quentin, this place? It's only a starting point, man. I'm just biding my time and saving my money until I can finish my education and make something of myself. Maddy knows that. And when she sees my townhouse and hears more about my plans for the future, she'll know I'm serious. She already gets that I'm not just another Jersey shore beach bum, slicing up pizza pies on the boardwalk like my brothers, going nowhere fast. You didn't see her face last night, the way she looked at me. I know she feels the way I do—"

Unmoved, Quentin rebuffed him, "Sure man, you'll be good for one thing, but she'll tire of that eventually!"

An enraged Ken grabbed his friend by the collar. "Don't you ever speak like that about her again! Madeline is a real lady, not one of your cheap Somers Point bimbos! But you wouldn't know what a real lady is now, would you?"

A stocky, slightly overweight man a few inches shorter than Ken, Quentin didn't take too kindly to that last statement. His ruddy face took on a deeper shade of scarlet as he threw a punch in Kenny's direction, which he easily deflected. Twisting Quentin's arm around his back, Ken pinned him against the wall.

"This conversation is over," he informed him before storming off.

Noticing the crowd that had gathered in anticipation of a knock-down, drag-out brawl, Ken informed them in a loud voice that the show was finished. "Mind your own business and get back to work!" he ordered them.

Rubbing his arm, Quentin called after him, "You know I'm right, man! One day you're gonna find out!"

"Kenny!" she couldn't hide her excitement when she opened the front door and saw him standing there with a big bouquet of flowers in one hand and a box of chocolates in the other. Dressed in a pair of khaki pants and a white buttoned-down shirt, he was the image of the quintessential clean-cut boy of summer. His ever-present smile radiated warmth and sincerity. And as he pulled her into a tight hug, mindful of the presents he was still holding, he realized there was nowhere else in the world he wanted to be at that precise moment.

"Hiya, sweetheart!" his words were muffled as he kissed her hair.

"It's so good to see you!" she said, releasing herself long enough to take the flowers and lead him into the foyer. "These are so beautiful, thank you!" She brought the assortment of white orchids and red and pink roses to her nose, breathing in their sweet fragrance.

"Uh, where are the ladies?" he asked, hoping they might actually be alone, respect for her family notwithstanding.

Pulling out a glass vase and setting it on the kitchen counter, Maddy informed him they were still at the beach. But before she could even cut the flowers out of the plastic, she felt his arms slip around her waist and his hot breath in her ear.

"You mean, we're alone?" he whispered sexily, placing a soft kiss on her neck as he gathered her long hair to one side. She was wearing her favorite black knit halter top, studded with gold and multi-colored gemstones, and a pair of dressy black shorts. Around her waist, she wore a matching gold belt, with a pretty rhinestone buckle.

"Afraid so, sailor," she softly confirmed. She turned to face him as he drew her into another delectable kiss. She wished it could go on forever as she felt his hands caress her bare upper back, then move to her waist and back up again. All of the day's stress melted away for Ken, as thoughts of his earlier confrontation with Quentin and his own nagging insecurities were obliterated by the satin feel of her skin, the warmth of her body against his and the rush of emotion that electrified his entire being at the mere sight of her.

When their lips finally parted, Maddy placed her head against his chest and held him close.

"God, you feel so good, Kenny," she sighed.

"So do you, baby," he whispered. "I never want to let you go."

"Kathy, you here?" Ken called out for his roommate as he and Maddy entered through the doorway of his Foxtail Court townhouse. They'd just had a great meal of spaghetti and mussels at her place after Mom and Aunt Maria had insisted he stay for dinner. The four of them had a marvelous time laughing over Aunt Maria's classic stories—well known within the family, but always funnier when retold with a new listener present.

Ken seemed to get a kick out them, particularly the one about a hot and humid day in August 1973 when she and Monica had decided to take all of the kids to Great Adventure. About midway through the Safari—where even the lazy, sleeping animals seemed to have been affected by the intense heat—the air conditioning had broken down in the car. As a woman who was often "roasting" on even the most bitter cold winter days, Aunt Maria had insisted on rolling the windows down, only to have the park ranger scold them over the P.A. system. Good thing he had, though, because right after that, a mob of baboons descended upon them, apparently hell-bent on "christening" Monica's brand- new white station wagon.

And of course, having insisted on wearing her cute new sandals instead of practical shoes to the park, Aunt Maria had ended up in the First-Aid building with blisters all over her feet. After throwing the shoes away, she'd "stolen" her teenaged son's tube socks so she could walk around in comfort—but not before they'd wasted most of the day waiting for someone to help her. Maddy laughed as she recalled the memory of her frustrated mother finally taking her by the hand and saying, "C'mon, Maddy, this is ridiculous! You and I are going on some rides. I didn't pay all this money so we could tend to your aunt's sore feet!"

But thanks to extremely long lines, they wound up riding a grand total of two amusements after being there nearly twelve hours.

Next, Mom shared stories of summer evenings at Phillies games when she'd pile five kids in the car and head down to the Vet at least four times a week. Maddy groaned as she remembered having to get out of the pool—her favorite thing in the world—so she could dry off, get dressed and join her siblings for yet another long nine innings, assuming it didn't go into extras.

"Don't you like baseball, Mad?" Ken had asked.

"It's okay, but I am definitely more of a football girl. I just love the Eagles. I grew up going to the games, and we still have our season tickets." He listened jealously once more as she recalled her presence, along with Lori and Damian, at the NFC Championship Game in 1981, when she'd thought she might freeze to death in the sub-zero wind chills. But it had been such a pleasure to watch the Eagles thrash the Cowboys in person. She cracked up as she recalled Wilbert Montgomery's touchdown in the first quarter—made in their end zone—and Damian jumping up and down so hard, Maddy and Lori were positive he would end up on the field. Fun times, for sure.

"Well, Ken, maybe you can come up and go to a game with Madeline this season," her mother suggested. "As much as I love them my husband and I prefer to watch the games at home now. With Damian living in Nashville and Greg and Lori so busy, we usually end up with at least one extra ticket."

"Wow, that'd be great!" He squeezed Maddy's hand under the table. She grinned at the thought of it.

Ken had a few good stories of his own, including one in which his mom—against her husband's wishes—took him and his older brothers to Yankee Stadium in New York to see a game, only to get stuck there during the frightening blackout of 1977. A young boy of 10 at the time he remembered well the panic and mayhem, though they all eventually returned home safely. His dad had not been amused.

And as a man who appreciated good food, and in fact, made a pretty decent meal himself, Kenny went crazy over Monica's tangy red sauce, the perfect companion to the mussels and spaghetti. He thanked her profusely every time he accepted another offer of more.

"Please eat, Kenny," Monica had said. "I don't want it to go to waste and Maddy sure isn't going to put a dent into it."

"Yeah, sweetheart, this is delicious. Why aren't you eating more?" Kenny asked, looking at her barren plate. "Aren't you hungry?"

"Oh, I try not to eat too much pasta," she explained. "Usually goes right to my hips."

"Are you kidding?" he asked, raising his eyebrows. "You're beautiful!"

He laughed at the ludicrousness of Maddy thinking she was fat.

"Yes, well, that's what we keep telling her," Aunt Maria added, exchanging an approving look with her sister at Ken's reaction. This guy definitely seemed like a keeper.

"Ok, well you all can make fun of me, but I know my body. Besides, it just means there's more for you, my teddy bear!" She playfully poked him in the ribs.

"I guess so!" he laughed. "But I still think you're beautiful, just the way you are."

"Guess she's working at the Taj tonight," Ken shrugged when no one responded to his calls. He led Maddy into the nicely furnished, cozy living area, where she observed with admiration the built-in bookshelves, modern entertainment center and rich leather couch and loveseat. There were some family photos hanging on the cream-colored walls, including one of Ken looking all handsome and serious in his Navy uniform.

"My gosh, look at you!" she said, smiling.

"Oh yeah, that's me, sailor man," he laughed.

"Ken, you should be very proud of yourself," she admonished him. "I am," she added softly.

"Thank you, sweetheart," he replied, kissing her on the head. "Hey, you thirsty? Want a beer—uh, soda?" he asked, remembering her distaste for pretty much any kind of alcohol.

"Water?" she asked as she followed him into the eat-in kitchen, adorned with granite countertops and white appliances.

Built just over a year ago, everything in the home was practically right out of the showroom. Maddy was in awe of Ken's housekeeping habits, which shattered the myth of the carefree bachelor. That he truly took pride in his living space was evident from the moment they pulled into his driveway. A small, well-manicured lawn led to a short walkway, framed by rows of impatiens; two hanging flower pots on either side of the front door held more of the same red, pink and white flowers. Upon entering, the home had a neat, yet welcoming aura, offering a perfect haven after a long, stressful day.

"I think I've got some bottled water for you, sweetheart," he promised, scouting out the fridge. "You know, instead of a beer, I think I'll have one, too," he said, pulling out two bottles of Poland Spring. She reached up to kiss him as he handed one to her.

"C'mon, I want to show you something," he announced, taking her hand and leading her up the stairs.

He opened the door to reveal his pride and joy, and the centerpiece of his bedroom—his king waterbed.

"Very nice!" she approved, smiling. Suddenly she felt a bit nervous. Although she trusted Ken, the thought of the two of them alone in such a provocative setting gave her pause. Attuned to her vibe, he gave her a quick kiss on the cheek and assured her his intentions were totally honorable. Pulling some photo albums down from the headboard shelves, he invited her to see some pictures.

"They're from my Navy days," he explained. With that, he propped up some pillows and sat upright on the bed, then patted the space next to him for her to do the same. She smiled in response to his mischievous grin but hesitated for a moment.

"Madeline, I promise you, I won't try anything," he coaxed her. "I know what kind of girl you are, and it's such a nice change. Please! I promise I won't hurt you." His azure eyes were earnest, prompting her to feel like an idiot for doubting him. She finally acquiesced and joined him on the bed.

"Whoa!" she laughed, trying to get used to the motion. "I've never been on one of these!"

"Then you don't know what you've been missing!" he joked, placing an arm securely around her. She snuggled in close as they pored over photo after photo, each with its own unique tale to tell.

As the sultry sounds of Earth, Wind and Fire's *After the Love is Gone* played softly in the background, Maddy suddenly stirred out of a sound sleep. For a split-second, she nearly panicked at the unfamiliar surroundings but when she spotted the skylight overhead showcasing yet another night of luminous beauty and felt the heat emanating from Ken's closely aligned body, the day's events came rushing back in a dizzying montage. She smiled as she noticed all the open photo albums strewn across the floor.

In the darkness, she could still discern some of the images Ken had explained in vivid detail—he and his buddies goofing around with pasties and hula skirts; Ken working diligently on the top deck of the aircraft carrier; and Ken and his former love Liz Anne, standing in front of the glorious redwood trees of northern California, during his leave. *Wow.* Now that was quite a story.

In fact, there had been many emotional narratives behind the pictures – some of which ignited a flow of tears from his eyes as he bared his soul to her. He didn't know what it was exactly that made her so damn easy to talk to, but as she sat beside him, transfixed by every word, he just couldn't help himself. It was as if she held some kind of power, some magical key that unlocked the impervious gates that had previously guarded his innermost thoughts.

She wondered what time it was as she settled back into her pillow, too comfortable for the moment to really care. She would've stayed wrapped up in his arms all night if she could, if only platonically. Unfortunately, even the literal act of sleeping together was going to have to wait for another time when Mom and Aunt Maria weren't hanging out on the other side of the 9th Street Causeway.

Actually, she was pretty sure they were gambling at one of the casinos right now, though it was anybody's guess which one. Mom loved Showboat; Aunt Maria was preferential to Caesar's. And though in all likelihood they'd probably be back late, she couldn't risk falling into one of her typical deep sleeps that would render her totally unconscious until morning, thus negating all of the high regard they now felt for Kenny. Not only would that be completely unfair to him, it might possibly kill their developing relationship. And after spending this precious time with him tonight, she definitely wasn't willing to take that chance.

"Mmmm, hi beautiful," he whispered as he softly smothered her neck in kisses and ignited shivers up and down her body as she nestled closer to him. "How are you?" he continued playfully.

"I'm good," she sighed. "How could I not be in the arms of a handsome sailor?" He laughed and held her even more tightly. "You know, you really are a teddy bear," she whispered.

"That's because I have a beautiful woman in my bed who I never want to let go of," he offered. "Ken?"

"Mmm-hmm?"

"I don't want to let go of you, either," she confessed. "Sweetheart, that's the best news I've heard all day."

With that, he leaned over her, taking great pains not to crush her under his weight. He stared into her eyes and stroked her auburn hair, which was fanned out against her pillow.

"Madeline?" His voice was hoarse and husky.

"Yes?"

"I think I'm falling in love with you."

Chapter 5

Madeline struggled to catch her breath as she gazed into his eyes. From beneath her palm, she felt the intense beating of his heart. There was a time not so long ago when she would have given anything to hear these very words from Jake. Now here she was, gasping for air.

She remembered back to a day when she and Jake had attended mass in a lovely church in Exton. She had remarked about the beautiful family that had been seated in front of them—an attractive mother and father probably in their mid-thirties, with six adorable children. It had been obvious from their Sunday best attire and joyful exuberance how deeply they loved and cared for their children and each other. Maddy had been awestruck by the family's simple expressions, like a touch on the elbow or a knowing glance and smile. Palpably moved by the entire scene, she'd whispered, "Wow Jake look at them! Isn't that the sweetest thing you've ever seen?"

"Yeah, that poor fool," he'd retorted sarcastically, nodding his head in the direction of the father. "He'll be working the rest of his life to feed and clothe all of those hungry mouths! Better him than me!"

The crushing disappointment she'd felt at his reaction marked the beginning of the end of their rocky relationship. In the second year of courtship, Jake had started to show his true revulsion for the traditional societal foundation of marriage, family, and responsibility. This incident, in particular, had awakened her to the fact that they shared divergent, incompatible goals and outlooks on life.

As for love, in hindsight, she realized he'd never felt anything close to that where she was concerned, which explained why the words had never crossed his lips. Of course, it's hard to love another when lost in one's own self-absorption.

Still, she doubted if she was ready to accept proclamations of love yet from anyone – even a handsome guy with whom she shared an amazing chemistry. It was only their third date. How could he know he loved her? Or was he just playing her?

She stared at him in silence as she tried to reconcile these conflicting thoughts. However, her lack of response had no deleterious effect on Kenny's enthusiasm or faith.

"Don't worry Madeline, you don't have to say a word right now," he whispered, gently placing his fingers on her delicate mouth. "I know you love me, and someday, you'll know it too."

"But how can you be so confident you love me? You don't even know me." Her words were firm but kind.

"See, there's where you're wrong." He leaned in for another kiss and she responded enthusiastically as their passion mounted. His tongue was soft and playful as he sought out hers; his hands roamed through her satiny hair, caressed her shoulders, and traveled down to her waist.

Temporarily lost in passion, she undid a few buttons on Ken's shirt to allow easier access to his broad, rippled chest. She couldn't get enough of his warmth, his unabashed masculinity as those new and overwhelming sensations rushed through her body. Ken broke away and sat up long enough to free himself completely from the garment. She looked at him with a mixture of awe and fear, fully cognizant of the dangerous line she was walking between adamant words and instigating actions.

"It's ok, baby, we won't go any farther than this," he promised in a husky whisper as he settled carefully back down on top of her. "God, you're so beautiful." He stroked her face before they melted into another spellbinding   interlude. Her small hands belied her underlying strength as she expertly massaged his back and weaved her slender fingers through his curly blond hair.

"You drive me crazy, sweetheart," he sighed. He slowly pulled her halter top out from the waistband of her shorts and slipped his hand beneath the knit material. He marveled at the smoothness of her skin as he moved closer to her breast.

Suddenly her mind wandered back to another time and place: the living room couch in Jake's parents' home where they'd returned from Lily Langtry's, her favorite dinner theater after seeing an amazing rock 'n roll review and a fabulous dinner. It was a biting cold night in February, the sort of weather that was much more conducive to snuggling in front of a fireplace than getting dressed up for a night on the town. But they'd had a wonderful date, and as they caught sight of the cozy fire his sleeping Mom and Dad had left for them, the only thing on their minds was romance. Their nascent relationship had been moving along swimmingly at that point, the result of a set-up from family friends.

Madeline had worn an ultra-feminine dress featuring a black velvet bodice that laced up the front and a floaty, detachable skirt that swirled as she moved. With her long hair pulled back at the crown with a black bow, she epitomized the sweet femininity of a Madame Alexander doll. Jake had noticed, though his somewhat tepid, "You look nice," compliment hadn't exactly inspired the dialogue of epic love stories.

Nevertheless, she found herself swept away as they began to enjoy each other's company in the soft glow of firelight. And as their fervor gradually amplified to a dizzying crescendo, she barely noticed when he began to untie the ribbons of her dress; before she knew it, she felt her black lace bra slip away from her shoulders. And then came the rush of icy cold water.

"Wow, you weren't kidding! You really are small!" he remarked without a hint of sensitivity as he laid his eyes on her bare chest.

A devastated Maddy quickly put herself back together before demanding a ride home; although he'd apologized profusely during the 20-minute trip back to Media, she'd been too hurt to even kiss him goodbye as she raced out of his car and into the comfort of her own bed. For most women, it would have been enough to end the relationship immediately; unfortunately, she tended to forgive a bit too easily, possibly due to a lack of self-love at the deepest core of her being.

"Kenny, no!" she cried out in a piercing voice as she forcefully pushed him away. She quickly tucked her top back into her waistband and sat up in bed.

"Mad, I'm so sorry!" His voice resonated with genuine remorse. "I just got caught up in the moment, and I guess I couldn't help myself. I didn't mean to scare or disrespect you, I swear," he pleaded, placing an arm around her shoulder and leaning his forehead gently against hers. "My God, the last thing I want to do is blow it with a girl like you."

She covered her face with her hands, more embarrassed by her reaction than anything he had done. What had happened wasn't exactly a surprise, considering they were all alone in his bedroom and shared an intense attraction. Gathering her composure, Maddy wanted desperately to find the right words to comfort him and clarify the root cause of her discomfort. But it was as if the synchronicity between her thoughts and the physical mechanisms necessary to express them had completely failed her. All she could do was sit there in silence.

But when he finally pulled her into a hug, she didn't resist. Instead, she buried her head in his chest and muffled an emotional apology.

"Nothing to apologize for, sweetheart," he comforted her. "It's ok. Everything's ok." His voice was a barely audible whisper as they held each other in the translucent beam of moonshine streaming from the window above them.

"Have a great day, hon!" Mom called out as Maddy pulled her white Le Baron back out of the driveway of the family's Pennsylvania home. It was Monday morning, and she'd just dropped off her mother and Aunt Maria before heading out into her territory to do some sales calls.

"Bye!" she blew them a final kiss before cruising down Martin's Run, on her way to Cedar Grove Road, then ultimately, Route 252, which she would take into Paoli. She was planning on hitting some hot prospects in the Chester County area today. The summer doldrums had begun to transition into a post-Labor Day mindset as companies returned their attention to their hiring needs.

Although she enjoyed the flexibility of her outside sales position, along with endless opportunities to meet new people, she was growing weary of its constant demands, ever-increasing quotas, and often frustrating outcomes. Many times, when she'd finally lure a new client away from their preferred agency, the thrill of accomplishment would give way to sheer disappointment when her own company couldn't fill the open position with a qualified person – or worse, had to do damage control when one of their temps either didn't show up or did a lousy job.

Unfortunately, her quarterly commissions depended upon completed assignments, something totally out of her control. While it was nice when a new client called in with an order, it simply meant the beginning of an extremely arduous process.

However, on this cheerful morning, career dissatisfaction was the last thing on her mind—it was too occupied with thoughts of Ken to care about temporary or permanent placements. And when Jon Secada's song came on the radio as she headed down Lancaster Pike, it transported her right back to the previous evening at Kenny's townhouse. He sure was full of pleasant surprises; underneath that handsome, well-built exterior beat the heart of a truly sensitive Pisces, a man whose emotions seemed to run as deeply as her own.

Just several hours before, Maddy had gasped in admiration over Ken's Military accomplishments, conveyed through his captivating story-telling and vivid collection of photographs. Then he'd abruptly stopped. She'd been so engrossed in the pictures she'd failed to notice the storm clouds that had formed over his typically smiling face.

"Kenny? You ok?" she'd inquired softly when she noticed him wipe away a tear. That's when he turned to look at her, his blue eyes glistening.

"I just can't get over how interested you are in all of this. During my four years in the service, my own father never even once wrote to me. Hell, I don't think he's even forgiven me yet for enlisting in the first place. He never wanted me to."

"But why? I would think he'd be really proud of you."

"You don't know my father," he explained with an ironic laugh.

"He took it as a personal insult that I didn't want to stay in Ventnor and make meatball subs and Stromboli's for shoobies and tourists. Figured if living there was good enough for him and my brothers it should be good enough for me."

"Oh Kenny, I'm so sorry," she comforted, placing a hand on his shoulder. "I think it's amazing you had the maturity at that age to make such a huge, life-changing decision. I give you so much credit. At 18, I wasn't nearly that mature."

"Why do you seem to know just what to say to make me feel better?" he'd asked, rhetorically.

"I just call 'em as I see 'em," she'd chuckled, trying to lighten the mood. It seemed to have worked. Ken had kissed her forehead in response, then picked up right up where they'd left off with the next photo.

"Oh, my! Look at these beautiful redwood trees!" she exclaimed when he turned the page. Next came the shots of a petite young woman with long, ebony hair posing arm-in-arm with him in front of northern California's celebrated natural landscape.

"Who's this?" she'd inquired with more than curiosity. As crazy as it seemed, she felt a bit jealous.

"Oh, that's Liz Anne, my high school sweetheart." For the first time all evening, Ken seemed reluctant to talk.

"And?" she pressed on.

"Not much to tell," he shrugged. "We dated during our senior year. After graduation when I joined the Navy, we kept in close touch. Unlike my father, she wrote to me every week. So did my mother. They both came out to see me one time when I was on leave. That's what these pictures are from."

"Looks like you're having fun," Maddy noted, taking in the smiling faces at the airport, in front of the Golden Gate Bridge, and in the middle of Fisherman's Wharf.

"We did....for a while." His tone was serious again.

"What happened?"

"Maddy," he sighed. "I don't know if I want to get into this—No, you know what? I am going to tell you the truth." She braced for the worst. Were they still involved? Had they married and were now separated?

"Liz Anne was a nice girl like you," he began. "And I really loved her. I had no problem waiting for her until we got married, and I'd told her that over and over again. But she was kind of insecure, and she had these preconceived ideas about sailors, you know, the girl in every port thing. Her friends didn't help any; they just added fuel to the fire with their wild accusations."

He stopped for a second and ran his hands through his blond waves. Maddy waited quietly for him to continue, genuinely intrigued.

"She swore she trusted me, but kept saying that she knew all about the pressure I was under constantly, you know, from the other guys." He gave her a telling glance, and Maddy nodded her understanding. "Somewhere in her mind, she got this crazy thought that she owed me. It wasn't my idea, Maddy, I swear. I never pushed her to do anything. But on our last night together she insisted on consummating our relationship. And I was as gentle with her as I knew how to be.

"Still, afterward, she bawled her eyes out. And I felt so guilty; I wished it had never happened; I really did love her, and all I wanted to do was make her happy."

Maddy silently studied his face and ascertained the veracity of his words, struck by the obvious pain this memory held for him. He stared into the distance as he brought his arms back behind his head. Without any prompting, he continued, "So I decided to do something special for her— I gave her all of my personal journals as a gift, so she'd understand how much she'd meant to me."

Wow," she remarked, impressed. As someone who'd painstakingly kept journals since childhood, she was delighted they shared yet another trait in common. She was also amazed that he would actually love someone enough to entrust them with such an intensely personal gift.

"Gosh, Kenny, I am speechless. She must've been so overwhelmed when you gave those to her!"

He just shrugged as he went on. "Well, apparently it wasn't enough. When I got back home, I bought her a small engagement ring. I called it a promise ring because as soon as I'd gotten my career started, I'd planned on buying her something bigger."

"So then what happened? Did she accept it?"

"Yes, but she was still very suspicious. Kept wondering who'd I'd been with, knowing my affectionate nature."

"Oh." She watched as the tears formed again. For the life of her, she'd never understand some women.

"The sad part is, I really loved her parents, and they loved me. But we couldn't seem to get beyond this misunderstanding. Then, of course, I was fighting with my father over my future plans, so I moved into my own apartment. That's when I took the job parking cars at the Taj. It paid my bills and gave me time to think about my next move."

"Makes sense," she commented.

"I thought so," Ken continued. "I had gotten good engineering training in the Navy, but Atlantic Electric didn't have a position available for me yet. One of my buddies was making good money as a parking valet, so he got me in. I actually enjoyed it; it was fast-paced, and I got to meet a lot of people. And the tips were great."

"So, what about Liz Anne?"

"Well, one day she stopped by to inform me that she'd burned all of my journals," he explained with a twinge of bitterness. "That was just before she threw the ring in my face. After that, she eloped with another guy from our graduating class, who'd since become a cop in Pleasantville."

"No way! I am so sorry she did that to you."

She'd slipped her arm around him as she tried to shift her position on the rippling waterbed and ended up crashing into him in a welcome moment of comic relief. Kenny smoothed her long hair and kissed her forehead as she settled comfortably into his chest.

"I'm not. I'm glad it happened," he'd whispered. "I wouldn't be here right now holding you in my arms if it hadn't." She closed her eyes and luxuriated in the warmth of his body as they'd both drifted into a peaceful sleep.

"So do you think you can get down here this weekend, sweetheart?" his tone was hopeful as he awaited her response.

"Absolutely!"

She was beyond the point of putting on silly pretensions; with him, she didn't feel the need. Besides, he'd been pursuing her as a gentleman should ever since the morning he'd come looking for her on the beach. Why play hard to get when his interest in her was plain for anyone to see?

She stretched out on her twin bed, enjoying the exquisite privacy of her own exclusive phone line—well at least the one she shared with her sister, Lori. In the Ocean City house, there had been no need for such extravagances; they were really only there three months out of the year, except for an occasional fall weekend or possibly even a winter break, weather permitting. Were it not for Ken, she'd most likely see the cottage on Simpson Avenue eight months from now, when things finally began to thaw in May. Now here she was, anxious for the September days to fly by so she could head over the bridge again and into his waiting arms.

"I can't wait to see you," he cooed. "If you're definitely coming, then I am going to work a few extra shifts this week so I can get time off on the weekend."

"OK but don't work too hard. We can manage around your schedule if we have to. I don't mind."

"Sweetheart, I'd work seven days straight with no sleep if it meant spending more time with you." Her heart fluttered.

"Aw," she sighed. Then noticing a disruption in the background, asked what was going on. On his end of the line, Ken made a face at Quentin indicating in no uncertain terms that his presence in the room wasn't welcome; Quentin reminded him that they were at work where Ken's assistance was required. He gestured to his co-worker to give him a minute before focusing back on his phone conversation.

"Nothing, baby, but I do have to get back to work now. Can I call you when I get home?"

"Sure, but won't that be at 6 a.m.? You might be tired."

"Never too tired to hear your sweet voice," he replied softly, trying to hold the image of her beautiful face in his mind like a still photograph.

"In that case, it'll be the best wake-up call I could ask for."

After saying goodbye, she snuggled up under the covers, dreaming of his arms around her as she went to sleep.

"So you're heading down to the house after work on Friday?" Mom asked.

She and Maddy were standing at the counter in their ceramic tiled kitchen preparing a dinner of chicken cutlets, tomato salad, and broccoli. As had been her "job" with this particular menu since she was a little girl, Maddy carefully dipped each chicken breast in egg before submerging it in Italian breadcrumbs and adding it to the Pyrex dish that would then go into the oven after the cutlets had made a short stopover in the frying pan. Her mom had the more difficult task of slicing away any unwanted fat and pounding them to the desired thinness before moving them along in the assembly line.

"Yeah, Kenny was able to get most of the weekend off, so we're going to go to the beach if it's still warm enough, then maybe walk on the boards, go to dinner...I'm not really sure yet." Monica Rose looked a bit concerned as she opened the oven door and slid the Pyrex dish inside.

"Maddy, I don't think your father is going to be too happy with the idea of you being there alone. I mean, Ken's a nice guy and everything, but it doesn't look right."

Here we go, she thought to herself. My God, hadn't she already proven her loyalty to her upbringing? At 25, most girls her age had already discovered what life was about. Here she was, still innocent in the ways of the world, fully on-board with the concept of waiting until marriage before giving herself completely to a man, ever mindful of her own dignity and her parents' wishes and reputation.

"Mom, my God," she protested, "All of the times I've been out on dates with Jake, we were alone plenty of times. What difference does it make if I am somewhere in Pennsylvania or at the Jersey Shore? If I wanted to do something wrong, I sure don't have to drive over the Walt Whitman Bridge. And what do you mean, it doesn't look right? Look right to whom?"

She fought to keep the emotion out of her voice, but conversations like these could be exhausting. She knew her mother meant well but sometimes wondered if "what other people might think" was the overriding concern.

"Honey, I know," Mom's voice softened. "I know you, and I know you're a good kid. It's just that you two are still getting to know each other, and your father and I don't really know Kenny yet. What I've seen so far I really like. I mean, he's respectful, courteous...and it's obvious how much he likes you. But I still don't like the idea of you being there alone. Why doesn't he come here?"

"Well, for one thing, he has to work part of the weekend, and for another, I really want to go to the beach while I still can, before it gets too cold." Then after an inspired thought, she asked, "Why don't you and Daddy come down this weekend, too?"

"I think your father's on call," she explained.

"Oh, well do you think he'd mind if you and Aunt Maria came down without him?" Her father was so good about those things, never resenting anyone else for having the freedom to enjoy the fruits of his labor; on the contrary, it gave him such joy to know that those he loved were happy. And quite honestly, he wasn't much of a beach person to begin with.

While his wife and children were content to play in the sand and surf for hours, Joseph Rose would become restless and agitated after what seemed like only moments. Maddy and her siblings would crack up as he'd rise up out of his chair and announce with firm conviction, "I cannot sit!" Then, he'd head back to the house before venturing to the Ocean City Municipal Golf Course or the small airport, where he'd begun taking flying lessons.

Much to her mother's chagrin, the latter hobby had led to the purchase of a low-wing Piper Cub, a money-sucking toy whose significant burden on their finances was evident every month when she did the books. She certainly didn't begrudge her hard-working husband an outlet; but after years of funding college educations, such an unnecessary big- ticket item was beginning to prove just too much of a strain. And now, Lori's wedding loomed on the horizon. It was all a bit overwhelming.

"I don't know; I guess I can ask him. Your father's so good that way."

Maddy nodded in agreement. "I can just leave him with some food he can heat up. You know your Dad; he's happy with a sandwich, but I can leave some eggplant parmesan and some other stuff in the freezer.

He certainly won't starve!"

Visions of the casino danced in Monica's head as she went over to the phone to call her sister.

"Ah, the smell of the seashore!" Maddy enthused. She held the button down on the electric window and inhaled the salty air as they cruised over the 34th Street Bridge on their way into Ocean City. Her Down's brother Louis was sitting on the seat next to her; Mom and Aunt Maria followed closely behind in their own car.

"Smells good!" he agreed. Maddy was thrilled he'd been able to get the weekend off from his job in material services at the hospital; she'd told Kenny so much about him and his accomplishments and she couldn't wait for them to meet each other.

And though it was well into the middle of the month, the weather remained warm and pleasant, as if God was bestowing a consolation prize for a mostly rainy summer before the inevitable arrival of fall and winter. Right on cue "their song" played on the radio, bringing her right back to that magical first date in Atlantic City, and that funny night at the Point Diner when Ken kept calling out fruitlessly for their indifferent waitress while she rebuffed his cute, but slightly irritating affections. Who knew that such an inauspicious beginning would herald the promise of something so much better?

As she and Louis pulled into the driveway from the alley, her heart skipped a beat when she noticed a familiar figure waiting for them on the back porch. He'd been sitting there patiently on a cushioned patio chair ever since returning to Ocean City after stopping home to shower and change after his shift. He stood up the moment he'd noticed the headlights flooding the pavement and heard the familiar hum of the engine, feeling the blood rush through his veins. Even in the dark she could make out the radiance of his ever-present smile.

"Kenny!" she cried joyfully, slamming the car door shut.

"Heh-hey," he laughed in his inimitable manner, throwing his arms around her as she bounded the three stairs up to his level. He held her tightly as he picked her up off of the ground.

"Kenny put me down! I'm way too heavy."

"Are you nuts?" he asked in all seriousness. She felt light as a feather in his big, strong arms.

Then, noticing Louis behind her, he carefully set her back down on her feet while she made the proper introductions. Maddy smiled as the two of them shook hands and Kenny inquired about the latest John Grisham book Louis was holding. He never went anywhere without a book and at age 34, he'd pretty much shattered every dire prediction made by narrow-minded doctors who'd coldly advised her parents to place him in an institution just days after his birth. All these years later, Louis was a thriving, happy, and productive human being. Maddy couldn't imagine her life without him.

The trio stood talking and laughing until Mom and Aunt Maria pulled up. After exchanging pleasantries, they sat down in the family room with some iced tea before Monica announced their plans to head over to Harrah's in Brigantine with Aunt Maria and Louis.

"I just got some comps in the mail this week," she explained. "So we're going to try someplace different."

"Oh good!" Louis beamed, rubbing his hands together. "I feel lucky!" he added, prompting all of them to crack up.

"My sister has successfully corrupted my sweet little nephew," Aunt Maria laughed. "You should see him play that video poker. He's really good!"

"You like that, huh?" Ken asked.

"Oh yes," Louis affirmed, smiling.

"I don't even know how to play that," Maddy added.

"You my dear should be singing in one of the lounges," Aunt Maria stated. "That beautiful voice; you could make a lot of money. You and Kenny could create some kind of act," she added, jokingly.

"Ah, *no*," he piped up. "Afraid I'd have nothing good to contribute there." He laughed at the thought of it.

"Yeah, right," Maddy protested. "Re Re, you should see him dance. He's amazing!" Ken was a little embarrassed as she went on to describe how he'd displayed his moon-walking skills at Key Largo that night.

"Ok, that's just about enough of that, young lady," he teased.

"You are much too modest," she scolded.

"Look who's talking," he replied softly.

"Have a great time," Maddy waved as the three of them pulled out into the alley and set off on their quest for fun and fortune. Once they were safely gone, Kenny pulled her into his arms and another spellbinding kiss on the back porch. A warm, gentle breeze had begun to blow, dancing through her hair and complementing the goose bumps that had already formed on her skin in response to his touch.

"God, I've missed you," he admitted in a soft, sexy voice.

"I've missed you, too," she replied, reaching up on her toes to pull him even closer. She was wearing a strapless, sea foam green sundress, with a matching bolero jacket and a short, flared skirt, with off-white ankle strap sandals that had just a slight, two-inch heel. He had on a pair of nice jeans with a navy tee shirt. Maddy could feel the hardness of his chest muscles as she placed her palms against him. For a while, they just stood there holding each other.

"Hey, I have a surprise for you," he finally announced. In the warmth of their embrace, he'd almost forgotten about it.

"What?" she asked curiously, breaking away to look into his sparkling eyes.

"Oh, now if I told you, sweetheart, that would kind of ruin it, dont'cha think?"

He loved to tease her and watch the ensuing sparks light up her face. Predictably, she tried to tickle it out of him before he literally swept her off of her feet and into his car.

Chapter 6

Thank you, sir," Ken said to the worker in the Ocean Drive toll booth when the man gave him back some change. They were headed north over the Longport Causeway to some unknown—to Maddy at least—destination. Despite her many playful inquiries, he still wouldn't 'fess up to where they were going.

"You'll just have to find out when we get there, little lady!" he teased her, keeping one hand on her thigh and the other on the steering wheel. His favorite cassette, for the moment anyway—Earth, Wind and Fire's Greatest Hits, blasted out soulful rhythms through the speakers.

Amazingly it was another clear, star-studded evening and as they made their way towards the city of Longport, they passed through her favorite stretch of road, completely surrounded by water.

"I love this part of the ride!" she enthused, placing her hand on his. He lifted to his lips for an affectionate kiss.

"Me, too," he agreed.

"Ken?"

"Yes?"

"Aren't you even going to give me a *little* hint?" He broke out into gales of laughter. "You're a persistent one, aren't you? Don't worry sweetheart, we're almost there. The suspense will be over soon."

"You are such a tease!" Her tone was playful as they crossed into Ventnor City.

A few moments later the black Acura pulled into one of many available spaces on the block alongside the beach. Had they attempted this just a few weeks prior, they'd have been circling around for hours waiting for such a prime location. But with the summer season in the rearview mirror and Labor Day weekend a recent memory, the Shore once again belonged exclusively to its year-round residents, its native sons like Ken, who were thrilled to have it back to themselves. He only wished that the privilege also came with 365 days of annual sunshine and summertime temperatures; winters in South Jersey could be downright depressing, not to mention, endless.

Maddy was willingly obedient when he motioned for her to wait until he came around to open the door and help her out of the car. Having heard a few off-putting things about her ex-boyfriend Jake, Ken was determined to treat her with the respect she deserved, even if she still had difficulty adjusting to such simple gestures. It was the least he could do, although he looked forward to the day when he could financially afford to spoil her with more tangible tokens of love like expensive jewelry and exotic vacations. But only after he'd vowed his eternal commitment to her in front of God and witnesses, of course.

"Is this where you went to beach growing up?"

"One of the places," he answered, popping the trunk and pulling out a large, red Coleman cooler and a black duffle bag that looked as if it were bursting at the seams.

"What's all this?"

"Here, take my hand sweetheart and you'll find out," he responded, simultaneously slinging the bag over his shoulder and lifting the cooler off the ground before reaching out for her with his free hand.

"Ken! Let me carry something," she protested, to deaf ears.

"Madeline, will you let me treat you like a lady?" he answered sternly.

"Yes, sir," she replied, as they made their way up the wooden steps leading to the sand. The moonlight cast a string of sparkling diamonds on an otherwise darkened sea as Kenny spread out an enormous, fluffy blanket; she knelt down on one end, cognizant of the increasing strength of the early autumn breeze. He sat down on the other side and proceeded to remove the contents of the cooler. As she observed in gratitude, he set up a romantic picnic of some of her favorite foods including homemade tomato pie, provolone cheese from South Philly, and even some freshly baked Italian wedding cookies.

"Oh my gosh! When did you find the time go to South Philly?" she asked in amazement.

"Don't forget my roommate Kathy is from there. She drove up on her day off yesterday, and I asked her to pick up some provolone for me on 9th Street. There's this place there she always goes to. I think the owner is a family friend. Anyway, it's the good stuff."

"It sure is," she affirmed as she breathed in the enticing aroma. "My mom drives down there every so often to get cheese, mostly for special occasions like Christmas. It's the best. Can't find anything like it in the supermarket."

"Nah, this is the real deal," he laughed, "although the tomato pie comes from some new bakery that opened up here in Ventnor. I hope it's good."

"It sure looks good," she noted. "Mr. Lockhart, I do believe you are going to make me fat," she chuckled.

"Hey," he warned seriously, "No starvation tactics tonight. You and I are both going to enjoy this good food—no apologies. Oh, and you have to have some wedding cookies. Kathy made those especially for you."

"She did? How'd she know they're my favorite?"

"Cause I told her," he shrugged. "I had asked for her advice about how to win an Italian girl's heart – and not just any Italian girl but the most beautiful one I know—a girl I almost blew it with that night at Key Largo when I was stupid and bought a rose for her friend instead of her."

Maddy laughed at the memory.

"And she suggested wedding cookies?" Madeline raised an eyebrow.

"She said it was a good place to start considering they were on your top ten list," he smiled. "And she makes the best, believe me."

"Hmm, well my Aunt Maria might take issue with that. Still,

those do look pretty good," she admitted, eying the full plate of the familiar twisted knots covered with white icing and multi- colored sprinkles.

"Well, no dessert for you until you've eaten your dinner," he teased, setting the cookies aside. Then he removed two plastic stemmed glasses, along with a bottle of one of her favorite beverages.

"Asti!" she exclaimed. "Boy, you are full of surprises. What are we celebrating?"

"You," he answered softly, pouring the effervescent golden liquid into their beach-appropriate holders. He handed her one as he settled in next to her on the blanket. "We're celebrating you," he repeated, as they clinked champagne flutes. All a choked-up Maddy could do was smile back at him as he beamed at her in the night.

"Do you ever wonder what people are doing on the other side of the ocean?" she asked, as they lay side by side on the blanket. Having considered every contingency, he had brought along his black sweatshirt embroidered with the gold Taj Mahal logo. Maddy lay wrapped up in it now, relishing its warmth and the lingering scent of its owner's aftershave. He held his arms tightly around her as she laid her head on his chest. They'd eaten their fill of gourmet treats and were now content to just embrace the magnificent scene around them—as well as each other.

"Hmm, well I've actually gotten to see what many of them were up to firsthand during my Navy days," he explained. "Unfortunately, not all of it was good."

"We're very blessed to live in this country, aren't we?"

"Yes, we are," he agreed, kissing her forehead. "Kenny?"

"Yes?"

"No one has ever done anything this sweet or thoughtful for me— ever. At least no one I've ever dated, anyway." Then lifting her head up to look at him, she whispered, "Thank you."

He gently stroked her auburn hair with his hands as they first joined eyes and then lips.

"You deserve all of this and so much more, sweetheart," he assured her in his husky voice, in between soft, damp kisses that awakened their senses and ignited their passions.

"Looks like they're not back yet," she remarked, noticing the absence of her mother's red Dodge sedan. They had just pulled into the driveway from the alley; the little house sat in darkness, save for the subtle glow of the porch light.

"They must be winning big," she joked.

"Wow, it's pretty late," he agreed. "Louis must be cleaning up with video poker; maybe they can't tear him away from the machine."

Maddy cracked up at the thought.

"So, do you want to come in and keep me company 'til they get back?"

She tried not to think about her appearance at the moment. After several wonderful hours spent enjoying each other's company on an increasingly windy beach, her contact lenses felt like irritating pieces of sand in her eyes; her disheveled hair hung in knots past her shoulders. Little did she know it just endeared her even more to him.

He placed the clutch in park, and then turned to look at her, still clad in his black sweatshirt. Because it was way too big for her petite frame, it hung almost past her skirt, setting off her shapely dancer's legs. Ken glanced at them in appreciation before taking her tiny hand in his and lifting it to his lips, in what was now his typical fashion.

"Sure, sweetheart," he whispered.

A few moments later they were snuggled on the couch watching a movie, although he could never quite get comfortable. Gambling predilections aside, he had no idea when her family would saunter in through the sliding glass doors, full of funny tales of visiting New Yorkers with obnoxious accents and jackpots that never materialized. Although she'd assured him that the sound of the tires on the concrete would tip them off, he remained vigilant as he held his arm around her waist and rested his head on the pillow above hers. In spite of himself, he couldn't help but wonder how it would feel to truly make love to her; his heart raced at the thought.

"Maddy?" he asked softly, as he traced her arm from shoulder to wrist.

"Mm-hmm?"

"Don't you ever get curious?"

She turned her body so that she was now looking at him directly.

"Curious about what?"

"You *know*," he offered a telling glance and a raised eyebrow. Then he regretted asking the question. But relief washed over him when he saw a smile slowly form on her face.

"Well..." she began, her voice trailing off. As desirable as he made her feel there remained an underlying fear, an almost irrational insecurity when it came to this very intimate act between a man and a woman.

For her, it went far beyond the "your body is a temple of the Holy Spirit" teachings of the Catholic Church, repeated so often throughout her schooling she could almost hear them in her sleep. She'd long ago accepted the validity of these words; indeed, she took them to heart and wanted nothing more than to give herself to her husband—whoever he might turn out to be—for the very first time on their wedding night. It was simply that as she grew older, she realized how few people, *good people*, had applied the same beliefs in the real world.

Even Jake in all of his self- righteousness had admitted to sleeping with his college girlfriend, though he claimed that his ensuing guilt over it had been partially to blame for their break-up.

Beyond all of that she struggled with some deep-rooted insecurity about not being good enough, not having a body acceptable enough, and not adequately aware enough of how to please a man. *Hadn't she read stories in the hottest women's fashion magazines about men leaving their wives over sexual dissatisfaction? Hadn't she seen the endless articles about how to be better in bed?*

And now as she stared into his expressive blue eyes, sublimely at home in his arms, she struggled for an answer. He really did seem to love her for her, yet it had only been a few weeks. *How could she really trust in that?* True, she believed him when he told her about Liz Anne, but surely a virile young man like him had been intimate with other women. He could he not have been? He was simply too cute, warm, and appealing not to have indulged in the pleasures of the flesh with more than one participant.

Maddy didn't begrudge him; she was fairly certain her brother Greg, whose personality mirrored Ken's, had also tasted forbidden fruit on more than one occasion prior to his engagement to Vanessa. But would Kenny really be willing to wait for her over the long haul?

She wanted so much to confide in him her conflicted emotions, to explain what she held so deeply within. But as with that night in his waterbed, there was a frustrating disconnection between her innermost thoughts and their eloquent expression. All she could manage was some lame answer about how sex belonged within the confines of a marriage. Undeterred, he just smiled at her as he traced the curve of her face.

"I know, sweetheart and I respect that so much," he assured her in his deep, sexy voice. "I just wondered that's all. I know I'd like to know what it's like be with you. Guess I'll just have to marry you to find out."

Then, as if sensing her apprehension, he asked with some concern, "Does it bother you that I've been with a woman before?"

"Kenny, no," she sighed. "No...I don't judge you for that at all. I mean, it's completely normal. It's just that...well...I just wish that we were on the same level playing field in that regard, that's all. I know it's probably too much to hope for with any guy, but it kind of makes me feel bad; like I am not being fair to you."

"Shh," he replied softly, "Madeline, I am here with you because I wanna be. There's no one else like you out there. And if I have to wait for you until I can marry you, then that is exactly what I'm gonna do."

God, he really did melt her heart.

"Is Ken coming to the beach with us?" Aunt Maria asked as Maddy scooped some coffee into the metal filter of her Mom's percolator pot. Another morning had dawned bright and sunny, and they were preparing a breakfast of oatmeal, eggs, and fruit before heading out for what might possibly be their last bathing-suit day for 1992. The gambling trio had enjoyed a late, if not financially successful night at Harrah's; a spent Louis was still upstairs in his bed snoring, though

Maddy planned to wake him up soon. Mom was still getting ready in her bedroom.

"Hopefully. Although he may get called into work because one of the guys is out sick."

"You know, that young man is a really hard worker," Aunt Maria observed. "And all you have to do is look at him to know how crazy he is about you." A joyful expression lit up her face. With her own daughter, Cassie happily married with a toddler son and Lori set to walk down the aisle within the next two years, Aunt Maria couldn't wait for her favorite niece to experience the same joy of being in love and walking down the aisle. From the time of Maddy's somewhat unexpected birth, she had shared an especially close bond with her only sister's youngest child.

As Maddy grew up, people had routinely remarked about her striking resemblance to Maria. And as close as she was to her mother, as she got older she came to rely on Aunt Maria as the one person in the world with whom she could share her deepest feelings without fear of betrayal. She may have been "old school" but that didn't stop Aunt Maria from being wise in the ways of the current culture, even if she disagreed with some of its accepted standards of behavior.

Maddy couldn't hide her excitement as she looked at her. "Oh my gosh, Aunt Maria, you should have seen the picnic he made for me on the beach. It was the most romantic thing anyone has ever done for me."

"Oh honey, I am so glad. You deserve it."

"And he's so respectful. He never pressures me to do anything I don't want to. Last night, he insisted on waiting with me until you all came back, even though I was afraid it might be really late, knowing how much you're all addicted." They both laughed. "In case he did have to work, I didn't want him to be tired. Poor guy, I hope he was able to get some rest."

"Yes, he looked pretty tired when he left," Re Re agreed. "Guess that just proves my point about how much he cares for you." Just then, Monica Rose walked in, already arrayed in her beachwear.

"Morning, ladies," she greeted them. "Looks like a beautiful day out there. We're lucky."

"Hi Mom," Maddy kissed her on the cheek. "Coffee will be ready soon."

"And look, you started eggs and oatmeal…wow, I like this treatment," Monica laughed appreciatively. Moments later around the dining room table, Maddy filled them in on her unexpected evening on the beach.

"There are even some cookies left over if you want any. I put them in the fridge to keep away the ants." With that, she got up to retrieve them. When she set the plate on the table, she winked at Aunt Maria and assured her that hers were still the best.

"That was nice of Ken's roommate to make these," her mom noted, dipping a sprinkled iced knot into her coffee cup. "God, they're delicious," she declared a moment later. The telephone disrupted any further commentary.

"Bet I know who that is," Mom teased as Maddy ran into the kitchen.

"Hello?"

"Hiya sweetheart!"

"Kenny, how are you?"

"At work, unfortunately. I won't be able to meet you at the beach today, but I'm off at five. Can I see you then?"

"Sure," she responded. "I'll miss throwing the football with you, but you can make it up to me later." He laughed.

"Hey, Maddy?"

"Yes?"

"Uh, what time is Mass tonight, at St. Augustine, do you know?"

"Um, I am pretty sure it's still 6 p.m. on Saturday. Don't think they've gone back to winter hours yet. Why?"

"Because I'd like to go with you before we have dinner."

"Really?" She was happily surprised by his request. Although a regular churchgoer, it had never been her style to force anyone else to adopt her habits; as long as a man respected her right to pray and attend mass, she was fine with him staying home. She'd come to understand that the way in which he conducted his life was much more important. After all, Jake knelt in a pew every Sunday, and it hadn't prevented him from mistreating her.

"Sure," he said softly. "You inspire me, Madeline. I want to do everything the right way."

"Me?" No one had ever spoken such words to her.

"Yes, you," he affirmed. As she paced back and forth in front of the refrigerator, Aunt Maria politely motioned for her to move out of the way so she could get the butter. She and Maddy exchanged smiles.

"Ok, but I think Mom, Aunt Maria and Louis will be joining us, too. Mom mentioned something about evening mass rather than waiting until tomorrow."

"That's great," he replied sincerely. "I'd love to see them."

"Ok then, sounds good."

"Maddy?"

"Yes?"

"Do you think you might ever sing for me sometime?" he inquired, his heart racing at the very notion.

"Hmmm, well that's certainly a possibility," she teased. "Did you want a private performance?"

"Definitely," he smiled on his end of the line. Off in the distance, Quentin watched the unfolding scene with annoyance; he wanted nothing more than for the inevitable to take place, so his friend would finally get his mind back on work, at least while he was here. He didn't understand why Ken insisted on deluding himself, thinking that this high-class girl would keep slumming long-term with a power plant engineer, but if he wanted to play this dangerous game, it was his life. However, while he was at the plant, he needed to cut out these nauseating phone calls. It was enough to make anyone sick.

Sensing the negative energy, Ken looked up and saw his co-worker scowling a few feet away.

"So, uh, will you think about it for me, sweetheart?" he asked again. He knew she was ridiculously modest about her talents, but the thought of her serenading him stirred his soul. He was sure there was an angelic voice to complement the beautiful face.

"Sure, Kenny. As long as we're alone, I'd be glad to sing for you," she promised.

"I can't wait," he told her before wishing her a wonderful day and hanging up the phone.

"Hey, Louis, how'd you like to go on some rides?" Kenny asked as the group stepped out of the church vestibule. Mass had just ended, and they were plotting their next move as they stood in the twilight of another balmy evening.

"Oh, yes!" Louis responded his face lighting up. This weekend was the last hurrah before Gillian's Fun Deck closed for the winter.

"Aren't you guys hungry?" Monica asked. "We could get a bite to eat first, then Maria and I can walk the boards while you all go on the rides."

"Sure," Ken answered. "In fact, I know this great little place on 10th and Asbury. Delicious seafood and steaks."

Maddy appreciated the ease with which he blended in with her family; he truly seemed interested in getting to know them in spite of work demands having prevented the two of them from spending any time alone so far this evening. And since unknown to him, it had been the only way for her to get herself to Ocean City this weekend—at least without a fight – it meant that much more.

"Well, ok then, let's go," she agreed, squeezing his hand.

The casual restaurant welcomed them with a nice, oversized booth and baskets of hot rolls and butter while they perused the menus. By the time the waitress came by to take their order, they'd been pretty much sold on that evening's special – pecan encrusted salmon with sautéed vegetables and rice pilaf. Maddy sat in between Louis and Kenny, with the larger of the two enjoying the extra room afforded by a place on the end.

He continued to delight her mother and aunt with his gregarious personality. A shared love of Eagles football didn't hurt either, particularly with Monica. Opening day of the new NFL season was tomorrow, with the group's favorite team playing their NFC Division rivals, the New York Giants, in the Meadowlands. With kick-off at 1 p.m., the plan was to watch the game at the house, before driving back to Philly.

"Why don't you join us, Kenny?" Monica asked. "I'll get some steaks, and we can grill out."

"Thank you, Mrs. Rose, I really appreciate the invitation," he replied sincerely. "I'll just have to check in at the plant to make sure they won't need me. Hopefully, Sam will be well enough to work tomorrow."

"I hope so," Maddy intoned softly, wistfully thinking about how quickly the weekends pass by.

"So, you really work some long hours," Aunt Maria observed.

"Yes, but they pay me pretty well. Thanks to this job, I bought my townhouse and my car, plus some extras. I don't plan to be there the rest of my life, but for now, it's a start."

He glanced at Maddy, thinking of all the plans he now wanted to put in motion even faster than before.

"Where did you go to school?" Monica Rose followed up.

"Holy Spirit High School in Absecon. After graduation, I enlisted in the Navy, where I got some excellent engineering training. I've been so busy working ever since I got home, I haven't had a chance to enroll in college, although I do plan to get a four-year degree."

Watching her mother from across the table, Maddy could sense disapproval although to the casual observer, Monica's thoughtful expression, and accompanying silence would barely register a modicum of concern.

But Maddy knew her mother's reaction all too well. As a woman who'd poured her heart and soul into making sure each one of her children achieved a proper education consisting at a minimum of a Bachelor's Degree, this was distressing news indeed. No amount of charm—sincere as it may be—was going to help her swallow that pill. As if sensing the mood shift, Aunt Maria piped up.

"Well, Kenny, that's wonderful. It's not an easy thing to join the military; your parents must be very proud."

"My dad didn't talk to me at first, but he came around eventually. Mom was always supportive, but I guess that's what moms do best," he shrugged.

"I think it's great," Maddy added. "I am not sure I could have done the same thing in the same situation, and I was lucky I didn't have to make that choice. Besides, a girl can't resist a man in uniform," she smiled up at him as she spoke, thinking of the handsome portrait that hung in his living room.

Actually, it wasn't so much the uniform, but the character of the person wearing it that was so damn attractive. Surely Mom would come to realize that, too.

"Ok, Louis, you have to hold both of your arms up as we go around," Ken teased as the trio settled into their seat on the Ferris wheel. The young ride operator locked the bar into place before pulling a lever and setting them off on their skyward journey.

"I hope we don't get stuck at the top," Louis giggled.

"We better not," Maddy chimed in as the cool breeze blew through her hair. Odds were actually in her favor given the lack of patrons; it was such a dramatic departure from the teeming crowds of summer. And as they rotated around nonstop for about the fifth time, it appeared that any fears about that outcome were definitely unwarranted. Each time they made a rotation she felt a rush of exhilaration as she gazed down at the blackness of the ocean which contrasted with the lights of the boardwalk. Of course, those sensations were magnified by the exquisite feel of Ken's protective arm around her. Watching him laugh along with her special brother brought an indescribable joy to her heart. While it was certainly true that Louis had an uncanny ability to bring out the best in people, Maddy couldn't help but believe that he was simply tapping into an existing source of goodness that dwelt within Ken's handsome exterior package.

"That was fun!" Louis declared as they stepped off of the ride.

"Yes, it was," Ken agreed handily before the three of them began walking towards 9th Street to reunite with Monica and Maria.

"Wow, I thought he was never gonna let us off," Maddy laughed. "I love Ferris wheels, but even I was getting a little nervous."

"Did you hear that, Louis? Your sister was scared," Ken's tone was playful as Louis joined in the good-natured teasing.

"Poor Mads," he said, patting her on the shoulder.

"Fine, go ahead and make fun of me, see if I care." She feigned indignation. With that, Ken encircled her from behind in his arms and kissed her on the head.

"You know I'm just teasing, baby," he whispered. "I'm so crazy about you, I can't help myself."

And though her body felt electrified, all she could do was place her hands on top of his as they made their way down the boardwalk.

"Did you guys have fun?" Monica asked.

"Oh, yes," Louis affirmed. "Ken and I even played games in the arcade."

"And he beat me at all of them," Ken reported with a chuckle.

"C'mon Ken," Louis admonished, swatting his hand in the air in his inimitable style. It was a gesture he always used when vehemently disagreeing with someone.

"Whadd'ya mean, come on Ken? You beat me fair and square!" He was truly amused and impressed by Louis. The group shared a good laugh before Mom and Aunt Maria announced their plans to sneak off to Atlantic City for an hour or so. The night was still young.

"Oh, good, I get to do some gambling!" Louis squealed, rubbing his hands together.

"Well, win some money this time, Louie!" Maddy teased.

"You have your key, right?" Mom asked her.

"Yep, sure do," Maddy replied.

"Ok, well you guys have a good time. "Ken, thank you for dinner. That wasn't necessary."

"It was my pleasure, Mrs. Rose. It's the very least I could do for the privilege of spending time with your beautiful daughter."

Maddy's heart fluttered. His words were not lost on either her aunt or her mother, who for the moment at least, forgot all about his lack of a formal college education.

Chapter 7

Here you go sweetheart," Ken said with a smile, handing Maddy a small cup of one of her favorite treats—lemon water ice.

"Cool, it's got little pieces of lemon in it," she enthused, taking a spoonful into her mouth. They were sitting on a green- painted wooden bench facing the ocean.

"You know, I really could have splurged on a large, Madeline," he remarked, nudging her playfully. Then, just as she was about to speak, added, "Oh, I know, I know. We have to watch our calories!" He was teasing of course, but she took slight offense.

"Hey, just 'cause you don't understand what it was like to be the 'chubby girl' in school, don't make fun of me. I wish I didn't have to be so careful, but I was never one of those naturally thin girls like Carmen, who can eat whatever she wants and not even have to exercise. It's just the way it is."

As she spoke her eyes followed the graceful trail of a seagull as it rode the evening air currents. Ken lodged his plastic spoon back into his slushy cherry flavored concoction and then turned her shoulders so she was looking squarely at him.

"Madeline," he addressed her in a serious, but gentle voice. "Listen to me, please. You are absolutely beautiful. There is nothing you need to change about yourself, ok? You want to be healthy, fine. You want to stay in shape, that's great with me. You're *already* there. But how can I get you to understand how incredible you are when all you can see are flaws?"

His eyes were sincere as they gazed into hers. Maddy comprehended his words, appreciated them even, and yet still couldn't quite grasp the truth of what he was saying.

"Y-you really feel that way, don't you?"

"Yes, I *do*." Although frustrated on the inside, he never wavered for a second. "Look, Maddy, I don't know everything that last guy said or did to make you feel this way, but I am telling you he was an idiot. I just wish I could make you see what I see whenever I look at you."

"I think you just did," she finally answered after a short period of silence.

"Good," he declared, kissing her on the cheek. Then in his teasing style, added, "Now finish your water ice, young lady!"

She cracked up as they watched the waves rush to shore.

"Well, here we are again," Ken announced as he ushered her through the front door of the townhouse. They'd just returned after a nice stroll on the boards; it was still a safe assumption that Monica, Maria, and Louis were happily playing the slots, or even heading to yet another casino hotel in search of "hot" machines. Ken knew that Kathy was working the blackjack tables tonight, giving them some time to themselves. He offered her a seat on the couch while he excused himself for a minute to head upstairs. She'd promised that Jitterbug lesson on his back porch on the way over to his place, and he wanted to take a minute to clean himself up.

While he brushed his teeth and put on a new shirt, Maddy inspected herself in the downstairs powder room. Pulling a naturally bristled hairbrush out of her purse, she smoothed out some wind-blown tangles, powdered her nose and applied some lip gloss. As she stared at her reflection in the mirror, his words came rushing back to her. *You're beautiful.* And as she adjusted the scalloped elastic sleeves of her black, off- the shoulder blouse and smoothed her slightly wrinkled black linen pants, she tried her best to believe them. When a final tug of her silver chain belt revealed it was securely in place, she walked back out into the living room, where he was already waiting for her.

The sight of him standing there in a pumpkin-colored, button-down shirt and black jeans, wearing his ever-present smile nearly took her breath away. No matter how many times she saw him freshly put together and ready to devote his full attention to her, it always sent shivers down her spine. And as she moved towards him and took his hand in hers, he felt the bolt of electricity with which he'd become accustomed ever since that night on the Key Largo patio. Without uttering a sound, he pulled her close to him and into another kiss.

And as their lips and hands explored each other's bodies, all thoughts of college educations, taunting co-workers, and overprotective family members drifted away with the tide, along with the acknowledgment of Monday morning's impending arrival when they'd inevitably return to their respective sides of the river. In spite of himself, he wanted nothing more than to scoop her up in his arms and carry her upstairs, where he would make passionate love to her until sunrise.

For now, he contented himself with the softness of her skin, the curve of her back, and the sweetness of her mouth. After what seemed like an eternity, they paused, with his strong arms still holding her close.

"You know, you did promise me something else," he whispered.

"What was that?"

"You said you would sing for me," he reminded her. As a slow smile crossed her face, she affirmed, "Yes, I suppose I did."

"Well?"

"You want me to do it right here?"

"Sweetheart, do you have a better place in mind? You did say you wanted privacy."

"So I did. Do you have a special request?"

"Not really, other than a slow, beautiful ballad."

"You're sure Kathy's not coming back?"

"Very sure."

"Ok, then. I really love Vanessa Williams' new song, so I guess I'll go with that. One request, though."

"What's that?"

"Can we slow dance while I sing?"

"That's one of the easiest requests I've ever had to honor," he whispered as he began to sway slowly with her in the dimly-lit room. Maddy cleared her throat and then delivered her best performance. Everything he'd heard about her talents proved true as he savored every note of her soulful serenade. For a second he wondered if he'd conjured her up in his mind—his ideal match, his perfect woman, a phenomenon much too good to actually be real. And as his hands rested around her waist, he wished this moment never had to end.

When she finished, he enfolded her in a big bear hug and affirmed not just her impressive vocal abilities, but his enduring love and passion. He expressed the second part of that carefully to assure her he understood that his physical desires would not be satisfied tonight. His reaction thrilled her but also added to her anxiety. How often could these tempting interludes take place before he lost patience and dumped her?

It was becoming quite obvious to that Ken's normal manly longings weren't the only issue; with every consecutive minute spent in his embrace, her own body was beginning to want more than just tender kisses and anatomically safe caresses. Why didn't anyone ever bother to address the female's raging hormones in any of the morality lessons of her youth? Why did it always seem like such an easy task to wait?

"I'm sorry," was all she could whisper back.

"Nothing to apologize for, baby. I'm just standing here picturing you walking down the aisle in your beautiful white gown. God, what a vision you would be."

She was stunned into silence as she tried to absorb everything she'd just heard; it was all so overwhelming. As she buried her head in his chest and held him closer, she silently ordered her persistent inner demons back to their rightful place in some deep, dark abyss, where they'd no longer wield any power over her.

"Hey," he whispered into her hair. "Will you come with me upstairs? I promise you, it's just to hold you near me, that's all. I love you too much to do anything to scare you away. Please?"

"Yes."

Her voice was barely audible, though her heart was pounding furiously as Ken easily lifted her off the ground and carried her to his bedroom.

He closed the door gently with his body before easing her carefully onto the bed. Now somewhat accustomed to the rippling effect of the water-filled mattress, she mingled with its currents as she sank her head into a fluffy pillow, never taking her eyes off of his. She quickly kicked off her sandals as Ken maneuvered himself on top of her, ever-mindful of his weight. He gazed at her for a moment and then decided the less intimidating choice would be to lie on his back. He gathered her in a warm embrace, allowing her to settle into the crook of his arm while she placed a hand on his chest. Above them, the skylight showcased a billion twinkling stars.

"Comfortable?" His voice was low and masculine as he kissed her hair and forehead.

"Mm-hmm," she sighed. "This is so nice."

He covered her hand with his while the other one slowly massaged her shoulder. How he wished he could slide the cotton-blend material down to reveal more of her soft porcelain skin and the firm, perky breasts he could feel through her clothing every time they engaged in a passionate embrace.

The stimulating thought of tenderly working his way down her body, leaving a trail of warm, wet kisses as he went nearly overpowered him as he pulled her closer.

But as the Boz Scaggs ballad, *Harbor Lights* played subtly in the background, Ken contented himself by running his hands slowly through her beautiful hair and touching her bare shoulder, while his imagination conjured up visions of a wedding night that satisfied body and soul. He could picture her emerging from a fancy marble honeymoon suite bathroom, wearing a short, white lace negligee with sexy décolletage and flowing pale pink ribbons that exquisitely showcased her smooth, sexy legs.

She'd smile sweetly as she made her way towards him, holding out a celebratory crystal flute of Asti. They'd toast each other and once again pledge eternal love and devotion before Ken would set her glass aside and lift her up into his arms in one graceful motion. Then he'd carry her to a plush bed of buttery soft Egyptian linens and lay her down gently before tenderly making love to her for the very first time, ever-mindful of her innocence and accompanying, understandable nervousness. It would be one of the most cherished, sacred moments of his life; he was determined that it would come to pass eventually, though exactly where and when, he was not quite sure of yet.

"Kenny?" Her hushed whisper interrupted his reverie. "Yes?"

"Is this ok for you?" She could have remained there content all night had two conditions been met—being truly alone in Ocean City with him for the weekend, and knowing beyond a shadow of a doubt that she was being fair and considerate of his feelings. The last thing she wanted to be was a tease.

"This is perfect for me, sweetheart," he replied softly, kissing her forehead. "Why wouldn't it be?"

"I don't know," she sighed.

"Do you have any idea what you do to me?"

She was fully aware of the phenomenon to which he was referring; in the stillness, she could feel her effect on him against her thigh even through his black jeans.

"That's what worries me," she admitted as she traced circles on his chest. She'd unbuttoned his shirt a few moments before, wanting to feel the warmth of his skin and the pulsating rhythm of his heart. "Maybe it's not right for us to be here. Maybe I shouldn't put you in this position and expect you to be patient until God knows—"

"Shh," he comforted her. "I'm fine, Madeline. I'm fine just holding you here in my arms. The rest will happen in time and when it does it'll be beautiful for both of us. You'll see."

"Wow, Kenny, you really are amazing." She lifted her head to meet his gaze as she spoke.

"If that's true, it's only because you bring it out of me," he replied, before drawing her into another intoxicating dance involving soft lips, artful tongues, and tantalizing caresses.

"Hey, Maddy, baby!" Joseph Rose greeted his daughter with his customary exuberance as he climbed up the back porch stairs, where she was busying herself with turning burgers, steaks and chicken breasts on a flaming hot grill. She and her mother had gone to the SuperFresh market on West Avenue earlier that morning, where they'd purchased all of the game day provisions.

"Dad! When did you get here?" She wrapped him in a hug.

"I just flew in a few minutes ago," he reported with pride. "Got someone to cover for me at the last minute, so I fueled up the plane and decided to surprise all of you in Ocean City. I tried to get your Uncle Earl to join me, but you know what a scaredy cat he is about flying."

"I sure do," she laughed, holding one arm around her dad as she put the cover back down on the grill.

"What's this?" he teased. "You taking over my duties? I am so insulted!" She cracked up. If there was one thing her dad really enjoyed besides flying his Piper Cub and practicing his golf swing, it was playing Grill Master in the summertime. Before she could answer, she heard a familiar voice.

"Nah, Dr. Rose, we were just getting it warmed up for you!"

"Hey Ken, how are ya?" Joseph promptly turned and extended his hand in a warm welcome as Ken closed the sliding glass door behind him. Joseph was a truly outgoing man who loved meeting new people and entertaining family and friends. From the time she was a little girl, Maddy had admired father's easy rapport and genuine interest in others—whether they were complete strangers, loyal patients or crotchety old uncles.

No matter their station in life, Joseph consistently treated everyone with whom he came into contact with respect and compassion; though he was one of the most well-known neurosurgeons in suburban Philadelphia, he'd never forgotten his Germantown roots.

And while he had a tremendous passion for his profession, his guiding motivation for going into medicine had been to help

people get well and provide for his family, not brag about his accomplishments. In fact, much as he loved it surgery had been his second career choice behind baseball. But thanks to an irreversible shoulder injury his junior year in high school, his promising future as a Major League Baseball pitcher had reached an abrupt end.

"I'm just great, Dr. Rose, how are you?" Ken replied.

"Doing fine; just flew into Ocean City airport. Had a great ride over—no bumps at all! It was absolutely beautiful!"

"Good to hear!" Kenny laughed, thinking how different Madeline's father was from his.

"Hey, is halftime over?" Maddy asked. "No, not yet don't worry," Ken assured her with a quick shoulder squeeze. They'd been watching an exciting defensive dogfight between the Eagles and the Giants; at the half, their team was leading, but only by 7-6. While it was a good sign that the Giants had to settle for two field goals both times in the Red Zone, there was still a long second half to play, and anything could happen.

It was the kind of game where a momentum shift could easily lead to a blowout.

"Good," she said. "I think these are almost ready."

"See what happens, Ken? They come down for one weekend without me and start taking over!" Joseph winked at him, and he chuckled.

"Hey, you boys are welcome to it," Maddy announced with a grin, walking to the door. "I'm gonna go see what Mom's up to, anyway. We may need to make more tomato salad and corn. We bought the silver queen cobs today—my favorite."

"Mm, sounds great," Ken replied, smiling at her. She looked adorable in a green Eagles tee-shirt emblazoned with the team's logo, and a pair of black shorts with a silver belt. Her auburn hair was pulled up in a high ponytail and on her ears, she wore her pierced gold Eagles helmets. Ken could picture her now in an official cheerleader outfit, dancing on the sidelines, waving metallic green and white pom-poms; she'd be the prettiest one on the squad, no doubt.

"Mom!" Maddy called up the stairs. "Dad's here!"

"Wait a minute, Lori," Monica Rose said into the phone. She'd been sitting on the end of the bed, intently listening to her older daughter's wedding plans while simultaneously wondering how much time she had left before kick-off. But before she could call down to the first floor Maddy bounced into the room.

"What is it Mads?" Mom asked, rolling her eyes in deference to the phone. Maddy giggled. As much as her mother was fiercely devoted to her children, when the Eagles were playing, everything else took a back seat— well, except for the procurement of a good meal when there was a significant break in the action. Normally, the 15-minute halftime recess meant either getting food ready for after the game, or setting it out to enjoy once play resumed in the third quarter.

"Dad's here. He decided to surprise us."

"You father's *here*?" Maddy shook her head affirmatively. Turning back to the receiver Monica said, "Alright, Lori, let me go. Your sister just told me your father arrived. He must've been able to get someone to cover for him. We can talk about the bridesmaids' gowns later and one night this week I'll go with you to those boutiques. Anytime is fine with me; I don't have anything else planned."

Monica rolled her eyes again at her daughter, who easily surmised that her older sister was still too excited to hang up. Finally, her mother replaced the receiver to its cradle.

"Whew! Your sister drives herself crazy worrying about every little detail for this wedding," she confided. "I keep telling her everything's going to be beautiful, but she agonizes over every minute decision. She's gonna drive me crazy. And my God, it's still almost two years away! Between her and your soon-to-be sister-in-law, I'm gonna be ready for the funny farm!"

Maddy cracked up again.

"She's not watching the game with Vince?"

"Yeah, but you know her; she obsesses over every last detail. So when did your father get here?" Monica got up, and the two of them headed back down to the kitchen.

"Oh, just a few minutes ago. He and Kenny are outside on the patio. I think the burgers should be just about ready by now."

"Ok, can you throw the rest of the corn in the pot, hon? I was gonna take it home tonight for dinner tomorrow, but between Ken and your Dad, I think we're gonna need all of it for today."

"Sure Mom."

Monica went out back to greet her husband, still engrossed in conversation with her daughter's new boyfriend. Looking at the scene of the three of them talking and laughing on the back porch made Maddy smile; she only hoped the future held many more such occasions. She stifled a yawn as she added a few more ears to the pot and turned up the heat. She could hear the NFL Today commentators blathering on about the new season, current scores, and Super Bowl predictions. Well, that was good; it meant they

still had some time to set up the food in the family room before the Eagles—who were set to receive—took to the field again.

Aunt Re Re and Louis had decided to go to a movie since neither one of them cared about goalposts and pigskin. Their plans included a bite to eat afterward, so Maddy and Monica had only portioned for three, well aware of Kenny's healthy appetite. And now that her equally voracious father had surprised them, it was even more of a good thing that the two women weren't big eaters. Otherwise, they'd be calling Kenny's favorite pizza place for reinforcements.

Madeline's thoughts wandered back to the previous evening's events when had actually convinced her to sing for him. At first, she'd been incredibly nervous, but now that she'd finally done it, she could hardly wait for the next opportunity to create that same exquisite feeling. Swaying slowly with him in the middle of his living room while she heard him whisper in that deep voice how much he loved her; resting her head on his chest as they lay side by side in his bedroom, just staring up at the skylight and dreaming of things to come—it was all the stuff of fairytales. Yet here they were: two real and flawed people who'd somehow managed to manifest a miracle when the stars aligned to place them on each other's path. *Was this really an act of God or a mere coincidence, much too good to last for more than a few months?*

She prodded the corn with a fork before cutting up some more tomatoes and onions to add to the salad. Still exhausted from a late night, she covered her mouth as she yawned. Ken had driven her home well into the wee morning hours, once they'd found the discipline to break away from their idyllic waterbed retreat. It hadn't been easy. Nor had it been a simple task to keep her guard up, lest one passionate thing lead to another, until—wow! Maddy could hardly believe she was even thinking this way. It was a far cry from her days of dating Jake. When she heard the sliding doors open, along with the accompanying familiar voices she turned to see Ken carrying in a platter of their freshly grilled main course as Mom closed the door behind them. The tantalizing smells of barbecue sauce and charbroiled meat wafted through the air.

"Ken, you can just put that on the counter," Monica directed, pointing to the hot plates that awaited the Pyrex dish's arrival. Maddy quickly strode over to optimally rearrange the set-up to host all of the food. Ken caught her eye and winked at her as he carefully set the platter down.

"Hey, Maddy, your friend here has agreed to go flying with me!" Joseph announced, slapping Ken on the shoulder. Mom and Maddy looked rolled their eyes at each other before she shifted her gaze to her dad and boyfriend.

"Really?" She laughed out loud but felt two conflicted emotions within. It was exciting to witness how well Ken and her father were connecting, yet terrifying that part of their easy rapport involved a mutual passion for aviation. Her usual trepidation about aircraft—from jet planes to helicopters—ignited a firestorm in the pit of her stomach.

Not so long ago, Maddy relished the thrill of take-off and the mesmerizing view of a golden sun peeking through white, puffy clouds as an airplane sailed through infinite blue skies. She used to be glued to the window, mesmerized by the   patchwork ground below, in awe of the amazing piece of 20th-century machinery that could transport her anywhere she wanted to go in just a matter of hours.

Up to this point, she'd never been on a flight that exceeded three hours. Somewhere along the way, she'd lost that original sense of wonder, though she couldn't quite recall exactly why or when. Maybe it had something to do with being an adult now. Or perhaps her mother's fears had finally rubbed off on her, though Monica certainly boarded planes when necessary.

From a mother's perspective, aerophobia was understandable; but not yet having children of her own, Maddy was puzzled by her own reaction to something she once loved to do.

"Yes, your Dad's gonna fly us over Atlantic City, then down to Cape May and back. It's gonna be so cool!" To emphasize the point, he gave her a high-five.

"Um, us?"

"Oh yeah, sweetheart, you're coming, too."

"Ah, Madeline's just like her mother, she won't fly," Joseph's tone was playful, though the sentiment was serious. But when Ken's aquamarine eyes pleaded with hers, she realized that any further protest on her part was futile.

"Oh, alright, I'll come," she acquiesced. The thought of having to sit in the cramped quarters of the back seat didn't exactly thrill her. In spite of her small stature, Maddy was quite claustrophobic. Well, it would only be a half-hour at the most; she could deal with that. Besides, she didn't have the heart to disappoint Ken, or even her father, for that matter. As she glanced at her mother, however, she realized there was at least one person in the room who wasn't completely on-board with the idea.

"Don't worry, Mom, we'll be fine." She patted Monica's hand. "Ken here has dealt with much more dangerous situations so I am sure he and Dad can handle it. Flying in a small airplane over South Jersey's not exactly as challenging as working on an aircraft carrier in the Persian Gulf." They all laughed.

"You got that right," Ken agreed.

"Alright, well, let's start eating before the second half comes on," Monica said with resignation.

"Geez, they gotta make you sweat it out 'til the end!" Monica observed when a defensive goal-line stand with less than a minute to go salvaged the Eagles' narrow margin of victory over the Giants. Had the men in blue been successful in crossing the end-zone, they would have eked out a 13-10 victory—assuming a good PAT, thus deflating the hopes of Eagles fans all over the Delaware Valley—for the moment at least. Then after a few days' funk, the devoted population would fully rebound to cheer their team on passionately against next week's opponent.

"Ain't that the truth?" Maddy laughed as they all stood cheering, laughing and high-fiving each other. Just then, Re Re and Louis entered the ebullient scene.

"Looks like good news Louis, thank God," Aunt Maria joked. "Otherwise, it'd be a long ride home with your mother."

"I know," he agreed, giggling.

"Hey, Louis!" Ken called out, catching sight of him.

"Hi Ken," Louis beamed as he shook his new buddy's hand.

"Joe! When did you get here?" Re Re asked.

"Oh, I flew in a few hours ago. I'd called your husband to see if he wanted to join me, but you know, Earl. Wanted no parts of flying!"

"Just like his wife," she laughed melodiously. Then, looking at her watch, she turned to her sister. "Hey, Moni, you ready to go soon? Speaking of Earl, I want to get home before it gets too late. He'll worry if we're driving on the expressway in the dark."

"Oh, Maria, it's the same thing as driving during the day, for God's sake. The exact same roads just lit up by streetlights instead of daylight. Besides, I'm the one behind the wheel. And you know how much I love to drive. I'll get you home safe and sound, don't worry."

A fiercely independent woman, Monica was often frustrated by her sister's irrational anxieties, even though she shared similar tendencies for differing reasons and circumstances.

"Alright, girls, take it easy," Joseph laughed. Then, shifting gears, he added, "Well Ken, it's still early. How about I file that flight plan?"

"Great," Kenny agreed, giving her a wink and a shoulder squeeze. She and her mother had already cleaned up the kitchen in between game breaks, assisted by a thoughtful Ken. And since Maddy had her own car, she could easily head back to Pennsylvania after their twilight tour of the New Jersey coast from over a thousand feet in the air. She never minded driving alone; the radio and her motivational tapes would keep her going during the nearly two-hour trek.

A few minutes later, Monica, Maria, and Louis said their goodbyes to Joseph in the family room while Maddy and Ken loaded their bags into her mother's red car.

"You just be careful with the two of them," Monica warned her husband. We don't even know Ken's family. That's all I would need is for something to happen to this kid—or my daughter."

"Hey, what about your husband?" He teased.

"Yes, you too," she affirmed. "But I've never been able to talk you out of the plane, and I've given up trying." With that, she planted a quick kiss on his lips before heading out to the driveway.

"Ok, Mads, we're leaving." She gave her daughter a hug before pecking Ken on the cheek. "Thanks for your help in the kitchen today," she added sincerely.

"It was my pleasure, Mrs. Rose. Thank you for the great dinner!"

"Just be careful, please," Monica advised them before slipping into the driver's side. Then with another thought, she rolled down the window. "Madeline, make sure you call me before you get on the road."

"I will Mom, don't worry," she promised. "Bye Louie, bye Re Re!" She blew them a kiss as they pulled out.

"Oh my gosh, I am so excited, baby," Ken enthused, wrapping his arms around her waist from behind and lifting her slightly off the ground.

"I'm glad one of us is," she laughed. Just then, Joseph joined them on the patio.

"Alright kids, we're all set. Why don't we just head over to the airport on foot?"

Located at 26th and Bay Avenue, Ocean City Municipal Airport was well within easy walking distance of their home. Maddy welcomed the chance to burn off dinner and hoped maybe some brisk exercise would quell the butterflies that had begun to form in her stomach. And as the orange autumn sun started its descent on the horizon, the three of them made their way to the little plane that would afford them a birds-eye view of the Shore.

Chapter 8

This is 3-0, 4-0 Whiskey, requesting clearance for take-off." Joseph's voice sounded as official as any commercial pilot's as they taxied into position on the short runway. To the left, Maddy noticed the tall, ubiquitous marsh grass swaying in the breeze and the tower in close proximity. In front of her, she could see her dad and Ken nodding affirmatively at each other, arrayed in regulation headsets. She did her best to focus on the outside world with its wide open spaces and vividly painted skies as a distraction from her cramped quarters.

She was about to take a deep breath when Ken turned back to look at her with a reassuring smile and a thumbs-up. Maddy returned the gesture just as her father got clearance from the tower.

Ok, thank you!" His voice boomed as he revved up the engines and ignited the Piper Cub's ascent above the horizon. Amazingly, the little plane mimicked the identical take-off sensations of a large, lumbering jet, at least in Maddy's mind. A deafening amount of noise was accompanied by a rush of energy and the subsequent, haunting, free-fall feeling that always ensued once they were off the ground and it was safe to cut power.

In a matter of moments, they were soaring high above meticulous blocks populated with duplexes, colonials, and seasonal businesses. Joseph then directed the plane on an easterly course out over the ocean, leaving the magnificent sunset behind. Ahead of them, the waters were dark, but as soon as they made the turn north, the twinkling lights of the boardwalk and in the distance, the Atlantic City skyline, provided comforting context.

Not that Ken or Dr. Rose needed any consoling; they were happily engaged in loud discussions with the tower and each other. Kenny observed intently as Joseph explained the myriad of controls and switches, their flight path, and typical operational procedures. He was awed by Joseph's passion for his hobby, and the willingness with which he shared it with him—a guy who for right now at least, was simply someone his daughter was currently dating.

The good doctor's hectic schedule had prevented any meaningful interaction up until this point, save for one family breakfast and a scant few hours at the beach. And even then, Ken had spent more time with Maddy's mother and siblings that he had with her father, though he'd appreciated Joseph's down-to-earth demeanor. He didn't seem to be affected by his status at all; on the contrary, he came across as a pretty affable man, who also happened to be brilliant and successful. And that was something to emulate.

"Look, Maddy, casinos ahead!" Joseph called to his daughter, who struggled to control her claustrophobia in spite of the fascinating scenery. She leaned forward and peered out through the front windshield. Now close ahead, the glittering towers appeared like a magical kingdom in an enchanted fairytale. Even from high in the air she recognized their familiar layout and characteristics, from the Golden Nugget to the Tropicana.

"It's really beautiful!" she yelled over the amplified hum of the single engine.

"You ok?" Kenny asked, catching her eye.

"Fine!"

He winked at her again.

She settled back in her seat as she heard her father announce to his co-pilot that they were about to bank to the left as a prelude to a turnaround to a southern trajectory towards Cape May. Of all aspects of flying, Maddy hated this one the most. Unlike many aerophobia sufferers, she didn't mind the process of landing, mostly because it meant a return to solid ground was imminent. If she closed her eyes, she could reasonably cope with take-off. But something about these in-air turns petrified her – and making matters worse,

the only thing below them was a deep, black ocean.

But by the time she recognized the glitzy excess of neon and honky-tonk that defined the Wildwood boardwalk, she returned to a mindset of fascination. It had been years since she'd even set foot in this particular Shore town, though as a child and adolescent she'd often visited as the guests of her two favorite cousins— Lyle and Daphne, on her dad's side of the family.

The older son of Joseph's now-deceased eldest brother, Lyle, a fun- loving, warmhearted guy had been married to the lovely, generous Daphne since Maddy was a toddler. Damian, then a child of about six, had even acted as ring bearer in their wedding. Having had no sons or daughters of their own, over the years, they had taken great pleasure in celebrating the milestones of the Rose children— including graduations, Holy Communions, and Confirmations—as well as traditional holidays like Christmas.

Maddy smiled as she recalled the many Christmas Eves where Daphne's uncle would dress up as Santa Claus for the delight of her and her siblings and the neighborhood children. They'd all gather around and take turns sitting on Santa's lap, expressing their fondest wishes before the bearded one would hand them a present with their name on it—prepared in advance by Monica Rose, of course. An exceptionally loving mother, she always made sure that all holidays, especially Christmas, were festive and bright for her kids.

"Hey, Dad, look—The Towers!"

She was referring to Lyle and Daphne's boardwalk condo building. As a young teen, she'd spent countless weekends there as their special guest. Kids at heart themselves, they'd play with her in the ocean, take her on rides on the pier and challenge her to miniature golf tournaments at the somewhat difficult course that was spread out alongside the boardwalk on the building's mezzanine level.

Oh, and after a long day of fun, they'd head over to Duffer's where the best ice cream sundaes at the Shore, if not all of the Delaware Valley, could be found. Lyle's eyes would light up, and he'd playfully rub his hands together when the waitress presented him with an obscene concoction of three oversized scoops of varying flavors, hot fudge, wet walnuts, and a mound of whipped cream topped with a signature cherry. Maddy laughed out loud at the memory.

"There they are!" Dad affirmed.

The flying bug had also bitten Lyle and Daphne, who became licensed pilots a few years after Joseph. Lately, though, they hadn't been much into it mostly due to its burdensome financial constraints. Still, they joined Joseph for rides on his plane whenever they could.

Ken looked back and smiled at her again. He loved it whenever something would incite her natural exuberance; when Madeline felt passion for anything, it was an irresistible sight to witness. And as she looked back at him, still in his Randall Cunningham jersey and nice blue jeans, the headset flattening some of his beautiful blond waves, she couldn't help but wish it was Friday night, instead of Sunday.

Finally, the little plane entered the skies above Cape May, a beautiful town noted for its Victorian charm and historic B & B's. Even amid a now darkened, post-sunrise atmosphere there was enough illumination below to perceive the telltale point that extended dramatically into the water, marking the southernmost boundary of the Garden State.

Though she'd only been in Cape May on a few occasions the resort held some interesting memories involving the Coast Guard base and a young woman she'd once considered her very best friend. Where Amy was now, and for that matter, whoever she was married to or shacking up with, was anybody's guess. That was a long, sad story, one that still both puzzled and angered Maddy, though it had led to an even closer bond with Amy's parents and younger brother Christian. Oh well, something good emerges from even the most upsetting situations.

Moments later, Dr. Rose began to maneuver the plane into a descent pattern, guiding the nose carefully in the direction of the ground. Now on a northerly course, it would be just minutes before Ocean City's familiar landscape would emerge from the shadows. Maddy had not only survived but actually enjoyed their 30-minute aerial tour, encouraged by her dad and Ken's free flowing conversation and obvious enjoyment of each other's company. Perhaps the issue of a college degree wouldn't be as much of a problem with her father, who seemed genuinely impressed by his daughter's new guy. That would be sort of ironic, considering his level of education.

Dr. Rose expertly orchestrated a smooth landing as the wheels gracefully touched down and glided across the runway; by the time he'd parked the plane in its usual spot, the propeller had begun to decrease in intensity. However, for safety reasons they had to wait another few minutes before exiting. She leaned back and closed her eyes, imagining sitting at the water's edge and staring at an infinite ocean. Somehow the claustrophobia eased when high above the ground; now that they were sitting on the runway the twinges of anxiety had begun to well within.

She laughed to herself remembering a time a few years back when she'd rushed out to greet her Dad, Lyle and Daphne, who'd just landed in the very same spot. It wasn't until she'd gotten perilously close to the rotating propellers that she noticed them waving and yelling furiously for her to retreat; unknown to her at the time, it was a basic rule of flying that you never approached a plane whose propellers were still in motion. If God forbid, one of them would dislodge from the nose, it could result in decapitation. That had been one of the few occasions she could recall any of them being truly angry with her.

At last, she found herself reaching for Ken's outstretched arms as he assisted her off of the wing and back onto the pavement.

"Wow, that was great!" he enthused, slipping his arm around her as they all headed back towards the hangar.

"Yeah, it really was beautiful," she agreed.

The world was incredibly magical from high altitudes; even the very ordinary places with which they were intimately acquainted took on an ethereal quality.

"Glad you enjoyed it, Ken," Dr. Rose slapped him on the shoulder as they entered through the glass doors. "Anytime you want to go up, just let me know. You're welcome to fly with me anytime."

"Thank you, Doctor," he replied appreciatively.

"Ok, kids, I've gotta go file another flight plan back to Chester County airport. I have a busy day of surgery tomorrow, and I don't want to get back too late. Gotta fuel up the plane, too. You're welcome to wait and watch me take off if you want." He winked at Maddy, a sure sign of his affection and genuine desire for a good send-off.

"Sure, Dad, we'll be glad to watch you." She took Ken's hand, and they walked back outside, where they sat on a bench facing the runway.

"You know Mad, your dad is really amazing. No one would ever know he's a famous surgeon, he's so humble and easy to talk to."

"Yes, well both of my parents have always remembered their roots," she explained. "I was never taught that we were better than anyone else just because my father was a surgeon. As proud as I am to be his daughter, I know that's his accomplishment, not mine. I have no right to be a snob based on someone else's achievements. I'm just thankful to have been born into a loving family. "

"Wow."

"What?"

"I've known plenty of people born into similar situations who did think the world revolved around them, that's all. When I was in high school, kids whose parents were professionals walked around with chips on their shoulders. Not everyone but most. None of the girls would give a guy like me from a working-class family a chance."

"That's too bad," she remarked. "I hate snobs. Actually, because I was so shy in high school, many kids thought I had my nose in the air, that I was, you know, a spoiled rich girl. I wasn't, but that didn't matter. Jealousy makes people do and say cruel things. Heck, I even had a nun in first grade who hated me because my dad was a doctor. She used to lecture me all the time about the poor kids in West Philly who didn't have enough to eat. And every time I'd wear a hand-me-down jacket from my sister Lori that was still in mint condition, she'd comment sarcastically,

'Oh, I see Daddy bought you another jacket!'"

"Oh my God, you're kidding."

"I wish I were," she sighed. "It got so bad that my mother actually went down to the school to talk to her. That was after I announced one day in the car that I wished my dad was a trash collector, because if he were, maybe Sister Timothy Ann would like me. That was all my mother needed to hear."

"I'm sure," he said, sympathetically.

"My mom reminded me that my father worked very hard for everything we had, and that was something to be proud of; he wasn't robbing banks he was helping people. Just as my grandfather—her dad, had done as a pharmacist."

"Your mom was right," he agreed. "Americans just don't get it. They have no idea how lucky we are to live in a country where you can work your way into any profession you want; to be able to do and be anything at all is a right that doesn't exist in most of the world. I've seen that with my own eyes."

"By the way, thank you for defending that right." She smiled as he leaned over and kissed her cheek.

"You are most welcome, Madeline Rose."

"Have a great flight, Dad!" She gave her father a hug and a kiss before he shook Ken's hand and reminded him of their future plans to do this again soon. They watched as Joseph strode out to the waiting Piper Cub, now fueled and ready to transport him back across the river. In the distance, he waved at them one final time before settling into the cockpit and starting the engine; once the propellers reached maximum speed, he directed the plane out to the runway. And then, in a perfect combination of thrust, lift, and timing, the small aircraft rose above the marshes and into the star-studded heavens.

"There he goes!" Maddy exclaimed. "It's amazing, he'll be home in a half-hour, and my mom will probably still be on the road." She glanced at her watch which revealed that a little over an hour had passed from the time they'd said their goodbyes to Mom, Aunt Maria, and Louis in the driveway. It hardly seemed possible.

She suppressed a yawn, then apologized, assuring him that the cause wasn't the company, but a lack of sufficient sleep. He grinned at her knowingly, before his face turned serious again.

"You gonna be OK driving tonight? Why don't you just stay over and head back in the morning?"

She hesitated for a moment, thinking how wonderful it would be to just be able to go home and crash, rather than deal with Expressway traffic. While Maddy typically preferred the back roads that ran through small towns like Franklinville, Swedesboro and Mullica Hill she avoided using them late at night when alone at the wheel.

If something should happen to her car, she stood a much greater chance of getting help alongside a heavily-trafficked route. Besides, friendly mystique aside, small towns were not devoid of criminals; it wasn't a great idea for a single woman to ride by herself through dark, two-lane "highways."

"God, I would love to," she sighed.

"So then, why don't you?"

His voice was soft. Little did he know she was also afraid of staying alone in the house overnight. And while she knew he'd probably be more than willing to either stay with her or have her sleep at his place, there was also the small matter of getting it past her family. As if reading her mind, he added, "Look, we can go back to the house, get your stuff and have you sleep at my house. You know by now you can trust me, right?" His blue eyes penetrated her brown ones.

"Yes, Kenny, it's not that," she whispered, slipping her arms around his waist. "It's just—well how am I supposed to explain it to my parents? You know how they are about these things, even if you and I know nothing's going to happen."

"Isn't it better than you falling asleep at the wheel?"

"Of course," she agreed. Then with a sudden thought, "Hey, what if I tell my mom you have to work a graveyard shift?"

He looked at her skeptically. "Are you sure you want to lie?"

"No, I don't *want* to lie. I hate lying especially after dating someone who lies to me for two years. But in this case, I don't have a choice. If anyone thinks I just want to stay here to be with you alone, there's gonna be a fight. Besides, it's believable that you would get called into work. And I am positive my mother would rather I got a good night's sleep than trying to keep my eyes open while driving."

"Ok, it's your call," he replied. "But let's stay at my place since it'll be easier for both of us to get to work in the morning."

"Whatever you want, sailor," she stood up on her toes to kiss him.

"Are you kidding me?" she was incredulous as she climbed into the waterbed. She was dressed in her pink short set pajamas but had pulled an Ocean City sweatshirt over the tank top. When she thought he was naked, though, she'd jumped right back out.

"Alright, alright, actually I am kidding," he laughed. "But normally I do sleep in the raw. Not used to even wearing boxer shorts to bed."

"Well that's the rule if you want me to sleep here," she reminded him.

"I know, sweetheart, I know. I just like teasing you, that's all. Come on, let's go to sleep now," he coaxed, extending his arm. She hesitated, prompting him to pull down the covers to reveal his Navy bottoms.

"See?" he asked.

"Oh, ok," she agreed, feigning indignation. That nagging feeling of behaving like a tease persisted, his good nature notwithstanding. Nevertheless, she snuggled in close, relishing a chance to spend an entire night together at last. Her mom had truly been relieved when she'd announced her plans to drive back from Ocean City in the morning, prompting a twinge of guilt, along with excitement. Now as they lay in the quiet, beneath the light of the moon, they drifted off to a peaceful, contented sleep.

"Maddy, sweetheart? Madeline?" he did his best to awaken her from her usual sound slumber. Although it was only 4 a.m. he'd gotten a call from the plant asking if he could head over there right away; apparently someone had a family emergency, and they needed him to fill in. And as Ken had expressed since the day he'd been hired nearly two years ago, as the only single guy in the entire operation, he wanted to be the designated go-to employee under such circumstances. Not only was the extra income welcome, he'd hoped his good work ethic would serve as a springboard to something better, whatever that might be.

But as he gazed down at her in the soft light of early morning— the long, reddish hair spread out across the pillowcase, the tiny hands tucked beneath her chin as she lay on her side, and the petite, curvy body outlined under the burgundy, satin sheet, the last thing on his mind was work. Funny, she never even moved when the phone rang, nor did she wake up when he'd stepped into a hot shower. He thought for sure by the time he put on his uniform and sat on the edge of the bed to put on his work boots, she'd at least stir in her sleep.

Finally, he leaned over and kissed her cheek. Stroking her shoulder, he whispered, "Maddy, please wake up."

And then, at last, she shifted in bed to face him.

"Is it time to get up already?" she asked groggily as she rubbed her eyes.

"Not for you, baby. But I just got a call, and I have to go in. I wanted to get up this morning and make breakfast for you before you went back, but one of the guys had an emergency, and they really need me. I am so sorry, but I will make it up to you, I promise." He stroked her cheek as he spoke, then sat down beside her.

"Wow, look at you in your official work clothes," she remarked.

"Yes, well, it's not forever," he reminded her.

"Kenny, it doesn't matter what you do; it's who you are on the inside that matters most to me." She took his hand in hers as they remained silent for a moment. Then she sat up and embraced him tightly. He buried his head in the softness of her neck and shoulder, his arms holding her firmly against him. "You know that, right?"

"I know baby; I just want to make something of myself that's all."

"And you can do anything you set your mind to, I have no doubt. I just want you to understand you're good enough for me right now. Besides you already have so much to be proud of, sailor man."

"How come you always know just what to say to make me feel better?"

His low, masculine voice ignited her passions. She planted kisses on his neck and inhaled his irresistible, shower-fresh smell. He moved his hands rhythmically up and down her back before bringing her face close to his.

"I love you, Maddy," he whispered, drawing her lips to his before she could utter a sound. A moment later, he was carefully situated on top of her in the bed as their passion began to mount.

"Kenny," she laughed, finally coming up for air. "Hey, you have to go to work. I don't want to get you in trouble!"

"This is exactly the kind of trouble I like, Madeline," he affirmed with a wink, moving back in for another kiss.

o

Maddy adjusted the straps of her lacy white bra before slipping into a crisp, forest green blouse and flared black skirt. She'd just applied her make-up in the mirror of Ken's bathroom and brushed her hair into a smooth, sleek ponytail. She slipped into a pair of black pumps before folding her matching black jacket over her arm and picking her purple and pink duffle bag off the floor. With one final glance around his room, she closed the door behind her, confident she'd scooped up all of her belongings.

As she bounded down the stairs, a panicked thought came to mind: she'd promised her mother she'd contact her before getting on the road.

And even though there was really no way for Monica to trace the origin of the call, Maddy quickly decided against using Ken's phone. Instead, she'd stop at a Wawa or Dunkin Donuts for coffee, where there would surely be a pay phone available. Besides, it was only 6:30 a.m.

But before she could walk out the front door, something caught her eye on the coffee table. As she got closer, she saw it was a white envelope with her name on it. She smiled as she recognized the handwriting, then opened it up to read Ken's thoughtful note:

"Sorry, I had to leave you this morning, beautiful. Sleeping with you in my arms was heavenly. Please drive safely and have a wonderful day. I'll be thinking of you. Call me when you get home. Love, Ken."

She held the note to her heart for a moment, before locking the door behind her and leaving the key in the mailbox as planned. She'd just thrown her bag in the back seat of the car and was about to get behind the wheel when she noticed an unfamiliar vehicle pulling into the driveway. Maddy recognized the woman behind the wheel from here photos, though they'd never met: it was Kathy, Ken's roommate. But what caused a shiver to run up and down her spine was the sight of Ken in the back seat, with an obviously pained expression on his face.

"Oh my God, what happened?" she asked the plump blonde as she got out of the car. Uncharacteristically, Maddy discarded formalities, too upset to think about anything but her boyfriend. Kathy understood.

"Ken just had a little accident at work, honey. Nothing to be worried about. I'm his emergency contact, and since I was getting off work anyway, I went to pick him up at Shore Memorial."

Maddy ran over to open his door.

"Heh-hey," he greeted her, summoning a smile in spite of his agony. That's when she noticed the brace around his leg.

"My God, Kenny, what did you do?" He was struck by the genuine concern in her voice as he gathered his crutches and handed them to her.

"Nothing baby, it was just a dumb accident. I fell, that's all."

"Yeah, so why the leg brace?"

"I tore some ligaments, but the good news is nothing's broken."

"Thank God!"

"Ok, well let's see if we can help this big guy out of the car," Kathy suggested. The two women carefully maneuvered him onto the driveway as he held an arm around each of their shoulders. Maddy then reached for the crutches, situating them in place before he quickly made his way to the front door.

"Wow, already he's a pro!" Kathy laughed. Then turning to the young woman who'd been occupying her roommate's every waking thought, held out a hand.

"Hi, I'm Kathy. Nice to meet you, Madeline. I've heard so many good things about you."

"Likewise," Maddy smiled. "Oh, and thank you for the delicious wedding cookies."

"You're welcome." Kathy's raspy voice was oddly appealing. Then, suddenly remembering, Maddy ran up to the mailbox to get the key, as Ken stood waiting for them.

"Oops, sorry." She quickly unlocked the door and followed closely behind. Once inside, he sank into the leather couch and elevated his injured leg.

"Can I get you anything? Water? Orange juice? Coffee?"

"No sweetheart thanks. I just want to rest for a minute. Will you stay and keep me company for a while?"

Maddy thought of her boss, as well as the temp who was supposed to show up this morning for the first day of work at a new client's office. Typically, as the account executive she'd show up with donuts and coffee in a gesture of gratitude to the hiring manager and company for their business; maybe Betty wouldn't mind taking on that honor on her behalf today.

And as she sat down on the space he carved out for her and took his hand in hers, she suddenly didn't care. Surely the office could survive without her for one day. When Kathy excused herself to get some shut-eye, it cemented her decision.

"Don't worry, Kenny, I'm not going anywhere," she promised softly.

Chapter 9

"Here you go, baby." Madeline handed him a prescription pain pill and a glass of water. He was propped against a mound of pillows on the leather couch, having thought the better of climbing the stairs to his bedroom.

"Thank you," he whispered, in a tone that betrayed his acute pain, though he tried valiantly to mask it. She had gone out to the pharmacy to pick up the Darvocet the doctor had phoned in for him, in spite of his protests against taking medication. Hardly a pill-popper herself, she'd understood his resistance though she managed to convince him that in this case, an MD-approved prescription was warranted.

"No reason to suffer," she smiled, taking the glass and setting it back down on the coffee table after he'd chased down his medicine. He stared at her in the beam of sunlight flooding through the picture window. After making the decision to stay, she had changed out of her work attire and was now sporting a comfortable outfit consisting of denim shorts and a red, cotton-blend cropped top with a V-neck surrounded by gold rivets. She'd added a gauzy red bow with matching gold flecks to her ponytail to complete her look; on her ears, she wore her shiny hoops.

He took in the sight of her, wanting nothing more than to pull her onto the couch and smother her with kisses, though his temporary physical limitation made that impossible.

"Kenny, did you hear me?" she asked, waking him from his stupor.

"I'm sorry, what did you say?" She pretended to be annoyed.

"Geez, the Darvocet couldn't possibly have kicked in already."

"It's not the Darvocet, it's you," he said sweetly. Maddy blushed. "You're just not used to sincere compliments, are you? Well, you'd better get used to it. I couldn't have asked for a more beautiful caretaker. Thank you for staying with me today."

"You're welcome. But as I was saying, I have something else for you." She then presented him with a gift bag, much to his delight and surprise. He was visibly touched as he pulled out the Jon Secada and Earth, Wind and Fire CDs, a small stuffed teddy bear, a one-pound bag of plain M&Ms, and a chain of authentic Philly soft pretzels from Wawa.

"Thank you."

He reached out for her, and she knelt down on the floor to hug him tightly before they exchanged a few delicious kisses.

"Kenny!" She giggled when he refused to release her. "Come on, now, you need your rest."

"I'll sleep so much better if you join me," he teased, sliding over a bit and then patting the empty space. A slow smile spread across her face as she carefully snuggled in beside him.

Maddy gingerly extricated herself from a deeply slumbering Ken's embrace; it was already late morning, and she wanted to make him a few meals before heading back home to Media. Thank goodness Betty had understood when she phoned in her request to take an impromptu vacation day. Mondays weren't auspicious days for sales, at least in the employment industry. Most of her agenda was going to consist of visiting existing clients rather than cold-calling prospects anyway. And since schmoozing was an activity Betty rather enjoyed, she'd been more than happy to deliver the donuts to the new account.

Over at the SuperFresh, she had purchased the supplies she needed to make some of Ken's favorites—including the spicy marinara sauce he'd raved over the night they had dinner with her mother and Aunt Maria. Instead of mussels, though, she bought scallops and shrimp, figuring they might fare better in the freezer. Then all he'd have to do is boil some spaghetti and, voila! Dinner. There was just one minor problem: Despite her heritage, she wasn't quite as learned in the methods of making Italian sauce as her elder female family members. In fact, it had only been in recent years she'd even developed a taste for it herself.

As a child and adolescent, she'd always asked her mother for "plain" pasta, tossed in olive oil and garlic instead of tomato sauce. For whatever reason, she just couldn't understand why everyone was so enamored with what some in her family had often called "gravy." Of course, once she'd grown into a young adult that had all changed, though pesto was still her preferred choice. In fact, she could have made it easy on herself by buying a container of the olive oil, basil and pinola nut mixture at the store and simply leaving it in Ken's refrigerator. But when she remembered how much he loved the spaghetti and mussels, she didn't have the heart to deny him.

"Guess I'll just have to call Mom," she thought, walking over to his phone. Though long distance, she was pretty sure he wouldn't mind. Besides, the conversation was on his behalf and anyway, how long could it possibly take to write down a recipe? Monica Rose answered on the second ring.

"Hello?"

"Hi, Mom," Maddy spoke in a hushed whisper.

"Hi, hon, where are you?" Monica's tone was cheerful as she set down the bridal magazine she'd been reading. Lori had asked for her opinion on a few more gowns she'd discovered since their conversation the previous day. They were planning to go to some boutiques that evening.

"I'm still at Ken's."

"How's he doing?"

"He's sleeping right now, so that's a good thing. It's nothing serious, thank God; the doctor thinks he'll be as good as new in a few days."

"That's good. Well when he wakes up, tell him I was asking for him."

"I will."

"So when are you heading back?"

"Uh, in a few hours. I want to leave him with some food for the week, which is why I'm calling. He really loved your sauce that night, but I am not exactly sure how you make it. Can you give me the recipe?"

Monica laughed. "Sure, honey. You're not going to believe how easy it is."

"I'm sure. I guess I never really paid attention when you cooked it."

As she jotted down her mother's instructions, Kathy entered the kitchen, clad in her bathrobe. They exchanged smiles before Kathy pulled out the coffee pot to brew eight strong cups in preparation for work.

"Ok, Mom, that sounds great. No, don't worry; I am definitely going to leave before it gets dark. I'll call you."

"Alright, sweetie. I may still be out with your sister when you get back, but Louis and your father should be here."

"Thanks for the recipe. I love you."

Maddy replaced the receiver and then turned to Kathy, who was now seated at the table.

"Good morning! I hope I didn't wake you?" Kathy looked at her with warm green eyes.

"No doll, you didn't wake me up." Her voice was enthusiastic and raspy. "I'm not much of a sleeper, which is one reason why I love my job so much. Constant activity, noise, people—it's what I live for."

Maddy cracked up.

"Growing up in a family of five kids, I've definitely had my share of

that," she replied. "I must admit, though, sometimes quiet works really well for me, too!"

"So what's all this?" Kathy asked, motioning to the ingredients that were spread out all over the counter.

"Oh, I just thought I'd make some meals for Ken before I go home today." Then remembering her manners added, "There's plenty here for both of you. I just hope I can make it taste as good as my mother's."

"Well, I can sure tell why he's so crazy about you," Kathy stated, as she began to blush. "Adorable and thoughtful. You don't see that in too many girls today. They're either users, liars, sleazes or a combination of all three. They see a nice guy like him, and they pounce. Use him for whatever they can get, and then break his heart." Kathy spoke with a mixture of disdain and concern.

"Wow, Ken sure is lucky to have a friend like you looking out for him," she stated sincerely. "You really seem to have his best interests at heart."

"Well, he's like a son to me. Did he tell you about Liz Anne? What that girl did to him was nothing short of cruel." Kathy whispered loudly as she glanced back towards the living room.

"Um, yes, he did share that with me." Fearing he might wake up and overhear them, Maddy tried to discourage any further commentary on the topic. Kathy, however, remained undeterred.

"I mean; did she have any idea what she was giving up? How could she hurt him like that? Men like him don't grow on trees. Believe me, I know!"

"Yeah, he got a little choked up when he told me about it. And about his dad, too. I felt really bad for him." She busied herself with food preparation, feeling strangely intrusive, though Kathy's narrative mirrored everything Ken had already shared with her.

"Thank God, he and his dad patched things up," Kathy confirmed.

"And now that you've come along—a nice girl, the kind of girl he's been looking for, he's finally rid of that tramp, Roseanne!"

Roseanne?

"Uh, who?"

"Oh, don't worry, honey, she's just some local bimbo," Kathy shrugged. "She can't hold a candle to you, but you know how it is for men. Even if they want to settle down and get married with the right girl, they still have their needs. So do women but it's easier for us, somehow. Trashy Roseanne has probably been with every single guy under 30 in Atlantic County— provided they have the means to wine her and dine her, of course."

Maddy felt a knot tightening in her stomach as she sautéed onion and garlic in a frying pan. Why hadn't he ever mentioned her?

"I-I guess we never got around to discussing Roseanne," she admitted.

"That's because she's insignificant. Just a girl he knows, that's all. After Liz Anne broke his heart, he needed a distraction, and she just happened to be there. There was never anything serious between them— on either of their parts." Then sensing her discomfort, added, "Madeline, I hope I didn't upset you. I swear there's nothing between Ken and Roseanne. It's been months since I've seen her around here.

And you are all he's talked about since the night he met you. There's nothing to worry about!"

Kathy spooned some sugar into her coffee mug before adding a dollop of cream. Raising it to her lips, she looked Maddy in the eye.

"Please don't get mad at him. Knowing Ken, I bet he was planning to tell you all about it, even if it was just a mutually convenient kind of thing. The fact that he didn't proves my point—she wasn't even worth mentioning."

Kathy placed her hands on Maddy's shoulders. "Honey, look, I share your background, even though I'm from the city, and I'm not a college girl like you. I know how you were raised, probably just like me in many ways. Did you go to Catholic school, too?"

She nodded in silent response.

"St. Maria Goretti," Kathy announced, patting her chest.

"Cardinal O'Hara," Maddy declared softly. She really didn't enjoy dredging up old adolescent memories.

"So, you know how it is, then," Kathy went on. "They teach us how to live, right from wrong, and that's a good thing. And I come from a big, close family like yours. Only one sister, but lots of cousins around the neighborhood. My family wasn't rich, but my parents were very proud. They worked really hard to send us to Catholic school. And they taught us all of the same things; took us to Mass every Sunday. The whole bit.

"And then one day, my older sister Donna announced she was pregnant at age 18. Hoo-boy! My parents were devastated!"

"I can only imagine," Maddy sympathized, shuddering at the thought of ever being in that position herself. She was fairly certain her parents would never disown her although it would be a very long nine months filled with recriminations and lectures about her future; hopefully after the birth of an adorable grandchild, all would have been forgotten, if not actually forgiven. But for the rest of her life she'd live with guilt over "embarrassing" her family. Definitely not a good scenario.

"So what happened?" Maddy asked.

"Well, Donna had been seeing the boy—the father of her baby, for over two years. He was also from the neighborhood; in fact, he was like the son my father never had. So, once my parents got over the shock, they accepted it."

"Just like that?"

"Well, what are you gonna do?" Kathy shrugged again. "It's not like Donna was out tramping around; this was her steady boyfriend. And they loved each other very much."

"So did they get married?"

"They sure did, but in a quiet, low-key ceremony. Our parish priest was a good friend of the family, and he agreed to marry them. And guess what? They're still happily married! Even had two more kids."

"Wow, that's great," Maddy noted, still trying to put herself in the same position with the exact same result. Somehow, it just didn't seem possible.

"Yeah, and here I am 50, and still single. Go figure!" Kathy let out a loud, gravelly belly laugh before announcing her intention to go smoke a cigarette out on the patio.

"And don't give a second thought to what I told you!" she reminded Ken's young girlfriend as she opened the sliding glass door off of the kitchen and stepped outside.

"Thank you, sweetheart."

Ken had awakened to find Madeline busily setting up a tray table with a turkey and cheese hoagie from Wawa, a pickle and a bag of Herr's potato chips. He looked adorably groggy as he rubbed his eyes and sat up on the couch.

"Damn," he laughed. "How long have I been out? And what smells so good?"

Placing the tray in front of him, Maddy smiled. "Well to answer your first question, I'd say at least an hour and a half. As for the second, I'm taking a crack at my mom's mussels marinara sauce.

There's plenty, so you can have some tonight for dinner and freeze the rest. I'm also leaving you chicken cutlets and a pan of eggplant parm. Wouldn't want you to starve or anything, just 'cause you have a bad leg."

Her tone was playful as she unscrewed the lid to a cold bottle of Turkey Hill iced tea.

"Do you want a cup with ice?" She held up a drinking straw.

"Uh, no, that's fine," he replied, visibly touched by everything she'd done. "You're amazing," he added softly.

"Ok, well I am going to get my tuna sandwich; be right back," she announced, heading back into the kitchen. Kathy's words about Roseanne were still reverberating in her brain, but she decided to confront him about it on another day. Or maybe not at all. She'd have to wait and see.

Ken and Maddy spent another afternoon laughing and talking. All thoughts of old girlfriends and local tramps melted away as they listened to the new CD's and enjoyed each other's company. He still couldn't get over what a kind, decent person she was; they'd only been dating a short time and already she'd shown more concern and consideration for his wellbeing than any other girl he'd ever dated. And although she lived less than two hours away, it seemed like there was an entire continent between them when they were apart. It was almost as if he was still sailing around the world, and Madeline—not Liz Anne, was the girl waiting for him back home.

"Kenny?" her voice was a hushed whisper as they lay on the couch. She hated to see her time with him come to an end, but dusk was quickly approaching, and she wanted to get on the road. They'd both fallen asleep again, with Madeline the first to stir.

"Mm-hm?"

"I have to get going," she announced wistfully. His arms felt so good around her, and her head still rested comfortably on his chest. "Not that I really want to or anything," she added. "My parents will be worried if I get on the road too late. I know that probably sounds kind of silly, given the situations you've been in."

"No, it doesn't, sweetheart," he whispered, kissing her temple. "I worry about you, too. Will you call me when you get in?"

"Of course."

It was still such a new and exhilarating feeling to have someone in her life who truly cared—someone other than a family member. She looked up at him and smiled before he leaned down to kiss her lips. She shifted carefully on the couch, mindful of his injury as she responded, feeling his hands through her hair and the strength of his warm body beneath her.

"Kenny," she giggled, finally coming up for air. "You're not making it easy to leave."

"That's the idea," he laughed, moving in again.

"I'll be back this weekend," she promised, in between kisses. "Hopefully, you'll be out of the brace by then."

"Oh, I'll be out of it long before the weekend, baby," he promised. "I want to get back to work so I can spend time with you."

"Well just don't overdo it. You know I don't mind waiting for you. I can entertain myself on the beach or boardwalk until you get done. The most important thing is that your leg heals properly."

"Yes, ma'am," he teased.

And then with another soft exchange and a promise to call, she reluctantly got up off the couch and gathered her belongings.

"Hi Pop!" she called out brightly as she entered the house from the garage. He was watching his beloved Phillies on television with as much enthusiasm and excitement as if they were actually fighting for a shot at the World Series. Unfortunately, in spite of all of the hopeful springtime predictions, they'd let him down again this season. Such was the fate of a die-hard Philadelphia sports fan.

"Hiya, Maddy, baby how are ya?" Her dad got up to give her a hug and a kiss as she approached him, duffle bag still slung over her shoulder.

"I'm great, how are you? How was work today?"

"Not bad, not bad at all! You know, saved a few lives; nothing special." They both laughed. "How's Ken doing?"

"He's fine; really taking his injury in stride. He's determined to be back at work in a day or so. I made him promise to wait and see what the doctor says; no reason to push it." She put her bag on the floor and sat next to him on the couch just as a Tastykake commercial came on.

"What's the score?"

"Bah! They had a 5-0 lead at one point, and they blew it. The Mets are up 8-5." He sounded completely disgusted.

"Oh, I'm sorry, Pop," she consoled him, patting him on the shoulder.

"Eh, what are you gonna do? It's only the 7th inning, so they still have some time to come back." Then switching gears, Joseph remarked, "You know, Maddy that Ken is really a special guy. I enjoyed flying with him last night. He's a decent, respectful young man. I was really impressed with him." Relief washed over her.

"You really think so, Dad?" she pursued.

"Absolutely! And I can tell how much he likes you, but of course, why wouldn't he feel that way about my beautiful daughter?" He squeezed her shoulder and gave her a peck on the temple, prompting her to crack up.

"You have to say that because you're my dad!" she teased him.

"No, I'd have to love you as your father, but I wouldn't have to tell you you're beautiful if that weren't true. But in your case, it definitely is."

"Well thanks for being president of my fan club," she said, giving him a peck on the cheek. As she stood up again, she asked, "Where's Louie?"

"Oh, he's out in the pool, getting in his last kicks before we close it for the winter. They're coming tomorrow to cover it."

Her heart sank; she hated this time of year, knowing a long, cold, dreary season lay just ahead. As much as she loved the ocean, the pool was her favorite place to swim—no seaweed or jellyfish, and you could actually see your feet in the clear, blue water.

"Isn't it a little chilly?" She'd noticed when she'd gotten out of the car that the air felt a lot cooler than it had in New Jersey.

"Yeah, I turned the heater on for him earlier," Joseph explained. "Actually, it's about time he came out anyway. It's getting late, and he has to work tomorrow."

"I'll go tell him," she offered, walking into the adjoining family room, and then slipping through the sliding glass door and onto the enclosed porch. She smiled as she caught sight of Louis through the window, steadily backstroking towards the deep end of the illuminated, Roman-style pool. He was truly amazing. She remembered when they were kids of about 12 and 19, respectively. They would challenge each other to see who could swim the fastest under water up and back, without coming up for air.

Though she was an excellent swimmer, Maddy could never quite beat her older, "special" brother, who seemed to have invincible lungs. Ever the gracious champion, he was always good-natured about his victory, assuring her she'd do better the next time.

She opened the screen door and called out to him once he'd stopped. He was now holding onto the diving board, surveying the scene; his face lit up when he saw his sister.

"Hi, Mads!" He waved as he called her name.

"Dad wants you to come in now. It's getting cold, and you have to work tomorrow."

"Ok, I'll be in in a minute," he promised. As she turned to go back inside, she heard his voice again. "How's Ken?"

"He's doing much better, thanks," she assured him.

"He's a nice guy, Mads. I really like him," Louie offered.

"Good to hear." She always trusted his ability to read people. "He likes you a lot, too, Louie. He told me he wants a rematch at the arcade." Louis laughed out loud. Then he asked, "Maybe this weekend?"

"That's a possibility. We'll see," she promised. Although she intended to head back to the Jersey Shore, she wasn't certain how it would all pan out with her family. If Louis didn't have to work this weekend, it might actually help her. She had no problem bringing him along and was positive Ken wouldn't mind, either. It might actually be fun.

As she entered the kitchen, she heard the phone ring and answered it to hear a familiar, welcome voice.

"Hey," Ken greeted her playfully. "You were supposed to call me when you got in young lady."

"Sorry, Kenny, I just walked in the door and got distracted by my father and brother. I was just about to pick up the phone."

"How was the ride home?"

"Pretty good; not too much traffic."

"I miss you already, baby. Actually, I missed you as soon as you walked out the door."

"Aw, I miss you, too. Wish I didn't have to come back. How's your leg?"

"It's fine," he replied dismissively, though if truth be told, he was definitely struggling a little. "Hey, the sauce was great sweetheart, thank you."

"Really? Don't just say that to make me feel good!"

The sound of her laughter prompted longings within him.

"No, I'm telling ya the truth; it was delicious. You can ask Kathy, I ate almost a pound of pasta myself. She loved it, too." "She's really nice, Ken. I like her a lot."

"Yeah? What did you two talk about while I was crashed out on the couch?" She hesitated for a second before deciding this was not the moment to broach the subject of Roseanne. Besides, Mom and Lori would be walking through the front door any minute.

"Nothing much—growing up in South Philly, food, recipes, Catholic schooling—the usual stuff." He cracked up. "Oh, and I think she did mention a thing or two about your greatness."

"Oh, come on!"

"No, really, she truly loves you like a son, Ken. It's a wonderful thing to see."

"Yeah, she is a nice lady," he agreed. "And she takes good care of my place." Then, with another thought, he asked, "So do think you can you come back down this weekend, sweetheart?"

"Absolutely." She spoke with confidence, though she wondered if her plans would prompt another disagreement with her mom. It was so rare that they argued over anything, and she hated it. But this was one instance where she was prepared to do respectful battle if need be. After two hurtful years with Jake, she deserved some happiness.

"I may have to bring Louis with me, though, if no one else can make it," she explained. "I know it's silly, but—"

"I'd love to see Louis!" Ken exclaimed. Not only did he feel genuine affection for her brother, he was willing to abide by any rules necessary to see her beautiful face.

"Well, great. I know he feels the same way about you."

Just then she heard a key turn in the lock, followed by the chattering voices of her mother and sister. As they made their way into the kitchen, she smiled and waved at them. Cupping her hand over the mouthpiece, she whispered, "It's Ken," in response to her mother's quizzical look.

"Hey, uh, Kenny, can I call you back in a little bit from my own line? Mom and Lori just walked in."

"Look forward to it, sweetheart," he replied softly. "Give them my best."

"I will," she murmured.

"Maddy?"

"Yes?"

"I love you."

"Ok, I'll talk to you soon, baby," she cooed, feeling suddenly nervous.

Chapter 10

So, how did you ladies, do?" Maddy inquired, joining them at the kitchen table over glasses of iced tea.

"Ah, just alright," Lori sighed. "None of the gowns looked as great in person as they did in the magazines. And let's not even talk about the prices."

"Well, we'll just keep on looking, Lori. My God, you've got plenty of time," Monica assured her. Maddy detected something else in her voice, something that had little to do with overpriced wedding gowns.

"What's wrong?" Maddy asked, noticing the clouds forming over her mother's face. She exchanged a knowing look with Lori.

"What else? Your sister-in-law," Monica replied curtly. "You know, I
told your brother not to marry that girl. I knew she wasn't right for him from the start. Nobody ever listens to me."

While Madeline sympathized with the sentiment, her stomach flipped over at the thought of rehashing this old, tired story. Yes, her mother spoke the truth, but after seven years of dating, three years of marriage and now, newborn twins, Madeline figured it was an issue for her brother Damian to resolve. Her heart did ache for her parents, however, who couldn't seem to really enjoy being first-time grandparents, thanks to these seemingly endless theatrics.

"Laura? What'd she do now?"

"Your brother has an opportunity to do a six-week anesthesiology program at Penn," Monica explained. "It's an honor to have even been asked. Damian wants to do it, but she's giving him a hard time because she doesn't want to stay here with us. She says I intimidate her."

"Can you believe that? Ugh, how ungrateful can she get? You'd think she'd be excited because it's a chance for her husband to advance his career, especially now that they have kids," Lori chimed in. "My God, he has a chance to participate in a program that's only going to benefit his career and his family and instead of being happy, she's being a pain-in-the-ass and refusing to come here."

"I'm sure she'd have no problem if the program was in Des Moines, where they could stay with her family. Sure, it'd be alright then," Monica was justifiably angry, no doubt about it.

"Well, is that what Damian said?" Maddy inquired.

"Pretty much," Lori replied.

"When's the program?"

Monica explained, "It runs from just after Thanksgiving through the second week in January, which means they'd be here for Christmas. The babies would spend their very first Christmas with us, not *her* family. And I know she can't stand the thought of that. I'm only ok when I am doing things for them, like flying down there at my own expense to take care of the babies while they attended her sister's wedding. And don't get me wrong, her parents were wonderful; they took really good care of Lily and me. But I mean this is the thanks I get. My son has an opportunity to better himself, and because I am such an ogre, she doesn't want him to take it."

"Oh boy," Maddy sighed. It had only been two months since her mother and Lily, a family friend whose daughter had once been Maddy's very best girlfriend—from the 6th grade until their first year of college— had flown to Nashville. Her mother had even paid for Lily's ticket since she was doing her a favor by coming. Two-month-old twins were a handful for just one person—even a seasoned veteran like Monica Rose, mother of five. At the time, Lori and Madeline had argued that Damian and Laura should have underwritten the trip; after all, weren't Monica and Lily doing them a good deed?

"The whole thing is ridiculous," Lori cried. "But he needs to stand up to her. Right now, she's not working, and he's the sole breadwinner. I say that decides it right there. He's the one who has to tell her that."

"Do you think he will?" Maddy pressed.

"We'll see," Monica said. "He has to give Penn an answer soon. They're not going to wait forever. It just cracks me up. Your father and I paid for all of his expenses for medical school, hers basically told her 'you're on your own,' and yet she worships the ground they walk on. I just don't get it."

"Neither do I," Maddy remarked, patting her mother's hand. "I'm really sorry about this, Mom. I hate to see you and Dad have to deal with more of Laura's crap. It's not right; you're good people and great parents."

Just then, Joseph strode into the room, his Phillies having inevitably gone down to defeat. He quickly ascertained the scene of his three "girls" commiserating with long faces and exasperated sighs.

"Aw, Moni, you still upset about Laura? Forget it! Our son's a grown man, he's gotta learn how to handle his own problems. I'm done worrying about it." His booming voice seemed to fill the entire room.

"Dad, that's easy to say," Lori retorted, "But it's Damian's future. You mean his wife can't put up with staying here for six weeks? It's not like we're all a bunch of monsters, for God's sake. She should look at it this way—they'll have plenty of babysitters. They can even go out on dates if they want to."

"Yeah, good point," Maddy agreed, wishing there was some way to wave a magic wand and cast an infinite spell of good will over her entire family and dissolve all conflict forever. Sadly, that was only the stuff of fairytales.

"Lori, your brother's a grown man," Joseph repeated. "It's his life. I paid for him to become a doctor, now the rest is up to him. If he wants to blow a chance to work at Penn because of his wife, that's his choice. I'm done with it."

"Well, I'm his mother, and it bothers me that my son could miss out on something so important just because his small-town, mini-minded wife has no self-esteem. She may have an M.D., but she has no common sense, and certainly no social skills. For God's sake, her parents don't even have any friends. She told Damian, she's amazed by all of the people we know. They never had parties or anything growing up; they all lived in this little cocoon with just their immediate family."

"Well, Moni, he chose to marry her," Joseph reminded. "He knew what he was getting into."

As her parents and Lori continued the debate, Maddy stifled a yawn and looked at her watch. Oh my, ten o'clock already. She wanted to call Kenny back before it got too late. Besides, as badly as she felt about this latest disruption, she'd long grown weary of the constant turmoil that had defined their lives ever since Damian brought Laura home for Thanksgiving all those years ago. And now Greg was on the verge of marrying Vanessa, who so far was fitting in quite nicely, though she did have an irrational tendency towards perfection. In that regard, she was much like Lori, who agonized over every buying decision, from a simple sweater to a formal evening gown.

Madeline loved everybody dearly, but was beginning to feel lost in this never-ending drama; she didn't really want to offer an opinion on this or that, though she was more than willing to listen and sympathize. Yet others would insist on involving her in the scuffle as if she somehow had control over the outcome. Maybe it had to do with her Zodiac sign, but whatever the cause, Maddy had a distinct proclivity towards absorbing the feelings of others—not a bad thing when all was well, but when tensions were high, it could be downright exhausting. Was this what devoted daughters were supposed to do? Was this the price you paid for having a close, loving family?

Caught up in their own dialogue, no one noticed when she quietly slipped away to the sanctuary of her bedroom. Judging from the sounds of it, Lori wouldn't be joining her anytime soon. And Greg was apparently on his way home from Vanessa's; no doubt he'd have a few things to say, too. Hopefully, his natural optimism and sense of humor would help calm a few nerves.

Maddy quickly brushed her teeth, completed her nighttime facial regimen and slipped into a pair of comfy pajamas. Then she snuggled under the covers and dialed Ken's number. Her heart skipped a beat when she heard his voice.

"Hey teddy bear, it's me!"

"How are you, sweetheart?" He'd been dozing on the couch while he waited for her call, still feeling a little woozy from the pain meds. He rubbed his shirtless chest as he spoke to her. Although it had cooled off outside, he still felt hot. And since he was temporarily sleeping in the living room, he had to at least wear boxer shorts, out of respect for Kathy.

"Great, now that I'm talking to you," she whispered.

"Aw, thanks." She could almost see his smile through the telephone.

"So, what's the plan for this weekend?" His tone was hopeful.

"Well, I'm definitely coming, and as I said before, I know at least one person who'd really love to join me, provided he doesn't have to work."

"Louis," Ken said softly. He laughed as he remembered their fun times in the arcade and on the boardwalk rides. "That'd be great. We could all go to a movie, maybe even take him gambling at one of the casinos."

"Sounds wonderful," she agreed. "Of course, if he does have to work, I could always see what Carmen is up to."

"She still seeing that Iranian guy?"

"Nah, I don't think so. Last time I talked to her, she was thinking about going back to her old boyfriend. I told you she's flighty," Maddy laughed.

"Hey, I owe her a lot. If not for her, I would have never met you."

"Yeah, well, you could've bought that rose for me," she teased. "I would have accepted it *and* been your exclusive date for the evening. Guess it took an exotic brunette to get your attention first."

"C'mon, Madeline, you know how I feel about you." He sounded somewhat frustrated. And as he lay there in the dark, he was still embarrassed by the whole incident. But what did he have to do to prove his love for her? He thought for sure he'd done everything right up to this point, if not perfectly.

"Oh, Kenny, I'm sorry. I didn't mean to upset you; I was just joking around," she explained. She made a mental note never to bring it up again.

"It's ok, sweetheart, I think I'm kind of cranky with this leg thing, anyway. I just want to get back to work and get on with life."

"And you will. My goodness, it's only been one day."

"By the way, my mom was here, and I gave her some of your sauce for her and my dad. She was very impressed that you made all of that food for me. Told me to thank you for her. She can't wait to meet you."

"I look forward to meeting her, too." Maddy was certain she must be a wonderful woman, to have raised such an unbelievable son.

"Maddy?"

"Yes?"

"I wish you were right here next to me."

"Me, too."

"You still awake?" Lori's voice penetrated the darkness, interrupting her imminent transition into blissful unconsciousness. Madeline rolled over and rubbed her eyes as Lori flipped on the light.

"Well, I guess I am now," she replied, with a twinge of annoyance.

"Oh, I'm sorry Mads; it's just that, you're never around on weekends anymore, and I miss talking to my baby sister," Lori sat down on her bed and proceeded to tickle her. "And the suspense about what's going on with you and Ken is killing me. You never tell me anything!"

Impossibly sensitive, Maddy threw her head back and laughed out loud before ordering her sister to cease and desist. Lori complied but remained seated next to her.

"Maybe that's because all you ever want to talk about are wedding gowns," Maddy teased, prompting her sister to jokingly threaten more tickling.

"Ok, ok, I'll share some stuff with you! He's a really great guy, and I like him a lot."

"And?" Lori pressed.

"What? We get along really well, we both love the same things, and he makes me laugh all the time. And he's the most affectionate guy I've ever met. In fact, sometimes he gets on my nerves because he always has to be touching me. But he really is a big teddy bear. Guess I'm not used to it, after the way Jake treated me."

Lori frowned at the memory of that horrible late-night phone call at the beginning of the summer. She felt the anger well up within as she recalled how she pretended to be asleep while Jake proceeded to confess his sins – a myriad of hurtful lies and fabrications – to her blindsided sister, basically admitting that there had always been a ticket for Maddy to his cousin's comedy show in Baltimore. But because he hadn't wanted her "tagging along" with his family, he'd deceived his girlfriend of two years into believing there was a shortage, a claim hotly disputed by Monica and Lori, who'd definitely smelled a rat. Yet, gullible, trusting Maddy had believed in his sincerity. Adding insult to injury, he'd also feigned anger about having to leave her behind.

And lacking the manliness to face Maddy in person, he'd hidden on the other end of a phone line while he told her in no uncertain terms that it was over between them. It was all Lori could do to remain quiet in her bed as she overheard her younger sister's visceral anguish. This had been her first real boyfriend, after all, and Lori was no stranger to that kind of indescribable heartache. Yet, she also recognized it as a necessary, albeit painful, process on the road to personal growth. Still, watching someone you love—especially someone as sweet as her little sister—having to endure that kind of mistreatment was not easy.

When the call ended, Maddy had thrown herself under the covers, crying into her pillow, so as not to wake Lori. But seconds later, she jumped into her bed and, throwing her arms around her, simply said, "I know exactly how you feel." Those genuine words prompted a rush of fresh tears, along with an intense feeling of comfort; it was hard to imagine Lori saying anything more appropriate in that situation. It was one of many occasions that would forever stand out in Maddy's memory.

"Hey, baby girl, you just enjoy it," Lori's tone was firm and serious. "I could tell right away that day on the beach that Ken is truly crazy about you. And why wouldn't he be? Besides, he's really cute. And isn't nice to date a manly man for a change?" Maddy cracked up.

"It sure is!"

"Let him treat you with the respect you deserve. And enjoy every second you have with him. If he ever makes you feel less than the beautiful girl you are, you'll know it's time to walk away. But something tells me that's never gonna happen with this guy. He's definitely a keeper, according to Aunt Maria. And you know she prides herself on being psychic."

Maddy laughed again before a panicked thought occurred to her.

"Lori?"

"Yes?"

"Does Mom ever mention anything about Ken? I mean, she seems to like him, but I can't really get a good grip on what's going through her mind. Dad I know is crazy about him, but I'm not so sure about Mom."

"You mean the college degree thing?" Lori spoke softly, but her annoyance was obvious as she rolled her eyes. Maddy nodded.

"Look, Maddy, I love Mom dearly, too, and I know she only wants the best for us, but that doesn't mean she's always right."

"So she has said something to you."

"Only in passing. I told her what mattered most was how you felt about him. If the two of you could talk, laugh and relate to each other on a lot of different levels, Ken's lack of a college degree wasn't important. Not that he shouldn't pursue one if that's what he wants. Just saying that intelligence and level of education are not necessarily the same thing."

"That's exactly how I feel," Maddy exclaimed, uplifted by the words of wisdom. "He's smart, Lori. He teaches me things. I could listen to his Navy stories for hours. And while I was living at home and studying British and American literature, he was working on an aircraft carrier, sometimes in hostile places around the world. What have I ever done that compares to that?"

"Well, don't put yourself down just to lift him up. It sounds to me like you both have valuable things to bring to the relationship."

"Yes, I guess when you put it that way, it's true."

"So don't worry about Mom or anything else." With that, Lori gave her sister a hug and announced her plans to get ready for bed and disappeared into the bathroom.

"Hey, Lori, thanks," Maddy called after her, before rolling over on her side and settling into a sound sleep.

"Well, well, look who decided to show up for work today," Betty Stewart's lilting Scottish accent and exuberant laughter greeted her as she stepped through the door of the Kingston Personnel office in

Wayne.

"How are you, sweetie?"

"I'm great, Betty, how are you?" Maddy smiled at the vision of her boss behind her desk—a disorganized cacophony of papers, files, and photographs that stood in stark contrast to her crisp, grey-and-white pinstripe suit, perfectly twisted French knot and professionally manicured nails. Though a plump woman, Betty never had a hair out of place; her scattered office, however, was another story.

"I'm doin' fine sweetheart, come on in," she motioned to Maddy with her hand.

"Guess what?" she teased, as Maddy pulled out a chair and sat down. Betty was grinning from ear-to-ear; whatever it was had to be good.

"What?"

"Your new client? The one I delivered the donuts to yesterday? They love Alexandra, and they want to keep her on a long-term, temporary basis, at least six months or more. And, not only that but they gave me an order for five more temporaries for their customer service department. Isn't that great?" Her accent intensified as the excitement in her voice rose exponentially with each new piece of good news. When she finished, she positively beamed at her protégé.

"Oh my gosh, that's fabulous!" Maddy cried out joyfully. She jumped out of her chair and answered Betty's high-five.

"I'm so proud of you, Madeline. This was a tough nut to crack, but you hung in there and persisted with it. I've been trying to get the American Enterprise account for years now—and you managed to do it after just a few short months. Congratulations!"

"Thank you," she said again, as a warm feeling of accomplishment radiated through her being. It was a welcome phenomenon after a long day of cold-calling in the field, though she had come away with a few excellent leads.

"So how's Kenny doin'?"

"Much better, thanks. I really appreciated your flexibility yesterday, Betty. Thanks for understanding."

"Well sweetheart, I was once young and in love myself," she chuckled. "Of course you'd want to take care of your honey after something like that. And I'm sure he appreciated your TLC."

"Yes, he did." *Wow, did Betty really think this was love after such a short time, too?*

"He sounds like a wonderful young man for you Maddy Rose. I have a really good feelin' about it."

"Thanks, I hope you're right," she replied, picking up her briefcase and heading into her office to sort through her latest crop of business cards.

"You just relax and let things unfold. You'll see it'll all work out great."

Maddy heard her musical accent all the way down the hallway as she wondered how her handsome patient was feeling. She contemplated calling him briefly from the office phone before her thoughts were suddenly interrupted by Arlene, their placement coordinator. A young, attractive woman around Maddy's age, Arlene was prone to discontentment, in spite of a generally good nature. Whenever she entered Maddy's office, it was typically not to celebrate or engage in idle chit-chat.

"Hey, Arlene," she greeted her brightly as she glanced up at her from behind the desk. In spite of her sometimes difficult personality, Maddy always admired Arlene's artful make-up application, long reddish ringlets, and hazel eyes. And at nearly 5' 7", she was a statuesque presence in the tradition of Carmen, Lori and Vanessa. Today she looked especially stunning in a cream-colored suit and a royal blue silk blouse.

"So I heard about the new client, congratulations."

What it lacked in enthusiasm, it made up for in—well, Maddy couldn't be quite sure. It was difficult to ascertain Arlene's sincerity, based on her monotone voice and expressionless face.

"Uh, thanks," she finally replied. "What's up?"

"I just want you to know these positions may not be easy to fill. So, don't put any pressure on me. I'll do my best, and we'll see what happens. I am placing the ad in this Sunday's paper, and going through my files to call qualified temps."

"Well, Arlene, that's all you can do," Maddy sympathized. "And if you need help, just let me know. Betty wants me to focus my time out in the field, but if you want me to stay in one day and help you make calls, as long as it's ok with her, I'll do it."

Arlene continued to stand there.

"Anything else?" Maddy asked, beginning to get annoyed.

"You know, Betty never congratulates me like that when I fill a position; you get a new client, and it's like you gave her a million dollars."

"Oh, Arlene, I don't think she means anything by it. It's just that, we're an industry driven by sales, and it's tough out there. When you get a new account, you have to celebrate it. Believe me, cold calling is really hard. I still have days when I dread it. But the home office pressures Betty for new clients, and she pressures us—me to bring them in and you to fill them. That's how it works."

Although she spoke calmly, Maddy had long begun to tire of her co-worker's "poor me" routine; it was hard enough doing her own job. But while she felt like screaming, she maintained a sweet façade and a tranquil demeanor.

"Yeah, I guess you're right," Arlene conceded with a sigh. "Thanks for listening."

"Anytime," Maddy called out as she left. She quickly picked up the phone to dial Ken before she returned for another gripe session. He picked it up after the first ring.

"Hello?" Maddy's heart skipped a beat at the sound of his deep voice.

"Hey, Kenny, it's me. How're you feeling?"

"A helluva lot better now," They both laughed.

"Uh, I can't talk long since I'm on the company phone. Just wanted to check in with you after a long day in the field. How's the leg?"

"Much better today." He was propped up on his pillows on the couch, his new CDs playing in the background. As he spoke to her, he held the teddy bear she gave him in his hand. "But let's talk about you. How's your day going?"

"Well, my new account just gave us five more orders; my boss is really happy."

"Sweetheart, that's great. Congratulations!" He felt genuine pride as he listened to her recount the whole story.

"We'll have to do something special this weekend to celebrate," he said.

"That sounds wonderful. I'm pretty sure Lori is coming down with me. Vince's sister lives in Ocean City, and it's her husband's birthday this weekend. They're going to his party, so they'll be staying at the house with me."

"Great!" Whatever made it possible for Maddy to return was fine with Ken.

"Ok, baby, I'd better go. I'm on the company's dime here, and I don't want to get myself in trouble, especially after landing such a big fish."

"Alright, sweetheart. Can I call you later?"

"Absolutely."

Maddy smiled inside and out as she suddenly felt refreshed and ready to make the sometimes harrowing, but always necessary, follow-up phone calls.

Chapter 11

Mads, you ready to go?" An impatient Lori stood at the bottom of the stairs calling up to her sister.

"Coming!" she cried out, slinging her pink and purple duffle bag over one shoulder and folding a garment bag containing dresses of varying textures and styles over her other arm. Now that they were well into the month of September, she couldn't be certain of what to expect weather-wise at the Shore; chances were temperatures would still be warm and pleasant during the day, but evenings this time of year could be downright chilly. And though Ken had assured her his leg had healed, she figured they might just end up at a movie theater or hanging out at his place—two perfectly acceptable options. As long as they were together, she didn't care. Besides, she didn't want him to overdo it; it was bad enough he went back to work already.

She bounded down the stairs with her usual energy, dressed in a pair of lime green leggings with an oversized coordinating top and a pair of Keds sneakers. Even in her mid-20s, she didn't look a day over sixteen. Since Ken would be working until at least ten, she figured she'd have plenty of time to change into something else once they arrived in Ocean City.

"Don't look at me like that," Lori laughed in spite of herself. "I don't want to be late getting to Peggy's house; I promised I'd help her get ready for the party tomorrow night, and it's already almost seven." She reached out to playfully pat her younger sister on the head.

"I'm sorry," she apologized. "Today was crazy for a Friday— all of these orders came in for temps, and Betty had me making phone calls with Arlene most of the afternoon, trying to fill them. Ugh! I was ready to pull my hair out working with that girl. She's such a whiner; I still have a headache from listening to her."

"Well, let's not waste any more time," Lori chided. "I'm excited about taking my new car on its first long road trip."

"Uh, Lori, the Jersey Shore's not exactly a long road trip. It's what, like 80 miles from here? Disney World, now that's what I consider a long ride; remember when we all went in Mom's old station wagon?"

"How could I forget? You drove us crazy trying to find a bathroom in the middle of nowhere," Maddy laughed recalling the incident, though as a twelve-year-old, it hadn't been quite so funny.

"You girls ready to go?" Monica Rose walked into the ceramic-tiled foyer from the kitchen. She was on her way into the office, where she was planning to write out some bills before her husband arrived home from his weekly tennis outing. They had plans to go to dinner at a new restaurant in Devon with their friends Nick and Nancy, and she wanted to tie up loose ends so she could simply relax and enjoy herself.

"Yeah Mom, we're heading out now that Madeline's finally ready. I'm supposed to help Peggy make some food for the party. As it is, I probably won't get to her house until after nine."

"Well, just be careful," Monica went on with a concerned expression, "It's Friday night and I'm sure the Expressway will be mobbed. Why don't you take the Commodore Barry and go over the back roads?"

"Yeah!" Maddy exclaimed. "Let's go that way, Lor, it'll be much more scenic, and we'll move the whole time."

"No, it's too dark. Besides it's already late; I'm sure the Expressway is fine by now."

"I don't know," Mom replied, "Not with all the casino traffic, Lori. But you do what you want."

Monica and Maddy exchanged a knowing look; the two of them had spent many a Friday evening driving to Ocean City via rural routes like 538, enjoying the passing countryside and singing along to the radio. Once they'd discovered this alternate route, they rarely ever used the Walt Whitman, save for those rare occasions when truly pressed for time. Even so, the longest it had ever taken them on the scenic course was just over two hours.

"Well I'm taking the Bonneville, and I want to see how it handles on the highway," Lori explained.

"And you have that new car phone installed in there too," Monica remarked. "Makes me feel better, should something happen."

Maddy laughed. "It's a brand-new car, Mom. I should hope nothing would happen."

"Yeah well, it's not the car; it's the other nuts on the road. Anyway, you girls have a good time," She pecked each of them on the cheek. "What're you and Ken doing Maddy?"

"Oh, well he's working tonight, so we'll probably just hang out and watch a movie. We're spending the whole day together tomorrow— probably drive around, go to the Hamilton Mall; he says he needs some new winter clothes."

"How's his leg?"

"Much better; he doesn't have to wear the brace anymore."

"Well if didn't have to work such a labor-intensive job he wouldn't have to worry about accidents like that. That's why an education is so important."

"Ok, Mom, we're going," Lori announced, taking Maddy by the shoulder before a disagreement erupted. Maddy's heart sank, but she silently followed her sister's lead as they headed out the front door. She knew as soon as she laid eyes on Ken's beaming face, nothing else would matter.

The white Bonneville cruised smoothly along the Garden State Parkway, just a few miles now from Exit 7S that would take them through Somers Point and over the 9th Street Bridge into Ocean City. In spite of traffic concerns, the trip had been relatively uneventful, with congestion at a minimum in spite of an abundance of vehicles. Throughout the trip, Lori and Madeline had delighted in the car's luxurious features including a CD player, from which they blasted their favorite songs. Still in search of a ballad for her wedding, Lori had subjected Madeline to repeated listening to everything from classic 70's artists to early 90's bands.

"You know you're going to sing the song for our first dance, right?" Lori asked.

"If you really want me to," she sighed. "You know how nervous I get in front of an audience but for you, I'll do it."

"Thanks."

"So where's Vince again?"

"Basketball practice. He's getting ready for a big fundraising tournament and the other guys were only free after work today— which is actually better considering the party is tomorrow night. He's gonna drive down in the morning."

"Oh, ok. Lori?"

"Yes?"

"Do you think I should stop seeing Ken?"

"Why? Is that what you want?"

"No, I really like him. He's so different, you know, from anyone I've ever met, but I just don't want this to end up causing problems between me and Mom."

"Madeline, we've talked about this. You have every right to date whomever you want, if it makes you happy, no matter what anybody says. You're 25 years old for God's sake. And Ken's such a nice guy— we all liked him right away that day he came to the beach with us, including Mom. He was really polite, he blended in easily with everybody, he sat and waited for you for two hours and then tracked you down in the phone book when he couldn't find you. I'd say he's definitely sincere. And from what you've told me he treats you well. He's funny, outgoing, cute, smart...why on earth would you give that up?"

"I don't know," she sighed. "I keep waiting for the other shoe to drop, that's all. Something just doesn't feel right."

"Madeline, listen to me. We all have to live our own lives. As much as I hate to think about it, Mom and Dad aren't going to be here forever. They got to live their lives, and we have to live ours. If you were dating a derelict or a drug-dealer, I'd be the first one to come down on you. But here's a guy who respects you, makes you laugh and thinks you're beautiful. Take it from your older sister, who has a lot more dating experience—guys like Ken are hard to find. Don't walk away if you don't want to."

Maddy took her words to heart as they made the turn onto the causeway and sighted the familiar landscape of Ocean City in the distance.

"I think someone's on our porch," Lori teased as the wheels rolled over the paved driveway. And as the headlights illuminated the darkness, Madeline shivered with excitement.

"Kenny!" she exclaimed in recognition. Her sister had barely put the car in park before she bounced out of the passenger side door and into his arms, hardly noticing the palpable chill in the autumn air.

"Hey!" He scooped her up off of the ground and gave her a quick kiss on the lips before Lori joined them on the wooden structure.

"Lori! Hey, how ya doin'." He greeted her with a peck on the cheek.

"Hey Ken, how are you?"

"Great; the leg's all better," he announced.

"You sure? I thought you had to work until ten? Are you sure you didn't leave early 'cause it was bothering you?" Maddy quizzed him skeptically.

"No, I left early because they didn't really need me. And since all I wanted to do was come over her to meet you, I was happy about that." He gazed into her eyes as he spoke and she felt the electric sensations intensify throughout her body.

"Aw, isn't that sweet," she teased, throwing her arms around him.

"Uh, Maddy do you have the house key? It's cold out here!"

"Yeah, it's here in my purse somewhere."

She fished through the contents of her bag; a moment later, they were all standing in the family room. That's when Maddy noticed how incredibly handsome he looked in a mock burgundy turtleneck and pair of belted jeans. A healthy glow had returned to his cheeks, and his aquamarine eyes sparkled with excitement.

"So what do you want to do tonight, baby? I'm starving, so after we go out and get something to eat, we can do anything you want."

"Mm, I'm hungry too," she agreed, rubbing her arms to ward of a chill. That's when he wrapped her up in another comforting embrace.

"I hope you brought heavier clothes, sweetheart. You look great, but that outfit's not gonna keep you warm." He kissed her head.

"Speaking of which, Maddy come get your stuff out of the car. I gotta head over to Peggy's place," Lori announced.

"Ken you have to see her new Bonneville. It's awesome!" Madeline exclaimed, taking him by the hand and back out to the driveway. The trio shared a few lighthearted moments, as Lori eagerly demonstrated all of the features of her proud new purchase. Ken appropriately responded with genuine interest, particularly to the mounted car phone and CD player.

"Yeah, Maddy and I definitely took advantage of the CD player driving down here tonight. She's helping me pick out some good music for my wedding. And even though she's the maid of honor, I think I finally convinced her to do at least one solo at the reception." She winked at her younger sister.

"Wow, now that I'd love to see," Ken replied softly, hugging her shoulder. "Provided, of course, I'm lucky enough to be your date."

"Oh, I think that can be arranged," she assured him softly.

"Well ok guys, I'm off," Lori stated. "Mads, you have the key, right?"

"Yes, but why don't you take it? You'll probably be back before me and Ken anyway. Besides, we can always hang out at his place until you get home."

"Good idea."

She caught Maddy's lob before sliding behind the wheel. "See you later. Have fun!"

"Bye, Lor!" They waved as she honked at them from the alley. Then Ken lifted her off the ground again and buried his head in her neck. "Maddy I've missed you so much."

"Likewise." She breathed in his scent and delighted in the sheer strength of his body as they held each other in the moonlight.

"I can't believe we're back here at the Point, Madeline. I wanted to take you to a nice restaurant, not a stupid Jersey diner," he remarked, rolling his eyes.

"Hey, don't be dissin' Jersey diners," she teased. "I've eaten some of the best meals of my life in this state."

"Yeah, well, believe it or not, there are actually other kinds of restaurants here—and I can also afford to take you to them."

She looked up at him from behind her plastic-coated menu. "I know that. Why is it so hard to believe that I really want to eat here? It's kind of late to eat a full-course meal, anyway. Besides, I'm really in the mood for a good breakfast—maybe a cheddar cheese omelet with bacon on the side or even a short stack of pancakes. They were so yummy that night we were here. Then again, that burger that guy's eating over there looks really good."

"Are you sure this is all you want? I've dated women not nearly as classy as you who always insisted on going to the best places or else."

"Women like Roseanne?"

She couldn't help herself, feeling a bit insulted by his suggestion— at least in her mind—that she was some snobby doctor's daughter from an upscale Philly suburb who expected him to spend wads of cash on her. And though that hadn't been his intention at all, it transported her back to unhappy memories of high school, and most recently, Jake. Unfounded accusations of elitism were quite common with her old boyfriend.

The first time they'd spent a Christmas together, he'd taken offense to her family's "dressy" attire, which contrasted sharply with the casual sweat-suits preferred by his side. Rather than compliment Maddy on her pretty red satin dress, he'd admonished her for "trying to show everyone else up."

Having been raised with the belief that special occasions merited special clothing, she had just assumed everyone else engaged in the same customs. After all, wasn't that one of the things that distinguished a holiday from every other day of the year? And while on the surface it appeared to be a superficial debate, it had been just one of many differences that doomed the relationship.

"Roseanne? How do you know about her?" he shot back with a twinge of anger.

"Uh, her name came up in conversation with someone." She was suddenly filled with regret for bringing up the subject; her tendency to overreact was one of her worst shortcomings, one she struggled to overcome.

"Someone?" he repeated.

"Ken, why are you so upset?" She mustered the discipline to keep her tone calm and understanding.

"Tell me please." Although he spoke in a firm voice, he appeared to calm down a bit as he reached out for her hand.

"Ok, it was Kathy. The other day when you were sleeping on the couch, and I was making sauce for in the kitchen, we had a little conversation. It was no big deal. Please, don't be mad at her."

"What did she tell you?"

Maddy took a deep breath. "Just that Roseanne was someone you used to date and that she was glad you weren't seeing her anymore. Said that she used guys for whatever she could get out of them and then moved on to the next when she got bored."

"What else?"

"That's it really. Ok, look, it bothered me a little until Kathy swore she hadn't seen her around in a while—at least not since you and I had started dating." She purposely omitted the part about her extreme insecurity regarding physical intimacy; after being with someone so willing to "put out" how long could Kenny really tolerate chaste kissing and hand-holding with her?

His expression became thoughtful as he caressed her small hand and looked deeply into her eyes. "It's true, Madeline. There's been no one else for me but you since the night I met you. And Roseanne had long been out of the picture even before that. Besides, we were never an exclusive thing; it was never even a real relationship—she was just a girl I knew from high school, an old friend I hung out with for a while."

"A friend with benefits?" she pressed. There was no trace of malice in her voice; just an element of sadness and concern.

"I'm not gonna lie to you. Did I sleep with Roseanne? Yes. Guilty as charged. But you know what? Liz Anne had broken my heart, my dad was giving me a hard time, and my career was up in the air. I didn't know what the hell I was supposed to do with my life. And Roseanne was there for me; no pressures, no hassles, we just had a good time together. So yeah—I gave into temptation for some fleeting moments of pleasure. Is it what I really wanted? No. Am I proud of it? Not really. But Maddy, you have to understand, I didn't even know you then. I didn't know that there were still girls like you out there." He leaned in closer to stare deeply into her eyes. "Don't you get it? I love you, Madeline Rose."

Speechless, all she could do was sit there until a waitress interrupted the silence. She smiled as she placed two glasses of water on the table, and then asked if they were ready to order.

"I think we need a little more time," Ken advised her politely. After she'd walked away, he turned back to face Maddy again. "You do believe me, don't you?" He searched for some kind of sign in her expression—anything to let him know she took him at his word. It seemed an eternity before she finally responded.

"Kenny, it's ok. I understand, and I don't hold it against you. I was just upset that I hadn't heard about it from you first, that's all. It was kind of a shock when Kathy blurted it out that day."

"I was planning to tell you. Just wasn't sure how or when. I wasn't purposely trying to deceive you. God, I've never met anyone like you before in my life, Madeline. This is all so new to me."

"Me too," she whispered.

"So are we good now?"

"Yeah, we're good," she laughed softly as she playfully punched his arm. "Thank you for your honesty. I do appreciate it."

"You're welcome." Then with another thought, he spoke up again. "Maddy?" "Yes?"

"You know you can talk to me about anything, right?"

"Yes, of course."

"Good. Because I want you to be honest with me, especially if something is bothering you. I will always listen without judging you, I promise."

"Thank you. And I promise you the same."

She was truly touched—and more than a little disappointed in herself. In spite of her genuine affection for him, she couldn't bring herself to say the words that so easily rolled off his tongue. Worse, when it came to issues of real import, she morphed into a helpless, petrified child from an outwardly mature young woman. But why? What was there to fear, really? So far, Ken had proven himself a man of honor. He called when he said he would, treated her with utmost respect, and always made her laugh—surely everything else would just work itself out.

After all, if he was this great now, it stood to reason that if they ever did get married, he'd be more than patient with her. And how scary could it be anyway? Lots of people she knew, her parents included, were married with kids. Obviously, sex wasn't frightening for them— at least not now. Probably a lot of people felt the way she did at one time but got over it after the initial foray into the unknown. If God Himself had set up it this way, sex was for sure a normal activity to be enjoyed within the boundaries of a marriage, right? That was the thing, though; it was hard for her to fathom the pleasure aspect; while she firmly believed that a good kiss was one of the very best things in life, the rest of it—beyond the sweet caresses and warm embraces, just seemed sort of...frightening. That is until Ken entered her world and turned it upside down. Now she didn't know what to do about all of these new sensations.

"Madeline, did you hear me?" His deep voice brought her back to reality. "Let's not ever let anything come between us, ok?"

"Ok," she smiled again.

"Alright then, enough of that. Let's eat already."

He laughed as they reopened their menus and mulled over that evening's choices.

Ken wrapped his arms around her tightly as they snuggled up on a blanket beneath the boardwalk. They'd taken a quiet stroll after dinner, during which she'd told him about a rumba dance routine she'd once performed to a remake of the old Drifters classic, *Under the Boardwalk*. That had prompted an observation that, while she always loved the song, she couldn't really relate to it, having never actually spent time with anyone special in such a romantic setting. So of course, when they arrived back at the car, he'd opened his trunk, pulled out a big beach blanket and extended an irresistible invitation.

And though there was a noticeable crispness in the air, neither one of them cared as they held each other close and gazed out a rolling, majestic sea.

"Are you warm enough?"

"Mm-hm," she sighed, resting her head back against his chest. He was leaning against a wooden support beam, with Maddy situated in front of him, wearing his black Taj sweatshirt.

"This is so nice," she purred.

"Maddy?"

"Yes?"

"Do you think you might ever invite me to your house in Pennsylvania?"

She lifted her head and turned to face him. "Of course; I'd love for you to come up for a weekend—I'm sorry, it's not that I didn't want you to, just that I guess I was trying to squeeze out as much of the summer as I could. We had such a rainy one this year, I hardly went to the beach. And coming down here on the weekends is such a nice change of scenery."

"Well, for *you* it is. For me, it's home. Don't get me wrong; I love spending time with you here. It's just that I want to know more about you, see where you grew up, what your neighborhood is like, you know, experience something different. And I haven't really spent that much time in Philly."

"Oh my gosh, there are so many things I want to share with you! If you want, we could go to this great dinner theater in Valley Forge, maybe do some sightseeing downtown, visit Longwood Gardens and of course, watch the Eagles game." Her enthusiasm increased with each new idea.

"Hey! How 'bout next weekend? Do you think you can get off from work?"

"I will beg for the time—or just work extra shifts during the week," he replied, thrilled by her reaction.

"Damn!" she cried suddenly.

"What?"

"The Eagles play away next week, I think. Otherwise, I could've taken you to a game at the Vet. We only have three season tickets, but my parents don't really like to go anymore. Remember how my mom was telling you about that? They like to watch in the comfort of the family room—can't say I blame them the way some of those fans are. Normally it's Greg, Lori and me since Louis isn't into football and Damian lives far away."

"Well, there will be other games; we can watch this one on TV, don't worry," he laughed. "Just watching them with you is an experience, live or on television." He cracked up remembering the Eagles-Giants battle the week before and his utter astonishment at Maddy's passion and intelligence for the game. It was yet another area in which she stood head and shoulders above every other female he'd ever dated.

"Yeah well, you'll get to see me in action again on Sunday," she joked.

"I think they play at 1 p.m. And you know what? I believe they're up against your second-favorite team, the Vikings, this year."

"December 6," He confirmed.

"Well, if you go with me, you have to promise to cheer for the Eagles, or I might have to do something crazy, like paint your face green."

She giggled at the thought before an amorous Ken suddenly pulled her close to him and drew her into another tender kiss as the cool breeze gently rustled their hair.

Chapter 12

What time is Ken getting here, hon?" Monica Rose inquired of her daughter as they pored over a crossword puzzle at the kitchen table. From the time Madeline was in elementary school, it had been one of their favorite shared hobbies. An avid reader practically from the time she was a toddler, she excelled in writing, literature and word games, thoroughly enjoying the challenge of deciphering the cryptic clues and then coming up with the correct letters. Usually, she and her mom were doggedly persistent, able to crack just about everyone they attempted. Tonight, however, The Philadelphia Inquirer's Friday night crossword edition had been particularly tough.

"Oh, he called me while I was still at the office earlier; said he was leaving Somers Point around 5:30. Since he lives right near the Parkway, I just gave him directions from the A.C. Expressway. It didn't make sense to have him drive several miles south and then take all of those back roads. Besides, most traffic is heading to the Shore, and not away from it, I would think."

"Yeah, that makes sense," her mom agreed. "I would imagine he'll be here by 7:30 at the latest. What do you guys have planned?"

"Tonight we'll probably just go to dinner and maybe see a

movie, if it's not too late. Tomorrow night he's taking me to Lily Langtry's. The Eagles are playing the Cardinals on the road on Sunday, so I guess we'll watch it here with everybody."

"Yeah, that'll be good, honey. We can make something easy like spaghetti with clams for dinner, and I'll go pick up some tomato pie and other stuff to snack on. Maybe Lyle and Daphne will come over, too, although if she comes she has to watch the game or hang out with Louis in the other room. I don't want to be distracted."

Maddy laughed, knowing how tough it could be for her mom to play hostess for non-football enthusiasts. She certainly sympathized with the sentiment; none of her girlfriends gave a damn about the sport, either.

"I just don't understand how anyone could not enjoy football, Mom. I'm addicted to it!" Then, changing the subject, "Oh, I forgot to tell you, Kenny invited me to a wedding!"

"Really? Who's getting married?"

"One of his cousins who lives in Ventnor. I don't know the guy. Actually, I haven't met anyone in his family yet, although he's shown me lots of pictures. I guess this'll be a great opportunity to get to know them. His mom sounds really nice; I'm looking forward to meeting her."

"Wow, that's a big step, going to a wedding with him," Monica remarked softly. Maddy shrugged her shoulders.

"I guess, but we've pretty much been seeing each other nonstop for a month, plus talking on the phone all the time. Neither one of us is seeing anybody else. He needed a date, so he asked me. Makes perfect sense. Ugh! Now, I have to figure out what to wear. I have a few ideas, but I have to ask him again what time of day it is, so—"

"Madeline, don't you think this is moving a little too fast?"

"Why because he invited me to a wedding?"

"Don't get me wrong, Maddy. Ken's a very respectful kid, and a pleasure to be around. He's nice and all, but—"

"It's the college degree thing again, right?" she felt her blood beginning to boil, but she fought to keep the emotion out of her voice. Her father would be walking through the door at any minute, and she certainly didn't relish the thought of the three of them butting heads over the issue. True, Dad was on her side; but the idea of her parents arguing over something else when they were already stressed out over Damian and Laura pained her deeply.

"Madeline, honey, it's just that you come from a highly educated family," Monica pleaded as calmly as possible. Like every good mother, her fondest wish was for her daughter to marry the right guy and live happily ever after. And though she truly did like Ken, she lacked her daughter's intuitive faith and spiritual vision when it came to detecting the inner spark that fueled his passion and work ethic. "My goodness, your grandfather was a pharmacist back when most immigrants were still working hard labor."

"Mom I'm proud of our family, too, but what does that have to do with anything? Ken treats me like a lady; he respects me, he makes me laugh all the time. We have fun together, and I never have to pretend I'm someone else when I'm with him. After all of the crap I took from Jake, doesn't that count for anything? Why can't you just be happy that I met a decent guy?"

"Madeline—"

"Oh, and by the way, here I am a college educated *girl*, living at home with mom and dad. I don't even make enough money working a job I hate to even buy or rent my own place. Maybe you don't like what Ken does for a living, but he makes a helluva lot more money than me, owns his own house and has a nice car. You know what? He's ten times more accomplished than MBA Jake, who still lives at home while he's trying to find himself!" In spite of her best efforts, the tears were flowing freely.

"Well, what do you two even have in common? I mean, what do you talk about?"

Monica spoke in a soothing voice now, hoping to pacify the situation before her husband walked through the door. She hadn't planned on having this exchange right now, considering the weekend plans ahead, but Madeline's wedding news had acted like kerosene on a smoldering fire. She'd initially dismissed the concern that her daughter might be speeding ahead precipitously in this relationship, but it appeared her instincts had been correct.

If Ken was at the point of including Maddy in important family celebrations, no doubt his intentions were serious. And who could blame him? But not just anybody was going to get Madeline's hand; she was simply too special to settle for anything less than she deserved.

"Everything! We talk about everything, including all of the amazing things he's done and seen in the Navy. You know, not all kids are lucky enough to have their parents foot the bill for college. But unlike Jake, Ken doesn't hate me for not having to take out loans to finance my education. He took it upon himself to enlist because he wanted a better life. I admire him for that. Hasn't just about every man in our family also served in the military, with the exception of Greg, Damian and Louis? You're proud of them! Why can't you be proud of Ken?"

"Honey, I do admire that. Your Uncle Dan was an Admiral in the Navy and look at all he's done. But there's no substitute for education, that's all I'm saying. And I just hate to see you get too serious with this guy too soon, that's all."

"Mom, how long has it been since you've been in the dating world, about 36 or so years? Do you have any idea what it's like out there, especially for nice girls? 'Cause if you did, you wouldn't be giving me a hard time right now."

"Hey, what the hell is going on in here?" Maddy closed her eyes for a second when she recognized her father's booming voice. "I can hear the two of you all the way out in the garage."

"Mom doesn't want me to see Ken anymore."

"Madeline, that's not what I—"

"You listen to me, Maddy," Joseph Rose said firmly, striding up closely to his daughter to emphasize his viewpoint. He was still dressed in his tennis garb, having just come from his Friday night session. "You are 25 years old. You can date anybody you want!"

A shell-shocked Maddy remained silent for a moment, grateful for her father's support, but dismayed that she'd become the cause of discord between her parents.

"Joe, all I was saying is that you can't discount the importance of education in today's world," his wife explained. And while he conceded that point to her, he opposed her on everything else. Madeline watched sadly as their disagreement escalated into a shouting match, with Joseph extolling Ken's praises and Maddy's right to choose her own boyfriend, and Monica expressing heartfelt motherly concern. It had never been her style to interfere before. That's what made this even more difficult for Madeline to cope with; it was completely unknown territory.

And as she stood there, a bystander in a battle she'd indirectly instigated, she was rendered speechless. Her stomach in knots, she suddenly panicked when she looked at the clock.

"Mom, Dad, please stop fighting!" she ordered them. "Ken's going to be here any minute. I'm going upstairs now to clean myself up before he does. Then I am going to spend a nice weekend with him before I end things for good." And with one final glance at her mother, she added, "I hope that makes you happy." With that, she turned and ran upstairs to redo her make-up.

"I guess you heard all of that," Maddy sighed to her sister, entering the comfort of their large pink and white bedroom. Lori had been in the bathroom, wrapping her hair up in hot rollers, in anticipation of a night out with Vince. She'd heard the drama unfolding downstairs, but had made a conscious decision to stay out of it, preferring to speak with one- on-one with both her Mom and sister once the storm clouds had passed.

"She's ridiculous," Lori remarked. Then, seeing her sister's eyes fill up again, threw her arms around her. "Mads, don't cry. It's gonna be alright, you'll see. She'll come around."

"I just can't stand it," Maddy sobbed, "All this turmoil with Damian and Laura and she has to pick a fight over Ken? He's the best thing that's happened to me in a long time. I'm happy with him. Why doesn't that matter?"

"Hey Mads, what's up, darling?" Greg addressed her by one of his many terms of endearment for his youngest sister as he walked in on the unfolding scene. He'd heard the commotion, too, but had been chatting with Vanessa on the phone about their plans for the evening.

"Oh, it's just Mom being overprotective," Lori explained. "She's hung up on the education thing with Ken. I don't know what the problem is; he's a nice guy, he works hard, has his own place; most importantly, he makes her happy." She nodded her head toward her sister as she held an arm around her.

"Pfft! Is that what this is about?" He waved his arm dismissively in the air in imitation of Louis.

"Maddy, you have every right to keep dating him—my God, you're an adult. And if the two of you get along, it's no one else's business. If the guy was mistreating you, I'd be the first one to beat the hell out of him, you know that. But so far, I really like him. He seems like a nice kid."

Madeline looked up at her six-foot, two-inch tall brother, whose hazel eyes emanated sincerity and solidarity. From the time she was born, they'd shared a special bond; now as a grown woman, his support was all the more meaningful to her.

"I'm just tired, Greg. I'm tired of everything being a problem around here, whether it's Damian and Laura, everyone else's wedding plans or even the latest saga with Uncle Nick and Aunt Susan."

Maddy was referring to their mother's brother, whose wife had been generating drama in the family with her insane jealousy for over 30 years. Aunt Maria, in particular, had been at the receiving end of most of Susan's bile, for reasons that defied logic.

After all, Aunt Maria and Uncle Earl were two of the nicest people anyone would ever want to meet. But for as long as Maddy could remember, Nick and Susan's presence, along with their three children, at family events tended to cause nothing but friction and the distinctive feeling of walking on eggshells. They possessed the dubious ability to destroy an otherwise festive occasion simply by arriving at the party.

"Don't get me wrong; I agree with Mom. She's absolutely right about Laura, although it probably wasn't a good idea to have written that letter to Damian a few years back. And yes, who can forget all of the tension at their wedding and the way Mom, Aunt Maria, and Lori had to go clean Laura's apartment. Lori and I were so hurt when they had a luncheon for all of the bridesmaids and conveniently forgot to invite us. If we wanted to stay mad, we could. But you know what? It's Damian's problem. And if he turns down the Penn program because of her, he's crazy; but it's still his decision to make. And I am just tired of being wrapped up in all of this conflict.

"When I'm with Ken, I forget about it all. I forget all about Jake and the nasty things he said and did. Now this great guy comes along, and just because he doesn't have a formal education, I'm supposed to throw it all away." She broke down in sobs again.

"Hey, don't cry," he consoled her. "You have to just do your own thing; don't let anyone else dictate who you can see. If you like this guy, that's all that matters."

"Yeah, Mads," Lori chimed in. "You know we support you. And I think the more Mom gets to know Ken, the more she'll like him. But guess what? It's your life. You're the one who gets to decide—not Mom or anyone else."

"She doesn't want me to go to a wedding with him. Says if I go, I'm just getting myself in deeper." Maddy's voice was muffled.

"Madeline, listen to me; go to the wedding with him if you want. Don't cave into that kind of unfair pressure. Mom is wrong in this case; she has no right to do that to you." Lori was furious.

"I just hate seeing Mom and Dad fight over this," Maddy remarked."I can't stand that they're fighting because of me."

"They're not fighting because of you; they're fighting because Mom has unrealistic expectations. For God's sake, we're talking about a well-adjusted, self-supporting guy here. And there are lots of people in our family without degrees—people who are pretty damn successful by most standards. Mom doesn't love them any less because they didn't go to college."

Lori made a silent note to herself to discuss the matter with their mother at a more conducive time; she knew if she went downstairs now, it might only make things worse. And with Ken due to arrive any second, it also had the potential to embarrass the entire family.

"C'mon," Greg encouraged. "Get yourself together. It's almost seven-fifteen; the guy's gonna be here soon." Maddy released herself from his hug and looked up at them with a tear- stained face.

"Yeah, I guess you're right. I'm sure my make-up is a mess; I'd better go wash my face and redo it. I don't want him to know what's been going on around here." Greg kissed her cheek.

She made one final observation before moving on.

"You know what else is really sad, that I just can't seem to get across to her? Ken is so very respectful, even though he's dated other girls before who—weren't like me if you know what I mean. And even though we're incredibly attracted to one another, he has never once crossed the line or pressured me to do anything. Not once. And we've been alone plenty of times, believe me."

"Well, take it from your big brother—when it's true love, you're willing to wait. That's the way it is for me and Vanessa, anyway. She wants to wait until we're married and that is great with me. And you know I haven't always been a saint." He laughed as he patted her on the head. Both girls cracked up.

"Uh yeah, we're well aware of that, Greg," Lori chuckled. "But it's nice to hear you've changed for the right one. Vince is the same way with me."

"I just hope Kenny can stay patient. He's told me he loves me so many times already. And it's like I'm so closed off inside, I don't even know what I'm feeling anymore. But I do know I care about him a lot. And I love being with him."

The ringing of the doorbell pierced the subsequent silence, causing Maddy's heart to catch in her throat.

"Oh my God, it's him."

"Hurry and get cleaned up; I'll get the door." With that, Lori ran out of the room.

"Remember what I said," Greg cautioned, before following Lori out of the room. Maddy collected her thoughts as she entered the bathroom to wash away all visible traces of anguish.

She brushed her long hair and then inspected her face in the mirror again. Though still slightly puffy, artful make-up application had concealed the worst of the damage from the evening's earlier discord. She smoothed some gloss over her lips as a finishing touch on her rosy lipstick, adjusted the wide waistband of her black, knit slacks and tucked in the folds of her purple, silk blouse. With its scoop neck, puffy sleeves and gathered bustline, it created an attractive illusion. On her feet, she wore a pair of high-heeled black pumps.

To her great relief, she'd overheard good-natured laughter and uplifting conversation coming from downstairs while she quickly reassembled herself. And when she finally walked into the kitchen, Ken was happily interacting with Louis, who'd just arrived home from work, as well as her parents. Before she could even utter a sound, however, he looked up, as if psychically sensing her presence.

"Hello beautiful," he said, almost imperceptibly. As always, she felt faint when his sparkling eyes met hers. Their mesmerizing color was set off nicely by a patterned pullover sweater in varying shades of blue that coordinated perfectly with his neatly pressed navy pants. Maddy recognized the outfit as one of their purchases at the Hamilton Mall the previous weekend, where she and Ken had passed several joyful hours securing his new fall wardrobe.

He met her halfway between the table and the folding door that separated the foyer and the kitchen, planting a kiss on her cheek and enfolding his arms around her.

"Kenny!" she exclaimed. "It's so good to see you—you look so great in that."

"You have good taste," he laughed, releasing her. He was well aware that her family was still in the room.

"Well, welcome to Pennsylvania. How was the drive? Were my directions ok?"

"Perfect," he smiled.

"Uh Maddy, guess what? Ken brought us two big boxes of tomato pie for the game on Sunday," Mom announced.

"From that bakery in Ventnor, same place I got it for our beach picnic," he added.

"Oh, wow, thanks."

"Hey Mads," Louis piped up, "Ken bought me a book."

"Really? Let me see." She walked over to the table and sat down next to her brother, who promptly showed her his new copy of *A Time to Kill*, by his favorite author, John Grisham.

"I took a chance, hoping he didn't already have it," Ken explained.

"No, I have *Pelican Brief*, but I didn't have this one," Louis clarified.

"Aw, that was really nice." Maddy's earlier inner turmoil had now been replaced by a warm, comforting sense of calm.

"Nah, it was the least I could do. Besides, Louis is my buddy, right?" Ken and Louis exchanged a high-five.

"Oh yes," Louis agreed.

Maddy exchanged a knowing glance with her father, seated at his usual place at the head, still dressed in his tennis clothes. In front of him, a red-stained plate provided telltale evidence of his spaghetti-

and-meatball dinner. Mom busied herself at the stove, preparing a dish for Louis. Setting it in front of him, she remarked, "Don't mind us, Ken, it's a typical Friday night around here, with everyone eating in shifts. There's plenty of food, though, if you want some."

"It looks delicious Mrs. Rose, thank you. But I want to take Madeline out for a nice dinner tonight." He picked up her hand and kissed it.

"I hope you don't mind, but I did a little research, and someone recommended The Ship Inn in Exton. So I made us a reservation at eight-thirty. It's not too far from here, is it?"

Pleasantly taken aback, she replied, "Uh, no Ken. Not at all; in fact, it's one of my favorite restaurants." She conveniently omitted the fact that Jake had originally introduced her to the establishment, contemplating silently how nice it was to have the opportunity to create new memories. Ken sure was full of welcome surprises.

"Well Maddy, you two should get going. It's still a good half-hour from here, and it's almost eight now." Her father spoke in a congenial tone, delighted by what this young man had demonstrated so far.

"You're right," she agreed, rising to her feet. She gave each of her parents a parting kiss before taking Ken's hand and heading for the front door.

"You are so beautiful," Ken said softly from across the rounded, white linen table for two. A glowing votive sat in the middle, surrounded by a ring of ivy. Even in the subdued light, he saw her blush.

"Hey, you have to learn to deal with compliments, 'cause there's plenty more where that came from."

"It's a new experience," she explained softly.

"Well, as long as you're my girl, that's how it's gonna be. Which reminds me, I have something for you." He reached into his pocket and produced a small, gift-wrapped box. Maddy's heart thumped in her chest as she accepted it from his hands.

"Um, it's just something I saw that reminded me of the two of us," he explained. "You'll see when you open it."

She tore away the paper and lifted the lid to reveal a gold, diamond-cut pendant in the shape of the Pisces symbol, attached to a braided gold chain. As she stared at the two fish, Maddy was overcome with guilt for ever entertaining the notion of breaking up with him. If he'd only known what had transpired at her house just moments before his arrival, no doubt he'd be completely devastated. How could she have thought so easily about letting him go? It must've been a fleeting moment of insanity.

"Do you like it?" His face was beaming as he noted her reaction.

"It's absolutely gorgeous. I love it!"

"Here, let me put it on you," he said, moving around behind her. Maddy lifted her hair as he closed the lobster clasp around her neck; the necklace glittered exquisitely against her porcelain skin, a striking contrast to the deep purple fabric of her blouse.

"Perfect," he declared as he sat back down in his chair.

"Thank you so much, Kenny. That was sweet."

"You're more than welcome, baby. Oh—by the way, I bought myself one, too, although mine is actually on a nice pen. I'm not much of a jewelry kind of guy, but I wanted us both to have the same one as a reminder of our shared zodiac sign and birthday."

"You're too much," she remarked. "Hard to believe you're for real."

"Well, I'm here, and I'm not going anywhere. I love you." He squeezed her hand as he spoke. But before she could reply, he added, "And don't worry, I know you love me too, even if you can't say it yet. Someday when you're ready, those words will be music to my ears."

Maddy intertwined her fingers with his, silently praying for God to give her the wisdom and guidance to do the right thing by everybody.

Chapter 13

Maddy? You in here?" Monica's voice was soft as she tread lightly through the darkened room and sat down gingerly on her daughter's twin bed, where she now lay quietly in the stillness. Madeline acknowledged her mother's presence, but her tear-stained eyes remained focused on the big picture window a few feet away. Although the crimson and orange late-autumn sunset was on the verge of succumbing to the blackness of night, she hadn't bothered to switch on the lamp on the nightstand. Somehow the darkness just seemed appropriate.

"Uh, your dad and I were going to go out for a bite to eat. Would you like to join us?" A guilt-ridden Monica inquired hopefully.

Witnessing the dramatic changes in Madeline over the last few weeks had been nothing short of torturous; in what seemed like the blink of an eye, her bubbly, energetic daughter had transformed into a withdrawn, troubled young woman who'd lost all interest in everything that had once incited her passion and energy. To Monica's chagrin, she stubbornly refused to go out; consistently rebuffing Carmen's repeated attempts to lure her to their favorite dance clubs, including the new KP Corral that had opened up in King of Prussia.

Having recently developed a love for country line dancing, Madeline had added it to her dance syllabus at the behest of her Pottstown students at the beginning of the fall semester this year. Though technically her weekly back-to-back classes were supposed to focus strictly on ballroom, she'd decided it couldn't hurt to throw in something a little different. Besides, after three years, she knew everyone in the class well enough to have earned a bit of flexibility with the curriculum. When KP Corral opened, Carmen and Maddy frequented the place regularly after work so they could have some free-spirited fun while Maddy picked up some new moves for her classes. That was of course before she succumbed to pressure and wrote Kenny a goodbye letter.

"No, thanks, I'm not hungry," she informed her mother, before rolling over to face Lori's closet. Wasn't it enough that she'd caved into unreasonable demands and broken Kenny's heart? She was also expected to carry on as if he'd never existed? Here it was, the night before Thanksgiving and all she wanted to do was crawl under the covers, crying over what might have been; for all she knew, she could've been spending the long weekend with Kenny's family in Ventnor, or driving and laughing with him in the car as they toured suburban Philadelphia on rambling, country roads. Instead, here she was, lonely, frustrated, sad and angry—mostly at herself.

After all, Dad, Lori, and Greg had all taken her side, offering complete support and encouraging her to follow her heart. Dad had even stressed on more than one occasion that Maddy could always talk to him whenever she felt the need. There was no question that, had she proceeded with the relationship, Mom would've accepted it eventually. But Maddy was self- aware enough to acknowledge the truth—she'd used her mother's disapproval as an escape route when her own intense feelings for Ken had become too frightening to handle.

Looking down at the gold Pisces pendant in her hand, she thought back to that beautiful weekend, and their romantic dinner at The Ship Inn. He had such an incredible way of making her feel as if she was the only woman in a room; being with him had been so easy. No pangs of inadequacy, borne out of some misguided notion of failing to live up to the accomplishments of her ambitious family. Ken saw her as that rare and complete woman—smart, beautiful, principled and sweet.

She was everything he never thought he'd find. And towards the end, he'd nearly accomplished the impossible by edging her ever so closer to seeing what had been clear to him from day one.

"Maddy, you have to eat, hon," Monica encouraged her soothingly.

"Mom, please, just leave me alone."

A saddened Monica smoothed her daughter's hair and offered another sincere apology, along with unprecedented encouragement.

"Please listen to me, honey. I was wrong. Very wrong. And I am deeply sorry." Madeline remained quiet as she absorbed her mother's words. "Look, your father and I have talked about this a lot. All we want is for you to be happy. And we both saw the way Kenny looked at you, the way he treated you with such devotion and respect. He made you happy."

"Well, apparently that wasn't enough without a college degree," she sniped.

"I'm sorry, Madeline," Mrs. Rose repeated. "I was so wrong about everything. I liked Kenny from the very beginning; what a refreshing and welcome change he was from Jake. And you were right—he's ambitious, smart, and hardworking. I have no doubt he'd take good care of you if you two ever got serious. I guess I was just being a little too overprotective of my baby. Even your Aunt Maria is mad at me for that."

"Yeah, like she has a lot of room to talk," she commented sarcastically, thinking of her cousins who'd oftentimes felt smothered by such focused attention.

"You're right," Monica laughed. "Your aunt and I are both guilty of loving our children dearly—perhaps too much. But Re Re is also a good judge of character and she liked Kenny right away too. She thinks he's adorable and so do I. Honey, why don't you call him?"

"Mom, I've broken the guy's heart," she sighed. "I crushed it into a million little pieces after he was nothing but good to me. I stood him up for his cousin's wedding, and for a work party—my God, how could I do something like that? The guy was so proud of me, all he wanted to do was show me off to his family and his co-workers, and look what I did to him. Why would he want anything to do with me now? Besides, it's been several weeks since I mailed that stupid letter with the pictures from his visit. I'm sure he just loved reading the part about slowing things down for a while. Obviously, it's over."

"Honey, I am just so sorry for my role in all of this." Monica's tone was somber. "Will you forgive me?"

Touched by her mother's sincerity, she sat up in bed to face her; her blue eyes glistened with tears, and her expression resonated with real love and   concern. Wrapping her in a hug, she whispered, "Yes. Yes, of course, I forgive you, Mom." They sat there holding each other for a moment.

"Maddy, I pray to God every day for you, for you to find all of the happiness you deserve, not just with the right guy, but also with a career that lets you use all of your talents and skills. I know you don't feel very passionate about your work now, but I know something better is coming soon."

Breaking away, Madeline added, "Thanks, Mom. You know, maybe it's all for the best, the way things happened with Kenny."

She thought back to the indelible moments of intimacy that had been a simultaneous source of pleasure and conflict. Maybe her initial fears were on target; maybe it had been terribly unfair of her to expect Kenny to wait until some mythical wedding night to consummate their relationship. In the long run, he was probably much better off finding a girl who didn't have Maddy's sexual hang-ups. Surely he'd find someone wonderful who could satisfy him on all levels.

In the meantime, now that Damian and Laura had reconciled their differences with the family, she'd have the sweet distraction of infant twins to pull her out of her funk. They were due to arrive in a few days for a six-week stay. Perhaps the pain would dissolve amid the distraction of diaper changes, nursery rhymes and bottle feedings. But for now, Maddy just wanted to be left alone to her misery as her worried mother reluctantly closed the door behind her.

"C'mon, will you just tackle the guy!" Greg yelled at the television set, on the off-chance that an Eagles defensive player might hear his pleas all the way in San Francisco, where the Forty-Niners were currently driving for a touchdown against the Rose family's beloved team. They all let out a collective groan a few plays later when the west coast opponents successfully got the ball into the end zone. Welcoming the distraction from her problems, Maddy sat on the couch between her mother and oldest brother, eagerly participating in this fall Sunday ritual. She'd been so caught up in the excitement she'd barely noticed when her mother got up to answer a ringing telephone.

"Uh yes, one moment please," she heard Monica advise the caller, before stepping back down into the game room to summon her daughter. "Maddy, it's for you. I think it's *him*." She spoke in an excited whisper. Maddy felt her heart catch in her throat but climbed the two stairs into the office with renewed hopefulness. She took a deep breath before picking up the red receiver.

"H-hello?"

"Hey, Madeline, it's Kenny." He paced back and forth in his living room, trying to keep his emotions in check. While his heart was beating furiously, he was determined to come off as calm and collected. After all, he'd had plenty of time to work through the anger; he wanted to prove to her that he was mature enough to accept her decision graciously.

"Hi, Kenny. How are you?"

"I'm fine, how are you? You watchin' the game?"

"Yeah, looks like they're gonna lose this one. I'm just sitting here, commiserating with the family; you know how it is." The sound of his laughter revived a longing from deep within.

"Well, Maddy the reason I called is I just wanted to thank you for the pictures. They turned out great. And I want you to know, there're no hard feelings. I understand and accept your decision. But I hope we can still be friends."

"I-I'd like that, Kenny," she replied, once again resigned to the notion that he needed a real woman, not a scared little girl. Still, she was thrilled that he bore no ill will towards her.

"Well, keep in touch, ok?"

"Will do," she promised. "Please take care, Kenny." And with that, she hung up the phone and rejoined the group.

"How is he?" Monica asked, surprised by the brevity of the conversation.

"He's fine; just called to say hello and to ask if we could still be friends. No hard feelings about the letter, thank God."

"That's it? That's all you had to say to him?"

"Yeah, what else is there to say?"

"Look, Maddy, why don't you call him back and invite him to the Eagles game next week? We have an extra ticket. And they're playing the Vikings, too. Didn't you tell me they were his next favorite team behind the Eagles?" Her tone was laced with enthusiasm for a do-over of the relationship.

"Yes, but—Mom, I don't know. I'm still so embarrassed about the whole thing. And what if he turns me down? He probably has to work anyway."

"So why don't you call him back right now and ask him so he has time to find someone to cover for him?" Mrs. Rose asked forthrightly. This young man was obviously still interested in Madeline. Perhaps the football game would be a perfect vehicle for getting them back together again.

Madeline gave herself a mental pep talk just before dialing the 609 South Jersey number, knowing there was a very real possibility of rejection. And if he did indeed turn her down, she'd only have herself to blame. He sounded so upbeat and positive during their short conversation; maybe he'd already moved on with someone else— someone who wouldn't appreciate him driving to Pennsylvania to share an afternoon at the Vet with an old girlfriend.

Regardless, she was going ahead with it. If he did express an interest in coming, it might be a good chance to truly heal the wounds and salvage a friendship—or maybe something more. She closed her eyes as the phone began to ring, comfortably stretched out on her bed.

"Hello?"

"Kenny? Hey, it's me again." He felt a bolt of electricity through his body at the sound of her voice.

"Maddy, how are you?"

"Good, thanks. Listen, we have an extra ticket to the game on Sunday. And since you're also a Vikings fan, I wondered if you'd like to go with Lori and me? You can drive to my house, and we can all go from there."

"Really?" He was simultaneously puzzled and excited.

"Yeah, really. I remember our conversation under the boardwalk awhile back; I'm sorry it's such short notice for work and everything, but if you can get the time off it would be so much fun. We have awesome seats in section 242, just behind the goalpost. And we know most of the people around us from going to the games all these years. They're really cool. Maybe we can even tailgate if you want."

"That sounds great, but I can't promise anything, though. I'm gonna have to do a lot of begging to get the time off. We've been really short-staffed lately."

"Ok, I'll tell you what: make your calls and get back to me in a few days. I can wait for you."

"Alright then, I will do my best. But I'm just warning you, if they make me work extra shifts, I may not be able to get to your house until really late Saturday night."

"That's ok, Kenny. I'll stay up and wait for you no matter what time it is."

"Ok, then, I hope to have an answer soon."

As they said their goodbyes, each was filled with a mixture of hope, optimism, and nervousness.

"Well that was great, but now I'm going to bed; I'm tired. Good night hon," said Monica, stifling a yawn as she stood up. "What time is Kenny getting here?" They'd just finished watching *The Cutting Edge*, a cute romantic comedy about two Olympic ice skaters. Now well past midnight, Louis and Dr. Rose had already retired, along with Damian, Laura, and the twins; Lori and Greg were out at a party with their fiancées.

"Um, not until around 2 a.m.," she replied. "Poor guy; he's probably just getting off work now. He's gonna be tired after doing a double-shift."

"Well I put fresh sheets on the guest room bed, and there are plenty of clean towels in the hall bathroom. If he's hungry when he gets here, you can heat up some leftovers from dinner. I know how much he likes Italian food."

"Ok Mom sounds good." Then, getting up off the couch, she announced her intention to brush her hair and reapply her make-up.

"And don't forget to put some lipstick on," Monica teased, prompting her daughter to roll her eyes in mock exasperation.

Ken headed west on the Atlantic City Expressway, cruising along at a pretty good pace, thanks to the late hour. Though weary from a long workday, the biting cold air funneling in from a slightly open window, along with real excitement over seeing Madeline again, provided the caffeine benefits of a hot cup of Wawa coffee—something he'd forgotten to purchase prior to hitting the road.

From the speakers, *Just Another Day* blasted out its soulful anthem to love and heartbreak. Ken laughed out loud as he wondered about the wisdom of choosing this particular number as his and Maddy's "song"; perhaps it had been a bad omen from the beginning. Funny, a few short months ago, he'd made this exact same trip under very different circumstances. Back then he was so sure of Madeline's feelings for him, though she never could quite articulate the words "I love you."

But there was always something in her eyes that made him trust in her deep feelings for him; something about the way she'd always listen with empathy to his innermost thoughts and most cherished dreams; and of course, something in the warmth of her kiss that told him she really did love him, in spite of her reluctance to say the words.

He smiled now, thinking back to that weekend in Pennsylvania when he'd decided to teach her how to drive a stick-shift.

They'd driven his black Acura to her high school parking lot, where Maddy made a valiant effort to master the nuances of shifting gears. Ken patiently encouraged her even as the car lurched forward and back, sputtering under the clumsiness of a novice who couldn't effectively maneuver the clutch. "It's ok, sweetheart, you're doing fine," he'd soothe her, lifting her tiny hand to his lips. The driving lesson had been one of the many highlights of a perfect weekend.

The night they'd gone to Lily Langtry's had also been unforgettable—she'd looked breathtakingly beautiful in a hot pink dress, studded with rhinestones in the bodice and set off by a filmy, full skirt that accentuated her sexy legs. When he saw her coming down the stairs, her auburn hair flowing sensually past her shoulders and her smile lighting up her face, he knew beyond a shadow of a doubt that he would one day make her his wife. Then a few weeks later, she'd effectively deflated every hope he'd had of ever seeing her walk down the aisle in a stunning white gown.

Now here he was, blindly throwing caution to the wind. Was there still a chance for him and Madeline, or was this simply the beginning of a new phase in their relationship, one he'd have to learn to accept? As he looked up at the blinking red lights of the Walt Whitman Bridge and the illuminated Philadelphia skyline, he suddenly felt nervous.

In spite of her genuine elation at the prospect of seeing Kenny again, Maddy struggled to keep her eyes open as she lay on the couch in the game room. She'd replayed the movie, hoping it would prevent her from dozing off, but not even a romantic love story involving one of her favorite sports could accomplish that task. The emotional upheaval of the last two months had simply drained her. Finally, she stood up and began pacing around the room, before checking herself out in the large mirror behind the bar.

She was wearing a heavy forest green oversized sweater over matching leggings and a pair of her favorite leather boots. Nearby, her quilted winter jacket was strewn across a chair, in anticipation of greeting him in the driveway. Maddy glanced at her watch just as she noticed a pair of headlights turning into the driveway from the window; the butterflies began to dance in her stomach.

Tentatively, she slipped out into the cold night air and down the first few slate steps of the front entrance. As she peered around the walkway, her heart skipped a beat when she caught a glimpse of Kenny opening the trunk—a vision of total masculinity in his winter parka and work boots. Suddenly consumed with a mixture of fear, remorse and longing, she hesitated at first.

"Ken?"

"Yeah."

Though his tone didn't inspire much confidence, she ran right up and threw her arms around him, as if spurred on by an invisible force. For a while, she was unable to speak. He buried his head in her neck, fighting his own inner battle between love, desire, and anger. She finally broke the silence by whispering over and over, "It's so good to see you."

She wanted so desperately to say "I'm sorry," to beg for his forgiveness and ask for a second chance; but as with the phrase "I love you," she remained involuntarily mute. For some unknown reason, she just couldn't break down the barriers that prevented her from being completely vulnerable with him. Still, he seemed happy to see her as they walked arm-in-arm back to the house.

"Good morning, handsome," Maddy called out softly as she lightly knocked on the guest room door.

"Hey," he replied groggily, rubbing his eyes. In spite of the season, he slept bare-chested; Maddy took note of his broad shoulders and toned muscles as she sat down next to him, still clad in her fluffy pink bathrobe. With her hair back in a ponytail and her face devoid of make-up, he thought she looked like a porcelain doll.

"Did you sleep well?" she asked as he took one of her hands in his.

"Yeah, great thanks. How 'bout you?"

"One of my usual dead sleeps!" They both laughed. "I just didn't know if you heard all of the commotion this morning with the babies," she continued. "Little Tommy was fussing, and Ava really didn't want to get dressed for Mass this morning. I told everyone I'd stay home and watch them, but Damian and Laura insisted on going to church with the rest of the family. It's so cold to take them out, but I guess it's not my call. Anyway, I can't wait for you to see them; they're so adorable."

"Like their aunt," he replied, stroking her cheek.

"I'm so glad you still feel that way," she whispered.

Lori, Maddy, and Kenny spent a glorious Sunday afternoon watching the Eagles defeat the Vikings, 28-17. They'd all bundled up in ski suits, gloves, scarves, and hats, fighting a wind chill close to zero, thanks to December's brutal winds. But not even the intense cold could break their spirits as the three of them screamed, cheered and booed, along with65,000 other rabid fans. And for Maddy, it seemed as if things were blissfully back to normal; Ken appeared at ease and just as crazy about her as ever, occasionally kissing her on the head and staring at her in his inimitable way. The only brief moment of tension had occurred earlier when Ken and Monica first saw each other, but Mrs. Rose had quickly diffused that situation by offering a warm and sincere welcome.

More striking was Ken's instant rapport with the babies, Ava in particular. She'd been crying profusely as they all shared breakfast in the dining room, but when Ken lifted her in his arms and began consoling her in a soft, comforting voice, her entire demeanor changed immediately. And as the infant she smiled up at him with her big blue eyes, Laura remarked, "Ken, I think we're gonna have to keep you around for a while!"

Possessing an avid desire for a family of his own someday, Ken had always felt comfortable with infants and children. And he knew if he was lucky enough to produce offspring with Madeline, he would love them beyond understanding.

Chapter 14

A raging winter storm blanketed the Delaware Valley in several inches of snow and ice, complemented by the plaintive howls of a frigid wind. Maddy paced around the kitchen, holding baby Ava in her arms and staring out at the unfolding weather scene with trepidation. Here it was, New Year's Eve and Kenny was driving up from New Jersey to be her date. Greg and Vanessa, Lori and Vince, and Damian and Laura were all joining them for a dinner celebration at the nearby Media Inn, the one establishment in the area offering live music, food and drink at a reasonable cost.

As Maddy cooed sweetly to a receptive, smiling Ava, Laura entered the room holding Tommy.

"Wow, it's really coming down out there," she noted. "Reminds me so much of Des Moines."

"I guess winters were pretty brutal there," Maddy offered, noting how pretty her sister-in-law looked in a blue taffeta dress with a wide sash and a ruffled neckline. She'd curled her dirty-blonde hair, and it hung in a full- bodied bob that framed her attractive face.

"Wow Laura, you look great."

"Oh, thank you." She laughed nervously in her typical way. Laura was truly a good person at heart, but the boisterousness of the Rose home with its constant activity was sometimes intimidating to her. Still, Maddy was impressed by the way she'd conducted herself so far.

"I just hope Kenny gets here safely. It scares me thinking of him driving over the bridge and then on all of the narrow windy roads around here."

"I'm sure he'll be fine," Laura offered. "He seems like a capable, smart guy. He'll be careful."

Just then, Damian joined them in the kitchen, clad in a beige suit. As soon as Ava saw him, she held out her arms; Maddy happily transferred the tot to the embrace of her waiting father.

"My gosh, I'd better go get in the shower," she said. "Otherwise, you'll all be waiting for me when it's time to go."

A little while later, Madeline and Lori were standing side by side in their shared bathroom, the older sister wrapping her hair in hot rollers and the younger, applying make-up. As an accompaniment to this customary ritual, their favorite radio station played in the background, tonight showcasing the top 100 hits of 1992. Monica Rose walked into the pink and white bedroom to relay a message.

"Maddy, Ken just called to let you know he's on his way. His cousin's wife just had a baby, and he stopped by to see him on his way over. He says it is really bad driving, but he'll be here soon."

"Ok, thanks, Mom. I don't care if he's late; I just want him to get here safely."

"I know," her mother sympathized, "It looks pretty scary out there.

But I'm sure the Expressway and the bridge are clear. They're usually pretty good about salting the main roads. It's Paxon Hollow I worry about the most."

She thought back to countless moments when her children were younger, picking them up from school early and then navigating the car precariously on the windy road that led to their street. The toughest trick of all came just as they were about to approach Martins Run; it was there that a sharp bend came perilously close the adjacent golf course. On more than one occasion, her metallic green station wagon had slid right into this treacherous trap, its wheels caught in a stubborn, icy—and seemingly inescapable, predicament.

"Me too," Maddy sighed. "I wish he had a car phone like Lori. At least he could call us if he needed help."

"Don't worry Mads, I'm sure he'll get here," Lori offered, as she used a pick on her freshly coiffed mane. Maddy got out of the way when she saw her reach for a big can of Aqua Net; she hated the smell of that stuff, not to mention the way it made her hair feel like cardboard. But she was more fortunate than Lori; while her naturally wavy hair was also fine, it was much more abundant and able to hold a style on its own. Left to its own devices, Lori's dark, straight hair hung listlessly to her shoulders.

"Ok girls, I'll be downstairs," Mom announced, before starting for the bedroom door. Then with another thought, "Madeline, what are you wearing tonight, hon?"

"Oh, my black dress from Gantos," she replied, pulling it out of the big walk-in closet where all three of them stored their formal attire. "Remember, I wore this for a dance showcase once? I want to wear it again while I have the opportunity." With its gathered waist, accented by a matching rosette, handkerchief-hem and sequined bodice, it was one of her special occasion favorites.

"Yes I almost forgot about that one," Monica commented. "You look great in that; I'm sure Ken will love it."

"If he gets here in one piece," she said worriedly.

"Honey, I'm sure he'll be fine." With that, her mother kissed her on the cheek and headed back down to the kitchen.

Madeline inspected herself from head to toe in the full-length mirror. Pulling on the bodice of her strapless dress, she adjusted it to create an illusion of cleavage, made possible by a padded, underwire bra. She'd pulled her hair back at the crown with a sequined bow, and let the rest fall in soft waves midway down her back. On her feet, she wore a pair of formal, satin pumps, though she worried about their functionality on slippery outdoor driveways and sidewalks. She was contemplating whether or not wear her winter boots and then change into her dancing shoes once safely indoors when she heard her mother calling from the foyer.

"Maddy, Kenny's here!" Her heart leapt in her chest. With one last glance in the mirror, she ran to the top of the banister, where the image below sent shivers of excitement up and down her spine. She looked down to see Ken standing by the front door, gazing up at her with his ever-present smile from behind a gorgeous bouquet of white roses. Her equally enthralled mother took in the scene with delight.

"Oh my gosh, I am so glad you made it here safely!" she exclaimed, rushing down the stairs to throw her arms around him. He gave her a chaste kiss on the cheek as he carefully held the flowers around her back.

"Ken, these are beautiful," Monica stated. "Why don't I go put them in some water?" With that, she took the blooms and went off in search of the perfect vase.

"You look incredible, Maddy," he whispered, taking in the sight of her, which had been well worth the harrowing ride in the blinding snow.

"You're pretty handsome yourself," she replied, hugging him tightly. He looked like a department store catalog model in his black suit and double-breasted winter coat, which he'd unbuttoned but had not yet taken off. She could still feel the cool moisture of melted ice as she pressed up against him.

"I'm so thankful you're here; I was so worried about you."

"Nah," he laughed. "It's gonna take a lot more than ice and snow to keep me away from you, sweetheart."

Maddy felt a wave of gratitude wash over her as she contemplated what this New Year would bring.

"Go, Kenny!" Greg and Damian egged on as Ken displayed his break-dancing skills for the group. Even the band members seemed pleasantly amused by the sight of a six-foot, two-inch male spinning around on his back on the hardwood floor. Maddy, Lori, Vanessa, and Laura were equally entertained, laughing and clapping along. At Maddy's request, Ken also showed off his Michael Jackson moonwalk, to the amazement of her whole family, particularly her brother Greg, who couldn't seem to get the hang of it, try as he might.

Throughout the evening, Madeline's heart was warmed by the easy rapport Ken shared with her brothers, laughing and joking along heartily with them. She realized if she could ever get beyond her irrational fears and marry Kenny, he'd fit into her family perfectly. And from what she knew of his relatives, especially his mom, she'd enjoy them immensely, too. At one point, while she and Lori were powdering their noses in the Ladies room, Lori remarked, "Maddy, that guy is absolutely gaga over you! He keeps telling all of us how beautiful you are, how he's gonna marry you, the whole bit. Ooh, I'm so excited for you, baby girl!"

"I'm just relieved we got beyond that little misunderstanding," Maddy sighed. "God, I was so stupid to write him that letter. But I don't know; this reunion almost feels too good to be true. It's like I'm waiting for the other shoe to drop."

"Don't do that to yourself," Lori admonished. "He looks perfectly content to me right now.Frankly as much as I love you, I'm getting tired of hearing about how wonderful you are!" Her tone was playful.

"Lori? Do you ever get scared about sex?" Maddy asked, suddenly serious. "You're getting married soon. Do you ever think about it?"

"Of course," her sister replied. "But I figure, it's a natural part of life. Look at it this way—if it was so horrible, the human race would've ended a long time ago."

"Yeah, I guess you're right. Kenny's so good about waiting, but sometimes I wonder how long that can go on."

"Well, like Greg said, when it's real love, the guy's willing to wait. Look at all of us."

"True," she agreed.

"C'mon," Lori urged, placing an arm around her, "Let's get back out there and dance. Our dates are waiting."

It felt like heaven as Ken held her close in his arms and swayed with her to the Prince ballad, *Diamonds and Pearls*. As always, he sang softly in her ear, creating a flood of warm sensations throughout her body and soul.

A crackling fireplace provided a romantic ambiance as Ken and

Maddy snuggled up under a blanket on a plush sofa in the family room. It was now past 1 a.m., the rest of the house was fast asleep, and they were enjoying their first private interlude since his arrival several hours ago. They'd all greeted 1993 with noisemakers, confetti, and silly party hats, toasting each other with champagne and looking forward to new possibilities ahead. Now dressed in winter pajamas, Ken and Madeline reveled in each other's company, reacquainting themselves with the passionate kisses and tender embraces that had characterized their relationship since that summer night at the Taj Mahal.

"You are so incredibly beautiful, Madeline. I love you so much," he whispered. While his words were music to her ears, she was unable to do anything more than listen as she rested her head against his chest.

"You know," he vowed, "I am going back to school to get my degree and then I'm coming back for you. I can still picture you walking down the aisle, sweetheart. And I swear I am gonna marry you someday."

While Maddy wondered what he meant by "coming back for her," since the local area was rife with excellent universities, all she could do was assure him that—degree or no degree—he was certainly more than good enough.

"Kenny, if you want to go back to school, I totally support you. But do it for yourself; not for me. You don't have to have a degree to be my boyfriend. Look, my mother admitted she was wrong; she told me how sorry she was and how much she truly likes you.

"I'm sorry I caved into that kind of pressure because none of that education stuff ever mattered to me. You and I talk about so many things, and we share the same values. That's what counts. But I guess I was feeling powerless, you know, living at home with my parents," she sighed. "I didn't like fighting with my mom and thought I was doing the right thing by everyone. I was wrong. But all of that is behind us now."

"Maddy, how could you think you were doing right by me? I can understand the parental thing, but how could you think dumping me like that was helping me? I was crazy about you; I still am," he said forthrightly.

Overcome with shame and remorse, she couldn't bring herself to look at him, though she held him closer in her arms. And as he felt that familiar bolt of energy and all-consuming passion, he remained frustrated and confused. Why couldn't she admit she loved him, too? What was stopping her?

Though he wanted to explore the issue, he decided it best to save it for another day. Right now he just wanted to taste the sweetness of her mouth as they held each other in the stillness.

"Looks like the roads are clear!" Maddy announced, closing the large white front door to shut out the cold. She was dressed in a pair of rust corduroy pants and an off-white cowl-neck sweater. They'd all just shared a nice breakfast in the dining room, where Dr. Rose had made a beautiful mimosa toast to the New Year. Lori then left to hang out with Vince and his family; Vanessa and Greg took Louis to a movie and Damian and Laura were content to spend the day indoors with the babies.

Ken was busy clearing the table as Maddy walked back into the kitchen, where her mother was loading dirty plates into the dishwasher. Wordlessly, she joined in the effort.

"That Ken is such a good kid," her mother remarked. "He helps out around here more than your father or brothers." Maddy laughed as she saw him balancing a pile of soiled platters as he carefully strode up to the counter.

"Thank you, Kenny," Mrs. Rose said. "But you've done enough now. You and Madeline should go out and have some fun."

"Oh, it'll only take another few minutes, Mrs. Rose. Why should we leave you with a big mess to clean up?"

"You're the best," Maddy piped up, giving him a quick kiss on the lips. "Hey, Kenny, you feel like taking a ride to the King of Prussia Mall? We can take the back roads, and I can show you where my office is. It's a really nice ride."

"Sure, that'd be great." And while he flashed her his trademark smile, Maddy observed the wistfulness in his voice and an element of sadness in his expression. She made a silent note to herself to get to the bottom of it once they were safely in the car.

They cruised by snow-capped rolling hills and endless stretches of farmland as she directed him over suburban Philadelphia's picturesque byways, which had fortunately been cleared of any lingering ice. He looked as handsome as ever in his burgundy turtleneck and jeans, wearing his parka from the Eagles game. But his sparkling blue eyes were devoid of their usual luster as he gazed out at the road in front of them.

"Kenny? What's wrong?"

"Oh, uh I guess I was just thinking about my dad. It's New Year's Day, and I really should call him, but I'm dreading it."

"Oh," she replied, remembering the tension between the two of them. "Does he even know you're here with me?"

"No, I didn't tell them anything; just that I was spending the New Year with some friends. Actually, I told my mom that; I haven't even spoken to my father since Christmas Day."

"Hey, this is just my two-cents' worth, but I think you should call him and wish him a Happy New Year. If nothing else, it'll make you feel better."

He turned to look at her briefly, his expression conveying a mixture of disgust, trepidation, and hopefulness.

"Look," she went on, "Calling him doesn't make him right about anything. It just clears your conscience by doing the right thing. I mean, he's still your father, and you still love him, even though he's wrong. And you have a chance to show him that you are the bigger person, here."

"You think so?"

"Yes, I do," she replied honestly in a soft, encouraging voice. "And if you want, I'll be right there next to you—or close by in the next room."

"You really are a sweetheart; you know that?"

"You are so good to me; this is the least I can do for you."

She stood right by as Ken picked up the office phone and dialed his parents' number, incredibly proud of him for taking this simple but profound step—hopefully, the first small one on the road to reconciliation. Much of course, depended upon Carl Lockhart; but regardless of the outcome, Kenny could put his mind at ease knowing he made a valiant attempt.

"Hello, Dad? It's Ken," he said brightly. "I just wanted to call and wish you and Mom a happy New Year." Though not privy to the other side of the conversation, judging from the smile on Ken's face, his call must've been warmly received. And as Ken became further engrossed in conversation, Maddy slipped away to give him some privacy. A few minutes later, he joined her on the couch.

"So how'd it go?" she asked as he placed an arm securely around her.

"Pretty well," he grinned. "We didn't solve all our problems, but at least it was cordial. Mom was out so I didn't get to talk to her."

"I'm proud of you," she remarked, settling into the crook of his arm. "I know that wasn't easy."

"You're a good influence on me," he noted, kissing her temple. "You're good for me in so many ways."

"Kenny, let's go see Aladdin tonight," Madeline bubbled over, thinking of Robin Williams' hilarious performance as the blue genie; she never tired of the Disney brand, whether in the form of movies, theme parks or music. They'd just finished another wonderful family dinner after which Ken contemplated calling the plant and begging them for extra time off. His carefree hours with Maddy and her family were passing much too quickly, and he wanted at least one more day with them.

"Ok, but haven't you already seen that?"

"Well yes, but not with you." He cracked up; she was like a little kid at times.

"Alright then," he acquiesced.

"Do you mind if I ask Laura and Damian? They haven't really gone anywhere today, and I know they'd both like it."

"Of course," he replied.

Laura enthusiastically accepted their sincere invitation, despite her misgivings about "intruding" on their date. Maddy and Ken both assured her the sentiment was genuine; besides, they'd find plenty of alone time later.

"Well ok, but I don't think your brother will come with us," she remarked. "He's sound asleep on the easy chair with Tommy on his chest. But I sure would like to get out."

And so the trio made the twenty-minute trek to the AMC Multiplex in Painter's Crossing, where they spent a joyful two hours in a time and place where there were only complete resolutions to life's most difficult problems and happy endings for all of the good people involved.

"Well?" she asked hopefully.

"Quentin says he'll cover for me," Ken beamed. "He could use the extra hours after the Christmas Holiday." With that, he picked her up off the ground, spinning her around in jubilation.

"This means you can watch the playoff game with us!" Her enthusiasm was running over at the thought of all them cheering on the Eagles against the New Orleans Saints. Since they were playing away, Mom had invited some relatives and friends to catch the action at their house.

In the company of Madeline's warm, wonderful family the two of them watched their favorite football team advance to the divisional playoff game against their archrival Dallas Cowboys, by defeating the Saints 36-20 in the Louisiana Superdome. For Maddy, the euphoria of that moment was only superseded by the indescribable joy of being reconciled with Ken, and looking ahead to a bright and beautiful future.

Throughout the month of January, Ken and Madeline spent as much time as possible together, weather permitting. And though Old Man Winter hadn't been feeling particularly generous, constantly slamming the area with brutal snowstorms, bitter winds, and sub-zero temperatures, they managed to see quite a bit of each other on the weekends. Ken had even made another trip to Pennsylvania to take Maddy to a dinner dance with her parents, along with Aunt Maria and Uncle Earl. And though they'd had a fabulous time, she started to notice something troubling in his demeanor—a more pronounced restlessness, and a palpable sense of frustration.

From a professional standpoint, she could certainly relate; after all, in spite of having an understanding boss, Maddy had long since tired of outside sales. It was especially grueling in inclement weather such as they were experiencing now. From deep within, she knew that God's purpose for her life went much deeper than cold-calling for new accounts and obtaining coveted employment contracts.

And though there was a certain amount of satisfaction in connecting the right employer with the right job seeker, it was no longer enough to placate her. Then there was the added matter of a small profit-margin, which definitively limited her earning potential. But worst of all, in a family of professionals, Maddy felt completely inferior and inadequate; even her handicapped brother had far exceeded the direst expectations. What was so wrong with her that she couldn't even fulfill her own potential?

Despite being raised in a loving, supportive home, for as long as she could remember, she'd been plagued by a haunting feeling of not being good enough, of always coming up short of the mark, no matter how hard she tried. As a Catholic school girl, she'd studied hard and earned excellent grades; yet at the end of every school year, the teachers invariably awarded the coveted "plaque" to her academic rival, Megan Kelly. It didn't matter if the two had identical grade-point averages— somehow the nuns consistently favored Megan over Madeline.

Combined with her perennial struggle with just enough extra poundage to be the butt of cruel jokes and the perception some classmates had of her being a "spoiled rich girl," it had amounted to a sometimes lonely, hurtful and frustrating childhood and adolescence. And while Maddy did have her fair share of friends, none of them had merited the status of inclusion in the "in" crowd that hung out after elementary school on the "hill" near the convent or—in later years, drove around to the local malls and other "cool" hangouts.

Through it all, her family had been a source of comfort and unconditional love. So while her educational years had been tumultuous, the drama had been balanced by strong family ties, supported by fun vacations at the Shore and Pocono Mountains, thrilling hours spent at the Phillies and Eagles games, and endless, joyful celebrations of milestones including Holy Communions, graduations, and other assorted, uplifting events.

Whenever her academic experience got too heavy, Maddy simply reminded herself of the blissful haven awaiting her at home. Once there she'd either bury her nose in a book, dance with Louis to the latest hits or play football with Greg and Damian.

The last activity had led to her first "sports injury" at age seven, when Greg accidentally landed on her arm after both of them had fallen to the ground in an attempt to catch Damian's pass. At first, they'd both laughed at loud in the crisp, fall air—that is, until she heard a distinctive "crack," followed by a searing, shooting pain.

It felt like her arm was on fire as a spooked Greg scooped her up in his arms and carried her to the front landing. As she wailed uncontrollably, "My arm! My arm!" a panicked Greg kissed her forehead and comforted her, while the other kids ran into the house to get the adults. Yes, the pain had been formidable, but combined with the gruesome sight of her mangled arm protruding from her sweater sleeve, it heightened her fear and hysteria. She was certain they'd have to amputate.

At the same time, she sympathized with Greg, who as the oldest sibling was sure to take heat from Mom and Dad for failing to "know better." After all, moments before the accident, Mom had come outside to admonish them to stop running around in the dark and get inside, "before someone got hurt." As Maddy recalled, her frantic mother had not been pleased by this outcome, prompting the child to refrain from crying as she snuggled up in the back of the car with Aunt Maria on the way to the hospital. While Dr. Rose drove, Monica continuously looked back at her "baby" with a look of utter anguish from the front passenger seat.

Fortunately, age had been on Maddy's side, and her arm healed beautifully. But that evening when she returned home, she made a point of going into Greg's room to tell him it was an accident and that she didn't blame him for anything, no matter what Mom and Dad might think. He'd been sitting at the end of the bed with his head hanging in shame until he saw his little sister's smiling face.

"Don't worry, Greg," she'd told him. "All I have to do is wear this cast for six weeks and then my arm will be all better."

Relieved, he presented her with the ultimate token of regret, at least for 1974—Elton John's *Goodbye Yellow Brick Road* album. Even at that immature age, Maddy had been profoundly touched by the gesture.

"Kenny? Kathy?" she called out as she quietly closed the screen- door behind her. After knocking a few times with no answer, she finally just turned the knob in the hope that he'd left it unlocked; it was freezing outside, and all she wanted was the shelter of a warm living room. She'd just arrived in Somers Point, where the bone-chilling winds were whipping around with much greater fury than two hours ago in Media.

Maddy stepped into the familiar surroundings, seating herself on the couch and rubbed her arms vigorously. A minute later, Ken was standing in front of her.

"Hi, sweetheart, sorry about that!" He pulled her into a bear hug.

"Hey, it's ok; it's just so cold outside I can't stand it."

"I know; me either. Except that, I like warming you up." He laughed before drawing her into a temperature-raising kiss.

"Hmm, now that was worth every second of being out in the cold," she praised him.

"Hey, you feel like taking a drive? These last few rounds of storms have really eroded the beaches around here; you have to see it to believe it. It's kind of depressing, actually. But we can also stop off and say "hi" to my cousin if you want."

"Sure, you know how much I love riding around in the car with you. And it would be nice to meet some of your family. God knows, you've spent enough time with mine."

They passed another nice afternoon together, in spite of noticeable boardwalk damage and the general malaise of an overcast winter day at the Jersey Shore. She enjoyed hanging out at the home of Ken's cousin and his wife, where she met their newborn son and engaged in pleasant conversation. But there was something different about him this time, something she couldn't quite put her finger on. Yes, she was aware of his nagging restlessness and overall discontentment—two emotions she herself was dealing with – yet she knew without a doubt that something else was going on. And it didn't feel particularly good.

"Thank you," Ken said to the cashier at SuperFresh, where he'd just purchased ingredients to make fajitas. They planned to head back to his place so he could pack an overnight bag and then spend the night with Maddy at the Ocean City house, where he would also cook their dinner.

Although it was fun preparing the sizzling steak, chicken, and accompanying veggies, Maddy's heart was heavy. Far from being the fun- loving, attentive boyfriend, Ken now appeared to be simply going through the motions in order to appease her. Still, she said nothing as they sat at the glass-top table, enjoying his perfectly seasoned creations, while outside, the wind gusted furiously.

Chapter 15

Maddy finished brushing her teeth and applied a dab of moisturizer to her face before exiting the bathroom. It was late at night, and she and Kenny had just finished watching a movie downstairs. Though the heater was working just fine, there was a marked chill in the air, thanks to the relentless winter winds that forcefully enveloped the little Cape Cod; it was hard to believe that less than five months ago, she'd paraded around the home in her shorts. Now here she was, bundled up in heavy winter pajamas, struggling to keep warm.

She strode into her bedroom and saw Ken comfortably ensconced under the covers of Lori's twin bed. "Hey," he whispered.

"Hey, you ready to go to sleep?"

"Mm-hm."

With that, she flipped off the light switch and crawled under the blankets of her own bed, separated from Kenny by a nightstand as well as total blackness. She'd never realized just how dreary Ocean City could be in the wintertime, with seasonal businesses boarded up, quiet streets devoid of pedestrians and cars, and an oppressive darkness that seemed to invade every corner once the sun went down.

It all seemed sadly appropriate, given the pall that had hung over the entire evening, but a moment later, Ken made her giggle uncontrollably by leaping out of the blackness and into the bed with her.

"Kenny! What are you doing?"

"Do you actually think I'm going to sleep apart from you?" he teased, pulling her into a close embrace that soothed her soul and heated her body.

"Does this mean you're not mad at me?" she asked, listening to his heart beating fast in her ear.

"Why would I be mad at you?" He stroked her hair as he spoke in a calm, gentle voice.

"I don't know, but something's wrong. You're not yourself today at all."

"You're right," he sighed. "But it's not because of you."

"Then what's the matter?"

"I'm just—it's just, Maddy I don't know what I'm doing here. I mean, professionally. Do you really think I want to work at Atlantic Electric the rest of my life? God, I am so sick of that place. I'm smart, I want to go back to school; I want to do something meaningful and financially rewarding, and it's like I can't seem to figure out exactly what that is. I just know I don't want to be stuck at the Jersey Shore the rest of my life."

"I get it. And you are incredibly smart; I noticed that about you right away. I have no doubt you can do and be anything you want. My God, look at everything you've accomplished already. Do you know how amazed I am by you? You didn't have the luxury of being born into a family that could pay for you to go to college, so you enlisted and served your country for four years. How many people can say that? I mean, as much as I respect and appreciate our military, I know I could never do what you did. It takes discipline and character to pull that off. And you did it."

"Wow," he laughed. "You really know how to make a guy feel better."

"I *mean* it," she emphasized, running her hand up and down his sweater-clad chest.

"I know you do," he replied softly, kissing her hair. "You have no idea what it does to me to hear you say those words."

"Kenny, you'll figure it out. Just don't give up; keep believing that there's so much more ahead of you—all kinds of great things. Because there's definitely a plan for you. You just have to let things unfold while you put one foot in front of the other. And be patient with yourself; this isn't a contest."

"How'd you get to be so smart?"

"It's a genetic condition," she joked.

With that, he pulled her close to him and placed his lips on hers, filled with a burning desire he knew would not be satisfied that evening. She closed her eyes, savoring the feel of his strong body and the subtle rhythm of his tongue as it playfully sought out hers. When they finally came up for air, she was situated beneath him, staring into sparkling aquamarine eyes that pierced the darkness and seemed to see through to her innermost being.

"I wonder what it would be like to be with you," he whispered, moving a stray hair away from her face. "Guess I'll just have to marry you to find out."

Once again, she was rendered speechless, though his words filled her with pure ecstasy as he moved in for another kiss.

For the next several hours they held each other close, alternating between meaningful conversation and passionate make-out sessions. And though their fully clothed bodies stopped well short of crossing any lines, they experienced an intimacy that rivaled the sweetest pleasures of the flesh. Kenny expressed his hope for a hot summer that would keep him busy at work so he could put some more money away for his education; Maddy confided her deeply held feelings of inadequacy, given her highly ambitious family ties. And each supported and understood the other's feelings perfectly—without any need for qualification. It was something they'd come to treasure more than they could ever know on that blustery January night.

"Hey, guess what?" she could hardly contain her enthusiasm as she held the receiver to her ear. It was early February, the twins had gone home with their parents, and the house was back to its normal routine.

"What, sweetheart?" Ken asked. He was spread out on his

waterbed, having just gotten home from work himself. Outside, a hard rain pelted the windows and the skylight above him.

"I got promoted to Assistant Branch Manager at the employment agency!" While it wasn't her life's ambition to remain in this difficult and tedious industry, Maddy still rejoiced in her accomplishment. While she was figuring out what to do with her life, she might as well achieve something else that was good. Unfortunately, Kenny unwittingly pulled an upsetting imitation of Jake by throwing cold water all over her news.

"Oh, that's just great," he said sarcastically.

"What? Why are you angry? I thought you'd be proud of me!" She sat down on her bed, deflated by his reaction.

"Well, it's just that—I thought you hated your job. And now this just ties you deeper to it, that's all. I mean, you don't even want to stay there."

"Well, that's true, but I have worked hard, and it's nice to be rewarded for it. Besides, it's a little more money and definitely less cold calling.

We're going to a hire a new Account Executive to focus on exclusively on sales."

"Oh." He lay there in the stillness, completely torn up inside.

Though he truly loved her with every fiber of his being, he just couldn't see a way clear for them anymore. At least, not right now. Until he had an actual degree and a powerful, high-paying job, he'd always feel inferior to her family, no matter how nice and welcoming they were. And while he ached to see her walking down the aisle as his bride and enjoy all of the bliss of their long-awaited conjugal union, he knew he'd never be satisfied as long as he lacked a formal education. Their marriage would be doomed from the start.

Unknown to her, he'd been contemplating a life-altering change for some time now—one that entailed major upheaval, both literally and figuratively. Ever since she mailed him that letter last fall, he'd been searching for signs to help him make the right decision; now it seemed God had finally answered, although it pained him to hurt her like this.

"Well, I guess I'm gonna hang up then. I'm really sorry you can't be happy for me," she remarked sadly. But before she could end the call, Ken stopped her.

"Wait! Maddy, I am so sorry. Of course I am proud of you."

"Then, what's the matter?"

"Nothing, honey. I just had a bad day at work, and I was taking it out on you. I'm sorry. Will you forgive me?"

"Yes."

"Hey, how 'bout if I take you out to dinner to celebrate? I can come up to PA this weekend."

"Really?" Though she was still a bit perplexed, she welcomed the chance to see him again; bad storms had prevented them from getting together the previous weekend, and she truly missed his company.

"Yeah, I can drive up Friday night after my shift. We can have dinner, maybe go out dancing; the whole bit." He sounded much more like the Kenny she fell in love with, though her feelings remained stubbornly unexpressed, locked away in some spiritual vault, just waiting for the right moment to break free.

"Ok then, I'll see you Friday night." "Maddy?"

"Yes."

"Congratulations, sweetheart. I really am proud of you."

"Thank you for a wonderful evening, Kenny," she whispered, snuggling in close to him in the guest room bed. It was a slightly dangerous game; however the sounds of her father snoring down the hall and the knowledge that everyone else was either asleep or out for the evening confirmed that they were safe—at least for a little while. Besides, she hadn't actually climbed under the sheet with him but was covered only by the blanket and the comforter. She rested her head on his bare chest as he stroked her hair.

"You're welcome," he whispered in the darkness, before bringing her in close for another intoxicating kiss. And as their passion mounted, he ran his hands through her hair and up and down her back, trying to preserve every moment for future reference. He wanted to remember everything about her—the softness of her skin and hair, the subtlety of her artful tongue, the curve of her body and of course, the irresistible appeal of her tiny, but agile hands.

They had been the first of many beautiful features that had jumped out at him that night at the Key Largo Club. There was so much he was going to miss about her, but he tried not to think about that as he held her tight. And then, Madeline shocked the hell out of him.

"Kenny?"

"Yes?"

"I love you."

God, why now? What was she trying to do to him? All of these months he'd desperately longed to hear these words from her; words he'd so eloquently expressed regularly, almost from the day they met, with no satisfaction. And now she chooses to tell him when his whole life is in turmoil?

"Well, just don't get crazy on me, Madeline." His tone was a firm warning; another unexpected rush of icy cold water.

"What?" she snapped, breaking away quickly to sit up. "What do you mean by that?"

"Oh, and guess what? I'm totally naked under this sheet." His outward coolness masked his inner heartbreak. But he knew the only way he could move on was to somehow make her hate him.

Unsure of how to react to this extreme turnabout, Maddy quietly rose to her feet.

"I don't know exactly what kind of game you're playing here, Ken, but I'm going to bed. Goodnight!"

She closed the door behind her, leaving him to wonder what to do next as he lay there in the darkness.

"Good morning, Dad," Maddy greeted her father enthusiastically as she entered the kitchen. He was sitting at his usual place at the head, drinking a cup of coffee.

"Morning, beautiful. Where's Kenny?"

"I think he's still getting dressed," she replied nonchalantly as she added some cream to her mug and then sat down to join him. Mom and Louis had gone to early Mass; Dr. Rose was preparing to make rounds. And while Maddy made pleasant small talk with her father, she kept thinking back to her puzzling conversation with Kenny the night before. Her heart felt as if someone had wrung every ounce of strength out of it. Here she'd finally mustered the courage to tell him how she felt, and he responded by promptly shooting her down. She simply didn't get it.

Ken pulled on a sweater before placing the rest of his things in his duffle bag. Guilt and remorse engulfed him like a tidal wave; still, he pressed on. He could hear her chatting downstairs with her father and quickly decided the best course of action would be to join them. At this point, it was probably best to avoid being alone with her. Besides, he'd pretty much engraved her sweet face in his mind forever; she'd never truly be far away.

But when Dr. Rose invited him to go skiing with him and Maddy a few minutes later, he cheerfully accepted the invitation. Preferring not to involve her father in their drama, a confused Madeline agreed to the plan for the following weekend, outwardly smiling while inwardly, her emotions spun out of control. And when Ken hugged her goodbye in the driveway, she really believed he was sincere when he told her how much he was looking forward to it. They'd decided to drive up on a Friday, necessitating a day off from work. However, Maddy was certain Betty would agree to it; as bosses went, she was fairly easygoing and reasonable.

So with one last kiss, Ken drove off in his black Acura, while Maddy stood shivering in the driveway, contemplating the uncertain road ahead.

"Where's Ken?" Dr. Rose asked, as he, Maddy and Monica sat around the kitchen table talking and laughing over their morning blend. Having injured his hip in a tennis match a few days prior, Dr. Rose had wisely decided to stay home, rather than risk further injury on the ski slopes. Though disappointed, at least he knew his daughter would have the pleasure of her boyfriend's company. That is if he ever showed up; he was supposed to arrive at 8 a.m., and it was now close to ten.

"Wow, it's not like him to be late," Monica commented. "I mean, the only time was New Year's Eve, but that was understandable given the weather conditions. And at least he called to say he was running behind. But it's beautiful out today. That's really strange that he hasn't even picked up the phone. I wonder if he's sick."

Maddy silently debated whether or not this was the official end of their relationship. Maybe it had been too good to be true after all.

Her mother continued, "God, I don't get it. I mean, when your aunt and I were at the Shore house this week for a few days, he called to check in on us, which I thought was really sweet. And he talked to me for a long time about how much money he makes, and how his townhouse is just a starter home. He made a point of telling me that he can provide for a wife and family. Why would he tell me that, unless he was serious about you, honey? Maybe you should call him, Maddy. Something's not right."

A minute later, as she stepped into the privacy of her bedroom, those words reverberated in her head. Something was definitely not right. And it would be five long months before she would even speak to Ken again, let alone understand what had just happened.

Chapter 16

The cleansing warm water rained down on her, rinsing away all traces of sand as she reached for the shampoo. It was mid-August, and Maddy had just returned from a rare solo afternoon at the beach. With Carmen relocated to Manhattan, Mom and Louis in Nashville, Dad on-call this weekend, and Greg and Lori preoccupied with wedding planning, she'd been left to soak up the sun on her own. She'd driven down after work on Friday evening, eager to enjoy the hot weather, regardless of the lack of company. And as she stood in the privacy of the enclosed, wooden outside shower, she basked in the joy of this simple—and strictly summertime—pleasure.

Ever since Ken had abruptly exited her life, she'd retreated a little more into herself each day, though outwardly she put on a brave front. She'd even gone on a few dates over the past several months, though her heart hadn't been truly engaged—and with good reason. At least two of the men had turned out to be complete jerks. And the contrast between their treatments of her versus Ken's could not possibly have been more dramatic. Still, she had given each of them a fair chance, determined to go on with her life. It wasn't as if she hadn't made a Herculean effort to get to the bottom of the Kenny story.

But despite countless phone calls to his home and even a few short conversations with his roommate, she never did find the resolution she sought. And while she hated that trite and ubiquitous word, "closure," she realized it was something she desperately needed; if she could at least understand what exactly had gone wrong, perhaps she could avoid the same mistakes in the future.

True, she'd hurt Kenny badly by writing him that letter last fall; but they'd been able to patch things up to the point of spending a good portion of December and January together. On New Year's Eve, he couldn't stop telling her siblings and future in-laws how much he adored her and couldn't wait to make her his wife. And while that particular holiday had never been one of her favorites, this year's celebration had been the happiest she could ever remember. Ken mingled so easily with her family, joking around, sharing stories, enjoying Sunday dinners and watching Eagles games; it all seemed so normal, a preview of life's coming attractions.

Yes, he'd been miserable in his career, but so had she. Why did it have to spell the end of their relationship? After demonstrating such consistent respect, he could've mustered the courtesy to break up with her to her face, instead of standing her up for their ski date without so much as a phone call. That was the kind of behavior she'd expect from Jake, not Kenny. Had this been payback for hurting him? He didn't strike her as the vengeful type, but what else was she to assume? None of it made any sense.

She turned off the spigot and wrapped herself up in a fluffy, oversized towel. As she undid the latch of the shower door, she peered around to check that there were no neighbors walking down the alley. Once assured the coast was clear, she ran up the porch steps and into the family room from the sliding glass doors. In the sanctuary of her bedroom, she quickly dried off and changed into a casual shorts-set before blow drying her long hair in the hall bathroom. The noisy hair appliance nearly drowned out the sound of a ringing phone a minute later; Maddy switched it off and ran into her parents' room to answer.

"Hello?" She responded brightly, thinking it was probably Mom checking in from Tennessee.

"Madeline?" Her heart lurched at the sound of the familiar, masculine voice.

"Yes?" Her tone exuded annoyance and anger.

"It's Kenny." From his Aventura apartment, he gazed out at the Intracoastal Waterway, in an attempt to calm his nerves. On his bedroom mirror, photos of him and Madeline evoked a happier time and place.

"Yes, I know. Nice of you to finally call." She stared out at the alley from the big picture window, where a large orange sun was painting colorful streaks on the horizon.

"Um...I'm sorry," he stammered. His words preceded a seemingly endless silence until Maddy spoke up again.

"For what? For standing me up for our ski date without calling? For disappearing off the face of the earth? What exactly are you sorry about, Ken?"

"For everything," he replied softly. While he acknowledged her right to be justifiably angry, it pained him to the core to hear the rancor in her voice. He'd witnessed much genuine emotion in Madeline, but this kind of hostility posed an unprecedented challenge, though he knew he bore the brunt of responsibility for it.

"Do you have any idea how you made me feel? I trusted you; I believed in you. And you just kicked me aside with no explanation, no proper goodbye, nothing."

"Maddy, I am truly sorry," he repeated. "That was such a bad time in my life; my whole world just fell apart. And I just couldn't take being in South Jersey anymore. I felt like I was gonna go crazy if I didn't get out of there!"

"Well, where are you now?"

"I moved to Florida."

"Florida?"

"Yeah, uh, I got tired of the winters and just needed a change. Besides, there's so much more happenin' down here business-wise. I got my real estate license, and I plan to get my mortgage broker license, too. Maddy, it's so beautiful here; you should see it! The beaches are clean, and the ocean is blue and clear; you can actually see your feet! And all of the Spanish-style homes, tropical flowers and things to do—it's so different from up north."

"That's great Ken, I'm glad you're happy," she replied somewhat sarcastically. Apparently, he wasn't suffering any anguish over her.

"Well, not totally," he admitted.

"Really? What could possibly be missing in Paradise?"

"You," he said softly.

"Me?"

"Maddy, I miss you so much."

"With all of the beach babes in South Florida, you expect me to believe that?"

"C'mon, Maddy, you know there's no one else like you."

"So, that's why you left me? Makes perfect sense."

"Maddy, I'm sorry. I thought you understood how frustrated I was up there."

"Yeah, Ken I get that because I felt the same way, remember? I still do. But I'm not the one who disappeared without a phone call; you are."

"I know. You are absolutely right, and I'm sorry. But Maddy, you should consider moving down. Ballroom dancing is so popular here, you could teach lots of classes until you figured out what you wanted to do. And there are all kinds of clubs that have live music, you could even sing on stage. I remember how beautiful your voice is; you could make a lot of money. Maybe even work for the Palm Beach Princess. I know you could be happy here."

"Right—away from everyone in my family, living in a strange place all alone. Sounds like just what I need!"

"You wouldn't be alone; you'd have me."

"You?"

"Madeline, I've never forgotten about you, or your family," he replied sincerely. "You inspired me—the entire Rose family inspired me to finish my education, start a good career, you know, make something of myself. And that's what I'm doing. But I miss you, sweetheart. I miss you so much."

"C'mon, Kenny. I'm glad we've all inspired you, I truly am. But you expect me to actually believe you miss me?"

"Madeline, it's the truth." Then with another thought, he suddenly asked, "Who's taking you to your brother's wedding?"

Caught off-guard, she couldn't quite conjure up a snappy comeback, and thus resorted to complete honesty.

"I don't know; I don't have a date yet."

"Well, can I take you?" His tone was hopeful.

"You want to take me? You're gonna fly up to Philly to take me to my brother's wedding?" The surreal overtone of this telephone session was beginning to wear on her. She sat back down on the bed, unsure of whether to laugh or cry.

"Well, yeah. If I can get the time off of work, absolutely."

"Ken, don't make promises you don't intend to keep. I'm glad you're ok, I'm glad you called, but please; don't say things you don't mean. Don't play with my feelings like that. It's not fair."

"Madeline, I love you. And I am sincere; I do want to be your date for the wedding. Please, you have to believe me." He thought back to the first time he ever kissed her, high atop the Taj Mahal Casino. What he would do to hold her in his arms again.

She sat there silently, lost in confusion and conflict. A significant part of her wanted so desperately to believe, yet none of it felt right. If he truly loved her, how could he just up and leave like that? Why did he have to turn her whole world upside down in order to change his?

"Look," he said, interrupting her internal debate, "I will try to get the time off from work and let you know within the next two weeks if I can make it, ok?"

"Ok," she agreed softly. Before hanging up, she jotted down his phone number and address, at his insistence. Back in her bedroom a moment later, she picked something up off the bureau. And as she stood there holding the glittering Pisces pendant in her hand, she felt more tortured than ever, while endless footage of recent events began to play vividly in her mind.

"Madeline, pick up line one darlin'; there's a gentleman named Jim Russo waiting for you."

Betty's lilting voice drifted musically down the hallway as Maddy reviewed the monthly report for the Kingston Personnel Agency's Wayne branch. Despite the fact that her endless craving for something more out of her career had only intensified since her promotion, she was at least grateful that business had picked up dramatically. Unfortunately, their efforts to find a good Account

Executive had thus far been fruitless, necessitating continued time in the field.

During one of her unplanned cold calls, she knocked on the door of an insurance company located in a new office condo community in Exton. Dressed in a professional summer suit of red linen with gold buttons and navy accents, she'd looked particularly stylish when she spoke with a friendly receptionist who nevertheless informed her that the boss was out. However, she willingly gave Maddy his business card. A few days later, Maddy returned, bearing Kingston's promotional gift for decision- makers—a notepaper holder for the desk, decorated with his initials.

On that hot late-June day, she'd also looked stunning in a pale peach linen ensemble with a short, but tasteful skirt that buttoned up the side. It was all part of her conscious effort to maintain an attractive exterior, regardless of persistent inner turmoil. Lately, she'd begun to have sporadic episodes during which her heart would suddenly palpitate wildly, her head would begin to throb, and her stomach would ache as if someone were squeezing it in their fist. These strange sensations were also accompanied by an overwhelming and eerie desire to jump out of her skin.

Madeline couldn't quite pinpoint exactly how and why these occurrences were taking place, although puzzlingly, other people were usually around when they did. She'd be enjoying lunch or dinner with a friend when—bam! It would hit her like a bolt out of the blue. And though these experiences were incredibly frightening, thus far she'd been able to hide her distress by simply excusing herself to go to the restroom. Once there, she'd take deep breaths until she felt safe again. Thank goodness, today she felt fine; she had much territory to cover with follow-ups, beginning with Future Insurance.

The green door of the office opened just as Maddy approached the bell; behind it stood a nice-looking man with sandy brown hair, blue eyes, and a mustache.

"Oh uh, hello," she smiled, extending her hand. "I was gonna ring but looks like you beat me to it. I'm Madeline Rose with the Kingston

Personnel Agency."

Returning her gesture, the man replied politely, "James Russo. Very nice to meet you." He looked at her for a moment before asking, "Weren't you here the other day?"

"Yes, I spoke with Karen. She told me you didn't use temps often, but that there may be a need in the near future. So I came back hoping to introduce myself to you and bring you this little reminder." She handed him the gift.

"Thank you," he said, "You know, she should have let you speak to me; I was on the phone with a client, but I was about to end the call. I would've given you a few minutes of my time."

"Well, thanks, Mr. Russo—"

"Jim," he stated.

"Jim," she repeated, "That's very nice, but now that we've had a chance to meet, you'll know who to call when your hiring needs change. I really appreciate your courtesy, though. Thank you." As she turned to leave, he stopped her.

"Wait!"

"Yes?" Madeline made eye contact again.

"Uh, do you get to this area often? Maybe we could have lunch sometime?"

"I'm usually in Exton about once a week," she admitted.

"Well let me know and we'll do lunch."

"Ok, that would be nice. Have a great afternoon," she called to him as she headed back to her car.

Although he seemed pleasant enough, she could tell he was probably a bit older than her, not that it really mattered. And maybe it would be fun to share a "safe" lunch with a new man—provided it didn't go any further. She was still reeling from Kenny's rejection and struggling to find the appropriate lesson embedded in the events of the past nine months. Besides, if this guy was already in his late-30's he wouldn't want to hang out with a child like her for long anyway.

But later that day, as she was sorting through business cards in her office, Arlene strode in holding a piece of paper from the fax machine.

"For you," she said handing her a handwritten invitation from Jim to join him for lunch the following Wednesday. As if to emphasize his interest, he'd drawn a huge smiley face beneath his signature.

"Well, I guess he's sincere," Maddy laughed, before calling to accept his offer.

Though she'd expected a venue along the lines of Bennigan's, Friday's or Chili's, Jim surprised her with a leisurely, upscale meal at the Duling- Kurtz House. While the white-glove service, elegant ambiance and extensive menu were impressive, Maddy hardly gave it a second thought until—when retelling the story that evening—a jubilant Vanessa exclaimed, "He took you to Duling-Kurtz! Madeline, I've never been to Duling-Kurtz; this guy must really be into you!"

And as they shared interesting conversation over Caesar's salads with shrimp, she was delighted to discover a mutual love of theater, the beach, and Frank Sinatra music. Her instincts had been correct; at 36, Jim was ten years her senior. However, his enthusiasm, spontaneous sense of humor and principled work ethic created an extremely attractive package. When she returned to the office, she'd faxed him a thank you note, to which he'd promptly responded, "The pleasure was all mine. Let's do it again, soon!" Despite her initial misgivings, a delighted Maddy felt ready to truly give him a fair chance.

The following morning, Betty and Madeline cracked up when Jim's faxed response to their "Day at the Beach" contest included the question, "Isn't there something missing from this package?" Maddy quickly faxed back, "What exactly is missing?" That was when an amused Jim called her at the office, claiming her fax had brightened his day. He informed her that what was missing was a beach companion, to which Maddy replied teasingly, "Betty is available," Jim roared with laughter.

Interestingly, his birthday had been March 8, the day after hers. But it wasn't long until his odd behavior made her question the wisdom of getting involved with another Pisces. While he pursued her relentlessly for a brief period via regular phone calls, faxes, and lunch dates, Maddy grew suspicious when their plans never evolved into after-hours dinners or Saturday evening concerts.

That is until a phone call from his receptionist revealed his impending marriage to his live-in fiancée in the coming fall. The woman had been so sympathetic when she'd spoken with Maddy, absolving her from guilt, and fully acknowledging that her boss had led her on under false pretenses.

And when a determined Maddy finally tracked Jim down to confirm the truth, the weasel didn't deny it, though he could offer no further explanation other than wanting to spend some "innocent" time with a pretty girl. For a disgusted and hurt Maddy, the incident had proven to be just another heartache in what was beginning to feel like a never-ending saga of cruelty and sorrow.

Back in her Ocean City bedroom, Madeline wiped away a tear as she struggled to come to terms with life as it stood right now. Why were men so unbelievably hurtful? First Jake, then Ken and now Jim—not to mention Gary. In each case, she'd been simply minding her own business, focused on enjoying the moment, not even consciously seeking male companionship. And when her natural exuberance attracted them, she'd behaved as a lady should, allowing them to pursue, while graciously accepting dates without a hint of coyness.

Unlike many others she knew, Madeline lacked the innate ability and burning desire required to effectively play head games and put on pretensions; that kind of childish, inauthentic behavior repulsed her. All she wanted was the love and devotion of a good man who would appreciate her for who she was. And when Ken came along, it appeared the search was over. But sadly, he turned out to be no different from the rest.

She reclined on her twin bed, staring up at the ceiling fan. God knew, she was trying – trying to uncover the hidden meaning in these experiences, searching for the lessons the experts on her motivational tapes assured her existed in every happenstance—which of course, was a misnomer since nothing in the Universe occurred at random. On the contrary, every seeming coincidence was actually a planned and purposeful event meant to aid in one's soul progression. Her job was to locate the underlying pattern so she could shift her awareness and create the life she always dreamed of. And while all of this sure sounded good in theory, in practice it was downright exhausting.

Her mind wandered back to a sunny early-summer afternoon when she'd cold called another insurance company in the Rosetree Corporate Center. Impeccably dressed for business in a navy and white pinstripe suit, Maddy had approached the "gatekeeper"—a friendly, middle-aged administrative assistant—to determine the competition and ascertain her agency's chances at filling personnel positions at this particular organization.

Engrossed in friendly chatter, she barely noticed the dark-haired gentleman who passed her by on his way back to his office, though he did call out a greeting to his fellow co-worker before closing the door behind him. And though she hadn't so much as said hello to this man, later on back at her place of employment she received an unexpected delivery—a gorgeous bouquet of white roses similar to the ones Ken had brought her on New Year's Eve.

Although they hadn't been properly introduced, the insurance guy—whose name was Gary Snyder—had tracked down her business card after she'd left. In the attached note, he'd expressed a sincere desire to get to know her.

Touched by the gesture, Maddy called to thank him with genuine appreciation, initiating a series of promising dates that seemed to be headed in the right direction—until one fateful night in Ocean City poured icy cold water on her renewed relationship hopes.

He'd invited her to come by his summer rental, which had been conveniently located on West Avenue, just a few blocks away from the Rose home. An ebullient Maddy drove to the Shore after work with an optimistic attitude, imagining a fun-filled weekend spent in Gary's company. Instead, she got the brush-off. When she arrived at his place as planned, an aloof and hostile Gary rudely canceled their evening and practically escorted her out the door with the dubious claim of having to pick up his drunken roommate in Sea Isle.

A dejected Maddy was left to explain what happened to her sympathetic and angry mother a few minutes later when she arrived back at the house.

"You know, I just don't understand these guys," Monica had sighed.

"Join the club," Maddy responded before her mother tried to lighten the mood with talk of her daughter's goodness and her fervent belief that

God had a special guy in mind for her; it was simply a matter of time.

Curling up on her side in her now darkened Ocean City bedroom, she held her pillow to her chest and cried herself to sleep.

Chapter 17

Maddy focused her eyes straight ahead as she crossed over the Walt Whitman Bridge on her way back into New Jersey. She'd driven to Malvern from Ocean City earlier that Saturday afternoon to teach country line dancing for the Cowboy Ball at the Chester Valley Golf Club, where two of her Pottstown students, a sweet couple named Ellie and Paul Johnson, were members. Around the same age as Madeline's parents, they'd been students of her ballroom dance classes since their inception four years prior and had been immediately struck by her poise and professionalism.

Each semester when the school district mailed out the Adult Education curriculum, Ellie and Paul would enthusiastically register for another ten-week session, eagerly anticipating Tuesday nights, which often came with the added bonus of sharing a pre-class meal with Maddy and Monica at the local Pottstown Diner. So when fellow country club members noticed their tremendous progress at a formal dinner dance one evening, the pair had attributed most of the credit to the wonderful young woman and her mother—who would good-naturedly, "lead" the single female students to make up for the lack of male participants.

The Tuesday night ritual had quickly become one of Maddy's favorite activities as well. She'd pick up her Mom after work, and the two of them would make the scenic, 45-minute trek west on Route 422, where they'd laugh and chat about nothing in particular while singing along with the radio. As they'd pass by the rolling green hills of Montgomery County, Maddy would regale her with funny stories of Betty—who was always entertaining, or the latest incident involving a crazy client, or a flaky temp who hadn't shown up for work. Oftentimes, they'd laugh over the antics of some of Maddy's quirky dance students, wondering what he or she might say or do during that evening's lesson.

But no matter what was discussed, the drive offered quality one-on- one time for mother and daughter, free from whatever family dramas might be unfolding at that moment. During those carefree hours spent in the car and in the elementary school gym, Maddy forgot all about her insecurities, career dissatisfaction and romantic troubles, uplifted by the warm, receptive class and the sheer joy of the dance.

However, during last winter's semester, she'd started to experience those weird physical twinges, where all of the sudden she'd feel as if she were having an out-of-body experience. On a few occasions prior to the start of the lesson, she'd actually feared getting sick in front of the class, though—blessed with a strong stomach—Maddy could only recall two times in her entire life when she'd actually thrown up. But as had become her habit, she'd excuse herself to step outside or into a ladies room, take a few deep breaths and then rejoin the class, without uttering a word about the episode to anyone. It was a pattern that would eventually come back to haunt her.

Now cruising effortlessly down the Atlantic City Expressway, she sang along to the latest Vince Gill and Colin Raye cassettes, still very much in a country mood, thanks to the evening's events. It had been a pleasure teaching the nice people at Chester Valley, who'd, in turn, raved about her exuberantly to Ellie and Paul. The Johnson couple had been extremely pleased—though certainly not surprised—by her excellent performance that evening, for which Maddy had been handsomely compensated.

However, the best satisfaction for her had been the knowledge that she'd done her friends proud; after all, they'd truly stuck their necks out to the members of the Board, most of whom had insisted on hiring someone with professional experience. Maddy cracked up as she recalled a meeting involving her, Ellie and a very finicky and skeptical woman named Suzanne, who'd grilled her relentlessly about her dancing skills. She had passed the test with flying colors, teaching them an impromptu class in the middle of Ellie's living room.

After Suzanne had left, Ellie apologized profusely for the woman's initial behavior, but Madeline had taken it all in stride. The only downside to getting the job had been the accompanying necessity to tear herself away from the beach, all too aware that precious days in the summer sun would soon be coming to an end. Thankfully, the weatherman was promising another hot, clear day tomorrow and she planned to take full advantage. As she drove on through the night, she tried to focus on the good things in her life, even as memories of last summer and Ken's recent phone call hung over her like a black cloud.

"You've got a great arm, beautiful," Joseph Rose complimented his daughter as they played a spirited round of beach football. She'd just tossed him a tight spiral, hitting him perfectly in the chest.

"Thanks, Dad!" she called as she ran after his return lob, which had sailed high over her head, nearly landing hard on the blanket of some sunbathers a few feet away. She laughed out an apology as she scooped it up before it could do any damage.

"Hey Maddy, whad'dya say we take a break and go for a swim? It's hot out here."

"Sure," she nodded in agreement, before depositing the ball on one of their colorful beach chairs, along with the tee-shirt she'd been wearing over her bathing suit. Though another year had passed, Madeline persistently clung to old and self-defeating habits, going so far as to blame Gary's rejection that night on the fact that it had been the first time he'd ever seen her in shorts.

While she looked good—even slim at times—in her flattering work attire, casual clothes tended to emphasize her flaws. A skewed perception to be sure, but one whose origins dated way back to early childhood. To this day, she bristled at the memory of elementary and high school gym class, when she'd have to change out of her camouflaging uniform and into exercise-appropriate clothing. Sometimes she could still hear the taunts of cruel classmates.

Despite their continual encouragement, those who loved Maddy the most were consistently frustrated in their efforts to reprogram her mind; to successfully convince her to acknowledge the beautiful young woman she'd grown into, both inside and out. In the wake of the Kenny situation, Mom, Dad, Lori, and Greg had each made even more of a conscious effort to boost her spirits, constantly reinforcing her psyche with talk of her accomplishments, intelligence, sweetness and physical attractiveness.

But though the genuine admiration of family members and friends was a welcome source of comfort, it also came with the unintended consequence of drawing an even greater distinction between life at home and life in the outside world. Maddy basked in the joy of close family ties but couldn't quite find the same unconditional acceptance among her peers, with a few notable exceptions. Certainly when it came to the dating scene, encountering men of honor and integrity like her father and brothers was becoming an increasingly daunting task as time went on.

Further, the never-ending dramas of Damian and Laura and more recently, Greg and Vanessa, had caused her to retreat further into a secret inner hiding place, where she'd store her most menacing fears and thoughts. With two weddings looming large—Greg and Vanessa's set to take place in a little over a month, financial pressures, upsets over the twin grandchildren and financial as well as other assorted difficulties, the last thing her parents needed was another cause for concern. Therefore, she held tightly to the misguided notion that submerging her problems was an integral component in the accomplishment of a greater good.

"I'm sorry, Maddy, but I don't get a good feeling about any of this," Daphne exclaimed over the telephone. Since an afternoon thunderstorm had put an abrupt end to their father-daughter beach time, Maddy snuck into her parents' bedroom to call one of her favorite cousins.

Dad was safely out of earshot downstairs, completely engrossed in the Phillies game, as evidenced by his loud, spirited reactions to strike-outs, home runs, and other typical baseball occurrences.

With Mom and Louis still in Nashville, and her other siblings caught up in their own activities, it was a great opportunity to seek out an objective opinion on Kenny's recent phone call. More than two weeks had passed since his promise to get back to her with a firm answer about Greg's wedding. And with a little over a month to go before the upstate Pennsylvania nuptials, the clock was definitely ticking on hotel reservations. If Ken was indeed serious about being her date, she needed to know—and not just for lodging considerations but for a whole host of important reasons, beginning with her parents. It was gonna take a helluva lot of effort on her part to smooth the way for that reunion, after the events of this past winter.

A beloved relative, Daphne had often filled the role of conscientious bystander and confidence-keeper for Madeline once she'd made it into adulthood. It was a role expertly shared by Aunt Maria, who would've also provided a sympathetic ear; however, since her mother's sister tended toward overprotection, Maddy concluded that her childless cousin would be the better choice in this particular case. While she trusted Aunt Maria, she just couldn't run the risk of her betraying her secret to Monica, all in the name of mutual motherly concern.

"You don't think he's sincere, Daph?"

"Honey, think about it. The guy stood you up for your ski date without even calling. For the next several months, he ignored all of your phone calls. You had no idea what happened if he'd been in an accident if he'd found someone else—nothing. And then one day calls you out of the blue to announce he's moved to Florida, and he wants to fly up here to be your date? And you're supposed to go, 'Sure, Ken! No problem; take me to my brother's wedding!' How can you even trust this guy? What if he tells you he's coming and then pulls another disappearing act? I just don't want you to get hurt again."

"Yeah, I guess you have a point," she softly agreed. "Daph, I just don't get it, though. I mean, I would have absolutely no idea where he was right now if he hadn't called me. Why would he bother unless he still has feelings for me? I never did meet his parents or his brothers so it's not as if I had some direct link to him or anything. So why contact me now? What could he possibly hope to gain?"

"I don't know," Daphne replied earnestly, shaking her blonde head as she gazed out at her backyard through the bay window in the kitchen. Like Maddy's Mom and Aunt Maria, Daphne longed for her younger cousin to find happiness with the right guy. And throughout Ken and Madeline's courtship, she'd listened excitedly to her cousin's tales of blissful walks on the boardwalk, dances on Ken's outdoor patio and countless moments of joyful discovery of yet another shared passion or personality trait.

"I don't know, Daphne, there's a part of me that wants to believe so much in his sincerity," Maddy sighed. "I mean, I keep thinking back to last summer and all of the fun we had. It was so easy with him; I never once felt inferior or unattractive, like I do with other guys. Ken always made me feel special—as if I were the most beautiful girl on the planet. And I know if he came to Greg's wedding we'd have a fantastic time. He loves to dance, he's got a great sense of humor, and he blends in with the family—"

"Madeline, all of that may be true, but honey, come on. Let's be realistic here; he hurt you badly. And I don't care what his reasons were; he had no business treating you like that. I know I've lost all respect for him; he's gonna have to go a very long way to prove himself to me again."

"Well, I do appreciate your honesty," Maddy admitted. "And I know you have my back. It's just—I don't know a part of me feels like I should call him, just to give him one more chance."

"Well, that's entirely up to you, sweetie. If you feel that's the right thing to do, then I can't stop you. And maybe he was testing you, too; who knows? But the wedding's around the corner; if he's coming, he needs to decide soon."

"Yeah, I know. Although the way Greg and Vanessa have been fighting, you'd think they were getting divorced, instead of getting married. And of course, Mom and Louis are having problems in Nashville with Damian and Laura, you know, the usual stuff. Just when it seems like things have been resolved, something else happens. I can't even catch a break at work 'cause now Arlene and Betty are constantly at each other's throats, screaming and yelling in the office—geez, why can't life be more like Disney World? I'm tired of all this conflict." Daphne laughed heartily.

"Get used to it sweetheart, cause there's lots more where that came from; you're only 26; I suggest you prepare yourself!" Then becoming serious, she added, "That's why you just have to pray to God for the answers. You have to keep the faith and do your best. That's all any of us can do."

"Yeah, I guess you're right, Daph," she conceded. "I am thankful to have a solid religious foundation. I think that's what's keeping me going right now."

"Well, you just hang onto that honey. And if you need to talk, you know I am always here for you."

"Thanks, Daph. I really appreciate it!"

"I love you, Madeline."

"I love you, too."

Maddy tiptoed across the pink and white shag carpet, mindful of her sleeping sister. It was close to 11 p.m. on Sunday night, and though she'd originally planned to leave the Shore much sooner, the nasty thunderstorms had prevented it. Dr. Rose had driven back with her, wisely choosing to leave the plane in its hangar at the Ocean City Airport, rather than take a foolish and unnecessary risk. Against her better judgment, she'd broached the subject of Ken's phone call with her father during the two-hour ride just in case he might actually be serious about flying to Philly for Greg's wedding. To her surprise, Dr. Rose actually expressed sympathy.

"You know, Maddy I think Kenny is a basically a nice kid. He was probably a little insecure about the whole degree issue, being around all of us. It's nice to hear we inspired him to finish his education; he's a bright guy, and I'm sure he'll do very well."

"I'm sure he will, too. But Dad, I knew he was smart from the moment I met him; it never mattered to me if he had a formal education or not. And I am happy for him that he's going for it; I really am. I guess I just wish he would've picked a school in the area, so we could still see each other. It might've even been fun helping him study. And of course, it would've been nice if he'd had the courtesy to call me months ago, instead of disappearing. It still hurts how he stood me up for our ski date that day."

"Well that was lousy," Dr. Rose agreed. "He definitely didn't handle that situation well at all. You know, he really surprised me? I never thought he was the type who would do something like that. I lost some respect for him that day, for sure."

"I just wish I knew what to do now, Dad,"she sighed. "Why now? Why did he have to call me now and get my hopes up?"

"Well, maybe you should call him back and demand some answers," her father suggested pragmatically. "And if he's still acting like a jerk, dump him and move on."

Madeline decided to make the call the moment she got home, the late hour notwithstanding.

"Hello?" The deep, gravelly voice was thick with sleep.

"Kenny?" She responded tentatively, upset that she'd awakened him.

"Uh...yeah," he cleared his throat and rubbed his eyes as he spoke.

Turning to consult the digital alarm clock, he took note of the hour. Though it was only half-past eleven, it felt like 3 a.m.

"Oh God, you were sleeping," she sighed, "You know, we can talk another time. Sorry, I woke you up."

"No—no Maddy, don't go." Ken flipped on the light as he propped himself up in bed. He'd just put in an arduous, labor-intensive day in the hot, tropical sun, planting palm trees and laying down sod for a friend's commercial landscaping business. While not a long-term career move, the work provided the income stream required to finance real estate school and undergraduate courses at Florida International University.

"How are you, sweetheart? Thank you for the card and pictures; I got them the other day. You look great!"

"Thanks. Look, the reason I'm calling is you never got back to me about being my date for Greg's wedding. And if you are serious about coming I need to know so I can book you a room at the Pocono Inn. Plus, figure out picking you up at the airport, driving up to Stroudsburg—"

"Oh, Maddy I'm so sorry; I can't make it. I really thought I was gonna be able to. Thoughts of upcoming cram sessions, school and state exams, work and other commitments flooded his mind. He berated himself silently for ever mentioning it, especially now that he and Erin had reconnected.

"Oh," she replied dejectedly.

"I'm sorry, Madeline," he mumbled.

"Yeah, I'm sorry too. Sorry, I ever fell for your nonsense!"

"Maddy, please—"

"You know what, Kenny? Do me a huge favor and lose my phone number!"

With that, she slammed down the receiver and, resting her head in her heads, sobbed uncontrollably in the solitude of her father's office.

The late September sun flooded through the filmy curtains of the Pocono Inn hotel room, stirring Maddy from a fitful sleep. For one brief second, she lost all concept of time and space, but one glance at Lori's slumbering figure in the adjacent bed transported her back to a very unpleasant reality. Ugh! Why did it seem every wedding in this family was wrought with controversy? As if it hadn't been bad enough that Vanessa's insane perfectionism about everything from church hymns to place cards had fueled endless fights with Greg over the last two months, another blowout in the run-up to the wedding had taken place at the rehearsal dinner the previous evening.

In his sheer jubilation over the presence of his grandchildren from Nashville, Dr. Rose had inadvertently neglected to acknowledge Vanessa's out-of-state relatives during an enthusiastic champagne toast. Beaming with pride, he'd mentioned one-year-old Tommy and Ava by name and expressed his gratitude to Damian and Laura for making the effort to attend. Given the fact that the discord stemming from Mom and Louis' summertime visit to Tennessee had threatened their attendance, the relieved grandfather's words had sprung forth out of genuine, heartfelt sentiment, and not malicious intent. However, they set off a firestorm of emotion that had raged into the wee hours of the morning.

Torn between both sides of the argument, Maddy chided her father for his actions, though considering no one else had been offended, the entire episode felt like much ado about nothing. Worse, the pained look on her father's face in reaction to her betrayal had devastated her. But how could he lavish so much praise on Damian and Laura after all of the turmoil of the last month? Was it really that easy to forget?

Maddy recalled her mother's homecoming three weeks ago, with its corresponding tales of ingratitude, abrasiveness, and inhospitality. While she reserved a certain amount of sympathy for her brother Damian — along with sisterly love and loyalty, she abhorred such despicable treatment of their mother. After all, Monica Rose had willingly responded to their call for help (a practice which had become her habit in spite of past difficulties), going so far as to procure extended vacation time for Louis, a highly competent babysitter in his own right. And like Monica and Lily's childcare sojourn for the nuptials of Laura's sister the previous year, the 800-mile trip—with its accompanying fuel, food, and other travel-related costs, had been financed out of Dr. and Mrs. Rose's bank account.

At the very least, Monica and Louis merited a basic level of respect afforded to grocery store clerks and strangers in elevators. Instead, they were made to feel like intruders; a necessary evil in order to juggle difficult work schedules with the demands of twin babies. And though Maddy could appreciate the private tensions that might naturally exist between even the most loving husband and wife, they were no excuse for bad behavior. The tough part was acknowledging that while her brother and sister-in-law possessed universal human flaws, many of their inexcusable actions had a basis in lingering hypersensitivity over past events.

Yes, perhaps their mother shouldn't have written that letter to Damian when he was a medical student; but her concerns were still valid, even if her methods might have been a bit harsh. Further, Damian should have confined the issue within the bounds of a private parental summit, rather than sharing the controversial correspondence with his future wife—who never could quite move beyond the incident despite repeated clarifying dialogue and ultimate acceptance into the family.

In fact, to many including Madeline, Lori, Daphne and Aunt Maria, Monica had more than adequately compensated for previous mistakes through her noticeable efforts to welcome Laura and keep the peace. It soon became apparent that Mrs. Rose's generosity and interest where her youngest son and his wife were concerned had far exceeded any demonstrated by Laura's own relatives. Although warm and gracious people, her parents had left her to fend for herself in terms of underwriting her medical school education and providing for basic living expenses incurred as a result of choosing a faraway school.

Most shockingly, when Tommy's traumatic birth nearly resulted in tragedy for both mother and baby, it took them six weeks to even make the trip to see their first grandchildren, and to personally confirm their daughter's successful recovery. The Rose family, by contrast—Monica, Lori, and Madeline—had shown up in advance of the event to help out, remaining in Nashville until both infants were well out of the woods.

And yet, Laura's parents still reigned supreme in terms of their daughter's unfailing accommodations and acquiescence. Monica, on the other hand, seemed to incur mostly second-class citizen status in spite of her selfless actions. Understandably, Dr. Rose despised this mistreatment of his wife, but usually defended his son vigorously, perhaps due to a mutual understanding of the pressures of the medical profession. Maddy and her siblings demonstrated equal ferocity in defense of their mother, all the while loving their brother and longing for a resolution that would satisfy everyone. As the youngest child, Madeline, in particular, was torn between fidelity to her mother and genuine sympathy for all involved parties.

Her interest had led to a heated phone confrontation with Damian, who demanded to know what their mother's "problem" was, apparently flummoxed by the fact that Monica might actually take offense to being regarded as a trespasser in his home after graciously responding to his pleas for help. In return, Maddy had unleashed her fury, thoroughly disgusted by the entire situation and simultaneously anguished that it necessitated a verbal boxing match with her brother. Then came the threats of staying home rather than attending Greg's nuptials—a move that would've incurred unspeakable humiliation and upset. Dr. Rose had quickly stepped in to avert disaster, thus unintentionally paving the way for last night's drama.

A sharp, shooting pain suddenly gripped Madeline, interrupting her morning ruminations. She abruptly sat up and clutched the affected area, just as Lori began to stir.

"You ok, Mads?" she asked groggily.

"Ugh, that's a loaded question," she sighed. "Between last night and this morning, this whole wedding is beginning to feel more like a funeral."

"Do you need some Advil? I packed some," Lori offered, throwing back the covers and walking over to the dresser.

"Yeah, thanks. It's just the usual—period late again."

"How long this time?" Lori sat down on the bed and handed her a bottle of water to go with the pills.

"Three months," Maddy admitted. "I really wish my body would correct itself. I don't care what the doctors say, there's no way artificial hormones can be good for you. I know if I'd just refill the stupid birth control prescription, I'd get it again. But it's only a band-aid, masking the real problem, whatever that might be. Plus, the Pill makes me sick—no matter how many times they adjust the dosage, it never seems to help."

"I know," Lori sympathized. "Hopefully, the Advil will kick in soon. We'll take it with us, 'cause God knows, it's gonna be a long day. You and I have to be at the hair salon at ten, then to the Andiario's at Noon for pictures with Vanessa and the other girls. The limo is picking us up from their house, so I can drive us over in my car, and someone can bring us back there after the reception to get it."

"I wonder how Greg is doing," Maddy wondered. "Why is it that every time someone gets married in this family, we have a problem?"

"I don't know, but Vanessa's being ridiculous. I mean, it bothers me that Dad had to go out of his way to praise Damian and Laura after what happened with Mom, but for God's sake, he wasn't slighting her relatives; the whole thing is so goddamn stupid! It's her wedding day for crying out loud—why is she picking fights with Greg and getting everyone all upset? He had nothing to do with it. You'd think she'd be so thankful to have found someone like him that she wouldn't have time for this crap."

"Tell me about it," Maddy agreed sadly. Here I am, dateless for this beautiful event, and Vanessa doesn't even have a clue how lucky she is. A handsome, funny, smart, genuine guy like Greg—maybe we should trade places for a day."

Thoughts of Jake, Ken, Jim, and Gary filled her mind, although Ken, as usual, dominated. In spite of everything, he still retained a special place in her heart. Forgetting him was not going to be easy, especially when faced with a glaring lack of decent male companionship. God willing, she'd find the right one soon; until then, she'd put on a sunny demeanor worthy of her loving, sweet and bubbly reputation.

Chapter 18

Madeline waited patiently while the seamstress conducted the final fitting for Lori's Cinderella-style wedding gown. Standing on the platform of the bridal boutique in front of a three-way mirror, Lori adjusted the oversized, puffy sleeves as the seamstress diligently examined the heavily laced hem of the white silk shantung creation. And while Maddy affixed an expression of pure, unadulterated interest on her face, her thoughts drifted back to another emotionally charged phone call, one that had differed dramatically from the others in terms of duration and gravity.

Over the course of the last several months, she'd grown accustomed to, if not exactly comfortable with, Kenny's regular communication, though, unlike his original contact that summer night in Ocean City, she'd kept these subsequent conversations a deeply held secret. Soliciting her well-meaning father and Daphne for advice had only created more confusion than clarity in the long-run, notwithstanding Ken's wedding-date letdown.

In the aftermath, she'd wrongly assumed the end of all ties with the man who had once made her heart beat incredibly fast merely by offering her an adoring gaze, a genuine smile or a sincere word of affection. That is until he proved her wrong by simply dialing her number. Somehow, she'd managed to stay calm and civil throughout the duration of these calls, in spite of her festering inner anger.

But their most recent contact, which had exceeded two hours, nearly came to a screeching halt before it ever got started, thanks an initial reaction borne out of sheer skepticism and exhaustion.

"Maddy, it's Kenny. God, I miss you so much." His voice betrayed an overwhelming loneliness, at first undetected by the recipient's emotional weariness.

"You know what, Ken? I've about had it with these phone calls. You're the one who moved away; please stop insulting me with talk of how much you miss me – I'm hanging up now."

"No, please—don't! Please talk to me for a while." Ken began to sob, prompting her natural compassion to compel her to remain on the line.

"What's the matter?" Her tone softened dramatically.

"I miss you, Madeline. I love you so much, and I can't stand being away from you. Is there any chance that you'll consider moving here? I'm telling you, there is so much going on in South Florida—I know you could find meaningful work. And with ballroom dancing being so popular here, Maddy, you could stay busy and make money just by teaching classes. I know you want to write, and you will. But in the meantime, you can make a living with your dancing and maybe even sing, too, who knows? And your family wouldn't have to worry; I'd take great care of you. They can visit anytime they want—it's only a two-hour flight."

"Kenny, we've been through all of this before," she sighed. Although tempted by his offer in the deep recesses of her heart and soul, she still couldn't quite wrap her mind around taking him up on it.

"Maddy, c'mon, I know you miss me too."

"How do you know what I'm feeling?" she snapped defensively. "You have no idea what it's been like for me all these months."

"I'm sorry sweetheart; I didn't mean to upset you. I only meant that I know you care for me as much as I care for you." In spite of his frustration, he remained patient and calm.

"Yeah well, I tried to express that once in person, but you told me not to get all crazy on you. If I remember correctly, that was just before you stood me up for a date and then disappeared for five months."

He shuddered at the recall of those terrible times. "I know, Madeline. I remember that. And I am so very sorry. That was an awful period in my life I never want to relive again. But like I've told you before, it just wasn't happening for me in South Jersey. And after being around your family,

learning about all of their accomplishments—it just made me want to be a better person so I could be good enough for you. Remember, I promised you I was going to get my education and then come back and marry you? I meant that, with every ounce of my being. I guess I just didn't realize how hard it was going to be to be away from you for so long." He'd barely gotten the words out before sadness overwhelmed him once more.

"Ok Ken, tell me honestly—how would you feel if I told you I was moving to Florida tomorrow?" she tested him.

"Pretty damn happy," he replied forthrightly, leaving her at a loss for words.

For a while, they remained silent, each awash in regret and remorse. Maddy wished she'd never given in to her fears in the first place by using her mother's initial disapproval as an excuse to break up with him. After they reunited, her misguided decision had only yielded more pain once she'd finally decided to trust in her feelings, only to be shot down harshly.

Kenny's bizarre reaction that evening had contradicted everything he'd previously said and done, as well as drawn an eerie similarity to Jake, who'd once sneered in response to a similar sentiment that she could not possibly know what it truly meant to love. At that moment, Madeline had arrived at the erroneous realization that, despite former evidence to the contrary, he was no different from Jake or every other pompous jerk that had since crossed her path.

Furthermore, as Ken struggled with work demands, school projects and the closing of real estate deals, it became increasingly more difficult to see the light at the end of the tunnel. From deep within, he knew his efforts would pay off if he could just remain focused and optimistic. But in the last several months, the oppressive scourge of competing love and guilt had created a formidable obstacle in the cultivation of a forward-thinking mind.

Additionally, his awareness of her dissatisfaction with her own life, whether willing to admit it or not, was quickly becoming a source of sheer frustration. He understood her closeness to her family, but for God's sake, Florida wasn't exactly a half-world away; hell, it wasn't even halfway across the country. Why was she being so damn stubborn?

On the other hand, why should she move after the way he mishandled things? When she was finally ready to express what he'd longed to hear

for months, he basically stomped all over her heart. And then to disappear without so much as a goodbye phone call—what did he really expect?

"Kenny, I don't know what to say, except it's hard for me, too," she confessed, at last, wiping away a tear.

"Thank God I'm not the only one," he replied softly. "Maddy, can I ask you something; please don't get mad at me, but it's just something I need to know."

"What?" She braced for the query.

"Are you still a virgin?"

"Kenny, I can't believe you're asking me that!" For a moment, she thought about sharing all of her dating horror stories, but quickly decided against it; she wasn't ready to give him the satisfaction of knowing he still ruled her heart.

"C'mon, Maddy, it's me you're talking to here; please just tell me." His voice remained steady and calm.

"Fine—yes, if you must know! Yes, I am still a virgin! Does that make you happy?"

"Yes, because I still want to be your first—and only," he confirmed softly. That led to another long silence as Maddy contemplated this simultaneously uplifting and confusing piece of information.

"Kenny," she finally said, "I-I don't know what you want me to say."

"Say you want it to," he pleaded.

"I do, but it's just not that easy," she sighed. She thought of the ongoing family drama involving Greg's temporary move back home after less than a year of marriage—a situation that thankfully appeared to be resolved, at least for the moment. Prudently, everyone had resisted taking sides, though plenty of colorful opinions had been expressed in the course of endless debate. Then there was Lori's upcoming wedding, which so far promised to be devoid of conflict.

As the maid of honor, Maddy couldn't simply up and run away from home, much as it was becoming an undeniably attractive option. Finally, there was the small matter of her parents' financial problems, the knowledge of which she feigned ignorance regardless of overhearing their detailed nightly conversations from across the hall as she struggled to drift off to another state of consciousness.

And with her strange physical episodes becoming increasingly prevalent, moving away seemed more like a recipe for disaster than a bold move toward a new life. Such events had even landed her in the hospital emergency room on a few occasions, though she spoke of them to no one. One February night, she and one of her fellow ballroom dance instructors had driven down to Ocean City for the weekend, attempting to shake off the winter blahs. That evening, they'd gone to Key Largo in the hopes of dancing the night away.

But soon after they'd arrived, the pulsating rhythms and flashing strobe lights suddenly changed from energizing dance accouterments to instruments of torture. In reaction to these typical nightclub accouterments, Maddy's heart began to race out of control, vying for first place with her head, which pounded ferociously. These sensations were accompanied by that frightening flight-or-fight response, compelling her to run as fast and as far as she could to some unknown destination. On this particular evening, Maddy followed her impulses back out to the parking lot, oblivious to the freezing temperatures.

Her dance partner had trailed right behind and insisted on taking her to Shore Memorial, where a nurse attached a clip to her finger and proclaimed that Maddy was getting plenty of oxygen, despite her protests to the contrary. And though she saw the blinking green indicators that confirmed this sound medical opinion, she remained unconvinced. That belief only intensified with the nurse's subsequent announcement that the patient was suffering from the flu—perfectly understandable given the recent outbreak.

Since that memorable evening, she'd managed to avoid emergency rooms. But though the acute onset of symptoms seemed to have subsided, a persistent, general feeling of uneasiness had taken over, accompanied by relentless headaches, stomach pains and occasional bouts with alternating sweats and chills. All of this continued apace without regard for the fact that she'd dutifully gone back on the Pill at her doctor's insistence, thus experiencing regular if "false" periods.

Yet through it all, Maddy did her best to maintain a happy façade, so as not to ruin Lori's wedding, worry her parents and otherwise negatively contribute to existing family difficulties. Besides, it wasn't all bad—she and her mom were spending plenty of quality time going to the movies, shopping and hanging out with Aunt Maria, who always made her laugh.

That particular phone conversation with Ken had ended with Maddy assuring him of her best wishes and her complete confidence in his ability to accomplish anything he set his mind to.

"It's not that I don't care about you because I do—so much," she'd said. "It's just that, I don't see how I can leave right now, if ever. I'm so sorry, Kenny."

The heart-wrenching call had concluded with both of them doubting the wisdom of staying in touch, though neither relished the thought of never speaking to the other again. Thus, the clandestine pattern of communication went on unabated, ultimately resulting in a decision that would shock everyone.

"Maddy, did you hear me?" Lori prodded her sister. "I want you to try your gown on one more time before we go to make sure it fits right. This is it, you know. The wedding's in less than two weeks."

"Sure," she complied, obediently taking the two-piece fuchsia formal into an available dressing room. When she emerged a few minutes later, Lori offered her hearty approval. The dress, with its sleeveless, scalloped portrait collar, three rhinestone buttons up the bodice and sheath skirt with a tasteful front-slit expertly flattered Maddy's curves, while elongating her frame. And its vibrant shade complemented her fair complexion and auburn hair.

"Perfect," Lori proclaimed. "You'll be the prettiest one in the bridal party."

"And the only one without a date," Madeline added in a mixture of sadness and disgust.

"Don't worry baby girl, between Vince's friends and co-workers, I'm sure there'll be some single guys there. And between Lyle and Louis, you'll have great dance partners. We'll all have fun, don't worry."

Maddy returned her sister's warm embrace, all the while pondering her next move. Soon, her final obligation would be fulfilled, paving the way for her to finally honor the voice within, which had grown incrementally louder with every passing day over the course of the preceding 18 months.

In an idea gleaned from one of her motivational tapes, Maddy had taken to creating "dream albums," a pastime to which she'd devoted countless, pleasant hours. Per the expert's advice, she'd painstakingly cut out photos from various magazines—vivid images of all that she wanted her life to include, from a beautiful, waterfront home in South Florida surrounded by palm trees, to a healthy, physically fit figure, as displayed by a current supermodel or actress. On those photographs, she would sometimes glue a picture of her face in order to more effectively drive the point home to the Universe.

During the long, dreary winter, this activity raised her spirits and helped her solidify her decision; by the time Indian summer rolled around, and with it, Lori's precious milestone occasion, Maddy's mind had been made up. She'd overcome her own reticence about leaving; the only remaining obstacle would be helping her family to do the same.

At work, she'd begun to drop hints to Betty in this regard, procuring a promise for an excellent recommendation to a business contact she had in the Sunshine State. Madeline planned to get out of the employment industry for good, yet recognized the value of having a job waiting for her when she arrived. It would pacify her parents as well as provide needed income for expenses while she plotted what to do next.

Madeline curled up under the plush covers of the queen-sized guest room bed in Damian and Laura's lovely five-bedroom home. Although it was only early November, evening temperatures in Nashville had been uncharacteristically cold, thus necessitating winter pajamas and a mug of hot chocolate, which sat on a coaster on the nightstand. She'd just spent the last month here, taking care of the twins while Damian and Laura sought out the services of a qualified nanny to replace the incompetent one they'd fired—coincidentally just after Maddy had made her big announcement. At Damian's urging, she'd postponed her first day of work on the new job in Pompano Beach long enough to allow for some quality time with her youngest brother and his family.

Just as she'd expected, it had been a difficult conversation with her parents, although her mother had not been surprised. An astute woman with a perceptive maternal instinct, Monica had been aware of her daughter's restlessness for quite some time. These last few years certainly had taken their toll, between constant GYN visits, a tense work environment, relentless wedding activities, and of course, the lousy late-20th-century dating scene. Poor Madeline had certainly encountered more than her fair share of toads; Monica just couldn't understand why someone as bright and beautiful as her daughter would have so much difficulty finding the right man.

Only Kenny had appeared to be a decent, upstanding guy, and in the end, he broke her heart, too. It was so unfair. And as much as she was going to miss her "baby," she acknowledged that at 27 years old, Madeline was an adult who possessed every right to live and work wherever she pleased. Of all her children, however, she'd never expected this one to fly the coop.

But Madeline had never gone away to college, so perhaps this was simply a way for her to experience another part of the country while she was still a young adult. The problem was, Florida was stiff competition. With year-round summertime temperatures and plenty of sunshine, Monica doubted Maddy would ever return home for good. Moreover, part of her wished she could go along as well. Like her daughter, she reveled in warm weather, sandy beaches and swaying palm trees, despite her northeastern upbringing.

Dr. Rose, however, felt quite differently. Perhaps due to his own busy surgical schedule, he'd failed to notice his daughter's discontent. He saw her working, teaching her dance classes and taking an interest in her usual hobbies, from Eagles football to epic movies. As a man who was passionate about his own livelihood, family ties, lifetime friendships and Philadelphia culture, it was nearly impossible for him to relate to Madeline's feelings.

Mainly, his thoughts focused upon missing her smiling face every day and worrying about her safety. But in heated moments, all he could do was raise his voice and insist that the Florida cities his daughter was so enamored of were truly crime-ridden places unfit for residency. Of course, having done her own research, coupled with the information Ken had been regularly supplying, Maddy knew better. But she refrained from contradicting her father, as per the habit she'd developed over the course of her childhood. Besides, she understood where he was coming from and his need—in fact, his right—to vent his dissatisfaction with her choice.

During those uncomfortable exchanges, Madeline would silently recall the quote from one of her Wayne Dyer books, "If you want a place in the sun, you must leave the shade of the family tree." She was more than willing to give up the shade; she just wished that doing so hadn't come at the expense of hurting the ones she loved the most. But agreeing to accept Carmella and Frank's gracious invitation to live with them temporarily until she found a place of her own had alleviated some of her parents' valid concerns. And though Maddy had never actually met this couple, their connection to her family gave her a welcome degree of comfort.

Now that the worst was over, there was just one potential wrinkle in her thus far perfect plan—Kenny. A few months back when she'd flown to Fort Lauderdale to meet with Betty's contact, she'd stopped by his real estate office to say hello, dressed in her favorite peach linen suit, a staple of her professional summer wardrobe from the previous year. The flattering ensemble featured side-fastening mother-of-pearl buttons on a short, but demure skirt, and a tailored jacket. With her long hair partially pulled back at the crown, save for a few wispy bangs around her face, she still embodied the youthful image of an exuberant college co-ed.

As she entered the sun-dappled, ceramic-tiled atrium of the Gold Coast Agency, a wave of excitement engulfed her. That is, until her bright smile and unbridled enthusiasm were met with simmering hostility and outright rudeness. From behind a mahogany and granite counter, the curt, middle-aged receptionist barely responded to her polite request to see Kenny. When she finally did pick up the receiver to dial his line, she shot Madeline a look of pure condescension, nonverbally expressing her distaste at the gall of the young woman to simply walk through the front door.

"You can go on back!" she ordered her a moment later.

Passing by seemingly endless cubicles housing more than 20 agents and brokers, she detected a palpable chill in the air. With the weight of this oppressive negativity surrounding her, Maddy plowed ahead, suddenly more anxious than ever to see Ken. When she finally caught his attention, prompting him to quickly rise to his feet and embrace her, she felt equal parts relief and joy. He looked as handsome as ever in a light blue suit, his radiance even more stunning, thanks to year-round sunshine. His blond waves displayed a richer golden hue, dramatically setting off his aquamarine eyes and slightly tanned cheeks.

"Hey Maddy, it's so good to see you!" he'd said warmly, though his greeting hadn't instilled much confidence. After all, they hadn't seen each other in close to two years; a little more enthusiasm would have been nice. And while his phone calls of late had lacked the passion and urgency of his earlier contacts, she'd attributed that to being severely overworked. Still, Madeline had such high expectations for this reunion; it was almost as if his co-workers had conspired to somehow turn him against her. Paranoid perhaps, but what else to make of this strange encounter?

"You too," she replied politely, releasing herself from his arms after a quick glance around the room revealed that their every move was being watched.

"Uh, you know Kenny I can only stay for a minute. My interview is in an hour, but I just had to see you. You look wonderful."

"As do you. But that's hardly surprising," he noted with a smile as he ushered her back toward the lobby, where he hoped to find some privacy. They ended up in an available conference room next to the reception area. Ken closed the door behind them as she took a seat on a plush leather chair.

"So what's the plan? Do you think you'll get the job?" he asked, sitting down next to her.

"With Betty as a reference, I'm sure I will as long as I ace the interview. And if all goes well, I'll be living here permanently in a month or so. My parents' friends have been so nice about everything; in fact, I'm staying at their place for the next few days. They have a really nice house off of A1A in Pompano, with their own private beach. I'm sure I'll love it there, but I don't plan to live with them for long—only until I get settled and find a place. Can you believe it? After all this time I'm finally doing it!" She laughed nervously as Kenny covered her hand with his.

"You are full of surprises," he noted. And though he seemed happy, she sensed a certain apprehension in his voice. Far from being a man in love, euphoric over his woman's return, he appeared somewhat distant and confused.

"Ken? Is everything alright? You sure don't seem like yourself."

"Oh—yes, yes, everything's fine. I've just been really swamped between work and school. You know, I'm still doing the landscaping thing for extra money until I can close a few more deals. Between that and studying for exams, I don't think I can spend any time with you this weekend like we planned, Maddy. I'm really sorry."

"Don't worry, I have a rental car and a private beach. I'll be fine." She maintained a pleasant, calm demeanor in spite of her disappointment.

"Well, stay in touch and let me know what's going on. And when you do get here, I can help you find an apartment if you want."

"Ok, that'd be great."

After a few more brief exchanges, Kenny escorted her back to her car, where he wished her good luck and wondered what the hell to do next as he watched her pull out of the parking lot.

"Lay wif Ava?" The sweet little voice of Maddy's two-year-old niece stirred her out of her reverie; she looked down to see the toddler's beautiful face beaming at her while her arms clutched her favorite stuffed teddy bear to her chest.

"Hi, bella girl!" Maddy scooped her up and brought her into the bed, where she immediately curled up in her aunt's embrace. And as with every other night since her arrival, Madeline knew that somehow

Ava would end up in a ball on the floor by the time the sunbeams flooded through the curtains. But as she smoothed the child's wavy light brown hair, she felt an amazing sense of gratitude for having this unexpected time with her and her twin brother. Who knew how long it would be before their paths crossed again, now that Maddy would be logging air miles to Philly in her free time? It seemed so strange, yet wonderful that she was finally about to embark on this life-changing adventure.

Though all of her siblings were supportive of her decision, leaving Louis behind had been especially difficult, but Maddy promised to write regularly and talk on the phone often. Although logically she recognized her right as an adult to make this move, a nagging guilt persisted over her special brother. How could he truly understand what was really going on? And besides assuring him repeatedly that she would always be there for him, there was little else she could do.

Damian, in particular, understood his sister's need to find her own way in a new place. He'd originally inquired about the possibility of a Nashville residency, but Maddy quickly squelched that idea for a myriad of reasons, not the least of which was its geographical distance from Kenny. However, with the entire Rose family in the dark over her primary motivation for relocating, she'd assured her brother that while she appreciated the gesture, her own personal growth required her to create a new life from scratch.

And though Carmella and Frank were generously offering temporary shelter, Maddy was determined to find her own apartment—and identity—as soon as possible. Fully accepting the mantra, "If it's meant to be, it's up to me," she was infused with determination to succeed on her own terms in an unchartered land where she would simply be Madeline Rose—not Dr. Rose's daughter, Lori's sister, spoiled rich girl or perennial loser in love.

As Ava drifted off to sleep, Maddy pulled out a special gift from Damian, a hardcover copy of William J. Bennett's *The Book of Virtues: A Treasury of Great Moral Stories*. Opening the cover, she re-read her brother's genuine, handwritten words and pondered their inherent truth:

Dear Madeline,

Wherever you find success and happiness, be assured that your values must also be there if your triumph is to endure. Many people will try to convince you otherwise—that there are shortcuts, that cheating just a little along the way does not hurt anyone. They lie. Remain true to yourself, confident in the knowledge that who you are is the truest measure of how successful you are.

I hope this book helps to keep you on the right course when others try to nudge you away from it. We love you, and you'll always have a safe place to return to so long as I live.

Love,
Damian

And with a final prayer of thanks, Maddy switched off the light and settled into her pillow, filled with renewed hope and optimism for the future.

South Florida
1995

Chapter 19

The intense late-April sun rose high above Florida's magnificent Gold Coast, warming the early morning temperatures to the mid-80's while the tranquil, blue ocean glistened beneath its golden rays. A few miles west, Maddy stirred from a restful night's sleep, a side benefit of her hectic schedule, which combined sales calls by day with dance instruction at the Fred Astaire Studio by night. As she rubbed her eyes and focused on the popcorn ceiling, she panicked for a split-second before realizing it was Saturday. She had a few precious hours to herself before joining her fellow ballroom dancers for rehearsal.

She threw back the covers of her recently purchased mica bed and scurried to the bathroom where a tube of mint toothpaste awaited her. As she brushed her teeth, she stared into the mirror, trying to make sense of the past five months. Thanks to Carmella and Frank, her arrival in the Sunshine State had been characterized by a whirlwind of activity, including regular socialization with the adult children of their closest friends, who'd graciously included her in outings to places like the Parrot Lounge, Las Olas, and The Cove.

She'd even had the pleasure of meeting Rita Conti—another classmate of her mother's from Germantown—and her married daughter Debbie, who worked as a hairdresser out of her home. While Maddy was truly appreciative of everyone's warmth and hospitality, her heart was still heavy with sorrow, disappointment and even a modicum of guilt. Soon after she'd taken up temporary residence in Carmella and Frank's home, Ken had informed her of his not-so-platonic living arrangement with another Philly-area transplant, Erin Mahoney. In the privacy of her hosts' guest room, a devastated Madeline struggled to maintain her composure while Ken, at last, came clean regarding this significant development—a confession he'd erroneously assumed he'd never have to make.

Slammed by this cold, hard dose of reality, she figured the truth had left her with two choices: she could cry all the way home to Pennsylvania or she could view Ken's purpose in her life as a means of forcing her to make some necessary changes. As beautiful as their romance had been, perhaps it was simply a prelude to real change and growth, and possibly something even better. In spite of a deep sense of dissatisfaction over the last several years, she knew she would never have made such a bold decision had Ken not entered the picture. Besides, why should he and his mystery woman get to live in such a gorgeous place and not her? She deserved a slice of heaven, too. With stalwart resolve, she vowed to find a way to make it work.

But despite the omnipresent palm trees, hibiscus and glorious beaches, there was plenty to dislike about her new home, from the crazy drivers to the silicon-enhanced residents. Most upsettingly, Betty's contact had turned out to be the boss from hell, slashing her previously agreed- upon salary in half on her first day at the office and openly bragging about his infidelity to his wife with the heiress of a major waste management company—a woman half his age. Combined with an insanely competitive personnel market, where it seemed every street corner housed an employment agency, Ken's gut-wrenching news cut even deeper. And yet, she refused to give in.

One respite from the insanity was her part-time employment at the studio, which led to the development of her own social circle in the form of fellow instructors including Lloyd and Rebecca, a married couple whose breathtaking performances delighted students and teachers alike. Another was the fishing pier at Deerfield Beach, an impressive structure that jutted out a mile into the ocean. Open

24-hours, Maddy would often go there late in the evening, uplifted by the balmy sea breeze and the enthusiastic activity of the fishermen. Last but certainly not least, weekly Mass at St. Ambrose Church provided much-needed comfort and a boon to her faith, not simply by reinforcing theology but by aping an activity simultaneously shared by her family 1,200 miles away.

She entered her apartment's tiny kitchen and put on a pot of coffee. Gazing up at the row of encouraging greeting cards and notes that adorned the top of her light oak entertainment center, she smiled. Most were from her supportive mother while others were derived from an assortment of well-wishers, including Aunt Maria, Daphne and Lily. Madeline would invariably take a few moments each day to re-read these handwritten sentiments which served as a reminder that she was indeed loved and thought of. And though incredibly busy, she did her best to mail weekly cards back to family and friends, particularly her parents and Louis.

All remained blissfully unaware of the Ken situation, due to Madeline's conscious decision to conceal this aspect of her life. After his initial phone call announcing his move to Florida, and her subsequent conversations with her father and Daphne, she'd come to the conclusion that objectivity couldn't possibly be found among those who cared so deeply for her. Just as none of them could wrap up a package of career satisfaction and hand it to her with a nicely tied bow, neither could they present her with the right relationship advice.

By keeping Ken's ongoing communication a closely guarded secret, none had suspected her move had anything to do with the guy at all. That's where the guilt came in. While logic dictated she was an adult, free and capable of making her own decisions, emotion tugged at her heartstrings, berating her for hurting the ones who loved her most.

As the distinctive aroma of freshly brewed coffee wafted through the air, Maddy changed into flared black shorts and a coordinating cap-sleeve spandex top, a sensible ensemble for practicing her tango routine which, much to her chagrin, involved more than a few lifts. While she loved the idea of a group formation, she preferred to stay on the ground during her dance performances; unfortunately, Lloyd and Rebecca had other ideas. They wanted the studio's premier production to garner rave reviews in the local paper, which would in turn, hopefully, yield an influx of new students. To that end, she'd also agreed to sing on stage, a decision that dovetailed brilliantly with her recently determined goal of facing every one of her fears head on.

She'd just finished applying her make-up and pulling her long hair into a ponytail when a knock on the door startled her. It was only 8:30 in the morning on a Saturday. Who on earth would be stopping by so early? A moment later that question was answered dramatically when she opened the door of her Boca Del Mar residence to find Ken standing before her, dressed in his work attire; his typical smile betrayed a trace of nervousness. Maddy nearly fainted at the sight of him, though she maintained a façade of nonchalance.

"Ken! What are you doing here?"

"Hey, I've been wanting to talk to you. I have some news to tell you, but I wanted to do it in person."

"You're engaged," she stated matter-of-factly as she closed the door behind him and offered him a seat on the couch.

"Yes," he replied, awestruck. How did she know? And why was she so calm?

Soundly defeated, Maddy nevertheless kept a sunny expression on her face while her stomach began to churn in distress. She willed it back into submission as he went on, barely able to look into her deep, brown eyes.

"Um, I finally decided that I didn't want to live in sin any longer than I had to," he explained. "She didn't either, so we got engaged back in September. We went up north to share the news with our families. My parents were happy; her parents were happy. But right now she and I are having a little problem. See, she's a bit insecure because she's an older woman—well, not older, but she's a few years older than me.

"Anyway, it all started on Valentine's Day. I had to work both jobs so we never got to spend any real time together and—Madeline I am just not good at relationships."

Hoping his admission would act as an entrée into a profound conversation about the two of them, Ken was disappointed when his plaintive sigh was met with silence. As usual, she was at a loss for words at a critical juncture, unable to determine if he was seeking counsel from her as his newly minted "buddy" or trying to convey something more significant. Either way, she wasn't willing to oblige.

"To make matters worse," he went on, "She wasn't happy with what I bought her. I got her a pair of rollerblades—"

"Oh, I learned how to do that!" Madeline exclaimed. "My friends from the dance studio taught me; we have the best time at the park in Pompano. It's actually much easier than I expected. I love it."

She was hoping to take the discussion in a new direction to remove the image of Ken pledging his love and fidelity to another woman in front of God and witnesses from her mind. Besides, it was the truth. Rollerblading was second only to dancing and swimming now on her list of preferred recreation.

"Good for you," he complimented, puzzled by her reaction. "It is fun, isn't it?"

"And it's great exercise," she added. Then for effect, "Gosh I'd be thrilled with a new pair of rollerblades, whether for Valentine's Day or any other occasion."

She recalled the beautiful sweater she'd purchased for him on Valentine's two years back—a gift she'd given to her brother Greg after he stood her up for their ski date. A comment Ken had made sometime prior to that about Valentine's Day being a "Hallmark Holiday" suddenly came to mind. Slowly, anger began to replace heartbreak, though she continued to listen politely.

"Yeah well, unfortunately, Erin didn't think rollerblades were a good choice. She accused me of not caring for her, of not having time for her. Anyway, we're just going through a tough time right now, but I'm sure we'll be alright."

"Yes, you will," Maddy affirmed while the voice inside her head kept repeating the mantra, *I am a tower of strength, I am a tower of strength*, over and over again. Then he hit her with an unexpected query.

"Now how do you feel?" he asked nervously.

How the hell do you think I feel Kenny? You were the one calling and crying on the phone for nearly two years about how much you loved me and missed me; the one who practically begged me to move here in the first place; and the one who kept your live-in girlfriend a secret until there was no turning back! How the hell do you think I feel after uprooting my entire life, hurting my family and having to face the consequences of a misinformed decision alone? How could you deceive me like that? Is this some sort of payback for hurting you?

"Hey, I think it's great," she replied brightly. "Congratulations; I've been dating a lot myself since I got here. Believe me; I have my own things going on."

"Well you sure seem as if you've changed," he noted with a twinge of sadness and more than a little confusion. This was not even close to the reaction he was expecting. Maybe Madeline hadn't loved him after all.

"If that's true, it's only in good ways," she stated plainly. For a moment, neither of them spoke. Ken finally broke the silence.

"Hey, I'm glad things are going well for you. Erin knows all about you, by the way. She knows we once dated and that we're now good friends. And since we're neighbors, what with us now living close by in Boca Bayou, you have to come over and hang out with us at night. We can rent movies, make sundaes, have cookouts..."

As his voice trailed off, Madeline remained mute, quietly pondering the ludicrousness of what he was proposing. *Did he really think the three of them were going to be pals? Was there any realistic hope of her pulling that off?*

"You know, I'd love for you and Erin to be friends," he continued. "She still doesn't know that many people here."

"But she's been here over a year, right?"

"Yeah, see I came down first and then Erin followed, months later."

Months later! Was that before or after you stood me up and then constantly called me on the phone to cry about being lonely? Or did Erin move to Florida after you led me on about being my date for Greg's wedding?

At least the reason for the change in the tone of his calls had been revealed, though she couldn't quite decipher the timeline of events. Not that it even mattered at this point. She wouldn't dare hurt a woman she'd never met by coming clean with Ken about her real feelings, about how she still loved him deeply in spite of everything. Even if she did go out on that limb, there was no guarantee he'd return the sentiment, or assuming he did, break off his engagement to Erin to pursue a renewed relationship with her.

"She kind of depends on me," he explained. "She has a good

job and everything but most of the people in the office have kids so they're busy with their families. And of course, most of them live in Miami anyway. But I know you two would get along so well. You could go out shopping, go to the beach or just do whatever girls do when they get together."

Ugh! Was he for real?

"Uh, well you know Ken I am pretty busy these days with dance rehearsals and everything. But you know, when football season rolls around, maybe we could all catch an Eagles game at a sports bar one Sunday."

"Oh—well Erin isn't much of a football fan. In fact, she despises it," he admitted wistfully.

"Well, that's too bad. She doesn't know what she's missing. I'm hoping to go to a Dolphins game this year if I can get tickets."

As she spoke, he recalled the fun they'd had at the Eagles-Vikings game at the Vet that December, and of course, the barbeque at her Ocean City place when their team squeaked by the Giants in a nail-biter. He'd almost forgotten what a pleasure it was to experience the NFL with her— yet another reminder of a shared interest sacrificed; another casualty of a residual tide of bad timing and misplaced good intentions.

"Maddy, by the way, I love your apartment," he complimented, trying to change the subject. He was suddenly feeling depressed.

"Thanks, I'm happy with it for now."

"You know, you could've called me when you were ready to move! I told you I'd help you find something."

"Nah, I know you're busy," she replied breezily. "Besides, as you can see, I did pretty well on my own." She didn't mention that she was struggling to pay the rent, but such matters were no longer any of his concern.

"You sure did. I'm very proud of you!"

"Thank you." Then glancing at the clock she announced, "My goodness, look at the time! I'm really sorry Ken, but they're expecting me at the studio any minute. I really have to get going."

With that, she abruptly got off the couch, a move he mimicked a second later.

"Well ok then, Maddy," he conceded with a hug and a kiss on the cheek. "I have to meet some clients soon anyway. You take care and remember I am just down the road if you need anything. You can call me anytime, day or night."

She mumbled a polite thank you, even though in the sacred confines of her heart and soul she vowed she'd never take him up on this tempting but inappropriate offer, then ushered him out the door. From the second-floor window, she watched him pull away in his pre-owned silver BMW convertible, before throwing herself on the bed and sobbing uncontrollably.

"Madeline!" Kelly called out over the speakerphone. "There's someone on line two for you; a guy who says he met you at the chamber of commerce business card exchange the other day? Says his name is Mark Donnelly."

"Who? I don't remember meeting anyone by that name," she ruminated to the temp agency's sweet receptionist. Kelly had been the only saving grace in a trying and oftentimes hostile work environment; her compassion and willingness to lend an ear had been a Godsend.

"Did he say anything else, Kel?"

"No, not really. Do you want me to take a message?"

"Nah, put him through. Now I'm curious," she laughed. Maddy cleared her throat, hoping the call might lead to a lucrative new account, and thus, a healthy commission check at the end of the month.

"Hello, this is Madeline Rose. How may I help you?" she greeted the mystery caller, whose face and name she valiantly attempted to reconcile. In spite of her best efforts she still fell short at times when it came to remembering such details. And the luncheon the other day had been so crowded it would've taken superhuman powers to recall every handshake and interaction with the community's movers and shakers.

"Madeline, hi, this is Mark Donnelly from Pinnacle Insurance. We met the other day at the Delray Chamber event at Lake Ida Inn?"

"Um, yes how are you, Mark?" She tried to exude a professional familiarity though his deep, baritone voice wasn't even vaguely familiar.

"I'm doing just fine, how are you?"

"I'm well, thanks. What can I do for you?"

"Well, first I wanted to compliment you on your follow-up skills with the handwritten thank you card. I should be so diligent about those things!" He laughed out loud in an appealing way that immediately put her at ease.

"Thanks for the compliment."

"You're welcome. We don't really use temps here, sorry to say, but should something come up I'll definitely keep you in mind. Just don't tell Isabella."

He was referring to a good friend of his—an attractive, ambitious woman of 60 who owned an employment agency in his building. Maddy remembered her well from the other day, having been immediately struck by the woman's perfectly coiffed hair, impeccable suit, and beautiful pearls.

During their brief conversation Isabella had even offered Maddy a job, an invitation she was seriously considering. God knew Charlie Dowling was never going to change his repulsive behavior. The only reason she was sticking it out was to salvage her résumé; she was hoping to last at least a year at this new employer before moving on. Still, with every passing day she was inching closer to arranging a one-on-one meeting with Isabella to discuss her options further.

"Ok, I won't," she assured him with a chuckle.

"Madeline, do you have a boyfriend?"

The question took her by surprise. "No...I've only been in South Florida about six months and I'm still getting to know my way around," she finally answered, hoping she didn't sound like a loser.

Selective amnesia notwithstanding, it seemed she'd made a positive impression on him.

"Well, do you know about Sunfest?"

"Uh, no what is that?"

"It's an art and music festival they have every year in West Palm Beach. Live bands, delicious food and all kinds of fun things. It's a really great time."

"Sounds like it," she agreed.

"Would you like to go with me tomorrow? I know it's short notice, but if you don't already have plans, I'd love to take you. Where do you live?"

"In Boca Del Mar. My apartment is off of Military Trail, just north of Southwest 18th Street."

"Oh, ok I know that area. I actually have a licensing class tomorrow in West Palm, but I can come back and get you. My sister and brothers are all going. It'll be a lot of fun!"

"Uh Mark, I'd really love to, but I have to check with the dance studio first. I teach ballroom dancing part-time at Fred Astaire in Royal Palm Plaza, and I'm in a professional showcase in a few weeks. Since most of us work other jobs, Saturday is our rehearsal day. But you know, I can ask them for the time off this evening since we have a practice. I'm sure it won't be a problem, but can I get back to you?"

"Wow, a woman of many talents," he noted with pleasant surprise. Actually, I was hoping you could meet me for a drink later, but I guess that's out of the question."

"Maybe I can. My rehearsal isn't until 7:30."

"Oh, well can we make it around 5:30?" He seemed enthused by the idea, judging from the tone of his voice.

"Yes, that sounds good. I'm wrapping up soon for the day anyway. How about Mizner Park? It's one of the few places I know how to get to," she laughed.

"Mizner it is, then. Do you know where Baci is?"

"Sure do."

"Let's meet there by the bar at 5:30. We can sit and talk for a while in a nice atmosphere. I have to be at my brother's place around 7:30 anyway, so this works out perfectly."

"Ok then Mark, see you at Baci."

"Looking forward to it."

"Same here."

As she hung up the phone, it occurred to her that she might have trouble identifying a man whose appearance she had no recollection of in a crowded, Happy Hour environment. Because he'd come across as a genuinely down-to-earth guy on the phone, she hadn't had the heart to ask for a description. With any luck, he'd arrive first and spot her in the crowd. Glancing at the clock, she realized she'd have plenty of time to stop home and freshen up before her mystery date—her first "official" one as a new Floridian.

Mizner Park was bustling with after-hours activity as Madeline searched for a parking spot, noticing the throng of every day "supermodels" with artificial cleavage and size-two figures as well as the impeccably dressed GQ wannabes exuding palpable conceit and pomposity. While she thoroughly enjoyed hanging out at this Spanish-style plaza with its plethora of outdoor cafés, upscale boutiques and beautiful fountains enhanced by flawless landscape design, she had little patience for the pretensions of most of its inhabitants.

Though looking pretty stylish herself in an ivory and brown pantsuit her mother had mailed to her, Maddy's insecurities had only intensified since learning of Ken's engagement. In fact, she was running late now as a result of agonizing over her appearance for nearly an hour in the bathroom mirror. After several wardrobe changes, she'd finally decided on the billowing slacks and coordinating sleeveless blouse that tied in the back and buttoned down the front in a tasteful, but sexy V-neck.

Despite the oppressive humidity, she'd decided to wear her hair loose after vigorously brushing it upside down. And doing her Mom proud, she'd remembered to paint her lips with a lovely shade of rosy gloss, setting off her artful make-up application. On her ears she wore her big, gold hoops, opting to forego any other accessories, save for her grandmother's engagement ring on her right hand. Nanny had left it in her will for her six-year-old namesake, who'd been devastated by her sudden death 21 years earlier. It was an heirloom of immeasurable sentimental value, a cherished, white-gold trinket she guarded with utmost care.

Satisfied with her appearance after one final inspection in the mirror, she grabbed her car keys and her quilted evening bag and excitedly headed out the door.

Chapter 20

The sun beat down on the crowded pink plaza as Maddy entered its main thoroughfare on foot after securing a parking space in the densely populated garage. Though excited, she remained cautiously optimistic; after all, the wounds were still fresh from Kenny's recent announcement. But perhaps this unexpected date was God's way of nudging her in the right direction. Even if it turned out to be a dud, she had to start somewhere. Getting over Kenny was a rough, yet necessary proposition. And as a wise person once noted, there was nothing like a new man to make a woman forget all about the one that got away.

But as she approached the horde of beautiful people gathered on the other side of Baci's floor-to-ceiling windows, a wave of inadequacy overpowered her again. How could she possibly compete with all that silicon, botox, and designer clothing? Worse, what if this guy Mark was just as shallow as the Happy Hour revelers assembled in this decidedly trendy watering hole? Suddenly regretful for having agreed to the blind date, she abruptly turned away from the main doors and took a seat on a hot bench situated in the line of fierce, direct sunlight.

Oblivious to the discomfort, she sat lost in thought while the rays beat down on her uncovered head and arms. *Should she stand him up? Nah, that would be incredibly rude, and besides, she'd never treat anyone that way, especially after having been on the receiving end of such deplorable behavior. It just wouldn't be right.*

Madeline took a few deep breaths in an attempt to calm the butterflies in her stomach. In spite of recent developments and a broken heart, she hadn't experienced those weird sensations in a while, not since having dinner with Damian her last night in Nashville.

She recalled how she'd started feeling strange a few hours before her brother returned home from work. A well-intentioned Laura had insisted on the two of them sharing some one-on-one brother and sister time, impervious to Maddy's protests that a "good luck" dinner at a nice restaurant wasn't necessary. Of course, Madeline hadn't told her sister-in-law or anyone else about her persistent problem; therefore, Laura had no way of knowing the real motivation for wanting to stay home with her and the babies.

And after some time alone in the bedroom and bathroom preparing for the evening, she had successfully—so it seemed—calmed herself down again. But when the waiter presented her meal, she'd suddenly lost her appetite. Damian had attributed her nausea and discomfort to nervousness about moving away, a conclusion with which his little sister had dutifully nodded in agreement. And though she knew instinctively there was something deeper at work, she brushed the problem aside, preferring to deal with what she considered her top priorities—reuniting with Ken, working hard, making friends and eventually launching a writing career.

Now that she'd failed at the first objective, making enough money to support herself had taken on an even greater urgency. She was determined to succeed in her new home; damned if she was going to give in and return to Pennsylvania a defeated and rejected woman. Of course, her family would welcome her back with open arms, but she'd never forgive herself for quitting without giving it her best shot. Win or lose, she vowed to see it through.

Her ruminations were interrupted by a deep, masculine voice. "Madeline?"

She looked up to see a handsome man whose beautiful smile,

blond hair and six-foot frame were reminiscent of Kenny, though his grey-blue eyes lacked the same sparkle and effervescence as those of her former boyfriend.

"Mark?" she replied, rising to her feet and accepting a handshake that quickly transitioned into a peck on the cheek.

"What are you doing out here? It's so hot! I just scanned the whole bar area and figured I'd look for you outside, but I didn't expect to see you sitting on a bench in the sun. Your blood couldn't possibly have thinned that much already—you haven't been here long enough."

"Oh, I love it," she answered with a laugh. "I may be from up north, but I have always been a warm-weather kind of person. Now that I live in the tropics, I can't seem to get enough of it."

"Well, let's get back into the air conditioning before I embarrass myself by sweating through my suit." He grinned at her as he spoke, taking her arm and leading her into Baci's main bar area where, amazingly enough, two barstools awaited them.

"What can I get you to drink?" he asked.

"Oh, just an iced tea—a regular iced tea," she clarified. He looked at her quizzically.

"You sure? Wouldn't you rather have a glass of Merlot or Chardonnay?"

"No, just iced tea, thanks. I have to dance in an hour."

"Oh yes, I'd forgotten about that. You know it's funny, every time I eat at La Viola, I always notice the people dancing on the second floor of that building and think, 'someday I'm actually going to take lessons.' But I never get around to it."

"It's a lot of fun," she encouraged, "Most people don't realize you can ballroom dance to pop music. And it's great exercise, too." But before

He could respond, an older gentleman who appeared to be in his late-60's clapped him on the shoulder.

"Sid! Hey, how are you?" Mark greeted him enthusiastically upon turning around.

"Just great, Mark, what's going on with you? How are the kids doing? Is Brian going to camp this year?"

Kids? Was this guy married?

"Yes, he's really looking forward to it! Lindsey isn't quite ready to go so I am not going to force her. Her mother wasn't too happy about it but that's too bad."

"Well, it looks like you have a lovely companion," Sid went on, nodding at Madeline. Mark made the proper introductions before the older man politely excused himself and sauntered off to the other end of the massive room.

"He's a great guy," Mark explained. "We worked together at First America Bank as mortgage loan officers back in the 80's. Now he runs an awesome camp for teenagers in Lake Okeechobee; my son is so excited about going to it this year."

"So you have two kids? Are you married?" Her tone bordered on anger as she thought of her philandering boss and his unsuspecting wife. If this guy thought she was just some lonely single girl looking for a quick hook-up he was terribly mistaken.

"What? Oh no, Madeline, I'm divorced. I've been divorced for five years, though I was recently engaged to someone." He looked at her sheepishly as her initial relief transformed into defensiveness again.

"Engaged?"

"Well I was until about a month ago."

"Really, what happened? You seem so charming." It wasn't like her to lace her words with sarcasm, but between recent heartache and job dissatisfaction, she was quickly losing patience for this kind of nonsense.

"No, the problem is she's from Connecticut, where her family owns a thriving restaurant business. I can't get her to relocate here and with my kids, I certainly can't move there. So there was really no way to work it out."

He was somewhat oblivious to her slightly harsh reaction, distracted by her pretty face and long, flowing hair.

"Oh, that makes sense," she concurred, softening. "So did you at least get the ring back?" He erupted in laughter.

"Yes—well, she agreed to give it back; I don't actually have it yet, but I will in a few weeks," he affirmed.

"Good for you, I suppose."

After that inauspicious beginning, the date took on new and enjoyable life as they chatted easily about everything from growing up in the northeast to admiring Ronald Reagan, though Madeline had been too young both times to vote for her favorite modern President. At ten years her senior, Mark recalled proudly pulling the lever twice, concurrently ushering in prosperity in the forms of a lucrative lending career and a successful real estate "flipping" business.

Funny, she never would've guessed his age; his youthful appearance and laid-back personality made him seem much younger. And his spontaneous sense of humor was a welcome change from most of the other men she'd observed in these parts. While no doubt an accomplished businessman, he didn't appear to be consumed by an inflated ego.

She learned of his upbringing in southeastern Connecticut, his ill-advised marriage at 21 to his high school sweetheart and his eventual move to Boca Raton more than a decade prior. Soon after the young family's arrival in the Sunshine State, his ex had embarked upon a string of secret affairs until he'd finally uncovered the truth. That led to an eventual divorce and tough financial times, from which he believed he was at last emerging. He relayed to her that while he currently lived in a nice villa in Windwood, a northeastern Boca community, he viewed it as nothing more than a transitional place—a temporary shelter until he could purchase another single family home.

When the conversation shifted to her and the inevitable question of what brought her to Florida, Madeline was prepared with a well-rehearsed answer.

"Oh, you know I was born and raised in the Philly area and never lived anywhere else. And though I'm really close to my family I just needed a change of scenery. When I did my research, it seemed like things were really happening here. So, one day when I realized I was free and single, I decided to just take a chance and do it."

"Wow, that's really brave," he complimented her. "I give you a lot of credit for making such a big move on your own. Most people come here with spouses or significant others. But after what happened to me, maybe you've got the right idea."

In spite of her modesty, his compliment warmed her heart; her story was usually met with skepticism and disapproval from those who thought she was crazy, or worse—insensitive to her family's feelings. And for the first time in forever, Ken was the farthest thing from her mind.

"Well Madeline, it was a pleasure," Mark affirmed, kissing her cheek once more. They stood in the parking lot, having unknowingly used the same one upon their separate arrivals. Mark's car was just up the ramp from her white Le Baron, beside which they lingered for a few minutes.

"So I look forward to tomorrow; I will give you a call in the morning, and we'll go from there. Of course, if you can't get out of rehearsal, just page me. You have all my numbers, right?"

"Uh yes," she confirmed. "But I am pretty sure Rebecca will say yes; she's very easy going and we've practiced this routine a million times. If we don't have it right by now, it's never gonna happen. Besides, SunFest sounds like a lot of fun."

"It'll be a great time, I promise," he returned her smile and bid her farewell.

"Take care, Maddy. See you tomorrow."

"Bye Mark."

She slipped behind the wheel with renewed excitement and vigor, hopeful that Mark Donnelly would at the very least turn out to be a good and trusted friend. Still, when she recalled his handsome face, warm disposition, and masculine build, thoughts of friendship took a back seat to fantasies of romance, in spite of his having kids. At 27, Maddy had never dated anyone with this so-called baggage, but she was certainly open-minded enough to give it a whirl. How bad could it be after everything she'd experienced with childless men? Maybe this guy would actually demonstrate some maturity.

Driving west on Glades Road on his way to his brother's home, Mark wondered what he'd gotten himself into. Sure, Madeline was a cute girl, but that was the problem—she was just a kid. And in spite of being smart, personable and pretty, there was something just too innocent about her; something he couldn't quite put his finger on. Then there was Gina, a woman with whom he'd planned to spend the rest of his life as recently as last month. In spite of the break-up, she still intended to fly down for Memorial Day weekend as planned.

True, the visit's real purpose was to return the two-carat diamond he'd given her, but still, it was going to be a long three days in the Keys. Maybe there was too much going on in his life to take on anyone new, particularly a recently relocated young woman. While she seemed fairly self-assured, the last thing he needed was somebody else depending on him. Maddy was a babe-in-the-woods where South Florida was concerned; she was in for a rude awakening.

"Of course, you can go!" Rebecca bubbled over, her cute face lit up with palpable enthusiasm. They'd just completed rehearsal, and she and Lloyd were preparing to lock up the studio. "I'm so thrilled you met a nice guy, and I hear SunFest is a blast. We had something like it in Sarasota where I grew up, but from what I've heard, this blows away every festival in the state."

"Thanks, Rebecca," she replied, hugging her friend.

"No problem, honey. You've got the routine down pat anyway; you and Scott make a great dance pair." She was referring to Maddy's partner, a genuinely nice guy with wavy dark hair and a neat beard and mustache. With his tall, lanky build, he defined the stereotype of a ballroom dancer, though Maddy was self-conscious about him having to lift her in the air during the course of their Addams Family tango routine.

Then again, the entire production made her uncomfortable, though she'd never dare back out. But as she began her short commute home, she vowed to get up early the next day and use the treadmill in her apartment complex. There were still a few weeks to go before the big night; perhaps she could shed a pound or two. And while it was too late to really make a difference for tomorrow, she'd still feel good for having made the effort.

She headed down scenic Southwest 18th Street, picturing the clothes that hung in her walk-in closet, imagining which one of her many ensembles would flatter her figure the most, in anticipation of her big date with Mark.

Madeline entered the stillness of the fitness room for a 7 a.m. session with the treadmill. Normally bustling during the work week, the small, but well-equipped gym was typically devoid of exercisers on the weekends. Armed with a Walkman and a bottle of water, she was ready for a vigorous, heart-pumping workout as she flipped on the light and quickly got started. Before long, she power-walked up to a speed of 4.9, her ponytail swinging wildly while she visualized the forthcoming day's activities, eagerly anticipating meeting Mark's family and enjoying a renowned South Florida event. Meanwhile, as Mark maneuvered through the heavy traffic on I-95 on his way to class, he came to a decision.

Entering the air-conditioned sanctuary of her apartment, a sweaty Madeline wiped her forehead with a towel as she proceeded directly into the shower. Invigorated by the pulsing stream of water and an elevated heart rate, she closed her eyes and imagined a new and fulfilling life without Kenny. It wasn't until a few minutes later when she tied her short terry-cloth robe around her waist and headed to the fridge for a cold bottle of water that she noticed the blinking red light on her answering machine. And as she listened to Mark's outgoing message, her heart was once again consumed by sorrow, anger and frustration.

Madeline, this is Mark. Uh, listen, I'm sorry about this, but there's been a change of plans. Since I am already in West Palm Beach, it's not really convenient to drive all the way back to Boca to pick you up. Actually...that's not the real reason...the real reason is that I'm kind of torn up by Catholic guilt. You know, I just broke off my engagement, and I just don't think it's right for me to start anything new right now. I'm really sorry. Uh, I hope you have a great weekend anyway. Take care.

She listened to his recording again to confirm its authenticity since her life was beginning to feel like an episode of The Twilight Zone, filled with surreal happenings that defied logic and understanding.

Had she somehow misread his interest in her in spite of their enjoyable conversation over drinks last night? Did she say or do something to turn him off as they sat at the bar talking? Had this whole thing been a ploy to determine if he really liked her enough in person to commit to taking her to SunFest? If so, why mention it all until he had a chance to hang out with her for a while?

She sank into the couch as she mentally replayed every detail of her experience with Mark Donnelly, beginning with his surprising phone call to her office. It was more than a bit ironic that she was the one who made the impression on him; when she recalled her embarrassment over her inability to remember his face, she laughed bitterly. Apparently, this man had so little regard for her feelings he had no qualms about brushing her off at the last minute for a date *he* initiated. It reminded her of Gary Snyder back in Ocean City that summer, though to his dubious credit, at least he'd had the guts to dump her in person.

A ringing phone suddenly pierced the silence, forcing her to her feet; she didn't bother to pick up until she heard the familiar voice begin to record another message.

"Mark," she greeted him sternly, "This is Madeline. I was at the gym when you called before."

"So I take it you got my message?"

"Loud and clear."

"Look, I'm sorry Madeline. It is the truth, though; I am feeling really guilty about taking another woman out so soon after breaking my engagement. I know it sounds crazy, but Gina is coming down in a few weeks to officially return the ring and until then it seems wrong to get involved with anyone else."

"Involved? Mark, we weren't picking out China patterns, we were going to a music festival with a bunch of other people. Remember, I even canceled my plans so I could go with you after you invited me? I don't know what kind of game you're playing here, but you can count me out."

"I'm really sorry, Maddy," he repeated sheepishly.

"So am I," she retorted as she hung up the phone.

"Maddy! What are you doing here?" Rebecca asked incredulously, looking up from the turntable that was set up on one end of the large, hardwood floor. Behind her, the rest of the dance team lined up in formation, with the studio's receptionist taking Madeline's place in front of Scott.

"Ugh; don't ask. Do you mind if I practice today? I'm so mad I have to burn off some energy."

"Of course, you can practice, sweetie." Rebecca placed an arm around her as they joined the rest of the group.

"Kel, you've got to be kidding me!" Maddy exclaimed.

"No honey, I'm not I swear. He's on line one. Do you want me to just take a message?"

"Nah, let's see what he wants."

"Madeline?" he responded to her curt greeting.

"Yes. What can I do for you?"

"Uh, I just wanted to see if you were going to the business card exchange tonight at the Colony Hotel on Atlantic Avenue."

"I'm aware of it, but I'm not going because I have dance rehearsal tonight." Her tone remained firm and polite, though inside she was seething. *He had some nerve contacting her after leading her on and ruining her weekend.*

"Oh, sorry I won't see you there," he replied. "You know, I heard you were in the building the other day; you should've stopped by to see me."

Was this guy serious?

"Well I was there to see Isabella on official business; I didn't have time for anything else."

"Ok, well if your plans change tonight, maybe I'll see you?"

"No, I doubt it. I also have to practice my solo. And I still have a lot to wrap up here before I can leave for the studio. Enjoy the card exchange."

With that, she returned the receiver to its cradle, confident she'd just had her final conversation with yet another master of mixed signals.

Chapter 21

Rebecca, Lloyd, and Madeline piled into Madeline's car and headed down Interstate 95 to the outdoor bazaar, where they hoped to find some inexpensive costumes for their routines after a long day of rehearsal. Rebecca sang along with the radio as she drove, while Lloyd and Madeline reclined in their seats, enjoying the rush of air from open windows. Between the blaring music and noisy wind, Madeline barely heard the familiar jingle of her pager. She pulled it off her belt buckle and looked at the screen.

Hmm, I don't recognize that number, she thought. Rebecca, catching her in the rearview mirror, yelled above the din.

"Who's paging you?"

"I have no idea!"

"Maybe it's the jerk from last weekend, calling to apologize."

"I doubt that very much."

But while skeptical, heart skipped a beat at the possibility. Even after everything he'd done, she still felt a strange affinity for him.

They arrived at the Swap Shop and pulled into the parking lot near the drive-in movie screens. Although it was nearly five o'clock, the place was still packed with bargain-hunters and vendors. Young children ran around the fairgrounds squealing while their parents searched for the best buys under the outdoor tents. As the threesome scanned endless rows of tables brimming with everything from signature perfumes to designer sunglasses, Madeline felt overwhelmed. The early summer heat was beginning to wear on her as she dutifully sorted through dresses with Rebecca.

"Hey, what do you think of this little black one for my opening number?" Rebecca asked, holding up a sequined mini-dress with a plunging neckline. "You don't think it's too sexy, do you?" She pressed the garment against her shapely body to get a rough idea of its dimensions.

"No, I don't think so," Madeline replied, noting Rebecca's ample figure with a twinge of jealousy. "You'll look stunning in that."

"Yeah, well I'll let you know how much of a stunner it is the morning after," joked. "With all of this rehearsing, Lloyd and I haven't had much time or energy for each other."

"That should solve the problem," Madeline remarked brightly, wishing she had a husband at home to dress up for. Thoughts of Ken and what might have been flashed through her mind until another musical page interrupted her musings.

"Ugh, sometimes I just hate this stupid thing," she groaned as she pulled the unit from her purse. The same unfamiliar phone number appeared again on the screen. She frowned, and then tossed the pager back into her bag.

"Aren't you even a little curious to see who it is?" Rebecca asked. "Someone is obviously hell-bent on getting in touch with you."

"Maybe it's just a wrong number?" Madeline wondered, noticing the skepticism on her friend's face.

"C'mon, aren't you just a tiny bit curious to see if it is Mark?"

"No," she protested, unconvincingly.

"I don't believe you. He's all you've talked about for the past week despite what he did. Look at it this way, maybe he's calling to sincerely apologize, and this could be your last big opportunity to let him have it...or give him another chance."

"What? I am still so ticked off about last weekend. Why on earth would I give him another chance to hurt me?"

She bristled as thoughts of Ken's engagement flooded her mind and tortured her heart; Mark's standing her up at the last minute had reopened a wound that was barely beginning to heal.

"Beats me," Rebecca shrugged. "But I don't think your cheeks are flushed because you are excited to be hanging out with me at the flea market."

"Oh, all right; I'll go find a phone and call."

"Atta girl!" Rebecca cheered, turning her attention back to the black dress.

Despite her lingering anger over the entire incident, Madeline secretly hoped the caller was Mark. And yet she was angry at herself for wishing so. After Ken, she swore she'd never let another man make a fool of her and here she was, frantically searching for a phone, negotiating her way through throngs of agitated shoppers under the blazing summer sun. At last, she spotted a phone booth in the distance. *Someday these will be all but extinct*, she thought. Although she did own a cell phone now, in true fashion, she had left it at home charging on the kitchen counter.

Madeline held the receiver to her ear and drew a deep breath as it rang.

"Hello?" A female voice at the other end of the line sounded rather annoyed as Madeline fought the urge to hang up.

"Uh, hello, my name is Madeline Rose, and I just received a call from someone at this number?" She cringed at her timidity.

"You're who?" the stern voice demanded.

"Madeline Rose," she repeated slowly. "I've received three pages today from this number. Maybe it's a mistake. I am sorry I bothered you."

"No, wait!" Her voice softened a little. "I think you're the girl Mark was trying to call. He's not here now, but he'll be back soon."

"Oh, ok. Well, could you just tell him—"

"Here, I am going to put his daughter on the phone. You can give her the message," the woman interrupted. Then Madeline heard her yell, "Lindsey!"

There was silence for a second, then a young girl's voice.

"Hello?" It was definitely a first for Madeline, speaking to a potential boyfriend's child.

"Hi, this is Madeline," she responded warmly. "Could you just tell your dad I am not at home right now, but I will be in about a half-hour? He can call me then."

"Ok, he'll be back soon. He had to take my brother to a party."

"Great, well just let him know I did get his page, and I'll be home soon. He has my number."

"Ok, I'll tell him," she promised sweetly. "Thanks, Lindsey."

"You're welcome. Bye!"

"Goodbye."

Madeline hung up the phone in disbelief – so it had been Mark trying to reach her, but why?

"Hot date tonight?" Lloyd's familiar voice startled her; she spun around to find him standing there, holding two plastic shopping bags.

"No, I don't," she replied indignantly. "At least not yet."

"So it was Mr. Sunfest calling?"

"Yes, but he wasn't there when I called back. I wonder what he wants."

"My guess would be you."

"So what's in the bags?" she asked brightly, changing the subject.

"Just some shirts I got on sale. Nothing I can use in the show, but good for work." He proudly removed his purchases from the plastic to show her.

"Nice," she responded approvingly. "Where's Rebecca? I'm ready to get out of this place. It's too hot to shop."

"She's coming. We're about ready for a swim in your apartment pool. Besides, it's almost closing time."

Rebecca joined them momentarily, and they returned to the car. As they headed north again towards Boca, Madeline hid her excitement as she wondered what the evening would bring.

"We'll see you down there Madeline!" Rebecca called with a smile as she and Lloyd headed out the door of the apartment.

"Ok," she called over her shoulder. She was waiting for a response from the other end of the line as she paced in her bedroom holding the cordless phone to her ear. When they'd arrived back at her place, a message from Mark was waiting for her; now hopefully they would actually connect although the prospect made her a bit nervous.

What was there to say? How was she supposed to act?

She didn't want to be too friendly, yet she didn't want to give him the satisfaction of knowing how deeply his actions had hurt her.

"Hello?"

Finally, the baritone voice she was happy to hear again, in spite of everything.

"Mark?"

"Hey, Madeline." His tone was warm and friendly.

"That wasn't your ex-wife or ex-fiancée was it?"

"Oh, no, that's Renee, my friend's wife."

"From the way she sounded, I wasn't sure. I felt like I was intruding or something. She didn't seem too happy to talk to me."

"I apologize. That's just her way when she hosts parties. She tends to get a little frazzled, but I'm sure she didn't mean to be rude. They had a birthday party for their two-year-old son today. That's where I am right now."

"Well, I am sorry for not getting in touch with you sooner, but we rehearsed all day, then headed down to the flea market and—"

"Did you eat?"

"Yes, well actually we had a big lunch, and I am still full."

"Are you sure? My friend Bill is a caterer and he made a terrific meal today. They have so much food they don't know what to do with it all. Can I interest you in coming over?" It was a tempting offer, but Madeline decided against it.

"Thanks, but my friends are down by the pool and I just can't be rude and leave them."

"Oh." He hesitated for only a second. "Well, what are you doing later? My brother is in town for the weekend, and we're going to the Acapulco Grill tonight. My daughter is babysitting his son so we can get away. Would you like to join us?"

"Where are you going?"

"It's this little neighborhood place. Nothing fancy but they have good bands. It gets pretty crowded on Saturday nights, so we're going over early. It gets crazy, though. People dance on the tables." He laughed, apparently amused by the thought.

"Do you?"

"Uh, depends on how much I've had to drink," he answered with a laugh. Something about the sound of his voice stirred those familiar sensations within her.

"I guess I could handle that," she replied evenly, masking her growing excitement. Ignoring her better judgment, she welcomed the idea of seeing him again. "What time are you going?"

"Around nine."

"Can I meet you there?" Though planning to show, she wanted to keep him guessing; he still wasn't off the hook for the previous weekend.

"Sure."

"Mark?"

"Yes?"

"You won't stand me up, this time, will you?"

"No, we'll both be there at nine o'clock," he promised sheepishly.

"Ok, I probably won't get there until about nine-thirty."

"That's fine. We'll be waiting."

Madeline inspected herself from head to toe as she stood in front of her full-length mirror. She and Rebecca had chosen a floral print mini-dress, a blend of cotton and lycra that would look sexy and help her stay cool in the heat. It buttoned down the front and tied loosely in the back, softly accentuating her waist. Its A-line skirt and short length set off her shapely legs, as did the black strappy sandals she wore.

She'd curled her long, auburn hair and secured it into a loose ponytail with a rhinestone clasp. Her preference had been to let it fall softly around her shoulders and down her back but she knew that was asking for trouble in the ever-increasing humidity. After applying a rosy shade of lipstick and tossing her ID and some money into a smaller bag, she hurried out the door.

"He sure wasn't kidding when he said this place wasn't fancy," she thought aloud as she pulled her car into a spot on the dirt in front of the railroad tracks. It was one of the few spaces left within comfortable walking distance. The music that had penetrated the glass of her car windows assaulted her eardrums as she made her way towards the entrance.

As she maneuvered through the crowd of partiers ranging in age from 21 to 50, Madeline wondered why on Earth she ever agreed to this. Not only was she sick to death of this scene, she hated walking into it alone. "God help him if he stands me up again," she muttered under her breath. A hand on her arm detained her from further entry.

"ID please!" a male voice demanded. She looked up to see a rather large, masculine bouncer whose baby face betrayed his young age, his impressive physique notwithstanding.

"Sure," she answered, fumbling for her driver's license.

He looked at the card and then studied her face for a second. "You sure don't look that old," he commented, knitting his brow.

"I'm well preserved," she retorted. "Can I go in now?"

"Go ahead," He chuckled as he watched her disappear into the crowd.

Replacing her ID to her purse, Madeline walked into the smoky room, feigning confidence. The odor of stale beer and cigarettes hung in the air, diffused only slightly by the ceiling fans that spun furiously overhead. She stared straight ahead as she made her way to the bar, ignoring the eyes she felt upon her.

People checking out other people, that's what these places were all about. Upscale or casual, it didn't matter. She felt a wave of relief when she spotted Mark sitting by the bar in a pair of jeans shorts and a white golf shirt. She almost didn't recognize him; up to this point, she'd only seen him in business suits. As if sensing her presence, he turned away from his conversation to look at her. He smiled as she approached.

"Madeline," he greeted her with a peck on the cheek.

"Hi," she smiled sweetly.

"Uh, this is my brother, John," he explained, motioning to the dark- haired man seated next to him.

"Nice to meet you," she called over the music. "Want a beer?"

"What?" She was straining to hear him. He gestured toward the mug sitting on the bar next to him.

"Oh, I'll just have some cranberry juice, thanks."

She didn't feel the need to offer an explanation, but Mark, of course, had already surmised she was a lightweight, based on their previous meeting at the Baci bar. It was just one of the many qualities that separated her from most of the women he knew.

The bartender set down her glass just as the band announced a short break.

"You were right," Madeline said, "The bands here are pretty good."

"Yeah, but deafening after a while," John noted.

"Not very conducive to conversation, I guess," Madeline smiled.

"Nope. But I warned you it got kind of crazy in here," Mark reminded her.

"I believe you told me there would be table dancing, but so far I haven't seen any. Unless you were both doing it before, I arrived."

"We haven't had nearly enough to drink yet," John explained, laughing in the same manner as his brother. But the similarities between them ended there since John had dark, wavy hair and mischievous brown eyes. He was slightly shorter than Mark, although just as well-built. As they chatted, Madeline discovered he worked for the fire department in West Palm Beach, had lost his wife over a year ago when she died in childbirth and spent most of his free time with his son, Michael. In spite of, or maybe because of the tragedy, he had a wonderful sense of humor.

As she sat on a bar stool in between the two brothers laughing and talking, Madeline was glad she came out. She felt right at home with them, discussing everything from politics to music to football. Amazingly, they shared the same conservative political views, along with a penchant for classic rock. But when she told them about her incredible experience at the final game of the 1980 World Series at Veterans Stadium, when the Phillies' Tug McGraw threw the final strike to beat the Kansas City Royals, Mark teasingly reminded her that she was "a Marlins girl now."

Every so often, though, John—who appeared somewhat preoccupied—would get up and leave for a few minutes. It never entered Madeline's mind that perhaps he was just trying to give his brother time alone with her, though considering where they were at the moment, it hardly seemed to matter. And as soon as the band returned, conversation would be nearly impossible again.

"Is something wrong?" she asked when he left them for the third time.

"No, he's just a little overprotective of his son. He keeps calling poor Lindsey to make sure everything is all right. I wish he would just relax. She watches Michael all the time, and there is never a problem. This is the first time he's been out like this in almost two years. I—everything ok?" Mark asked, acknowledging his brother's return. John nodded as the band took over again. Madeline couldn't help but dance in place when they cranked up one of her favorite dance songs.

"Why don't you two get out there?" John urged, motioning to the floor. Madeline wasted no time.

"Come on, let's dance," she ordered, taking Mark by the arm. "You have enough beers in you."

He followed her lead to the postage stamp-sized floor.

"Now, don't put me to shame just because you're a professional!" he called over the music. They sweated it out on the tiny floor to a set of upbeat songs, including the Gin Blossoms' *Jealousy*, a track Madeline hadn't heard in a while. Despite his earlier reticence, Mark demonstrated some excellent moves, much to her delight. It was nice to know Ken wasn't the only good-looking man who could cut a rug.

Taking Mark's hands in hers, she attempted to give him a crash lesson in swing, not an easy feat given the volume of the music and the limited area in which to move. She laughed as he teased her with his own original moves. The world spun around and around until finally, the music rose to a crashing crescendo, and then faded away.

"We're going to slow things down a bit," the lead singer announced, as a slow ballad began. Madeline's heart skipped a beat as she recognized the familiar notes of the intro. Then the drummer—a big, burly guy with an amazingly strong voice—launched into a haunting version of Elton John's *The One*.

Oh great! It isn't bad enough that out of all of the love songs in the world, they had to sing this one, but Mark's just standing there looking like a fish out of water. Now what?

They locked eyes awkwardly for a moment, but just as she was about to suggest going back to the bar, he slipped his arms around her waist. They began to sway to the music as he held her body close to his. Overlooking his embarrassment at having worked up a noticeable sweat, he focused on the feel of her against him, and as he caressed her neck and shoulders, he breathed in the sweet smell of her perfume. She rested her head against his chest and closed her eyes, wishing the moment could go on forever. It felt so good to be in a man's arms again, and his strong yet gentle embrace was intoxicating. The feel of his hands massaging their way up and down her back sent a current of electricity through her entire body.

There would be plenty of time to confront him once the dance was over. She still wanted, and in fact, *deserved* answers. But for now, it was enough to savor these incredible feelings. John, however, had other ideas as he abruptly interrupted them with a tap on Mark's shoulder.

"I'm ready to go," he loudly informed his brother.

Mark reluctantly released her, and the threesome made their way back to the bar. Madeline pulled her tousled hair out of the rhinestone clasp, which had lost its grip on the dance floor. She gathered it on top of her head in an effort to cool off, trying hard not to stare while the brothers had a private conference. Moving further down the counter, she picked up a napkin and pressed it against her face. A minute later she felt Mark's breath in her ear.

"John wants to leave," he whispered. "We came in one car."

"Well, what do you want to do?" she challenged, her eyes carefully studying his face.

"I'd like to stay here with you?" he asked, hopefully.

"I suppose I could drive you home later if you're nice to me," she teased. I'll even walk you to your door if you'd like."

She was glad John was heading out for more than one reason. Attraction notwithstanding, Mark was far from absolved from his past behavior. Somehow she would find the strength to confront him about Sunfest. That is, if her mounting passion didn't get in the way first.

Mark smiled, took her face in his hands and planted a light kiss on her cheek. "You're a sweetheart." He tossed the keys to John, who left after exchanging pleasantries. She watched him fade into the night and thought *no more excuses*. It was long past time to get her answers.

As she mentally rehearsed the proper way to approach everything, she felt his arm around her waist again. A shiver of excitement ran up and down her spine.

"Do you want some more cranberry juice?" he asked.

"Sure."

His blue eyes held her for a second before he motioned to the bartender again, glad to be alone with her, finally. Amid the loud, sultry atmosphere he didn't fight the urge to give her a real kiss, and before another word was said, he took her by the shoulders and placed his warm lips on hers. Startled, but enjoying the feel of his strong, warm body close to her, she responded happily until he slipped his tongue in her mouth, which prompted her to draw back.

"I have a question for you," she announced.

"What is it?" he asked reluctantly, staring straight ahead. He'd had a feeling this was coming. Not that he didn't deserve it.

Madeline continued, ignoring the butterflies in her stomach; confrontation was still not one of her favorite things. "What makes this weekend different from last weekend? I mean, last weekend you uninvited me to Sunfest because you were bothered by—as you put it—'Catholic guilt' over your ex-fiancée. Fine. Maybe you really did feel bad about taking another girl out so soon, but it was still a pretty crummy thing to do, especially since *you* were the one who asked *me* out. I didn't chase you. In fact, I couldn't even remember meeting you at the business card exchange the day you called me at work to invite me out for a drink. Never mind that all we were talking about was a day at a festival, not a lifetime commitment or anything."

She was on a roll as her pent-up frustration erupted in a flowing stream of consciousness. He remained quiet as he listened, realizing there were no excuses for his behavior.

"Being Catholic myself, I do understand guilt, although in this case it seems like it was just a B.S. excuse to get out of a date. What I don't understand is why you called me three times this past week and invited me here tonight. Are you suddenly over it, or was it that you just get a better offer last weekend?"

"You think I took someone else?" He was amazed that someone this attractive would believe that. True, she was a total departure from the fake, surgically altered women of South Florida, which was one of the reasons why he felt a strong attraction to her. Especially now that he was a legally a free man, Mark was constantly hit on by superficial females looking to latch onto a successful man. As arrogant as it sounded, he could basically have any woman he wanted.

But Mark was more than just a handsome face; he was a down-to- earth guy who wanted a real woman to share his life. And as a father, he was not about to subject his kids to more drama. They'd already been through quite enough. Unfortunately, his cold feet had led Madeline to believe he was just another shallow jerk, like most of the men – and women – in this town.

"It did cross my mind. What was I supposed to think after you dumped me at the last second? I thought maybe you and your fiancée had gotten back together or something."

"No, that's not true," he protested honestly. "Gina and I are over. She can't commit to me by moving here, and since I have no intention of leaving my kids, there was no way it could work. But for some reason, I did feel guilty about having a date with another woman so soon, especially one like you. I know I acted like a jerk— hell I am a jerk. But I am really sorry." He looked deeply into her eyes as he spoke, nearly mesmerized by their startling intensity.

"Do you feel guilty right now?" She desperately wanted to believe in his sincerity.

He responded by putting his arms around her.

"Do I look like I feel guilty?" He flashed a smile worthy of a toothpaste commercial.

She fought to maintain her composure while her body reacted to his touch with a display of inner fireworks.

"No, but you can understand why I am a little skeptical, can't you? I almost decided not to come here tonight so you could get a little dose of your own medicine." It was hard to ignore the chills running up and down her spine, but she was determined to at least appear strong and in control. She was no match for his charms, however.

"Then why did you come?" His voice was barely a whisper as he leaned in close to her ear. More shivers.

"I-I guess I wanted to give you another chance to redeem yourself. I was hoping you were really a nice guy who just did something stupid." She trembled as he stroked her hair.

"I'm sorry," he repeated softly. "Can I have another chance?" But before she could answer, he began kissing her hair, her ear, and her cheek, working his way to her neck while his hands remained on her waist. As she rested her hands on his shoulders, she felt his muscles twitch beneath her fingers.

"I think I could be persuaded," she managed to utter in response before his lips were on hers again. This time, she didn't resist when he slipped his tongue into her mouth.

Chapter 22

So, where to now?" Mark asked as they walked arm-in-arm to her car. The night air had turned cool as a gentle breeze rustled the palm trees. It was a welcome relief after four hours in a stuffy bar.

"How about the fishing pier in Deerfield? It's so beautiful out now, I'd like to walk by the ocean."

"Sure," he said, drawing her into another intoxicating kiss. Neither one of them could keep their hands off of each other; it was as if some magnetic force had taken over once the apology had been given and accepted. Still, she wondered what he might be anticipating from the evening, knowing she would not be consenting to consummating their budding relationship on this particular date. It was simply way too soon. And charisma and clean-cut good looks notwithstanding, they barely knew each other.

Coming up for air, Madeline ordered him to drive, and tossed him her keys. At every stoplight on the way, he leaned over to kiss her. Every ensuing kiss had an intensity that surpassed the previous one as if years of pent-up emotion were spilling out in gradual waves. Any lingering thoughts of Ken were completely eradicated as Madeline lost herself in Mark's touch. She ran her fingers through his thick hair and pursued his lips hungrily; it had been so long since she'd been held by a man, she'd almost forgotten how good it could feel.

Yet there was something she did not trust. Maybe she was still reeling inside from Ken's impending wedding announcement and of course, Mark's recent actions, in spite of his sincere apology. She couldn't help but wonder where this was all heading. Mark was a man with needs after all, and she realized she could only satisfy his burning desire to a certain extent tonight. Would he accept that? For goodness' sake, it was only their second date. But after living in her new area a relatively short amount of time, she'd discovered that its dating mores dramatically differed from the ones to which she'd been accustomed.

Worse, here was a man who'd been somebody's husband for 15 years, a father to two children, and a fiancée to another woman for God knows how long. He never did specify the length of his engagement, though obviously its demise had been fairly recent. Regardless, it was a safe bet that his experience in these matters far exceeded hers. Although she'd been in many intimate situations with Ken during the time they were together, he always maintained the proper boundaries, at Madeline's insistence; much to his credit, Ken had shown admirable restraint, despite their intense passion and chemistry.

But Ken had also been her exact same age—quite literally—and there was a comfort level knowing he'd never been committed to someone else in a legal sense. True, he'd been sexually involved with at least two other women she knew of, and possibly even a few he'd never told her about, but his heart had definitely been in finding the right girl to settle down with. One thing she'd known for sure: Kenny was not a player. The jury was still out on Mark.

Besides, the prospect of being with someone new—someone who'd not only been around the block but who could so easily and skillfully awaken the same simultaneously powerful and terrifying sensations within her—was unsettling. And the night was still young.

When they finally arrived at their destination, Madeline was grateful for the opportunity to get out and walk, hoping a stroll in the night air would help recover her poise. Mark pulled out two dollars and paid the clerk at the pier entrance, then took her by the hand and led her through the gate. Ahead of them, the fishing pier stretched out expansively toward the dark Atlantic, which was illuminated only by the gleaming full moon above. A blanket of stars twinkled above an array of determined fishermen positioned all along the railway. Upon reaching the end, Mark and Madeline paused to take in a view of the coastline; in the distance, the high rises lining A1A to the north and south spread out magically, as though forming an ethereal backdrop for an enchanted storybook land.

"I love it out here," she enthused. "When I first moved down I used to come here two to three times a week after work. But since I moved a little further west it hasn't been as convenient. I need to make the time, though, because I forget about everything when I'm out here. I suppose I should thank Ken in a way. If it weren't for him, I might never have moved here at tall. Maybe that was his real purpose in my life."

Having decided to drop the pretenses, she'd come clean with him about her real motivation for moving to Florida, somewhere between Palmetto Park Road and Hillsboro Boulevard during the short ride over.

"Whatever the reason, I'm glad you're here," he whispered, pulling her close to him. As he initiated another kiss, she breathed in the smell of spicy cologne mingled with salty sea air. Standing on her toes to reach him, she ran her fingers through his hair and lost herself in the moment. Their kiss would have gone on indefinitely if not for the obnoxious shouts of approaching teenagers; the vibrations caused by their running shoes hitting the boards created a striking contrast to the romantic interlude.

"I guess we should be moving along," he said, still holding his arms around her.

"I guess so." She wishing the night would never end.

They were halfway to the beach when he sat down on an empty bench, situating Madeline on his lap as he did so. Once settled, his lips sought hers demandingly, while his hands kneaded her back, moving from her waist to her shoulders. Fastening her arms around his neck, she tried to lose herself in the moment. Yet inner turmoil prevented her from fully dissolving. *Can someone like me handle a man ten years older than me with infinitely more life experience? Will he have the patience to take things slowly?*

After all, it hadn't been that long since Ken had broken her heart. And as much as she loved Florida, moving so far from family had been a big adjustment. True, she'd made friends along the way, but she wasn't quite ready to risk another heartbreak. As if jolted back to reality, she abruptly released her mouth from his. He looked up at her questioningly.

"What's wrong?"

"Nothing," she whispered. "Could you just hold me for a minute?"

"Sure," He wrapped his arms around her, and she rested her head against his chest, savoring the warmth of his body as he kissed her forehead.

"You're a very warm person, aren't you?" he whispered, burying his head in her hair.

"I suppose I am," she agreed, raising her head to look up at him. "You seem to be the same way."

He gazed into the depths of her brown eyes, noticing that she seemed completely unaware of their bewitching allure. All he wanted to do was act upon the burning impulses he felt for Madeline—to sweep her away and show her how truly desirable she was. Instead, he answered her statement with a powerful, wet kiss that left them both nearly breathless until she suddenly broke away again.

Moving to the rail, she closed her eyes and focused on the sensation of a rush of wind through her hair.

"Did I do something wrong?" She felt his hot breath on her neck and turned to face him again.

"No, of course not," she whispered. *Actually, the problem is that everything you are doing to me feels too good.* "It's just that...well, I-I was hoping I wouldn't have to deal with this so soon, but the way things are heating up here, I don't think I have a choice."

"What is it?" he asked, as he smoothed her hair with his hands. He couldn't imagine what could possibly be terrible enough to compel her to interrupt such a pleasant activity. Knowing instinctively that Madeline wasn't the typical self-absorbed *Boca babe*, he was truly puzzled. Besides, he'd seen and heard it all in his fifteen years of living here; there was nothing a sweet, girl-next-door-type like her could confess that would shock him, though he was impressed by the passion she'd demonstrated this evening.

"Mark, I've never really been with a man in the Biblical sense. I know it sounds far-fetched, given that I am twenty-eight-years-old, but it's true. As much as I loved Ken dearly, I wanted to wait—hopefully until the day we got married. And he was really good about it, although I felt like it was asking too much of him, even though, damn it, I just plain wanted to— wanted to satisfy my own curiosity. But I could never let it happen. Soon after, he disappeared from my life, and I felt that somehow I was being punished even though I'd done the right thing."

As she spoke, she held her head against his chest, staring out at the beach, yet not really focusing her vision on anything. Baring her soul to a man she'd only known a week was a thousand times more intimate than anything they'd done thus far; it seemed safer not to make eye contact. She was painfully embarrassed by her naiveté, but it was too late to turn back now. And when he kept holding her in silence, she continued.

"As you know, I also had the Catholic upbringing, close family, all of that thank God. My parents are wonderful, fun-loving people, but they do have high moral standards. From the time I was old enough to understand, I was told that sex was something reserved for marriage. Of course, that was all I was told. Any other information came either from my school friends or soap operas. I felt so guilty when Ken and I would get into these very intimate situations.

"But at least it was a long-term relationship; one I thought would lead to marriage, and our eventual union in every sense of the word. Anyway, unfairly or not, my Mom was not a big fan of his in the beginning, which almost ended things before they even got started. And then we moved beyond that and into what I thought was a lifetime relationship. To this day, she has no idea I moved here to be with him. Guess it doesn't matter now."

"So she assumes you're still a—"

"I guess," she finished the thought for him. "We never talk about it. Sort of an unspoken understanding we have. I know that when compared to most people my age, I'm a late-bloomer. And Ken hurt me so badly it may take a while to trust someone enough to ever give myself away like that at all. Are you disappointed?"

Having listened intently, he enveloped her in his arms as a stiff wind began to blow. Her vulnerability, combined with her undeniable beauty tugged at his heart. While he wanted her to the point he couldn't see straight, he also felt an uncontrollable desire to protect her; he only hoped he could live up to her expectations.

"If you are asking to move slowly, that's fine with me. I mean, don't get me wrong, I'd like nothing better than to go back to your place and make wild, passionate love to you all night. But I understand where you're coming from. I've been celibate for a long time myself... not as long as you, though," he added. They both cracked up at his joke.

"So, you're willing to give this a try? I won't make you wait forever; I just need a little time."

"It's ok," he assured her, hoping he'd be able to fulfill his promise.

Having had enough of the beach for one night, they returned to her white Le Baron. As Madeline strapped herself securely in the bucket seat, she was fairly certain that this time he would drive her to his villa, bid her goodnight and leave her to replay the evening's events alone in her apartment. Instead, he paused as he brought the key to the ignition, then turned his body toward her as far as the fastened seatbelt would allow.

She shifted in her seat to face him. Moonlight streamed through the windshield as their lips met again, gently at first, then with more force as he slipped his tongue into her mouth. The intensity of his probing both fascinated and frightened her; she froze for a moment, wanting to etch the sensation in her mind forever. When he stopped and pulled back a little, she looked at him questioningly.

"Go like this," he demanded with a whisper. She watched as he danced his tongue around the parameters of his own lips before fulfilling his request as best she could, expressing her growing passion as freely as her persistent self-control would allow.

"You're smooth," he whispered. She felt his hands on her waist and then sighed softly as they massaged her back, working their way up to her neck. With his left hand, he reached down to unlock his seatbelt, freeing himself to concentrate on her fully. Feeling flushed and breathless, she pressed her face close to his in an affectionate embrace, wanting to remember his scent forever. Mark complied and held her tightly for a moment. Then, placing a hand on her cheek, he turned her face to his and stared into her eyes.

"Kiss me, kiss me," he demanded firmly. In an instant, his mouth devoured hers once more as Madeline matched him in ferocity until it nearly overwhelmed her. Then he briefly paused again. She watched in admiration as he pulled his white golf shirt from the waistband of his jeans shorts and lifted it up, revealing a broad, masculine torso.

"Touch my chest." He reached for her hand and placed it on his skin as he moved in for another kiss. Madeline caressed his shoulders, agilely working her way down to his waist. Beneath her fingers, she felt the warmth of his skin and the rippling of well-toned muscles. His stomach contracted as she explored that area.

"Feels good," he groaned. Her hand lingered above his waist, moving back and forth slowly, lightly. "I'm afraid I've developed a beer belly from all the drinking I did tonight," he confessed.

Is he kidding?

"It's ok," was all she whispered in response as her hands continued their work. Mark gathered her auburn hair in his hands, holding it to one side while he hungrily pursued her neck.

"Is biting legal?" he asked, proceeding to nibble at her soft, inviting skin. Lost in her own emotions, she barely heard the question, which she left unanswered. Her silence did not hinder him; he moved to the front of her neck and inched his way lower as she closed her eyes and ran her hands through his sandy-colored hair. The nearby surf pounded with the rhythm of their breath. Then a touch in a new area shook her out of her reverie. She abruptly stopped and looked down at her inner thigh.

Reading her mind, he responded, "I promise I won't go any higher. I am trying to be really careful where I touch you. Too exhausted to argue, she gave into his tantalizing caresses. It was incredibly stupid in a way. After all, she was twenty-eight, not twelve. *What is really stopping me? It is technically only our second date. I don't even know him yet. He could hurt me if I'm not careful.*

Mark's hand stubbornly remained on her thigh, creating a rush of sensation in the part of her anatomy that defined her femininity. He buried his head in her chest, prying at the buttons on her dress with his teeth. Consumed by both desire and awe at his hunger for her, she did not resist when she felt the second button come undone, revealing the black lace of her bra.

His hands slowly fondled her breasts through the delicate fabric, sending chills throughout her body. He couldn't get enough of her silky soft skin, the floral scent of her perfume, the feel of her chest against his. He was about to free her from the bondage of lace and underwire when she suddenly caught his hand and pulled it away.

He moaned in protest, "I want to kiss your nipples."

Madeline straightened up in her seat and refastened the buttons on her dress as guilt overtook passion. "I'm so sorry," she whispered. "It's not that I don't want to. Please just give me some time." She lowered her eyes as she spoke, unable to look at him. Feeling a bit guilty for rushing her, he gently drew her into his arms.

"I'm the one who's sorry, Maddy. You just excite me so much I can barely control myself."

"The feeling is mutual."

Mark waved to the guard as he passed the security gate that marked the entrance to his neighborhood. Madeline, worn out from the night's adventures, rested her head against the soft velour of the car seat. Her eyes felt dry and tired, much in need of the re-wetting drops she'd forgotten when she switched to a smaller handbag. She almost never forgot them, especially when going out to a smoky bar, but her excitement over seeing Mark this evening had interfered with practical considerations. She quickly pulled out her compact to inspect her make-up and, as expected, her eyeliner and mascara were smudged on her pale skin, an inevitable side effect of hours of making out. She blinked her eyes in an attempt to moisten them.

In the darkness, it was difficult to distinguish the characteristics of Mark's community, though it appeared very secluded and quiet. Palm trees and hibiscus lined the main road, encircling alternating buildings of condos and villas. At this late hour, she was sure he'd send her off with a final goodnight kiss. She'd have to see his place another time.

But as they pulled into a parking space, he shut off the engine.

"Here we are," he announced. She quickly glanced at her watch. Two a.m. Had they really been together for five hours already?

"Want to come in?"

"It's late. What about your brother and the baby?" *What about my waning self-control?* "I don't want to wake anyone."

"We'll be quiet," he whispered. "They won't even know we're here."

In the dim light, the villa was quiet and still. Madeline followed Mark's lead into a ceramic tiled foyer, stepping gingerly as he held her hand behind him and brought her into a large kitchen, where the swirling air from a ceiling fan gently played with her disheveled hair. She watched as he opened a door and peered inside.

"John's out cold," he announced.

He then led her into a den with a light oak entertainment center on one wall and beautiful white leather sofas on the other. Most striking though, were the many decorative picture frames adorning the room. From them, smiling faces of family and friends put the finishing touches on a warm and cozy environment.

Still holding Madeline's hand, Mark carefully opened another door, revealing a small figure in the semi-darkness. A young girl was fast asleep in her bed, completely oblivious to their presence, her long brown hair falling to one side.

"That's my daughter, Lindsey," he whispered.

Madeline smiled as he closed the door. Arm-in-arm, they walked out to the screened-in patio. She closed her eyes, enjoying the cool breeze against her cheeks as he slid the glass panel back into place, then turned and caught sight of her smooth, shapely legs. She stood with her back to him, unaware of his appreciative gaze as she surveyed the golf course and palm trees. He imagined running his hands over her soft curves, feeling every inch of her sweet-smelling flesh, placing kisses upon her thigh and ultimately exploring the area that defined her womanhood, first with his fingers and then finally—

"It's such a beautiful night, isn't it?" she commented, interrupting his fantasy.

"Yes, it is," he agreed, slipping his arm around her waist as he joined her in star-gazing. Puffy clouds adorned the tropical sky, and the full moon shone on the lake in the distance. Madeline still marveled at the lightness of the Florida sky at night. Back home, the darkness had an almost oppressive quality. But here, as day turned into night, an aura of romance and tranquility settled in.

"Let's sit down," he whispered, leading her to a wrought-iron chaise lounge. He sprawled out on the floral cushion first, and then reached for her, pulling her down to rest on top of him. As he encircled her with his strong arms, she longed to stay in his embrace forever.

She smiled as the warm water enveloped her in the rise and fall of its gentle tide. Adrift on the ocean, she looked up at the cloudless sky, feeling the rush of wind through her hair as the sun's rays painted blush on her cheeks. Her body, firm and beautiful in a hot pink bikini, felt nearly weightless as it mingled with the waves. She closed her eyes and inhaled the salty sea air. Drifting, floating, dreaming—

A sudden movement startled her. Mark shifted on the lounge chair, lying on his side so that his face and body were closely aligned with hers. He put his arm around her waist and pulled her snugly against him. Her body trembled as the excitement of his manhood grazed against her thigh.

"Hi," he whispered seductively.

"Hey," she replied in a sleepy voice, smiling back at him. "What time is it?"

"I don't know. It must be pretty late...or early, depending on how you look at it." He proceeded to run his hands over her curves, tracing the length of her body from the nape of her neck to the back of her thighs. It was sweet torture for him, knowing that his desire for her would not be satisfied tonight, yet he had to touch her.

"I should be going. It's probably four a.m. by now. We must've both fallen asleep and lost track of time." She made a move to get up, but his powerful arms held her in place.

"Please don't go yet, Madeline." His breath was warm against her skin. He softly kissed her eyelids, her cheeks, and her neck before seeking out her soft lips again. She ran her fingers through his hair and massaged his neck and shoulders, feeling the rising passion mounting within her again.

"You excite me, you know that?" His voice was raw.

"You excite me, too," she whispered.

While his hands caressed her back, she wondered how she'd ever find the strength to leave. Before she knew it, their tongues met again in a sensual dance as her own hands, which seemed to have a will of their own, lifted his shirt. He willingly complied and lowered his head as she pulled the garment from his body.

Heat emanated from his skin as her fingers touched his chest. Now situated on top of him, her silky auburn hair spilled over her shoulders while he ran his fingers through its length, unable to get enough of her. In the moonlight, her pale skin took on an iridescent glow. As she leaned over him, her sundress opened slightly, tempting him with the curve of her breasts, which were still bound by black lace.

Mark struggled for control but was quickly losing the battle. He began to undo the buttons of her dress, slipping it off her shoulders until it pooled around her waist. Madeline did not resist when she felt the black bra fall away, though she was still self-conscious about her body. And when his warm hands reached up to caress her, and she closed her eyes, losing herself in his touch.

Then suddenly, as if jolted into wakefulness by a blaring alarm clock in the middle of an exquisite dream, she abruptly sat up. Reaching for her bra, she began to dress herself as her composure returned.

"What's wrong?" he asked, still holding her firmly to him by the waist.

"Nothing...well, yes, something is wrong. Everything you are doing to me feels right, but it's just too soon. And we both know if I stay any longer, neither one of us will be able to stop before it's too late. Besides, your kids are in the next room, for crying out loud! I'd be completely mortified if they were to walk in on us. Or, worse, if I were still here in the morning when they wake up. I'm sorry, I—"

"It's ok, Maddy. I understand," he replied, helping her to her feet. He knew it would create an awkward situation if Brian and Lindsey saw her there, especially since his break-up with Gina was still recent. Even though their mother had no inhibitions about parading her contingent of suitors in front of them, he was determined to have a little more regard for their feelings. Besides, it was not his style to date more than one woman at a time. Though he'd been married at a very young age and could choose to "play the field" as so many of his friends advised, he had no interest in casual flings. And from what he now knew and sensed about Madeline, neither did she. He'd have to tread lightly.

Thus, he led her back through the villa to the parking lot. They walked wordlessly into the early dawn, each lost in their own thoughts. She turned to face him before getting into the car.

"Thank you for a wonderful evening," she said with a smile. She reached up and placed a light kiss on his lips before opening the driver's side door. Just as she was about to get in, he placed his hand on her shoulder and stopped her.

"Wait a minute."

She looked at him quizzically.

"When are you going to invite me to your show?"

"You really want to go?" For some reason, his interest surprised her. "Of course, I do...if you want me there."

"Ok, I-I'd love for you to see it. We've all worked so hard. But are you sure you want to sit through two hours of Broadway show tunes and dance traditions? You seem like more of a rock n' roll kind of guy to me."

"Hey, I've seen you move on the dance floor, now I want to watch you on stage. And believe it or not, I like show tunes, especially if you're the one singing them," he responded.

"You are full of surprises," she noted. Butterflies fluttered in her stomach at the thought of seeing his handsome face in the audience. "But it makes me happy that you want to come. I'll drop off a ticket to your office on Monday—or rather, tomorrow," she promised, realizing that it was now early Sunday morning.

"Great," he said, pulling her into a tight hug. "You OK finding your way out of here?"

"I think I can manage."

He kissed her lips firmly and quickly. "Be careful driving."

"I will."

As he watched this strange and beautiful new woman drive away, he wondered what he's just gotten himself into.

Madeline collapsed into bed, exhausted in more ways than one. She nestled her body into the firm mattress and shut her eyes, grateful, in a sense to be alone again. Her body was still pulsating from her passionate interludes with Mark, and she knew the sensations would remain with her for at least the next several hours.

But since the rest of the day would be filled with taxing rehearsals, getting quality rest was absolutely essential. Yet even as the first wave of sleep washed over her, she knew that like Ken before him, Mark Donnelly was about to play a pivotal role in her life.

Chapter 23

Madeline entered the atrium of the modern, five-story office building at the corner of Palmetto Park and Jog Roads, where cascading fountains, lush greenery, and glass-enclosed elevators welcomed her into a relaxing, tropical ambiance. Wearing a beige and white sleeveless dress with a matching bolero jacket, her hair pulled back at the crown with a coordinating barrette, she looked especially lovely—and much younger than her chronological age. And as she came through the revolving doors, she caught the eye of a few well-dressed gentlemen, though as usual, Maddy was completely oblivious to their appreciative stares.

It was nearly 12:30 p.m. and she had two objectives for stopping by— lunch with Isabella and show ticket delivery to Mark. She looked forward to the former, having had several promising communications with the owner of Superlative Staffing. A self-made businesswoman with a good heart and a keen instinct, Isabella definitely wielded influence in the Boca Raton community; as far as mentors were concerned, Madeline couldn't ask for any finer. That is if she were lucky enough to get the job.

But when it came to live performances onstage, she preferred an auditorium full of strangers. The other night when Mark surprised her by asking for a ticket, she'd impulsively agreed to his request, only to have second thoughts the moment she drove away in her car. Of all the dances, tango was her least favorite, and this routine was by far the most challenging she'd ever taken part in. Throw in a demanding, though admittedly beautiful ballad from Les Misérables, her favorite musical, and it all added up to a ton of stress. The Coconut Palm Theater this Thursday night was no place for a new suitor. *What if she screwed up, or worse, fell onstage? What the hell was she thinking, anyway?*

As much as she loved Kenny, even he had to settle for private serenades, though by the time she'd met him she'd given up on dance showcases and talent shows. It took every ounce of courage just to belt out Lori and Vince's wedding song in front of a friendly crowd at their Dupont Hotel wedding reception. Now here she was about to perform for a guy she barely knew—one who just a short time ago had landed on her scumbag list by standing her up for Sunfest.

True, he'd sincerely apologized, ushering in the most passionate date she'd had since losing Kenny; but could she trust Mark enough to allow him into this very personal and private aspect of her life? Kisses and caresses in the heat of pleasure were one thing— potentially embarrassing herself in public with him as a witness was quite another. And it didn't help that she was still battling the same old female problems with their accompanying cramps, bloating and headaches. Miraculously, none of those weird episodes she'd been having for the last few years had taken place recently, despite her horrid work situation and lingering heartache over Kenny's decision to marry someone else.

"Well, things are about to change for the better," she promised herself silently as she slipped through the double glass doors of Superlative Staffing.

"Hi, Madeline!" Genie, the friendly placement coordinator who was around Maddy's age, greeted her warmly. "Isabella wanted me to ask you to take a seat. She's dealing with an unforeseen client emergency in her office at the moment. It shouldn't be too long if you don't mind waiting for a bit."

"Sure, thank you," she replied, settling into a comfortable leather chair in the reception area. Beyond the glass double-doors, she watched the endless parade of office workers and high-powered business people rushing in and out of the building.

Judging from the white paper bags and Styrofoam holders many of them were carrying, they were presumably on their way out to lunch or back from a quick stop for take-out. Knowing Mark had a meeting in Hallandale with a prospective client, she breathed a sigh of relief as she picked up an architectural magazine and began to flip through its colorful pages. She was slightly embarrassed about the other night and the ease with which she'd succumbed to their intense physical attraction, pleasurable as it had been.

After all, Mark was ten years older. Though it had not been her intention to blurt out her virginal status while they were making out on the fishing pier, it had been the only way to put the brakes on a passionate interlude that was quickly spiraling out of control. With Ken, there'd been no apprehensions in spite of their overpowering chemistry: he'd fully accepted and admired her determination to wait until marriage, even though he'd been with other women.

All of those unforgettable times they'd snuggled up together in his waterbed or on the couch in her parents' home, he'd never once pushed her to give in. On the contrary, he spoke of their future wedding night in glowing terms, eagerly anticipating the honor of being her first and forever. For Ken, her innocence had been an unexpected gift, a treasure beyond worth; it was still unclear how Mark felt about it, though he'd demonstrated a certain level of understanding during their hours spent together on the pier and at his villa.

But Maddy was still reeling over how far they did end up going that night on the chaise lounge on his screen-porch; she'd never once allowed Ken to see her that way after months of steady courting. *How could she let Mark nearly seduce her so easily on their second date? Was it a byproduct of loneliness or a reaction to heartbreak? Or was she simply wearing down after all these years of trying to be a good girl?* She tried to forgive herself as she grappled with these difficult questions.

She remembered back to the prior week in this very office, when during the course of conversation about potentially working for Superlative Staffing, Isabella had thrown her off-guard with an unexpected and personal question—made even trickier by the events of the preceding weekend.

"So, Madeline, what did you think of Mark?" Isabella's dark eyes sparkled with excitement, remembering the business card exchange and how her colleague had expressed an immediate attraction to the pretty young woman with the sweet smile, silky auburn hair and noticeably toned legs.

"Mark Donnelly?"

Maddy had momentarily debated the wisdom of confessing what had happened between them with respect to their Sunfest date, before deciding to tell all to Isabella. She certainly didn't owe him any loyalty or consideration, not in the wake of what he'd deliberately done to hurt her.

"Yes silly, Mark Donnelly. Believe me, he noticed you right away at the luncheon."

"Well, he has a strange way of expressing his interest," she'd retorted, before sharing the story of their meeting at Baci and his subsequent cancellation of their date the next morning.

"Gosh, I'm really surprised!" Isabella replied honestly. "That's not like him at all. I think he just got freaked out because you are exactly his type—a cute little Italian girl from the northeast. You know, his Mom's Italian, I don't know if he told you that. And I'll tell you, he's a great catch! A nice guy from a nice family and every one of them is good looking. All the girls swoon over Mark at these business events, though I have to say I think his brother Matt is even better looking. He's married, though."

"Well you know, Isabella, as nice as it is to hear I'm his type, any man who stands up a woman at the last minute like that is a jerk in my book, whatever his ethnic background. Maybe he was truly conflicted overtaking me out so soon after his engagement, but if that were true, he never should have initiated a date in the first place."

"Pfft! That girl from Connecticut?" Isabella swatted her hand in the air dismissively. "She's never going to move here, Madeline. Believe me; that is over. Of course, he does have kids. That's the only drawback."

"I don't mind kids," she insisted. "What I do mind is being led on and then dumped at the last second. I don't think much of Mark

Donnelly, sorry to say."

"Well, I guess I can't blame you. But don't give up on him just yet; he just might redeem himself still."

"Madeline! How are you? I am so sorry to keep you waiting." She looked up to see Isabella standing before her, impeccably dressed as always in a beige suit with a red silk blouse. She quickly stood up to shake the woman's extended hand.

"Hi, Isabella. Don't worry; I took the day off to meet with you before heading to the studio for show rehearsal."

"Oh that's right; your show is coming up. How exciting!" She ushered Maddy into her sunny corner office, where they quickly segued into a discussion about salary requirements, start dates and performance expectations. A thrilled Maddy accepted her generous offer, a definite improvement over her current paycheck. And while her goal of becoming a paid writer still lived on in the secret chambers of her heart, financial obligations, and a stable work environment took precedence for now.

Once assured of the ability to pay her rent and save for a rainy day, she'd tackle her larger objective in a series of small but critical steps. Perhaps she could find a local publication in need of contributors; from the moment she'd arrived in Florida, her hectic schedule had prevented her from investigating that further. Hopefully now that things were settled with her employment, she could focus on working towards her true career aspirations. In the meantime, she'd give her very best to Isabella, a woman for whom she harbored tremendous admiration and respect.

Maddy thrashed around the bed, desperate to fall back into a restful sleep, fully cognizant of the trying day ahead of her. While it thrilled her beyond description to hand in her resignation to Charlie Dowling, she shuddered to think of his reaction. Thank goodness she'd never been forced to sign a non-compete forbidding her to work for any other employment agency within 30 miles; otherwise, she'd have been forced to decline Isabella's offer.

However, Charlie's wrath—an unpleasant byproduct of his excessive ego—was something with which she was unfortunately well acquainted. Thanks to right-to-work laws, she was free to terminate their employer-employee relationship and thus save her sanity; but it was a safe bet that this despicable man would make every second of her resignation miserable. Hopefully, he'd waive the customary two-week notice, in light of the fact that she was a sales representative. Isabella had promised an earlier start date, should that occur.

Suddenly, a knock on the door startled her. After throwing on a short robe, she answered it to see Kenny's smiling face. "Can I come in Maddy?" he asked. "I really have to talk to you."

"Ken, come on now, you shouldn't be here." she admonished.

"Please, sweetheart? I have something really important to share with you." His sparkling blue eyes pleaded with her earnestly.

"Oh, ok," she agreed. "But please, make it quick; I have a busy day tomorrow." He entered the living room and sat down on the couch before motioning for her to join him. Against her better judgment, she sat down, tightening the belt of her robe as she did so.

"Maddy I wanted you to be the first to know I broke off my engagement to Erin. There was no way I could marry her when I am in love with someone else." Her heart jumped to her throat as she struggled to digest this shocking but welcome news. For a moment, she was speechless. That's when he took her hand in his and leaned in close to her.

"I love you, Madeline Rose. You're the woman I want. No one else comes close to you. Please forgive me for hurting you! I am so very sorry."

"Kenny, of course, I forgive you," she cried, throwing her arms around him. "I love you, too, so much!"

"Oh my God," he laughed. "I am the luckiest man alive! And in the very near future, I am going to make you my bride, just like I've always promised."

"Oh, Kenny, I can't wait to be your wife," she sighed before they melted into a passionate kiss.

Music blasted from the speakers of the nightstand alarm clock, rudely awakening her from this palpable, disturbing dream. As she shot up in bed and silenced Vanessa Williams' song, *The Sweetest Days*, she took some deep breaths and wiped the tears from her eyes, wondering when if ever, the torment would end.

Mark took a program as well as his assigned seat after thanking the usher for escorting him to the second row. He wasn't sure what to expect from tonight's performance, but he was definitely intrigued. Though the younger woman mystique had never really appealed to him, somehow Maddy had captured his interest with her refreshing blend of unpretentiousness, warmth, and sincerity. Sure, it bothered him somewhat that she was the same age as his youngest twin sisters, but he couldn't seem to stay away; it didn't help that she excited him beyond distraction. Not since the early days of his courtship with his ex had he experienced such an energizing physical attraction.

He thought back to the other night with its endless kisses and stimulating caresses. God, how he would have loved to have ended his dry spell by making love to her; long distance relationships were tough for more than one reason. It had been several months since he and Gina had even been in the same room, let alone the same bed. Between fatherhood and work responsibilities—not to mention the irrational demands of a bipolar spouse—it sometimes felt as if all the joy had been sucked out of his life. And yet, his two kids were a constant source of pride and reason for gratitude.

During their weekly sleepovers and alternating weekends, Mark would take them to the beach, rollerblade with them along A1A and talk to them about everything from his stalwart love and concern to whatever recent school issue happened to be unfolding. While acting as both mother and father could be exhausting, it was also necessary. His self-centered and oftentimes unstable ex left him no other choice. If it were up to him, his children would live under his roof full-time. Unfortunately, in spite of a glaring lack of maternal instincts, Tammy had been inexplicably awarded primary custody.

And between paying the mortgages for his villa and his former home in Hidden Valley, covering Catholic school tuition and fulfilling child support obligations, he sometimes felt like nothing more than a clearing house. During those moments, he'd remember his primary goal of bringing two self-assured and well-adjusted children into adulthood. Lately, he'd also taken to reading spiritual and motivational books, as well as running—a hobby he hoped would improve his health emotionally, mentally and physically.

Still it would be a welcome relief to have an accomplished, self-supporting and loving woman in his life, a woman who could satisfy him on all levels, genuinely care for his children and skillfully navigate the complexities of competing obligations.

Madeline was certainly beautiful, smart and kind; but when he considered the long-term, he had to admit age was a critical factor. While ten years wasn't exactly a lifetime apart, it was just enough to create irresolvable issues, not the least of which was his decision not to sire any more babies. The other night on the pier, Maddy had articulated her dream of having as many as five children, like her mother before her. At one point in his life, Mark had shared a similar goal; had his marriage been sound, he would've enjoyed rearing a larger family. After all, he himself was one of seven children. But thanks to his bad judgment in going through with a wedding in spite of persistent doubts, he long ago relinquished that fantasy.

So what was he doing here? If a long-term relationship with Maddy was out of the question, it was definitely wrong to lead her on. He already felt like a piece of dirt for having stood her up; why continue to give her false hope? True, she turned him on in a way that recalled the happier times of his adolescence. But he wasn't the kind of man who lived for the thrill of the chase, unrepentant of the trail of broken hearts he left behind. That was the profile of the typical Boca Raton male.

And though he certainly enjoyed living in this incredibly beautiful city, he unequivocally rejected the bankrupt values of some of its citizens. That was one of the things he loved most about his runners' club; nearly all of its members were down-to-earth, nice people in spite of their impressive resumes and palatial residences. While Mark was no lightweight when it came to focused ambition and stellar accomplishment, he retained a basic level of humility.

Like Ken, he'd grown up in a modest home where money was often tight.

He settled back in his seat, eager for the show to begin. Since his arrival, the rest of the row had been filled by an assortment of patrons, from neatly dressed elderly women to even a few young teenagers. And as the lights went down, he felt real excitement at the prospect of watching Maddy perform in a sexy costume that showed off her shapely legs and irresistible curves.

Backstage, Maddy breathed deeply as Scott, Lloyd and Rebecca offered the tango team their best pep talk, reminding them to simply have fun, secure in the knowledge that their last several practices had been flawless. But Madeline's case of bad nerves had more to do with Mark than with stage fright; after all, she knew the routine by heart and had even come to terms with Scott having to lift her in the air. A little while earlier, she'd peeked out from behind the curtains to see her handsome new guy sitting in the audience with a look of genuine interest on his face. All she wanted was to live up to his expectations and do herself proud.

And a few minutes later, adrenaline kicked in as the rousing music began, transporting her to another place and time while her body expertly executed the steps. When her partner spun her around in the air it actually felt exhilarating; during those moments of respite, all thoughts of newly engaged ex-boyfriends, blowhard bosses, and moral dilemmas were completely eradicated.

Mark watched her onstage with a mixture of admiration and desire. Dressed in a sexy, black costume with a short, filmy skirt and sequined bodice, her legs set off nicely by shimmering hose and high-heeled Latin dance sandals, she was a vision of smoldering femininity. And the way she moved around certainly piqued a man's interest. *Wow.* He could hardly wait to hear her sing.

Rebecca adjusted the puffy sleeves of Maddy's red velvet gown as she slipped into a pair of matching satin pumps. From the nearby stage, they could hear Lloyd belting out the Jean Val Jean solo, *Who Am I*. Like Maddy, he shared a special love of Les Misérables, though just about every musical inspired him. Judging from his performance tonight, however, it was obvious he'd made the right decision. Maddy and Rebecca were both moved to tears as they conducted a final inspection in the mirror.

Though a ratty costume would have been more appropriate for her chosen number, Madeline opted for a glamorous, early-19th-century look, mainly out of convenience—she didn't want to waste money when this perfectly acceptable option was already hanging in her closet. And as the audience thundered their applause, signaling Lloyd's exit, she felt suddenly calm as she made her entrance onstage. Upon seeing her, Mark's pulse quickened. With her porcelain skin, big brown eyes and flowing, silky hair, she epitomized his ideal woman. And when she soulfully began to belt out the lyrics to *On My Own*, he was completely captivated.

At the end of her solo, Maddy smiled, savoring the obvious approval of those assembled in the audience. But when she saw Mark rise to his feet, clapping boisterously as he winked and nodded at her, she felt the blood rush through her veins and the goose bumps form on her tingling body. It had been much too long since she'd felt this way; she wanted it to last forever. And as he stared at her under the theater lights, he was filled with an insatiable desire.

"Hey, do you want to join us for some champagne and Asti back at my apartment?" Maddy asked, still attired in her red ensemble. She'd been unsuccessfully trying to change for close to a half-hour, but had been continually deterred by the sincere compliments of various onlookers who'd made their way backstage after the show.

"Sure," he smiled, still in awe of what he'd just experienced.

"Great! I know it's getting late so I'll get back into my regular clothes now and meet you over there in fifteen minutes. It is a "school night" after all." She laughed as she made her way back into the dressing room, where Rebecca was busily getting herself together.

"Hey Maddy, great job again, girl! You were fantastic!"

"Thanks, Becca! You were pretty spectacular yourself!"

"You know, I think your new man was equally impressed; I saw the way he looked at you. Are you sure you want us all to come over? Maybe the two of you should spend some quality time alone."

Rebecca's green eyes sparkled with delight; she honestly believed she'd be doing her friend a favor by opting out. Unaware of Madeline's apprehensions regarding the opposite sex, she was perfectly content to postpone the celebration for another time.

"No, Rebecca please come over," Maddy pleaded. "We've all worked too hard not to congratulate each other on a job well done. Besides, Mark isn't totally out of the woods yet over Sunfest, in spite of the fun date we had."

Technically, that wasn't true, but Maddy thought it sounded plausible. Someone as ebullient and sexy as Rebecca would probably never understand the real motivations for wanting to avoid being alone with him.

"Well ok, but we're not staying long." She winked at Maddy as she slung her duffle bag over her shoulder.

"See you guys at the studio," Maddy called down the stairs as the last of her guests—save for Mark—bid her farewell. When she closed the door behind them, she felt his arms slip around her waist.

"Alone at last," he whispered sexily into her ear, before running his hands through her hair and planting sweet kisses down her neck.

"Mm-hm," she murmured, enjoying his affections yet simultaneously alarmed by the fact that there were no sleeping family members in the next room. While she trusted that his character precluded a criminal history, she was well aware of his normal, manly needs. As with Kenny, Madeline abhorred the idea of being a tease, though with her former boyfriend, serious intentions and a healthy respect for her parents helped keep things in check. Now that she was on her own, that sort of comfort level was nonexistent.

And as they fell on the couch together, she was temporarily

swept away by the taste of his mouth, the sultry feel of his stimulating caresses and the warmth of his masculine body. In spite of her haunting fears, she found herself unbuttoning his shirt and exploring his broad chest first with her hands, and then with her lips. He closed his eyes and sank his head back into a pillow while he savored her tantalizing ability to awaken every nerve ending in his body. Lost in a haze of pleasure, he was quickly losing control.

In one motion, he suddenly moved her beneath him and reached for the zipper of her hot pink, knit top. It wasn't until he'd nearly succeeded in removing it from her body that Maddy began to protest.

"Madeline, please let me touch you," he begged, his voice thick with desire.

"Mark please, I'm so small anyway, I doubt you'd like them!" The self-deprecating words were out of her mouth before she could recall them.

"Shh, baby they looked damned good to me the other night," he assured her. "Please let me show you just how desirable you are."

"I-I don't want you to get the wrong idea, about me inviting you here tonight. I'm not ready to—"

"Maddy please, I know that. I came over here because I wanted to. And we don't have to go all the way; I'd never force you to do that. Please, just let me touch and kiss you."

With that, he succeeded in removing her top, which fell to the floor gracefully as he discarded it. Her skin felt so smooth and warm as he gently ran his hands over her stomach and then across the lace fabric of her bra. Maddy was no match for his skillful caresses, morality concerns notwithstanding. Combined with sheer exhaustion over recent developments, she found herself fighting a losing battle; when she felt her bra slip away from her shoulders, she gave in to passion, relishing the feel of his tongue as she ran her hands through his hair.

"Are you sure you're ok with this?" she repeated as she climbed into bed next to him. She was wearing a new pair of floral print pajamas, the most demure set she could find in her lingerie drawer.

"Absolutely," he confirmed, still reeling with passion but appreciative of her offer to stay. While he wasn't actually drunk, a few celebratory beers and a glass of champagne, along with the late hour, were a potentially hazardous mix when faced with the prospect of getting behind the wheel. Maddy instinctively invited him to platonically share her bed, remembering similar innocent occurrences with Kenny, as well as the fact that Mark hadn't pushed her beyond a bare-chested make-out session.

Still, she felt a bit self-conscious as she slipped under the covers. For goodness sake, she barely knew this guy. *What was she thinking, asking him to stay over? True, part of her motivation involved his safety on the road, but what if he incorrectly concluded that she was really seeking more? What if he made a move on her during the night?*

"Sleep well, Mark," she smiled as she gave him a peck on the check before rolling over. "I really appreciate your coming to the show tonight."

"Hey I really enjoyed it," he replied sincerely. "You were fabulous."

"Thank you."

"You're welcome. Now go to sleep," he teased.

The illuminating rays of a golden sun filtered through the blinds, awakening Maddy ahead of the alarm clock. She quickly dialed down the volume before the blaring rhythms of whatever song 97.3 FM chose to play at 6:30 jolted Mark out of a sound sleep. She wanted to get up and dressed before he did, lest she find herself in another precarious situation. But just as she was about to swing her legs to the floor, she felt his strong arm encircle her.

"Good morning," he murmured seductively.

"Morning," she replied softly while attempting to extricate herself.

"Hey, where do you think you're going, Red?" he teased.

"Oh uh, I want to go brush my teeth; I can't get to the bathroom fast enough in the morning!"

She hoped her joke would transition him out of his amorous mood. Mark however, was still turned on by the events of the previous evening, from her breathtaking theatrical performance to the exquisite feel of her firm breasts against his chest.

"You know, it doesn't matter; you still excite me," he admitted before placing his lips on hers to initiate another arousing interlude. This time, she didn't argue when passion took over. Before she knew it, her pajama top joined the bedcovers in a crumpled heap by her feet, though she managed to retain her bottoms. Maddy lost herself in the familiar sensations, hoping to finally exorcise the ghost of Kenny and what might have been.

But when Mark guided her hand down his body, she resisted firmly.

"Madeline, can't you see how much you excite me? Please touch me," he whispered in a husky voice.

She finally acquiesced, at once enthralled and frightened by her effect on him. She recalled Kenny pointing out the same normal reaction, though he'd never forced her to confront it in this manner. Mark felt so warm and manly as she slowly allowed herself to stroke him.

"Does that hurt?" she asked naively.

"No, it feels good," he groaned, moving in to kiss her lips. But a few minutes later, he embarrassedly ran to the bathroom as nature took its course. Poor Madeline had been so shocked by this "first" she was at a loss as to what to do next. At her front door a few minutes later, she and Mark said an awkward goodbye, each silently questioning the wisdom of continuing this strange relationship.

Chapter 24

Madeline raced up the stairs on her way to the front door. It was Memorial Day weekend, and she was looking forward to relaxing at the beach and the pool, catching up on sleep and writing some long overdue notes to her mom and other family members. She'd just completed her first week at Superlative Staffing and thank God, so far things were going well. Isabella rather enjoyed accompanying Maddy into the field, giving her the opportunity to watch and learn from a professional in a "live" situation. And while the money was a big improvement over her last job, she was determined to save as much as possible to fulfill her dream of buying a place of her own, rather than squander her discretionary income on frivolous things.

As she fumbled for her keys, a white package caught her eye on the doorstep. She lifted it to find a note from Mark, along with her copy of *The Celestine Prophecy* by James Redfield, a book he'd borrowed from her a few weeks prior. She hadn't actually seen him since that uncomfortable morning-after, too embarrassed to face him in person. Thankfully, this past week she and Isabella had spent the majority of their time on the road, severely reducing the chances of bumping into him at their shared office building. And as she read his hastily scribbled lines, that familiar feeling of being doused with icy-cold water washed over her again.

Madeline,

Thank you for letting me borrow your book. I guess you could say I am one of those people who are very conscientious about returning things; I don't like to hold onto stuff that doesn't belong to me. Anyway, I am taking the kids to the Keys for the long weekend. Enjoy your Memorial Day!

Take care,
Mark

She entered the sanctuary of her air-conditioned apartment and sank into the couch, still holding the book in her hand. What a crazy time period this last month had turned out to be. Just when she thought things might finally be turning a corner—wham! Another crushing disappointment.

Still, there was much to be thankful for, from her new job to her overall good health, although she'd started having those strange episodes again. Thank God, most of them had taken place in the privacy of her apartment and not during the workday; otherwise, Isabella might've questioned her sanity. Just the other night she'd awakened out of a sound sleep for no obvious reason, a cold sweat overtaking her while her heart raced out of control.

Afterwards, she felt an invisible, oppressive weight on top of her head, as if someone had forced her to balance a ton of bricks while attempting to walk a straight line. It was a headache unlike any other she'd experienced before. Laying back into her pillow, she'd taken several deep breaths, repeated the affirmations she'd gleaned from her motivational tapes and prayed to God for protection and guidance. For one split second during the acute phase of the episode, she'd contemplated going to the emergency room, but quickly rejected the idea. *Why go there when all they were gonna do was tell her she was getting plenty of oxygen and that her vital signs were normal?*

Folding the note and returning it to its envelope, she walked into her bedroom and pulled her bathing suit out of a drawer. Instead of wallowing in self-pity, she was going to head to the pool for a swim. And a few minutes later, submerged in the crystalline water, she felt reinvigorated. After executing several laps, she lingered under the waterfall and gazed out at the row of palm trees swaying in the breeze, savoring a rare moment of solitude at this normally crowded spot. Somehow, everything was going to be alright. She'd get through this tough time and emerge on the other side even stronger for having endured.

She settled into a chaise lounge, soaking up the warmth of a lingering sun after applying a liberal amount of sunscreen. The golden rays reflected off of her auburn hair, creating a nice contrast with her black one-piece. And with her Brighton knock-off sunglasses from Festival Flea Market, she unknowingly exuded the air of a glamorous celebrity. Lost in her own thoughts, she barely noticed when a fairly attractive young man took a seat next to her—that is, until he initiated a conversation.

Maddy made polite small talk, grateful for the distraction. And as she interacted with this friendly stranger from Brooklyn, her faith was renewed, at least for a while. Then he threw her off-balance with an unexpected question.

"Can I ask you something? I mean, I'm a married man, but if I weren't married would you go out with me?"

"Excuse me?" she asked incredulously, noticing his lack of a wedding ring.

"You know, do you think I'm handsome? Would you go out with me if I weren't married?" he repeated.

An angry Maddy retorted, "The question is irrelevant, pal. The fact is, you are married, and I am not that kind of woman." *Sheesh! What was it with some of these men anyway?*

With that, she gathered her belongings, wrapped her towel around her waist and bid him goodnight as she stormed off. On the short walk back to her apartment, she began to question her judgment and wonder if the Universe was playing tricks on her for the sake of its own amusement.

Saturday morning dawned bright and sunny as expected. After a welcome night of restful sleep, Maddy propped herself up in bed with a few fluffy pillows and spent several minutes in quiet prayer. Recently, Mom had gifted her with a subscription to a nice little magazine called *Daily Word*, and as she read the scripture quote and thought for the day, she felt inspired. It was a simple pleasure to have this cherished time for soul contemplation, freed from the obligation of Saturday rehearsals at the studio.

After her reading, she got up and popped a Leo Buscgalia tape into her cassette player, listening to his distinctive voice and uplifting message while she brewed her coffee and thought about the day ahead. Though tempted to do nothing but lounge on the beach, a quick scan of her apartment revealed the necessity of accomplishing some mundane tasks as well. Somewhere along the way, she was going to have to dust, vacuum and do the laundry.

By the time early afternoon rolled around, she'd finished her chores and had changed into her bathing suit and cover-up. She was busily placing a towel, a magazine and a few bottles of water into her canvas tote bag when a knock at the door took her by surprise. Her heart lurched when she opened it to find Kenny standing before her, smiling in his typical fashion, dressed in shorts and a tee shirt. It bothered her that in spite of all the pain he'd inflicted, her body still tingled at the mere sight of him. Suddenly, she remembered the dream she'd recently had about him breaking off his engagement.

"Ken, I must say, this is an unexpected surprise." She fought to remain cordial and calm while keeping her hopes in check.

"Hey, how are you doing, Maddy? Can I come in?"

"Uh, I guess there's no harm in that." She offered him a seat and a cold bottle of water. *Was it her imagination or did he possess the unmistakable aura of a defeated man?*

There was no sparkle in his eyes, which appeared to be lost in thought as he stared off into the distance. And as he held the bottle of Zephyrhills in his hands, he leaned forward on the couch as if grappling with an unspoken, internal conflict.

"Is everything ok?" she inquired, settling in at a safe distance beside him. "You seem a bit preoccupied."

"Huh? Oh yeah, everything's fine. It's just that—well I guess I've turned into my father after all," he sighed. Madeline wasn't quite sure what to make of that statement, though it hardly coalesced with the profile of a happily engaged man eager to exchange vows with his beloved. *What exactly was he trying to convey?*

"Oh," she responded softly, recalling the difficulties he and his dad had endured in the course of their relationship. Though they'd seemed to patch things up that New Year's Day at her house in Pennsylvania, she had no idea where things stood with them at this point.

"Well is that such a bad thing?" she asked.

Kenny turned to face her, staring deeply into her amber eyes, nearly causing her to tumble to the floor.

"I hope the excitement comes back after Erin and I are married," he confessed.

Why was he telling her this? Was he just trying to spare her feelings by pretending not to be enthralled by the idea of marrying another woman? Or was he attempting to get her to open up about her feelings for him—feelings she still harbored in the infinite depths of her heart and soul, no matter how hard she fought to expel them?

"Kenny, I don't know what to say," she finally blurted out.

"Madeline, do you ever miss our conversations, you know, the way we used to talk? God, you were so easy to talk to." He ran a hand through his blond hair as he spoke.

"Well, I can tell you that no man before or after you has ever treated me the way you did. No one has come close to that level of affection, respect, and kindness." Her tone was wistful as her thoughts turned to Jake, Jim, Gary and now, Mark.

"It was all you, Maddy," he insisted. "It was all because of you. You always listened without judgment; I could talk to you for hours about anything."

Visions of shared moments spent relating to each other while curled up together in the comfort of his waterbed flooded her memory. She could almost see the moonshine filtering down on them from the skylight as they pored over his Navy photo albums, or kissed and caressed each other tenderly while their favorite love songs played in the background.

"Oh Kenny, I'm not sure what to say," she sighed, rising to her feet and walking over to the window, where outside, a group of rollerbladers glided along the sidewalk, talking and laughing. She almost fainted when she felt Ken's arms slip around her a minute later, but didn't put up a fight when he turned her to face him.

"I guess our timing was off," he commented sadly as a tear trickled down his cheek.

"I-I guess so," she agreed softly, resisting the urge to cry. But when he pulled her close to him in a tight bear hug, she couldn't hide her anguish as the water began to flow. Ken buried his face in her hair and neck, mourning what might have been with equal passion. They held each other for what felt like an eternity, contemplating a mishandled past and an uncertain future.

"If you want my opinion, the guy stopped by to see you so he could figure out if getting married is the right thing to do," Scott offered plainly as he dried himself off on a chaise lounge. Ken had just left after spending nearly four hours' poolside with Maddy and her friends from Fred Astaire.

"Or maybe he just wanted one last fling before he ties the knot," Lloyd teased, playfully punching her in the shoulder, unaware of the ludicrousness of his statement, considering Ken and Madeline's passionate, but chaste history. However, Maddy wasn't about to 'fess up to keeping her virginity intact to this new group of friends, nice as they were. Something gave her the distinct impression such news would raise a few eyebrows as well as concerns for her mental health.

"Nah, Kenny's not like that; he's an honorable guy, and he knows I have high standards. I don't go after other women's boyfriends, fiancées or husbands—it's just not my style. Besides, if he does break his engagement, I want it to be his decision with no influence from me. If he's having second thoughts about marrying Erin, he shouldn't go through with it, no matter how I feel or what I do."

"Yeah, you have a point," Rebecca concurred. "But I gotta say, Maddy, he gave you the perfect opening, to be honest with him. I don't know—if it was me and I still loved the guy, I'd tell him."

"But I can't hurt a woman I've never even met—a woman who's done nothing to me just because Kenny and I couldn't get our timing straight. It wouldn't be right; I wouldn't want someone hurting me like that. And even if I did admit my real feelings, there's no guarantee he'd end things with her anyway. I got the distinct impression he's resigned himself to his decision, even if it's wrong. I don't think he could live with the guilt of hurting her and her family by backing out now."

"Well maybe you have a point," Rebecca conceded. "Still, I'm amazed by you, though. Do you know how many women would move in for the kill in this situation? Hell, I've had girlfriends who had no qualms about stealing my boyfriends right out from under my nose!"

"It was strange when he called her on his cell from my apartment," Maddy admitted. He didn't tell her where he was, obviously. But it was more than that—it was almost as if he felt stifled by the whole conversation like she has him on a short leash or something. Anyway, he's not the upbeat, fun-loving guy I remember. And for someone about to get married, he's sure not excited about it."

"All I can say is for the guy to spend an entire Saturday afternoon on a holiday weekend with an old girlfriend, not his fiancée, something is terribly wrong," Lloyd commented.

"And Maddy, I saw the way he looked at you," Rebecca added, "Girlfriend, he's still in love with you—I don't care what you say or what he says!"

"Yeah well, love isn't the only issue here," Maddy stated sadly. "Or is that the problem? Isn't real love about letting go? If that's the case, I am strong enough to do that. Someday, if he ends up coming back to me, I will know for sure that his feelings for me are real—if I'm still available, of course."

"I still think it's rather odd that he wants you to go over to his place for a barbeque," Scott chimed in. "What's with this desire for you and his fiancée to be friends? If you ask me, that's just strange. Look, he's made his decision, even if he's not 100% sold on it. So why rub salt in the wound? He's got one helluva nerve as far as I'm concerned. He must know you're upset, even if you weren't open about how you really feel. I just can't figure him out; if he does still love you, he should at least let you maintain some dignity."

"You know," Maddy said, brightening, "Maybe in a way it would be good for me to take him up on his invitation; maybe if I meet her something will just finally snap inside, and I'll be able to move on."

"Uh, Madeline I think you may be spending too much time listening to those motivational tapes of yours," Rebecca noted with a hint of sarcasm and a raised eyebrow.

"Maybe that's the answer," she insisted. "And you know, Scott, if you were to come with me, it might not be so bad." She smiled as she playfully smacked him on the knee.

"Well, ok," he agreed. "But I want you to think long and hard before you do it."

Maddy slipped into a casual sundress and a comfortable pair of sandals as she mentally prepared herself for the evening ahead. For better or for worse, she'd made the decision to confront reality and at least try to forge a friendship with Ken and his fiancée. While the few people who were aware of the situation advised against taking such an action, she determined that meeting Erin would give her the opportunity to put any fantasies of marrying Ken to rest once and for all. Of course, it didn't help that poor Scott had a death in the family, necessitating a flight to California; but perhaps it was best for her to deal with things on her own, anyway. How bad could it be?

Several hours later, she would live to regret her decision after making the acquaintance of a woman who appeared to have nothing in common with the man Maddy still loved. From the moment she entered their two- bedroom condo on the fifth floor, she felt a distinctive yet subtle hostility in the air, similar to the one that had greeted her at Kenny's real estate office awhile back. And though physically attractive with a willowy figure, blue eyes and silky blonde hair, Erin definitely exuded a hard, urban vibe, notwithstanding her impressive career and level of education.

Yet it wasn't her tough Philly accent and rough-around-the-edges veneer that most impacted Madeline; it was her pervasive coldness and attitude of indifference. She barely engaged in conversation, though Ken's former flame conducted herself with as much dignity as she could possibly muster under the circumstances. And while Kenny did his best to facilitate the flow of conversation, it wasn't long before Maddy wished she'd never accepted his invitation in the first place. When Erin abruptly excused herself to go to bed— claiming a migraine headache— Madeline resolved to banish all thoughts of Ken and Erin from her mind forever.

"Ken, it's getting late, I think I should get going," she informed him, gathering her purse and walking toward the door.

"You don't have to leave," he insisted, filled with regret for Erin's inhospitable behavior.

"Kenny, don't you get it? You've made your choice. Now let me make mine."

She neglected to reveal that this would be the absolute last time he'd see her; it was just too painful to watch him acquiesce to the whims of such a disagreeable, insecure woman. And yet, Maddy silently acknowledged Erin's point of view. After all, how would she feel if the shoe was on the other foot? She might vehemently reject the idea of hosting her fiancée's old girlfriend for dinner too, no matter how well-intentioned the motivation.

"I just thought maybe we could hang out on the porch for awhile and talk," he went on.

"No, it's just not a good idea; you and I both know that. Look, I wish you well, I really do, but it's no longer appropriate for us to sit and talk the way we used to; we've both forfeited that privilege. So let's just be thankful for the time we had and move on.

I'll find my way, and you'll find yours. You and Erin will get married, have kids and build a life together—but you'll have to do it in my absence. No hard feelings, but that's just the way it has to be."

In spite of her best efforts, a determined tear slid down her face; she quickly brushed it away. Ken just stood there in solemn resignation, until she reached up to give him a peck on the cheek.

"Take care of yourself, Kenny," she whispered. Then she turned away and rushed to her car, leaving him alone with his conflicted emotions and second thoughts.

A cold autumn rain pounded the windows of Madeline's girlhood bedroom as she awoke from another dream-filled sleep. It was hard to believe almost three years had passed since her move to Florida and even harder to accept the circumstances of her current stay in Pennsylvania. In spite of faithful weekly attendance at Mass, daily prayer, regular yoga classes and constant reading and listening to motivational books and tapes, those terrible episodes had dramatically increased in intensity and scope. And while she'd done her absolute best to function in the world— particularly given the fact that she was now a homeowner, no longer could she calm herself down during the workday by simply breathing deeply in the privacy of a restroom stall.

And when she began behaving strangely during her parents' last visit, they'd insisted on bringing her back to Philly for tests to rule out the possibility of a brain tumor, based on the oppressive headaches that mimicked the overwhelming pressure of a vice and made it nearly impossible for her to focus. Worse, she was now experiencing an even more pronounced disassociation of her body and mind, causing her to feel as if her feet weren't actually touching the ground, even when she could clearly see that they were.

But most distressing was a new and chilling sensation she could only describe to her father as a "tightening of my spine." During these frequent and unpredictable moments, her legs and arms would suddenly feel limp and lifeless, though still fully functional. This was preceded by a strange sensation of at the base of her neck, whereby she'd swear some invisible "puppet master" was literally pulling her strings and forcing her into submission. All of these symptoms were now accompanied by vivid nightmares that typically featured disturbing images—from snake pits and fire-breathing dragons to evil men in masks wielding AK-47's.

In last night's dream, Madeline was scaling a Cobra-infested mountain in her bare feet, doing her best to avoid the venomous reptiles while she struggled to make it to the top. Along the way, she encountered several people from real life including Mark, who wordlessly smiled as he witnessed her impossible journey. He'd also been featured in previous dreams, such as the one where he and Maddy held each other close among the fallen leaves on a college campus, listening to the church bells ring in the distance.

Still another showcased Mark's mom—a woman Madeline had never met—encouraging her not to give up on her son "because I know he loves you." Oddly enough, that particular dream took place by the side of a crystal-clear river; usually, the water featured in these nocturnal mind movies was murky and dark. And yet, prior to her arrival back in Philly, her only relief from the madness came from completely submerging herself in the ocean or pool. Surrounded on all sides by the earth's purest substance, she experienced wholeness and peace, at least temporarily.

Monica Rose entered her daughter's bedroom, consumed with fear and worry for what might lay ahead. Though she'd seen Maddy at low points before, none had come close to what she was now experiencing. The emptiness of her expression, the lost look in her eyes and the seriousness of her physical symptoms combined to fill the devoted mother's heart with anguish. *Why did it seem her daughter was always getting the short end of the stick? What were they going to do if Maddy was suffering from a mental disorder?* Of all horrific problems, Monica felt least prepared to deal with that possibility.

Madeline smiled as her mom climbed into bed with her, recalling countless memories of growing up, when the two of them would linger for a few minutes prior to Maddy having to get ready for school.

"How are you, sweetie?" Monica asked.

"I'm fine," she replied softly.

"God, Maddy, I just don't want there to be anything wrong with your mind," Mrs. Rose blurted out emotionally. "I couldn't take it if something like that were to happen to you. You're my baby." She pulled her child close to her as she spoke and kissed her on the forehead. Madeline wordlessly held her arms around her mother as she said a silent prayer for help and wondered when this nightmare was finally going to end.

Chapter 25

Maddy smiled to herself as she cruised down I-95 on her way back to Boca Raton from Lake Worth. She'd just had a promising interview with an Oregon-based financial institution that had recently merged with First America Bank. It was hard to fathom that more than two years had passed since that awful time when she genuinely believed that her life—for all intents and purposes—was over. Those dark days had been characterized by abject fear and sorrow as family members, friends, licensed psychologists, group therapy sessions and prescription medications had only succeeded in raising her to a passable level of functionality.

After that fateful morning spent commiserating in bed with her mother, a battery of tests had ruled out suspected brain abnormalities as the root cause of her troubles. Later, a thorough exam and comprehensive blood work conducted by their family internist had proclaimed her to be the picture of health, at least physically. From her low-to-normal blood pressure and acceptable (if not perfect) weight to her supposedly "in-range" hormonal levels, Dr. Bingham expressed his delight with Maddy's excellent results and admirable nutritional habits, particularly her adherence to drinking at least 64 ounces of water a day.

However, the good doctor did give credence to her legitimate physical symptoms by offering her a "nerve pill" which he swore was non-addictive. Madeline gratefully accepted the samples in spite of her misgivings, planning to take them only as a means of assuaging her problems long enough to allow for an effective solution and a return to a normal routine. And though Dr. Bingham never verbalized a name for her malady, she discovered it on the prescription's packaging— panic and anxiety disorder. *Wow.* Well, at least she now knew what she was dealing with.

The information packet also touted cognitive and behavioral therapy and aerobic exercise as viable methods of coping with this miserable condition. Maddy had already employed the latter via bike riding, brisk walking, and swimming; pursuing the former hadn't even occurred to her until that very moment. She immediately determined that she would return to Florida, where she'd seek out professional help and finally put an end to this painful chapter of her life.

And though her parents harbored real and valid concerns, Madeline knew that the answers she sought were waiting for her in her adoptive state; as comforting as it was to be around those who loved her, it was time to deal with this newly defined issue in her own way.

Upon returning to her lakeside condo in Windwood, she began weekly therapy sessions with a highly respected psychologist in Hollywood. She also secured a marketing position with a local nonprofit organization, thanks to her involvement in the Professional Women of South Florida, a networking group she'd originally joined with Isabella, who'd since sold her business and embarked upon a new career in real estate.

At PWSF, Madeline formed solid friendships with many wonderful people including Elyse Lombard, whose family owned a successful moving business, Audrey Solomon, a brilliant foot and ankle surgeon and Carolyn Charlton, a gregarious and talented nurse in the home health field. During Madeline's absence, all three remained in regular contact out of authentic concern and interest. Once she'd made the decision to come back, Audrey and Carolyn had helped to ease her financial burdens by recommending her to the Down Syndrome Network, an advocacy group in need of assistance with publicity, programs and the procurement of funds.

And though Maddy lacked experience in the not-for-profit world, her intensely personal knowledge of the condition had fueled a natural passion and exuberance that came across quite dramatically during the interview process. Best of all, the office was located less than two miles from her Windwood condo, though she planned to sell it as soon as circumstances permitted.

Having managed to develop a genuine, platonic relationship with Mark Donnelly in the months following their initial meeting, he'd assisted her in purchasing her three-bedroom, two-bath residence by the water. It hadn't occurred to Madeline that living in the same community— sprawling as it was—might ultimately lead to more heartache by increasing the odds of bumping into him. And though she'd told herself she'd risen above any lingering romantic fantasies where he was concerned, her heart would skip a beat on those sporadic occasions when she'd see him rollerblading with his children, driving through the entrance or jogging along the trail that encircled the entire development.

But these innocuous incidents paled in comparison to witnessing Candice La Mont, the beautiful, middle-aged daughter of a Boca Raton business icon, move in with Mark almost one year after the infamous incident at Maddy's Boca Del Mar apartment. And though she'd discuss these and other issues in-depth with her therapist, countless sessions— while helpful to a certain extent—had led her to a frustrating plateau. Yes, she could now successfully hold a job and navigate through social situations again, but she still lacked a profound sense of complete wholeness and wellbeing.

Weekly yoga classes, continuous reading of spiritual books, daily prayer and consistent attendance at Mass were also contributing to her recovery, yet something remained elusive. Maddy couldn't quite pinpoint it, although she persistently researched other remedies. It was simply unacceptable that she had to learn to live with a perpetually sour stomach, fuzzy head and general feeling of unease.

And then one fateful night consumed with determined thoughts of relocating to another comparable condo community, and a palpable desire to finally end this relentless scourge of anxiety, she made an acquaintance that would alter her life forever.

"C'mon Maddy, you have to go to the meeting tonight. Audrey and Carolyn will be there, and I know how much they want to see you. And this month's speaker is supposed to be fabulous."

Maddy regarded Elyse's words with skepticism as she paced around her ceramic-tiled kitchen. Her beautiful blonde friend had been chatting nonstop in her typical effervescent manner, singing the praises of Ann Claire, a woman trained in the art of something called "remote viewing."

While Elyse was hazy on the details, her impression was that it had to do with psychic phenomena, much to Maddy's chagrin. A traditionalist at heart, she'd rejected such "nonsense" most of her life, though Aunt Maria regularly had her tarot cards read. She'd often report the uncanny findings back to her doubtful sister and niece, both of whom would chide her for wasting her money on charlatans.

Then there were the corrupt fortune tellers on the Atlantic City boardwalk, who lured unsuspecting patrons into their incense-saturated boutiques, where they'd scam them out of their money with horrid tales of hideous curses that could only be remedied by forking over $200 to the "all-knowing" sage. It was an old tale, one that held little appeal.

But surprisingly, Madeline's negative perceptions were shattered upon meeting Ann Claire that night, a serious businesswoman with a matter-of-fact attitude and a confident demeanor. Dressed in a stunning purple suit accessorized by chunky gold jewelry and cream-colored pumps, she looked more like a financial analyst than a spiritual guru. During her 45- minute speech addressing everything from reincarnation to the energy fields surrounding every human being's physical body, Madeline hung on every word, fascinated by the subject matter and the professionalism of the presenter.

And when Ann supported her claims with newspaper articles and other "hard" evidence, Maddy couldn't help but be impressed, regardless of her earlier apprehensions. But nothing could have prepared her for what unfolded next. Prior to heading back out to the parking lot, she approached the psychic to say a proper goodbye and thank her for an enlightening evening.

Upon shaking the younger woman's hand, Ann looked deeply into her eyes and stated without hesitation, "You're still in mourning for your grandmother, and she died well over twenty years ago. And you're harboring guilt over your handicapped brother. He's the middle brother, and you're feeling bad about leaving him behind."

Completely blindsided by these accurate yet shocking declarations, she felt her knees go weak as an astute and equally stunned Elyse pulled out a chair for her. Once seated, an emotional Maddy retorted that Louis was not the middle child, Lori was. An unfazed Ann responded, "I didn't say he was the middle child; I said he was the middle brother."

"Oh my God, you're absolutely right," she confirmed, feeling at once violated and awed. Everyone around her shared a similar reaction, having intimate knowledge of her family and her recent problems. They watched in absolute silence as Ann placed her hands on Madeline's shoulders and pronounced her awareness of the panic and anxiety disorder, along with an accompanying spiritual struggle characterized by a nagging inferiority complex.

"Have you ever felt that while other people's lives progress, yours never seems to go anywhere? Like you're constantly treading water?" Ann inquired sincerely. She nodded her head in response, too overwhelmed to verbalize an answer. *How could this woman, a total stranger, know so much about her?*

"Madeline, I am picking up on your grandmother's presence around you. She loves you dearly, but she's holding onto you too tightly. Do you have any idea why that is?"

"I-I think I do," Maddy admitted. "You see, I was born several months after my grandfather—her husband—died. And it's like I helped her overcome the pain by giving her something, someone else to think about. She was a warm, loving woman and she doted on me constantly. I remember her clearly even though I wasn't quite seven when she died.

"It was so awful; we were curled up on the couch watching a movie when she suddenly went into heart failure, only none of us kids knew what was happening. We saw her shivering violently, and we ran to get blankets to cover her up, made her tea, but nothing was helping. She just kept getting worse and worse. My parents were in the neighborhood visiting some friends and my oldest brother called them to come home.

"My dad immediately called for an ambulance and the last time I saw her, they were carrying her away on a stretcher. I was devastated; she was the only grandparent I knew. There isn't a day that goes by that I don't think about her. Even now, I still miss her."

Audrey handed Maddy a tissue and placed an arm around her as she dissolved into tears.

"Ok, that makes sense," Ann went on softly, "but I am also getting a message about incompletion like somehow you never got to say goodbye to her."

"Oh, well that's true," Maddy confirmed after taking a sip of water. "Even though I begged my mother to let me go to her viewing and funeral, she didn't think it was the right place for a child. So while everyone else went, I stayed home with a babysitter. Looking back, I agree with Mom's decision, though if it were up to me, viewings would be outlawed entirely. What's the point of staring at someone's dead body? It's barbaric. I've never quite figured out why people insist on having them."

"Yes, your mother did the right thing," Ann affirmed. "However because you never had the chance to properly mourn with other people, you never let go of her, and she never let go of you. I recommend that you hold your own private memorial service at home. You can light candles, talk to her, write her a letter—whatever makes you most comfortable.

"But you absolutely must tell her gently but firmly that while you will always love her, she has to let go a little; she must stop clinging to you. Tell her you will never forget her, but that it is ok for her to be at peace. You will see her again someday. As long as you are here on this earth, you have to be free to live your life and fulfill your purpose."

Maddy nodded her assent, actually looking forward to finally honoring her grandmother's memory in her own unique way. Then, overcome with anguish, she confessed her frustration at her failure to fully overcome the anxiety disorder, notwithstanding her embrace of just about every remedy known to mankind.

"Have one private session with me and it'll be gone forever," Ann promised with conviction. "We can talk on the phone or in person, it doesn't matter. But I can assure you, if you are willing to give me an hour of your time, you will never be plagued with this problem again."

She spoke with such confidence that a heartened Maddy eagerly took her up on her offer, securing an appointment with the busy psychic before walking out of the meeting. It was a decision that would eventually usher in a brand-new existence, free at last from the oppressive yoke of out-of-control emotion known as panic and anxiety disorder.

Back in the present moment, Madeline quickly unlocked her front door and rushed into the kitchen to answer the ringing phone. Having assumed it was either one of her good girlfriends, Lori or her mother calling to inquire about her interview, she was shocked to hear a voice from the very distant past—one she failed at first to recognize.

"Madeline?" It was obviously a man based on the tone, but beyond that she couldn't identify him.

"Yes?"

"Uh, it's Jake Winston." Though her ex-boyfriend did his best to sound confident, she detected a discernible trace of nervousness.

"Jake? Wow, this is a surprise!" she replied brightly. She'd long ago forgiven him in her mind for his past actions, thus she felt compelled to put him at ease, regardless of her bewilderment as to why he'd be contacting her now. It was certainly odd a full ten years after their break- up.

"I hope you don't mind my calling, Maddy. My mom actually ran into yours at the Acme a few weeks ago and asked for your number. You know, she always thought the world of you. But please don't be mad at your mom; she never thought for a minute that I'd be the one picking up the phone."

"No, it's ok," she assured him genuinely.

"Well, the reason I called is—Maddy, I've been doing an awful lot of soul-searching lately. And you came to mind; well more specifically,

334 / Water Signs

the awful way I treated you came to mind. God, the things I said and did—I am so ashamed of myself. Especially the way I ended things between us; my behavior was deplorable and immature, and I am just so sorry. I'm sorry for everything—for all of the hurtful things I said and did. I mean, the way I treated you was a disgrace. Do you think you can ever forgive me?"

Touched by this heartfelt apology, Maddy assured him that she harbored no ill feelings, stating that they were both older and wiser now. She also complimented him on his courage, genuinely impressed by his actions. Besides, the past was the past.

Although she would never consider dating him again, she did agree to a friendly get-together during her next trip to Philly. By the time they'd ended the conversation, both parties experienced a welcome relief and satisfaction. Unlike Madeline, however, Jake also retained a significant amount of regret for what might have been, though he wisely kept such musings to himself.

After hanging up, she settled into a cushioned chair on her screened-in patio and watched the swans glide around the sparkling lake. She remembered back again to the night she met Ann Claire, and their subsequent phone session a few weeks later, when Ann enumerated the details of Madeline's past lives to shed light on her current incarnation's hardships.

It did make sense, though it was still a difficult theory to swallow in many ways. The psychic had concluded the call by "putting a healing" on her client's previous lifetimes; on the other end of the line, Maddy heard very deep breathing, much like her yoga instructor's during a class. Prior to saying goodnight, Ann confirmed that the panic and anxiety issue was completely dissolved; however, it would take six months before Maddy would "know" that it was truly gone. She'd start to feel better incrementally, but one day there would be a patent realization that this horrendous phase was indeed over.

And exactly six months later, Maddy awoke with a clear head, a calm stomach and an overall feeling of excellent health for the first time in nearly eight years. It was as if a black cloud had finally been lifted, leaving clear blue skies in its place. Overcome with sheer gratitude, joy and relief, Madeline called Ann to share the wonderful news, exclaiming, "Ann, thank God I ran into you that night! I don't know what I would have done if I hadn't—I was at my wits' end!"

"Madeline," she replied dryly, "You manifested me into your life, don't you know that? God led you to me, based on your own intentions."

"Oh," she said, still somewhat puzzled. She sensed that Ann's words were wise and profound, but it wouldn't be until taking an interesting class at the Unity Church in Delray Beach that she would thoroughly comprehend the psychic's meaning.

Ken smiled as he looked down at his toddler daughter, sleeping soundly in her "big girl bed." A devoted father, he'd often get up in the middle of the night to check on his first-born, a habit he'd developed within days of bringing Bonnie home from the hospital. Lately, the child had been the only bright spot in his life, thanks to his sadly deteriorating marriage. Aside from Bonnie's birth, he could barely recall experiencing any sense of deep-rooted, overpowering happiness; on the contrary, in many ways he felt empty and alone.

Taking a seat in a nearby rocking chair, Ken leaned back and closed his eyes as thoughts of Maddy permeated his brain. How was she doing? Had she gotten married yet? Was she still writing? He hadn't seen an issue of *The Good News Gazette* in a while, though he'd secretly held onto the copy his mother had brought over to his house just weeks after Bonnie's birth. That was back when Erin had taken a corporate position in the creative department of a local cosmetics company before she'd decided to start a home-based business.

Paula Lockhart had entered Ken and Erin's home that morning, armed with a stack of newspapers and magazines, which she'd carefully set down on the coffee table before heading into the nursery. As Ken walked through the living room on his way to make breakfast, a photo of two familiar faces caught his eye. And when he picked up the publication to take a closer look, his heart was filled with pride and longing.

Beneath the headline, "My Brother, My Hero," and the byline bearing the author's name, Madeline and Louis smiled back at him, seated at a round dining table. *Wow.* She'd finally achieved her goal of becoming a published writer. He well remembered the endless conversations—by the ocean, snuggled up on the couch or wrapped up under the satin sheets of his waterbed—during which Maddy would eloquently share her dreams for the future. In spite of everything, he still missed that connection.

"Do you know her?" His mother's voice startled him out of his imaginings. Ken returned the paper to the top of the stack.

"Huh? Oh yeah, that's an old friend of mine. Remember Madeline Rose, the girl from Media I dated a long time ago? Back when I had my place in Somers Point?"

"The one who freaked you out by moving to Florida?" Paula replied, recalling a long ago mother-son summit at the Deerfield Beach Fishing Pier.

"Yeah, that's the one," he admitted sheepishly as his cheeks turned slightly crimson. Paula briefly scanned the article and photo.

"She looks like a very nice young woman," his mother proclaimed. "Cute, too. And she's obviously from a wonderful family. What an inspiring story."

With that, she strode back into the nursery, leaving Ken alone with his unexpressed thoughts.

"I'm sorry, Mr. Lockhart but I don't give out the personal phone numbers of my contributors," Colleen Smith, editor-in-chief of *The Good News Gazette* informed a frustrated Ken. He'd been at work for hours, yet unable to think about anything other than getting in touch with Madeline.

"It's ok," he persuaded her, "I am an old friend of Maddy's; she won't mind."

"I'll tell you what," Colleen had compromised, "Give me your number and I'll pass it along to her. That way, she can decide if she wants to talk to you."

"Ok, that sounds reasonable," a somewhat dejected Ken replied, doubtful that she would actually contact him.

And a few days later, it appeared his suspicions had been confirmed when there had been no word from Madeline. Unknown to him, she'd been debating the wisdom of returning the call ever since Colleen had given her the message. After all, she'd succeeded in banishing every thought of Ken and their past romance out of her mind, from the night of that terribly awkward barbeque. Why open up this can of worms now?

But in the end, curiosity got the better of her and she briefly reconnected with her old flame. It was a cordial but quick conversation, made purposely shorter once apprised of the birth of his daughter. Madeline warmly congratulated him on the joyous occasion while graciously accepting his sincere congratulations on her fledgling writing career.

Ken felt the same powerful eruptions within at the sound of her voice, though she gave no indication of her personal status, opting instead to update him about her parents and siblings. Madeline also omitted from the conversation her ongoing struggle with panic disorder, preferring to keep the tone light, so as not to encourage any unsolicited offers of help or worse—an invitation to dinner at his home. The last thing she needed was an evening with Ken, Erin, and their new baby.

At the call's conclusion, Maddy had immediately sealed off the part of her that stubbornly harbored intense love and desire for the guy who once bought a rose for her friend at a nightclub, and then went on to prove just how loving, kind and considerate a real man could be. And though Ken continued to honor his marriage vows, within the sacred boundaries of his heart, memories of another woman—and what might have been—persistently haunted him.

Chapter 26

Journey's End was a lovely community of single-family homes built around an impressive, man-made lake. As with many South Florida developments, its architecture boasted a distinctively Mediterranean influence, characterized by stucco walls, arched doorways, and wrought iron terraces.

Audrey Solomon lived in this beautiful neighborhood, along with her husband and toddler son. Over the years, she and Madeline had become quite close, to the point where each regarded the other as not simply a trusted friend, but a spiritual—if not biological—sister. Audrey had even selected Madeline to be her first child's Godmother, an honor she assumed gratefully and reverently.

Before proceeding beyond the gated entrance, Maddy smiled at the guard and offered a sincere wish for a pleasant afternoon, enthused by her own plans for the day. And as she made the left turn in front of the beautifully designed clubhouse on the way to the Grande Estates subsection, she fondly recalled an exciting event that had taken place there nearly a full year ago—her Forty Favorites birthday party.

Though initially upset about reaching that particular milestone, she perked up when she and Audrey developed the celebration's original theme, incorporating a lifetime of the birthday girl's most cherished things, from the Philadelphia Eagles to Italian wedding cookies. The catered event also included a deejay and personalized decorations including Madame Alexander dolls, original "books" written by Madeline as a child and even well-placed packages of Tastykakes.

But the most joyous part of her birthday had been the surprising arrival of Greg, Lori, Lyle and Daphne in a stealth plan orchestrated by none other than Elyse. She'd picked them up at Fort Lauderdale airport the Thursday evening before the party, and then invited Maddy over for a movie. Once there, she received the shock of her life as one-by-one, some of her favorite people in the world jumped out of the bushes framing Elyse's two-bedroom home. It had been one of the most meaningful and uplifting moments in her recent history; an evening she'd remember forever.

Mom, Dad, and Louis joined them the next day as expected. After taking her sister, brother and cousins to Deerfield Beach for breakfast, followed by a fun session at Maddy's functional training studio, the group had welcomed the rest of the family at the airport. The next several days were filled with laughter, good times and gratitude for the opportunity to reconnect in such a delightful way.

Buoyed by the love of family and friends, Madeline decided that 40 was a number to proud of. Besides, she still looked much younger than her age, thanks to a combination of good genes, a healthy lifestyle and a positive outlook; she was certain that the best was yet to come, a feeling that had only intensified since ringing in the New Year. Inexplicably, with the dawn of 2008, an authentic sense of coming "full circle" had consumed her.

And indeed, her intuition had been correct. Here she was, on her way to join her best girlfriends for a celebratory luncheon in honor of her recent promotion to content manager for a prestigious e-marketing company in downtown Fort Lauderdale. Specializing in the travel industry, the firm provided Internet support on behalf of their clients, most of whom were major cruise lines. After just over a year as an entry- level content writer, the astute higher-ups had rewarded her talent and work ethic with a significant pay raise and editorial responsibility for a team of six.

Ironically, she'd purchased a brand-new condo in Boca Bayou soon after landing her corporate communications position with Portland National Bank; however, her building was far removed from the one formerly inhabited by Ken and Erin. Though they'd briefly come to mind when she relocated several years ago, she'd swiftly relegated them back to that sealed-off area in her head, never to be recalled again—or so she'd assumed.

During the early days of her Boca Bayou residency, she'd embarked upon an ill-fated relationship with Tag Russell, a handsome loan officer whose office was just on the other side of Maddy's. For almost twelve months, she'd regarded his consistent flirting as nothing more than a pleasant workday diversion; after all, Tag never behaved inappropriately, nor did he initiate any gatherings outside of the office.

Even on that horrendous date of September 11, 2001, when Maddy had gone running hysterically into his office, his comforting hugs and soothing words had been completely platonic and above-board. However, one night after a company Christmas party, the two of them ended up having coffee at a local café, setting the stage for an involvement that would ultimately result in heartbreak.

The relationship's failure had mostly been a function of Tag's inability to move beyond the dissolution of his marriage and an early childhood tragedy—two events that had rendered him emotionally unavailable. A handsome man with wavy brown hair, blue eyes, a mischievous smile and a ready sense of humor, he and Maddy had shared an intense chemistry, along with a mutual affection. The former led to Madeline's full transition into womanhood.

But no amount of concerts, Marlins games, Harley rides or pool-playing sessions at Gatsby's could save this doomed relationship. Whereas Madeline fell in love with the highly successful, hard-working loan officer, the most he could offer her was an occasional good time—on his terms of course. And when his insecurity about being almost twelve years her senior finally got to him, he ended it altogether.

Somewhere before the transition from office friendship to a full-blown relationship with Tag, Maddy had briefly reconnected with Mark Donnelly, who at first appeared to be impressed with her successful banking career and obvious maturation. However, after three wonderful dates wherein they shared meaningful conversation as well as endless, passionate kisses, he disappeared again from her life. No goodbye call or farewell visit—just an abrupt departure after promising to contact her upon his return from California, site of his "all-boys" motorcycling vacation.

In an interesting twist, Tag had unknowingly referenced Maddy's former flame many months later when the two of them attended that year's Sunfest. Turned out, Tag and Mark had worked together in the lending department at First America Bank. And as Tag and Madeline browsed the multitude of artists' tents at the West Palm Beach festival, he told her all about his unexpected run-in at Publix with the newly engaged Mark, who'd happily announced his impending fall wedding. Though she did not disclose the details of her brief romance, Madeline silently pondered if Mark's fiancée had been the real reason for his disappearance the second time around. If so, it was certainly a strange and recurring pattern.

Then there was the trauma she'd endured at the hands of Ray Smith, yet another older man who'd deceived her into believing he was divorced and in the market for a meaningful relationship. Against her intuitive impulses, Madeline had allowed him to drive down from Jupiter to take her to dinner, after just a few casual lunches. Having met the retired police detective at a community awareness event, she'd erroneously assumed a good nature and a benign intention. But it wasn't long until the green-eyed, dark-haired deceiver proved her wrong.

When he refused to leave her place that evening, Madeline should have called the guard house, if not the police. Instead, she succumbed to his coercion instead of putting up a fight – a decision she regretted almost immediately. On the dark and dreary morning after when she felt violated and defeated, Elyse had been a Godsend, sympathizing and coaching Madeline through one of her most horrific experiences to date. Up until that point, she'd never understood the women she'd seen on the news or read about in articles who'd described similar incidents with dishonorable men. As a result, she could now empathize with their plight, even if an official crime had not been charged.

And yet, the silver lining had been the fact that Maddy never once regressed back to panic and anxiety disorder. In spite of the physical and emotional upheaval, she remained balanced and strong;

it was another testament to Ann Claire's validity and Madeline's faith and determination.

"Maddy, my gosh girl, you look great!" Audrey's bubbly voice greeted her as she opened the screen door of the atrium. Having just put her little boy down for a nap, she'd heard the familiar click of the handle as she walked by the foyer, prompting her to open the main doors before

Madeline could even ring the bell.

"Hey there, so do you," she replied, returning her friend's warm hug. A petite woman with a lovely face and gorgeous, waist-length dark ringlets, Audrey looked more like a Hollywood celebrity than an accomplished doctor. But her remarkable intelligence was evident to anyone who spent less than two minutes with her—along with her genuine sweetness, generosity, and commitment to her Catholic faith.

"Is Elyse here yet?"

"No, honey, but she called to say she's running late. I think she stopped by her sister's house to help out with the kids. You know, it's still so hard for them having to come to terms with Kevin's death. Being a mother myself, I don't know how that family is coping. I can't even imagine losing a five-year-old."

Audrey's eyes filled with tears, remembering the Lombard family's recent tragedy. Having supported Elyse throughout the entire ordeal, including the night the child passed away in his father's arms, Madeline fought the urge to cry, too.

"Some of your friends from your church class are here, though," Audrey added quickly, in an attempt to change the mood. Today was, after all, a celebration. "And we have a special guest, who was supposed to be a surprise, but since Elyse won't get here for at least a half-hour, we can't wait."

"Who is it?" Maddy asked, genuinely intrigued.

"You'll see!" Audrey exclaimed, taking her friend by the arm and leading her out to the enclosed patio, where a small group of women had gathered by the poolside bar. Nearby, a large table had been set up to host a healthy feast of homemade tuna, chicken, and egg salads, complemented by fresh fruit, multi-grain rolls and Audrey's famous tiramisu—one of Maddy's preferred desserts.

"Madeline, my goodness, look at you!" Carolyn Charlton exclaimed.

"Looks like you've reached your goal—congratulations." She pecked her younger friend on the cheek as she spoke. Though twenty years older than Madeline and Audrey, Carolyn had a natural exuberance for life and a sharp, spontaneous wit that made her seem ageless. And with her short blonde hair, impeccable make-up application, and stylish clothing, she always looked appropriately fashionable.

"I know, can you believe it? I finally knocked off those last stubborn ten pounds," Maddy laughed. "They've been dogging me my whole life, but I finally won."

"Well, you look fantastic. And I can't wait to hear all about your new promotion."

But before she could answer, Audrey entered through the sliding glass door, escorting a very special guest onto the patio.

"Ann, oh my God," Maddy cried out, astonished.

"Hello, Madeline," Ann Claire smiled, pecking her on the cheek. "I feel honored to have been invited here today."

"It's been awhile," Maddy offered, quickly embracing her. "How are you?"

"I'm just great, thanks. But I can't stay long, so I think you and I should go have a seat in the family room and talk."

"We hired Ann to give you a reading," Audrey explained. "Think of it as a special gift to celebrate your promotion."

"Aw, you're the best, thank you."

She smiled at them as she followed Ann back into the house, where they settled into the comfort of a plush sectional couch. Once relaxed through deep breathing techniques, Madeline nevertheless shot up in surprise reaction to the first thing out of Ann's mouth.

"Who's Kenneth?" the psychic asked her.

"W-what?" Her heart nearly caught in her throat at the sound of the name she'd forced herself to forget a lifetime ago. Even her closest friends knew nothing about him, believing Maddy had moved to Florida on a personal quest for a new identity and nicer weather.

"Kenneth," Ann repeated calmly. "I see someone named Kenneth cycling back in. I'm feeling that he's someone from your past— someone who loved you very much."

"Y-yes, that's true. He's someone I met when I was a much younger woman."

"And you loved him, too," Ann declared.

"Yes, well that was a long time ago, and he married someone else," she retorted.

"Really? Well, I don't think they're together anymore. I'm definitely sensing if he's not already divorced, he's on his way. What's being shown is that he's thought of you a lot over the years; in fact, he still thinks about you very much.

"There was no excitement in his marriage. Now don't get me wrong, he loved her. It's just that there was no 'wow!' kind of energy; it didn't go where he wanted it to go. He's had floating moments of happiness, but I'm feeling a joy-crisis dynamic around him. And he's kept himself busy— not necessarily happy busy. There's a real sense of dissatisfaction on his part; a tremendous amount of issues in this marriage. Right now I am feeling real bitterness about who didn't do what for the relationship. And there's a lot of concern and confusion over his kids. I'm getting that he has a boy and a girl. Did you know that?"

"Yes, I knew about his daughter because he'd contacted me right around the time she was born. I'd just had my first piece published in a local paper, and he called to congratulate me. That has to be close to 11 years ago. And then at one point a few years back we did reconnect very briefly over email, and he sent me a picture of the whole family, including his son. I could barely even look at it, so I ended up deleting it. And I immediately put him out of my mind again."

"Well, there's no doubt that you and he have the potential to recreate the relationship," Ann went on. "It's such an interesting energy. And I'm feeling that you were together in past lifetimes, but you both had karma to experience first in this lifetime before you could be together; it wasn't the right timing when you first met. Does that make sense?"

"It sure does," she concurred with a nod of her head. "The problem back then was that he was ready, and I wasn't, even though I really did love him. And even after I followed him to Florida to find out he was engaged, he pretty much admitted he wasn't excited about marrying her. But I refused to tell him how I really felt because I believed I was doing the honorable thing by stepping aside."

"Hmm," Ann replied, "I am getting a clear message that had you been honest with him he may not have gone through with the marriage. In fact, when the two of you do get together, he's going to tell you he never should have married her. It'll be interesting. You must definitely make contact. Absolutely call him."

"Are you really sure about that? I mean, the last thing I am is a home-wrecker, especially with two innocent children involved."

"Madeline," Ann stated emphatically. "The failure of Ken's marriage is not your fault. It's over because the two of them were never right for each other in the first place. If they couldn't make it work, that's directly attributable to Ken and his ex, not you. He had a lesson to learn about making good decisions and following his inner guidance. In spite of all of his misgivings and unresolved feelings for you, he still married her. And he's been a faithful husband all these years, but he's had it. Like I said, if he's not officially divorced, he's definitely in the middle of proceedings.

"But I cannot stress enough that you must contact him. He really wants to hear from you."

She took her words to heart, cognizant of Ann's remarkable abilities and pragmatic personality. She'd never advise her to do something this risky if she didn't truly see a positive outcome. The only problem now would be figuring out how to locate Ken's cell phone number or a personal email, though the Internet would most likely make that a fairly simple task. Beyond that, however, anything could happen, psychic phenomena notwithstanding.

"Girlfriend, I think it's great," Robin Aldridge exclaimed. One of Maddy's classmates from her Unity course, Robin, had been part of her prayer circle, a placement that had resulted in a beautiful friendship. For Robin, it had been all the more meaningful given the fact that she was a recent transplant to the Sunshine State. Delightfully satisfied after a healthy meal by the pool, the women now sat around chatting, while a pleasant breeze blew in off of the lake.

"It is kind of interesting," Maddy admitted. "All these weeks of praying for my perfect soul mate, the absolute right man for me and it turns out to be Kenny? I never would have guessed that in a million years."

"I still can't believe you never told any of us about him!" Elyse scolded playfully.

"That's because I truly did block him out. Except for a few fleeting moments over the years, it was as if he never existed at all. It's really scary to think how powerful the mind can be, but I should know that better than anyone after what I went through."

"So Maddy, when are you going to call him?" Audrey asked.

"As soon as I find a cell number. Ann had said I should call his house number and pretend to be an old friend from high school. But I am not the kind of girl that can play those sorts of games. It's just not in my nature."

"Me, either," Elyse added. "If you can't find a cell number, though, what are you going to do?"

"I honestly don't know," she replied.

"Well, Maddy I believe the answers will come to you," Robin proclaimed. "Look, you've been faithfully doing all of the homework assignments from class—the treasure mapping, volunteering your time to charity, getting up early so you can meditate and participating in our prayer circle. I have to believe that this is a sign for you. And what's the worst that can happen? You find out he's staying married? So what? At least you'll have a chance to start anew either way."

"That's a good point. One thing's for sure; I do have to take action. Whatever unfolds after that is up to God. I just hope He gives me the strength to accept whatever His will might be for this relationship."

"I have no doubt about that," Carolyn proclaimed. "And no matter what happens, you'll always have us."

A choked up Maddy smiled at them as she offered a silent prayer of thanks for all of the good people in her life.

Chapter 27

Madeline took a deep breath as she picked up her favorite pen. She'd decided on using one of her feminine note cards decorated with pink roses—along with a few sheets of matching pink writing paper, to showcase the extra thoughts she was certain would spill out of her heart and onto the pages. It was definitely a risk to mail such an intensely personal correspondence to the home of Ken's parents, though it was a far safer option than mailing it to the house he once shared—or might still possibly share, with his ex-wife.

In meditation earlier that morning, Maddy had a revelation: The "full circle" feeling that had consumed her since the dawn of the New Year had everything to do with Ken—and their unfinished business. While it might have been appropriate and even necessary way back when to banish him from her mind as if she'd never even met him, it was time to acknowledge the truth. Since the thought of posing as an old high school friend and calling his home terrified her, when she felt inspired to write him a letter, she followed the impulse.

And with the option of entrusting it to the care of his mom and dad, who perhaps not-so-coincidentally lived just down the road, her apprehensions were alleviated. Not completely gone, but calmed enough to compel her to act on her decision immediately, before accomplishing anything else on that sunny Monday. Filled with faith and hope, she began to form the cursive letters that would combine to create a beautiful mosaic of gratitude, remorse and affection.

Dear Ken,

How are you? I can't even imagine how you might feel right now, holding this letter in your hand. I mean, how long has it been? About a million years? And yet in so many ways, it feels like yesterday.

I don't know what it is about 2008, but ever since this year began, I have had a palpable feeling that everything was coming full circle somehow. It took me a few months to realize exactly what that meant, but now I have no doubt it involves you—and some important things I'd left undone and unsaid. Things you really need to know.

It's strange that you would be on my mind now; I can't explain why this is suddenly the case since I hadn't thought about you much at all over the years. For my own survival, I'd willfully blocked you out of my thoughts to the point where it was as if you never existed in the first place. There was just no way I could've been your friend, not in any sort of active way, at least. It was just too painful to see you with another woman, so I did the only thing I could do. You made your choice; I made mine. I even concocted a story to tell people whenever they would ask me why I moved to Florida. And the mind is such a powerful thing that I actually believed it myself.

Look, I know it is ancient history, but I am so very sorry for everything I ever said or did to hurt you. You were so good to me, so kind and caring. If I had a time machine, I am certain I would go back and make very different decisions where you were concerned. If I could go back with the knowledge I have now, I would understand just what I'd had in you. In many ways, you were so much more mature. You saw qualities within me that I was unable or unwilling to see for myself. And I never truly appreciated that.

You once told me that I inspired you; but the truth is you inspired me, too. I never realized just what a catalyst you have been in my life. These last fourteen years have been an incredible personal and spiritual growth journey, one that would not have been possible without you.

While I've had some pretty traumatic experiences (along with good ones), I can see now how every obstacle, hour of darkness, and tear shed in moments of anguish, have all contributed to making me the mature, self-adjusted woman I am today.

There are absolutely incredible people in my life that I am blessed to call friends, my writing career is finally in full swing, and my health is excellent (warm weather definitely agrees with me). Perhaps most significantly, my faith is stronger than it has ever been in my entire life. I owe all of this to you. Ken, you opened my eyes. You made me realize that the world—my world—was more expansive and wonderful than I'd ever imagined.

This may or may not be appropriate, but I want you to know that no man before or after you has ever treated me with the same amount of respect, affection, and concern. Sadly, at 25, I didn't know what I had. You were everything I didn't know I wanted. Yes, hindsight, as they say, really is 20/20. And no matter where you are or what you are doing, I hope it makes you feel good to know just how much you have positively impacted my life. At least, that is the intention of this letter.

Anyway, I am sure you are an awesome father, and I pray that you are well and happy. Take care of yourself and God bless!
Madeline
*P.S. If you are so inclined, I would love to hear from you. You can email me at **maddyrose67@goodmail.com** or call me at (561) 555-4257.*

After reading it over several times, she sealed the envelope, affixed a stamp and ran out to the mail slot to send her message on its way, while her confidence still remained strong. Then she curled up on her pale peach leather loveseat with a cup of Dunkin Donuts coffee and pondered how long it might be before her letter reached Ken's hands. Closing her eyes, she silently prayed to God to safely deliver her masterpiece to its intended recipient. Then she asked for the strength to let go, knowing that the ball was now in Ken's court.

Paula Lockhart looked at her pedometer and picked up the pace as she conducted her customary late-morning power walk. An attractive woman in her late-60's, she was diligent about remaining active and eating right to maintain good health. After all, she had two adorable grandchildren to see into adulthood. And now that her youngest son had endured a bitter custody battle and an acrimonious divorce, she was more determined than ever to support him and his offspring.

She'd always been so proud of Ken; from the time he was a little boy, he'd been her most affectionate and devoted son. Even as a newborn, she'd noticed something different—and wonderful—about her "baby." His soulful blue eyes showcased a natural exuberance and passion for life. And despite their modest means, she knew from the very beginning that her fourth and last child was destined to be a success in every sense of the word.

Too bad her former daughter-in-law hadn't shared that opinion. Oh sure, in the beginning, she used him like a security blanket after she'd accepted a lucrative position with an ad agency in Miami and relocated from Atlantic City. Oddly, for such a talented and successful girl, Erin had more than her fair share of insecurities, depending on Ken to provide everything from a social life to a comfortable place to live.

And while he was working hard as a mortgage broker and real estate agent by day, and taking classes in marketing and business at Florida International University four nights a week, she constantly harangued him over stupid things, like buying her the "wrong" gift or not spending enough time together. Paula sighed as she recalled one particular Valentine's Day when Ken had inadvertently provoked Erin's ire by buying her rollerblades—even though she'd been asking for them for months. That had been just one in a series of troubling incidents that should have prevented her son from walking down the aisle.

Alas, as a mother, Paula's policy was to listen, sympathize and offer only solicited advice—with no expectation that such advice would actually be accepted or followed. Thus, after countless heart-to-hearts with her son, she and her husband Carl supported him when he decided to marry Erin. It hadn't helped that Erin's parents had constantly chided them for "living in sin," until they'd both felt so guilty they couldn't wait to exchange vows just to shut them up. And while Paula and Carl hadn't exactly been thrilled with their son's living arrangements, they would have much preferred it if Ken had waited to at least finish school before committing to Erin in front of God and witnesses.

She rounded a corner of beautiful bougainvilleas as she took a sip of bottled water. Making her way past the lovely Old Florida two- and three- bedroom homes that comprised her Royal Oak Hills neighborhood, she suddenly had a flashback to another time and place. She and Ken were sitting on a bench at the Deerfield Beach Fishing Pier, watching the sun rise up over the horizon like a bright orange ball. He'd asked her to meet him there at daybreak, as was their usual custom when important matters needed to be discussed. Though Ken and Carl had long ago smoothed out their differences, his mother was still the parent he entrusted with his innermost thoughts and pressing conflicts.

She couldn't quite recall the name of the girl, but remembered their conversation had centered on someone her son had met and dated back in Somers Point. At the time, he'd been absolutely certain he would marry this Philadelphia-born, college-educated daughter of a successful neurosurgeon. And indeed, she'd appeared to return his feelings—that is, until she'd succumbed to family pressure to find someone who shared her level of education. But the break-up hadn't lasted long, and within a matter of months, they'd reconciled, only to go their separate ways again. Paula was still unclear about how it had all gone down.

But on that bright South Florida morning, Ken, who'd not yet presented Erin with an engagement ring, confided in his mother with a mixture of trepidation and excitement that this young woman from Pennsylvania, blissfully unaware of his live-in relationship, had finally announced her decision to move to Pompano Beach that fall. He'd begged her for an entire year to join him in the Sunshine

State—an offer she'd firmly and repeatedly refused. After giving up on ever attracting the girl of his dreams away from the Philly area, he'd resolved to focus exclusively on Erin, whose thriving career in advertising made such a move plausible, given the abundance of competitive agencies in Miami-Dade.

Now as he wrestled with his guilt, he asked Paula for her insights.

"Oh, honey, I can't tell you what to do. You've got to follow your heart," was all she'd offered. But it had been clear to her that Ken was going to take what he believed to be the "honorable" course of action: marrying Erin and somehow finding a way to be a good friend to his former flame, though it was hard to ignore the passionate history they'd shared. And though the thought of being a part of her wonderful, close family also thrilled him—especially where Louis was concerned, he'd decided he had to let go of such fantasies. After all, he'd pursued an unsuspecting Erin, who'd been able to return his affections with no apprehensions or geographical limitations.

"I wonder whatever became of that girl," Paula thought, wiping her forehead with a towel. She seemed to remember something about an article she'd written for *The Good News Gazette*, having to do with her Down syndrome brother who'd once been dismissed as a lost cause, only to have gone on to tremendous success, thanks to her determined parents.

As Paula recalled, when Ken had caught sight of it, he'd been blown away, though he'd said very little. But judging from the look in his eyes, she'd understood that her son still harbored very deep and complicated feelings for this young woman. And though she'd had no doubt he'd prove himself a devoted family man, it tugged at her heart to witness his obvious regret for what might have been. But that had transpired over ten years ago; no doubt this girl had gone on and married by now.

Now just a few steps away from her driveway, she caught sight of her mailman.

"Good morning, Dennis," she greeted him.

"Paula, how are you?" he replied. "Looks like you've got another good batch of mail today." He handed her a pile of bills, circulars and catalogs as she caught up with him.

"I sure do," she laughed. "Well, this should keep me busy for a while.

Thanks." She closed the door behind her as she entered the blissfully air-conditioned house, a welcome respite from the outdoor heat.

She settled into a recliner and proceeded to flip through the assortment until a pink envelope caught her eye. In neat handwriting that belied the writer's feminine gender, she noticed that the correspondence was addressed to Ken, in care of Mr. and Mrs. Carl Lockhart. Paula didn't know why, but she suddenly felt a shiver of excitement run up and down her spine. Walking to the phone, she immediately dialed her son's cell.

"Hey Mom, what's up?" Ken responded with his customary enthusiasm upon answering her call.

"Hi, honey. I am sorry to bother you while you're on the road. I know how swamped you've been with work."

"Never too busy for my mom," he assured her. She smiled on her end of the line.

"Well, honey I was just calling to let you know that a letter arrived here for you today. There's no name on it, just a return address of 27 Royal Palm Way. I don't know why whoever wrote it mailed it to me, but it'll be here whenever you have time to pick it up. Perhaps it's a belated birthday card?"

His heart skipped a beat as he remembered that Madeline lived in Boca Bayou. In fact, she was the only person he knew who lived in that community. Could it be that she somehow sensed that he'd been trying to find her? Or did she just want to wish an old friend with whom she shared the same birthday, a year of happiness? That would be kind of odd since she had never previously done that.

"Ken?" Paula wondered if they'd been disconnected.

"Yes, I'm here. Sorry about that, my phone must've cut out." He didn't want her to know he was lost in thought and emotion at the prospect of Madeline possibly coming back into his life.

"Do you have any idea who might have sent this to you?"

"Not really. Maybe it's an old friend from college or even the Navy. I'm really curious, now, but I doubt I can get over there until sometime this weekend."

"Ok hon, it'll be here waiting for you."

"Thanks, Mom."

"Ken?"

"Yes?"

"I don't know why, but I have a really good feeling about this."

Ken took a deep breath and dialed the number he'd located on Google a few short weeks ago. After he'd hung up with his mother, he'd pulled into a shopping center to collect his thoughts; he had 20 minutes to get to his next appointment, which was less than two miles away, creating a golden opportunity to make at least a brief contact. Funny, he'd been waiting for some sort of sign, and now that the Universe had delivered, using his mom as the messenger, he knew he had to act quickly.

However, an urgent incoming call from the office—informing him of a hot new lead—promptly put an end to his plans. No problem. It was probably better to call her over the weekend anyway when they would both have more time to talk. As he pulled onto I-95 from Hillsboro Boulevard, images of Madeline's smiling face flooded his brain as he maneuvered through the daunting South Florida traffic.

"All set Mom?" Madeline asked as she opened the front door of her condo and wheeled out the last of the luggage. It was 9 a.m. on Sunday morning, and they were about to hop on the Florida turnpike on their way to four days of fun in Disneyworld. They'd each gotten a good night's sleep and were excited about hanging out with Mickey, Minnie and the rest of the enchanting cast of characters.

"I'm ready, hon," Monica Rose replied, with a final check around the kitchen to ensure she'd picked up all of her medications. Though she and Maddy had taken Louis to Disney just five years prior, she was looking forward to experiencing some of the new attractions Maddy had told her so much about. And she always enjoyed visiting Epcot's

World Showcase, where various pavilions and attractions offered a glimpse into the customs and culinary traditions of various countries including Japan, Italy, Norway—and of course, the USA.

Maddy locked the door behind them as they made their way to her silver Honda, all tuned up and ready to safely transport them the 180 miles or so to Orlando. She'd loaded the car with some of her favorite CD's and motivational tapes to keep them entertained along the way. Blessed with sunny, comfortable weather, the trek north was sure to be a delightful one.

After confirming they'd loaded all of the bags with one last look around the car, Maddy backed out of her reserved space and lead the vehicle out to Dixie Highway, intending to access I-95 from Yamato Road, and then pick up the turnpike in Jupiter. It would be her last hurrah for a while as her new corporate position was set to begin in another week; she looked forward to spending this quality time with her mother.

Ken felt his heart pound in his chest as he listened to the familiar ring tone and eagerly anticipated hearing the sounds of her voice again. A few moments later he did, though it was via voicemail and not the live version. As her outgoing message played, suddenly, it was 1992 again, and he and Maddy were making out on his waterbed while the moonlight filtered through the skylight above them.

His hands caressed her face as he gazed into her expressive amber eyes. Nestled beneath his body, he could feel her heart beating fast while he placed his lips tenderly on hers, and then eventually tasted the sweetness of her mouth with his soft, subtle tongue. Maddy sighed, returning his advances with equal amounts of passion and fervor. In the background, the sensual sounds of their favorite music amplified their desires.

"Kenny?" Her voice was a mere whisper as he nibbled at her ear. He brought his face close to hers.

"Yes?" Her fingers traced the waves of his blond hair as she made her request.

"I want you to make love to me."

Happily stunned, but wanting to confirm the words he'd been longing to hear ever since meeting her, he studied her face for a moment before asking, "You sure, sweetheart? 'Cause you know I'd like nothing better than to make passionate love to you all night. I just need to know it's what you really want, too. Otherwise, it won't—"

Madeline answered him with a kiss that left him breathless as he proceeded to slowly unbutton her blouse to reveal her delicate, porcelain skin and the black lace of her bra. He began to trace kisses down her neck, working his way down to the curve of her breasts as he gently moved his hands over her. In the next moment, he carefully slid the garment off of her body and shifted her on top of him as he moved onto his back in one smooth move.

With her auburn hair cascading past her shoulders and her fair skin gleaming in the soft light, she far exceeded any vision of beauty he'd previously held in mind, both as an adolescent and a young man sailing around the world. He reached around her back to unhook the last trace of clothing from her chest, barely able to contain his excitement as delicious thoughts of finally seeing and experiencing every inch of her petite, curvy body conflicted with genuine concern for this being her very first time, and his desire to make it as beautiful for her as possible.

Back in the present, an intrusive beep interrupted Ken's fantasy. Though they'd never gotten nearly that far back in the day, his virtual interlude had felt so real to him that—for one brief second, he couldn't distinguish between reality and imagination. Caught off guard, his message kind of rambled on, in spite of his best efforts.

Madeline, hey it's Kenny. My Mom said she got a letter addressed from Royal Palm Way. I haven't read it yet, but...uh—I didn't say anything to her—but I assume that would be a Boca Bayou residence, and that would mean that you wrote me a letter. Uh, I guess it's a birthday... thing since you and I share the same birthday. Like I said, I haven't read it yet, 'cause I haven't been able to get over there, I've been so swamped with work.

So...uh, hope you're having a wonderful March, and that's about it. Thanks for the card. I haven't had the time to get over there, I've been so busy. But I will grab it, appreciate it, and hopefully...well, the reason I called is to make sure...uh...that you didn't need to talk to me. 'Cause

I'm not sure what's going on with you, what's happenin', but I hope everything's ok. It was such a pleasant surprise, and I'm gonna try to get over there this afternoon. So, um...thanks again...oh, and if you want to reach me, my cell number is (954) 555-1870. It's a business line, but you can call it anytime. Ok, talk to you later.

"Wasn't that great, Mom!" Maddy inquired enthusiastically as she and her mother disembarked from Soarin', Epcot's latest ride sensation.

"Wonderful," she agreed. "If the line wasn't so damn long, I'd get back on it again."

"To think, Lori was worried you'd be scared," Maddy laughed.

"Your sister thinks I'm a baby. That was absolutely beautiful. It's amazing how they can really make you feel as if you are hang-gliding over California."

"I know, wasn't it cool when it looked like we were landing on the aircraft carrier? That was my favorite part."

"Yes, and I loved the beginning when you come out of the clouds and see the Golden Gate Bridge and all that water; that was really something."

The two women boarded an escalator to bring them back up to the second floor, and the exit to the Land building. They were planning to head to Spaceship Earth next, where they'd board a slow-moving train within the geosphere globe, which would transport them through a historical journey of communication—from the dawn of civilization right up through modern times and beyond. However, they looked up to find a large crowd of soggy Disney vacationers, dressed in plastic ponchos and hanging around just inside the main doors.

"Uh-oh, looks like it's coming down pretty hard," Maddy sighed. "We should wait here for a while."

As she and her mother observed the endless parade of strollers, scooters and kids of all ages excitedly rushing in from the rain or walking determinedly towards the attraction of their choice, Maddy was consumed with thoughts of Ken. *Had her letter safely reached him? Did he have a chance to read it yet? How would he react? What if he wasn't really divorced, in spite of the evidence to the contrary?*

"Madeline, did you hear me? It stopped raining. I think we should make a run for it before the skies open up again." Monica spoke with urgency as she took her daughter by the arm.

It was only their first day and already her legs ached. Between running up and down ramps to catch monorails, maneuvering around hordes of people who wielded their baby transport systems as weapons, and standing in incredibly long lines, it was enough to test the mettle of someone half her age. It didn't help that a long, cold winter had prevented her from regularly walking the trail at Ridley Creek State Park.

Maddy shook her head in agreement as the two women dashed outside, taking care to avoid the endless, messy puddles as they hurried towards their next Epcot adventure.

"Hey, Mom! Dad!" Ken called out as he unlocked the front door and entered his parents' living room. He'd just dropped his son off at baseball practice, giving him the perfect chance to finally solve the mystery of the letter—not so much its author, as he was fairly certain of her identity—but surely its content. While he guessed it was a birthday card, he also hoped that all was well with Maddy. Was there a particular reason she needed to reach him? He fervently hoped it wasn't to tell him she was leaving the state, or worse—getting married. And since he assumed Madeline was in the dark about his current marital status, it made complete sense that she would seek out an alternative way to contact him.

When no one responded, he moved into the kitchen, where a note was waiting for him on the table with the explanation that Mr. and Mrs. Lockhart had accepted a friend's dinner invitation in Lighthouse Point. Unknown to her husband, Paula had specifically sought out an excuse to give their son some privacy; it was a safe bet he wouldn't get any with Erin still lurking around. Carl and Paula appreciated Ken's desire to make the divorce as painless as possible for the children. Still, they couldn't quite understand how Ken could tolerate living in the same home with a former spouse who seemed to relish tormenting him in word and action.

He set aside the note when he noticed the telltale pink envelope lying next to it. A shiver of excitement ran through his entire being as he sat down and proceeded to read the letter's sentiments, so eloquently expressed within a feminine card and three extra sheets of matching writing paper.

Chapter 28

Ken wiped away a tear as he absorbed the significance of her genuine revelations. It sure was a relief to know she still thought of him, and more importantly, that she didn't hate him. He'd been plagued with so many residual and conflicting emotions over the years—love, guilt, concern, desire, and regret—never quite knowing exactly how her life had been affected by his decision to marry another.

He'd assumed she was doing well, though he'd come up short on every online search he'd conducted recently. He had a vague idea that she was writing, based on the articles she used to contribute to *The Good News Gazette*, though that had been way back when Bonnie was an infant. And their brief email correspondence from a few years ago had revealed she lived in Boca Bayou.

But aside from that, there was very little he knew. And it went far beyond her career and place of residence. In spite of staggered moments of euphoria (which included the births of his daughter and son), and a purposely hectic schedule over the last several years, he'd never once forgotten about her. On the contrary, while he remained a faithful husband to Erin and a devoted father to Bonnie and Brian, within the sacred boundaries of his heart, he still harbored intense feelings of love and desire for Madeline, as well as an abundance of regret for what might have been.

In the tranquility of a tropical evening, he'd oftentimes lie awake in bed while Erin slept, as visions of Maddy's smiling face haunted him. Later, when he'd moved into the sanctuary of the spare bedroom following his marital separation, these visualizations took on new and uninhibited life as if now fully free to come into expression without fear of reprisal.

Of course, he'd done everything in his power to make his marriage work, mainly for the sake of his children. Occasional tensions notwithstanding, Ken had always appreciated growing up in a stable home with two parents who'd instilled traditional values. In fact, one of the many things that attracted him to Maddy initially was her similar upbringing. True, her dad was a professional who made a helluva lot more money than his own father. However, when it came down to the things that really mattered—close relationships, religious faith, love of country and an abiding passion for life, the Rose family and the Lockhart family were more alike than different.

But when Ken had stupidly abandoned all hope of him and Madeline ever making it to the altar, Erin entered his life, bringing with her the desired background, along with something else—a willingness to relocate to Florida. And though ashamed to admit it, it hadn't hurt that Erin had possessed no qualms about giving herself to a man before marriage. As a young man, he would've gladly waited for Madeline; but when he'd also grown to love another with whom he could satisfy his physical needs as well, lust had won out, at least for a while.

Months of pleading with her on the phone to move down here with him, endless conversations during which he'd be moved to tears out of a persistent longing for her, had accomplished nothing. Though frustrated with her job and her life, she had remained vehemently opposed to leaving her family for sunnier skies and a real chance at happiness. Erin, on the other hand, relished the thought of kissing Philly goodbye. And it hadn't hurt that she was a beautiful woman, too, though her statuesque frame, platinum blonde hair, and deep blue eyes were a striking contrast to Madeline's petite build and china doll looks.

In the beginning, Erin held true to her Catholic upbringing, having been raised in a humble household in southwest Philadelphia. As an only child, her parents had doted on her, nurturing her creative talents with piano lessons, art classes, and even a private acting coach. As she grew, Erin also discovered a passion for business, leading her to combine a fine arts degree with courses in marketing, advertising, and management. By the time she'd graduated from Drexel University after successful completion of a five-year co-op program, she'd garnered several lucrative job offers.

She began her career with a prestigious firm in Center City before the Trump Corporation wooed her away by doubling her salary and enhancing her already impressive resume. That move would impact her life in more ways than one as it soon led to her meeting with Ken Lockhart one evening, at the behest of a mutual friend. Ken had resisted the idea of a blind date at first, still reeling from his mishandling of the Madeline situation.

He remembered how they'd reconciled just before Christmas, prompting Maddy to invite him to attend the Eagles-Vikings game with her and Lori, for which they'd had an extra ticket. Since it had been a spur-of-the-moment decision, suggested by none other than Monica Rose, Ken had to do a lot of persuading to get someone to cover for him at the plant before officially accepting her invitation. And though Madeline hadn't formally apologized for writing him a Dear John letter several weeks prior, when he'd called her on the phone, he sensed the regret in her voice. He'd contacted her that evening to let her know he'd accepted her decision and harbored no bitterness.

Awhile later, she'd called him back out of the blue to ask him about driving to her house in Pennsylvania for the game, pointing out the irony that the Eagles' opponent that week just happened to be Ken's second-favorite football team. And lingering resentment aside, he'd been ecstatic about hearing from her again. No matter how much her rejection had stung, his heart exuded nothing but unconditional love, along with the indistinguishable hope of marrying her someday—once he'd completed his education, of course.

"Wow," he whispered aloud, to no one in particular. "You really know how to make a grown man weep." As he lingered in his parents' kitchen, he poured over every sentence, every sentiment repeatedly, as if needing unequivocal reassurance this was indeed real and not just some fabrication of a restless soul, longing for its twin flame.

He stared out the window as the fronds of a coconut palm gracefully danced in the gentle breeze and thought back to a day nearly fourteen years earlier, when a young Madeline had walked into his real estate office, impeccably dressed in a peach linen suit. She'd been fresh off a flight from Atlantic City to Fort Lauderdale, to meet with a prospective employer, in anticipation of her impending move to Pompano Beach a few weeks later. Family friends who'd lived there had offered her temporary shelter until she'd gotten her bearings and found an apartment in a safe area.

During the multitude of phone conversations that had preceded this particular visit, he had struggled in vain to find the words to tell her he'd been living with another woman—one whom he'd been excited to marry. That is until Madeline shocked the hell out of him. He never in a million years expected such an abrupt turnaround; for more than twelve months, she'd consistently rejected his pleas to join him in the Sunshine State. Now, with one 180-degree turn, she'd rocked his entire world.

But it was too late. And while he acknowledged at the deepest level that marrying Erin might possibly be the biggest mistake of his life, he just couldn't abandon her. After all, when he left New Jersey to pursue his dreams, they'd both felt the intense pain of separation. Yet Erin actively sought to remedy the situation by diligently working with a head hunter to secure a good position in Miami. Unlike Maddy, she'd placed no geographical restrictions on love.

Unfortunately, their live-in arrangement soon revealed significant differences—impediments that Ken hoped would either dissolve entirely or at least mitigate once they were united in the bonds of marriage. In hindsight, of course, he'd realized the error of his mindset; that while he truly did love Erin, it had been utterly foolish to believe they could actually go the distance with her relentless insecurities, self-centeredness, and proclivity towards distrust inflicting slow, steady and ultimately— unfixable, damage to their union.

Every female, whether Ken's boss, co-worker or fellow college student, provoked Erin's pervasive jealousy. On more than one occasion he recalled knock-down, drag-out arguments with her over innocuous incidents, from a study session in broad daylight over coffee at Starbucks, to mandatory after-hours socializing with the sales and operations teams at a company-sponsored event.

A respectful guy by nature, he despised fighting with his wife, particularly when the altercations had no basis in reality. Oftentimes, he'd simply retreat to the golf course or the beach when things deteriorated at home. And once they'd had both children, prompting Erin to set up her own business out of the spare bedroom, Ken found himself even less eager to engage her unfounded accusations. He didn't want his innocent kids to suffer the consequences of their parent's ill-advised decision to tie the knot, so he took great pains to avoid raising his voice around their mother—an effort that demanded a tremendous amount of restraint.

Then there was the negative influence of the Boca Raton culture. While an exceedingly beautiful city and a desirable place to live, Boca's downside was the extreme superficiality of many of its residents, some of whom held positions of power within the community, from the local paper's society page writer to the plethora of ambitious millionaires that populated upscale neighborhoods like Broken Sound, Royal Palm and the Sanctuary. While Ken envied no one, content to focus on his own goals, Erin got caught up in the web of botox, breast enhancements and liposuction that characterized the activities of the city's wealthiest females.

And as her business thrived, so did her vanity, leading her to undergo a seemingly endless parade of plastic surgeries, all to assuage her fears of growing older and help her keep pace with the women with whom she networked for both business and social purposes. After almost thirteen years of marriage, Ken didn't even recognize her—or was it perhaps more accurate to say that he was just beginning to?

Looking back down at Madeline's delicate handwriting, he re-read her line about how no man before or after him had ever treated her with the same amount of respect, affection, and concern. These words both thrilled and saddened him. On the one hand, he sensed a golden opportunity to rectify the mistakes of the past; on the other, it pained him that someone this special had failed to find the true love and commitment she so richly deserved. *What was wrong with some of these guys anyway? Didn't they recognize quality when they saw it?*

He folded the writing paper back into the note card before sliding it into the envelope. To think, just a few hours ago, he'd left her a message assuming her letter had been nothing more than a birthday greeting. Somehow, Madeline always did find a way to surprise him. Flipping open his cell phone, he checked the time and realized Brian's baseball practice was about to end. He raced out of the front door and into his white Lexus sedan. And as he drove past the flowering yellow trees that adorned the traffic islands separating eastbound and westbound traffic on Palmetto Park Road, for the first time in an eternity, he began to feel alive again.

"Home at last," Maddy announced, unlocking the tall, green door that marked the entrance to her condo and ushering her mother through the small foyer.

"Whew, feels good," Monica admitted a moment later as she propped her severely aching feet on the comfy leather couch in Maddy's living room. "I had a wonderful time, honey, but I think that's my swan song for Disney. Your mother's getting too old for that kind of walking."

She laughed out loud, attempting to hide her sadness in the face of this reality. It wasn't easy for either one of them to think of her that way.

"It was fun, though, you have to admit," Maddy suggested playfully.

"Oh, it sure was, sweetie," she replied. "And I had a great time, especially at Epcot. Actually, that's the one park I know your father would enjoy. I'd definitely consider taking him there."

Maddy wheeled her mother's suitcase into the guest room as they spoke, before heading into the kitchen to check her phone messages. Surely Ken must've gotten her letter by now.

"Madeline, when you're done I want to give your father a call," Monica requested from across the room.

"No problem, Mom. Let me check my voicemail real quick and it's all yours."

"Take your time. I'm just enjoying sitting here."

Nothing could have prepared her for the fireworks that erupted within at the mere sound of Ken's voice. As if afraid of her thoughts displaying on some sort of celestial cloud for the whole world to see, she moved to the recliner chair in her sitting area, which was located at the extreme front of her home. After listening to his message a few times, she pressed "2" to save it in the archives, and then jotted down Ken's cell phone number.

"It's all yours, Mom," she said as calmly as she could, handing over the cordless before taking her cell and retreating to the privacy of her bedroom.

Here it was, nearly 11 p.m. on a Wednesday evening. He'd mentioned specifically that the cell number he'd given her was a business line. Did she dare dial the number now? After a brief internal debate, she decided to go for it. After all, she'd been searching for him long enough. It was high time to just get on with it, knowing that whatever might transpire, she could handle the outcome well. Having successfully overcome truly horrific problems in the past, she could now effectively cope with anything else life threw at her. She'd been thoroughly tested and proven incredibly stronger for the experience.

This reconnection could, as Ann had predicted, lead to a renewal of her and Ken's relationship and a subsequent marriage; or it could simply usher in a final and welcome resolution on the past. Either way, it would smoothly transition her into a new phase of life—one she instinctively knew would lead to even greater happiness and peace.

Ken's phone immediately went into voicemail, and Madeline smiled as she listened to his professional, outgoing message. Then she sent her reply:

Kenny, hey it's Madeline. I apologize for not getting back to you sooner, but my Mom's here visiting until Sunday, and we just got back from Disney tonight. By now, I am sure you've read my letter, and I hope it didn't freak you out. I want you to know I meant everything I said, but I don't have to tell you that. You know me well enough to know I'm sincere. Anyway, it was great to hear back from you, and I hope we can talk real soon. Take care.

After bidding her mom goodnight a few minutes later, Maddy climbed into bed, hopeful and excited.

A few miles away, Ken stared at the tray ceiling and spinning overhead fan. Though it was getting late, he still didn't feel tired, as his mind raced from one scenario to another. From what he could ascertain from her letter, she was most likely single. *But had she married at some point? If so, what happened? He found it impossible to believe that someone hadn't snatched her up, yet why was she contacting him after all this time?*

Yes, he understood the purpose of her card, and it touched him deeply that she felt the need to apologize for past transgressions. And at the same time, he acknowledged that he was guilty of inflicting pain on her; in many ways, he should've been the one sending a letter.

Strange also that this particular year had brought her so much clarity; he'd just signed his divorce papers the previous fall. *Did Maddy somehow know that?* If she had been aware of his marital status, she offered no indication in her correspondence. His last recent search of public records had revealed no information whatsoever, which was understandable, given that his attorney had advised him it could take up to a year for such records to be updated on Internet databases. With no mutual friends or acquaintances to spread the word, she was most likely in the dark. And that made her gesture even more impressive.

He rolled over onto his side, kicking the cotton sheets down to the end of the bed. Ever since having children, he no longer enjoyed the luxury of sleeping in the raw and had taken to wearing boxer shorts. Tonight, he'd just happened to have chosen a green pair featuring the Philadelphia Eagles logo, though it had been ages since he'd actually slept in them; somehow, it felt appropriate. Funny, Erin despised football, one of the many activities Ken and Maddy had delighted in together.

It was also thrilling that she regarded him as a catalyst for positive change in her life, despite all of the heartbreak he'd caused her. And the thought that he'd somehow inspired her was the icing on the cake. All this time he feared she might actually feel nothing but contempt for him, though he completely understood her rationale for keeping her distance. He supposed it was selfish of him to want to keep her as a friend while he gave his love and devotion to another woman, but he'd truly missed her presence in his life. *Could there be a miracle, a second chance looming on the horizon for them?* God, he hoped so.

Madeline awoke to the sound of a ringing phone; good thing she'd had the wisdom to bring her cordless into the bedroom with her last night. When she glanced at the display, her heart skipped a beat. She quickly rubbed her eyes and cleared her throat in an attempt to remove all traces of lingering sleepiness.

"Hello?"

"Good morning, sunshine!" All of the familiar sensations rushed through her body at the sound of his enthusiastic greeting.

"Ken, how are you?"

"I'm doing just great. How are you?"

"Very well, thanks."

"So, what's been going on? It was so great to hear from you."

He was cruising down Interstate 95 on his way into the office. God, it was so nice to listen to her ebullient voice again; he well remembered the irresistible way she spoke in energetic bursts. Clearly, the passage of time hadn't diminished one of the many attractive qualities he'd loved most about her; he could just picture her smiling face and accompanying lively hand gestures as she filled him in on her current life. *Had thirteen years really passed since he'd seen her?* It hardly seemed possible.

Madeline struggled to focus on his words, thanks to the pulsating rhythm of her heart—a cadence that had dramatically accelerated upon being referred to as "sunshine." Try as she might, it was difficult to avoid jumping to the conclusion—based on one term of affection—that he was free in the legal sense. While he was obviously happy to talk to her, it was hardly conclusive evidence of his marital status.

But she noted with interest his accomplishment of an MBA degree, while working full-time as an outside sales rep for a telecommunications company—a career that was as lucrative as it was enjoyable. It thrilled her to witness the sheer excitement in his voice as he discussed his responsibilities and Palm Beach County territory. Because he only dealt with businesses employing a minimum of 100 people, his commissions tended to be high.

And yet, there was no trace of arrogance or smugness—only gratitude for having the ability to do something he loved and be rewarded handsomely for it. It was so adorably Ken for him to admit, "I've never made this much money in my life!"

But it was no surprise to Maddy that he'd come so far while retaining his innate humility; right from the beginning, she'd known he was destined for something greater.

All of the deep conversations they'd shared beneath the skylight, snuggled up in the waterbed of his Somers Point home had laid the foundation for this present reality. That inner spark he'd possessed from birth, that unquenchable desire to rise above his circumstances had partnered with a brilliant mind to produce spectacular results. It was a fitting tribute to the power of the human spirit when allowed to flourish in a free and democratic country—a nation that he himself had spent a portion of his life defending. Like so many in her family, Ken truly embodied the American dream.

Neither one of them dared mentioned children, spouses or even possible boyfriends, though Ken had the benefit of near-certainty of her single status, which had been implicitly stated in her letter. Still, he hesitated to ruin the joy of this reconnection by speaking of Erin, even for the express purpose of revealing his divorce. *Why remind either one of them of the pain of the past?* For now, he'd simply savor this long-overdue conversation with Madeline; he could fill her in on the details of his marital break-up when they finally met face-to-face again.

However, he couldn't resist "confessing" to Googling her and feeling frustrated when his searches came up empty. His admission sent shivers of excitement down her spine, proving Ann right on yet another point— Ken had ardently wanted Maddy to contact him. The psychic had been adamant about so many things, not the least of which was Ken and Madeline's ability to "recreate the relationship," now that he was out of his marriage. And though Ann's track record had been nearly flawless over the years, Madeline still yearned to hear him speak the words as she held the phone to her ear and paced around her bedroom.

But though no outright confirmation was forthcoming, he did surprise her by asking if they could get together the following week, a request she happily agreed to, while thoughts of seeing his handsome face again resonated ecstatically through her being. After giving her his personal email and confirming receipt of her cell phone number, he reluctantly ended the call to begin another hectic workday. With an even brighter smile than usual, he strode through the double-glass door of his office, invigorated and hopeful.

Chapter 29

Madeline applied a fresh coat of pinkish-red lipstick and tightened the belt of her floral print dress as she gazed into the ladies room mirror. It was nearly 1 p.m., and she was scheduled to meet Ken in a few minutes. Although she'd been overwhelmed with critical work projects, including an e-proposal and new website content for a major cruise line, it had been difficult to focus. Thoughts of Ken kept flooding her brain, and—in spite of her excitement, a twinge of regret for having opened this Pandora's Box in the first place.

Yes, she'd followed the divine guidance and written the letter, after which she'd felt a welcome sense of relief. Later, when they finally connected, her heart soared at the sound of his voice and his admission that he'd been trying to find her, too. Ann had insisted that the energies were indeed positive and that he was available in every sense of the word. So far, so good. *So why did she feel as if her heart was about to explode?*

She brushed her long, layered hair and spritzed just a tiny bit of Incanto, her new favorite perfume, behind her ears and onto her wrists. After taking one long, deep breath, she was about to head for the elevators when her cell phone rang, nearly causing her to faint from surprise. Relief washed over her when she saw that it was not Ken calling to cancel, but Elyse, ready to provide a last-minute pep talk.

"Hey, girl! You excited?"

"Oh Elyse, I can hardly breathe."

"C'mon, stay calm. This is what you've been waiting for forever; it's gonna be fantastic!"

"W-what if he's not divorced?" Maddy swallowed hard.

"For the last time, we have enough evidence to prove he's not married anymore—remember Erin's website and his MySpace listing? And as you've told me many times, he'd never play with your feelings by suggesting a get-together in the first place if he wasn't free. Besides, has Ann ever been wrong about anything really important? For goodness sake, this is the woman who solved your panic and anxiety problem. And she's been spot-on with my stuff; I say we trust her."

"Yeah, I guess you're right."

"So there it is," Elyse proclaimed. "Girl, you've paid your dues. It's time to accept your reward."

"Aw, thanks, Elyse." Maddy was truly appreciative of their genuine friendship, which had evolved into a close, sisterly bond in the wake of Kevin's untimely and horrible demise from that monstrous brain tumor. It was hard to believe over two years had passed since the day of her nephew's devastating diagnosis; Maddy recalled the absolute horror and utter helplessness the Lombard family had endured for over 10 arduous months as they fought against the inevitable.

"So, do you have your lipstick on? Is your hair cascading down in sexy waves? You're wearing a hot little dress, right?"

"Affirmative on all three!" Maddy cracked up. "And hey, you'll also be happy to know I am wearing a Victoria's Secret push-up bra. Not that there's much to push up, but—"

"I LOVE it!" Elyse mimicked her four-year-old niece's favorite expression, the ultimate seal of approval. Maddy laughed again; Elyse had a way of helping her work through just about every problem with her quirky sense of humor.

"You worked damn hard at Christine's studio to earn that toned body, girlfriend. And I worked damn hard on your wardrobe makeover—not that it needed a lot of help, just a tad more, uh, excitement. I wish I could be a fly on the wall today; it's gonna be tough getting through my appointments, wondering how you and Ken are doing."

"Ok Leese, let me run while I'm feeling much more relaxed."

"Where are you meeting him again?"

"The Samba Room."

"Ooh, it's gonna be great, Madeline. I'm so excited; call me later!"

"Will do. Bye for now."

Maddy floated to the elevator bank, positively glowing.

"May I help you?" A petite, attractive twenty-something hostess with big, dark eyes and a friendly demeanor looked up from behind the podium.

"Uh, yes I'm meeting someone here, but I just wanted to see if I could get a table for two outside. You look pretty busy, so I wasn't sure if you'd be willing to hold something for me until she gets here. She works just a block away, so I'm sure she'll be here any second."

A nervous Ken shot the young girl the most charming expression he could muster, an easy feat given his striking appearance. Though not required to wear a suit by his employer, he'd chosen one of his favorites for this very special day—a beige Armani he'd gotten for a steal at the Men's Wearhouse. Complemented by his neatly pressed pale blue shirt, toned body and boyish grin, he barely looked a day over 30.

"No problem, Sir," she replied with a slight Latin accent. "We still have a few patio tables available. If you'd like you can sit at the bar; I can—"

"Never mind, she's here," he replied in an almost imperceptible voice as he walked back out through the double glass doors, unable to wipe the Cheshire grin off his face. From her perch, the hostess witnessed the unfolding scene with fascination. Ken was rendered speechless as he watched Madeline—the same irresistible vision of femininity and sweetness he remembered well from their South Jersey days—stroll confidently towards him on the sidewalk. Upon meeting his stare, she grinned from ear to ear, as her earlier anxiety transitioned into a calm knowingness.

"Oh my God, you look great," he blurted out, immediately drawing her into a big bear hug.

"Is it really you?" she asked in a muffled voice, noting the familiar scent of his aftershave and the comforting feel of his warm embrace.

"Yeah, it's really me," he confirmed, before releasing her. They stood there face-to-face for a moment, their arms still connected. "My goodness, have you aged at all? You look fantastic!" His sparkling eyes penetrated hers.

"You too," she replied softly.

Touched by this emotional reunion, the young hostess strode over to escort them to the restaurant's most private outdoor table for two while it was still available; the lunch crowd was suddenly picking up, and she wanted them to have the best seat in the house. They followed her through the main dining room and onto the adjoining covered patio, where she led them to a secluded spot in the corner.

"This ok?" she asked.

"Perfect," Maddy confirmed, glancing at him.

"Well, enjoy your lunch." She winked at them before heading back to her station.

"Wow," he remarked, staring at her in his inimitable way. It felt as if they were back in Atlantic City, sharing their first dinner date at Frisanco's.

"What?"

"You just look incredible, that's all."

That was Maddy's cue to finally end the suspense. Folding her menu, she set it aside and, leaning slightly forward, politely but firmly demanded the truth. "Kenny, I need you to level with me, please. Look, nothing will ever change the way I feel about you. No matter what you tell me, I will always be thankful we reconnected, especially since there was a time I thought I never would ever again—at least not in person.

"But for my own sake, I want to know right here and now exactly where things stand. Is there a woman in your life whose world would be torn apart if she knew you were looking at me this way? Is it really appropriate for you to say these things, knowing how much I—"

"Do you honestly believe I would play with your feelings like that?"

Her heart leapt in her chest as he went on. "Sweetheart, I told you on the phone I'd been trying to find you. That wasn't just because I missed an old friend; it was because I realized how much I missed my one true love. When my marriage ended, I knew I had to at least look for you, though I also knew I was risking a huge disappointment. I mean, for someone like you to still be available—I just didn't think it was possible. Surely some guy would've scooped you up by now."

"Obviously, you are completely unfamiliar with the South Florida dating scene," she smiled.

But before either one of them could speak again, a waiter came by to take their drink order; Ken smiled when she asked for water with lemon. True, it was the middle of the afternoon on a work day, but somehow he knew she'd have made the same request had it been a Saturday night.

Fourteen years of living on the Gold Coast hadn't changed her a bit, thank God. Not that he would've cared had she ordered a glass of wine—it was just reassuring to know that Madeline Rose was the same phenomenal woman he remembered. Perhaps a bit more confident and relaxed, but still the same girl at the deepest level.

As their reunion lunch proceeded over Cuban steak and salmon, enhanced by Latin rhythms and warm, tropical breezes, both of them came to truly understand the significance of coming full-circle at last.

"I'm dyin' ova here! Give me details!" Maddy broke out into laughter in response to Elyse's exaggerated imitation of a New York accent. Of course, she was already giddy from the blissful hour she'd just spent with the man she now knew she was destined to marry—not that they'd actually discussed the topic or anything.

"You were right, he's single!" she revealed breathlessly. "And all of the same feelings are still there for both of us, only better somehow." From her office on the 22nd floor, Maddy gazed out at the Fort Lauderdale skyline. In the distance, a resident cruise ship made its way out into the turquoise ocean, headed off to distant islands.

"Oh Maddy, I'm so excited for you! This is the best news I've heard all day—just think; now we can all watch the Eagles games together at CJ's Draft House this season."

"God, that sounds so wonderful. I can actually double-date with you and Billy—amazing!"

"So, when are you seeing him again?"

"This weekend. He's finally moving into a house of his own, and he wants me to see it. He's taking a few days off from work this week to get it all together."

"And he didn't call my family's company to move him? Ok, screw him!" She was obviously teasing, though Maddy took her at her word.

"I'm sorry," she replied. "Had we connected sooner, you know I would've recommended that."

"Madeline, I'm kidding. Where's his house?"

"Uh, somewhere off of A1A in Boca. He told me where; I can't remember exactly, but I recall him saying that it's on water. I was kind of nervous and distracted."

"Well, that's understandable. Did he ask you about your life? I mean, you know, previous relationships?"

"I didn't get into any specifics; just let him know that while I've dated a lot, nothing really panned out. I don't know, Leese, I'm kind of scared to have to tell him about Ray. What if he can't handle it?"

Her face clouded over, thinking of that horrendous experience four years ago. And yet, she recalled clearly Ann's strict warning about up-front honesty; the psychic had been particularly harsh on that point, though she'd also described Maddy's husband as a loving man who happened to be stunningly successful in business. At the time of that particular reading, the name "Kenneth" had not yet been revealed, though looking back, Ann's physical description of him had been chillingly accurate, right down to the "electric blue eyes."

"Hey Mads, if Kenny is as great as you keep telling me, he won't let anything come between you two ever again. Besides, honey, you dealt with the problem admirably; you sought out counseling and handled it. I have to think he's going to be even more impressed by that."

"Yeah, I hope you're right, Leese. I guess I just have to trust that by doing the right thing, it'll make our relationship stronger. But right now, I just want to enjoy our reunion. The rest I can figure out later."

"Kenny!" Madeline offered a warm hug as he entered the small tiled entryway of her condo. It was another sunny Saturday, and he'd dropped by as planned to take her to breakfast, followed by a visit to his new home. Since it was Mothers' Day weekend, Bonnie and Brian were spending it with Erin and her new beau on Sanibel Island, where he owned a palatial beachfront getaway.

"Hey, sweetheart." He relished the feel of her petite body as he folded his arms around her waist and held her close. "God, you feel so good," he murmured, kissing her hair.

She was wearing a cute pair of white Capri pants and a hot pink, ruffled top; her hair was pulled back in a sleek ponytail with a rhinestone clip. On her feet, she wore her favorite Ann Marino thong sandals in a coordinating color, decorated with multi-colored flower and palm tree bangles.

She closed her eyes for a moment, savoring every second of their embrace until he pulled away to look at her. Dressed in a pair of casual Dockers and a navy golf shirt, he was the quintessential image of the successful South Florida male—minus the arrogance and conceit. And when he cupped her face in his hands, she felt as if she might actually fall to the floor before reaching to his forearms for support.

"Madeline, I know this isn't exactly romantic, considering it's broad daylight and all, but I can't wait any longer," he whispered.

With that he leaned down to place his lips on hers initiating a flood of emotion when tender hesitancy quickly transitioned into an artful and passionate fulfillment of what was once a relentlessly insatiable hunger.

"Oh God, you feel so good," he repeated in between kisses, luxuriating in the feel of her against him. As was the case all of those years ago, she still couldn't wrap her arms fully around his broad, muscular frame; it was a joyful return to a blissful time and place.

When they finally broke away, she gave him a brief tour of her model unit. Prior to his arrival, she'd removed her treasure maps from the bathroom mirror, along with her affirmations. Although willing to share these new lessons with him at some point in the future, she'd determined that today was reserved for simply reacquainting themselves with one another; there would be plenty of time for prosperity principles later. Besides, she already had a full agenda of difficult items to discuss when the moment was right.

"Madeline, I am so very proud of you," he remarked, just as she was gathering her purse and house keys. "You are truly a self-made woman, sweetheart. I always knew you could do it, but still you've blown me away!"

"Ah well, it's nice to know I can still surprise you, teddy bear," she teased.

His ears perked up at her use of that particular term of affection; it was one of the many things he'd desperately missed.

"I guess we never know what we're capable of until our backs are against the wall. But I was never truly alone—and I've bumped into many helpful; people along the way."

In addition to her parents and the rest of her family, thoughts of Carmella and Frank, Ann, Elyse, Audrey, Carolyn and countless other friends came to mind, along with, of course, the One Supreme Being that made everything possible. He was ultimately responsible for the accomplished life she'd managed to create up to this point—a beautiful existence she was still in the process of designing.

"I've always been in awe of you, sweetheart. Some things will never change."

He smiled at her again as he took her by the hand and led her out the front door.

"What do you think?" he asked. They were standing in the middle of an expansive, ceramic-tiled living room, beyond which panoramic sliding glass doors beckoned to a spacious lanai with a built-in swimming pool, cabana bathroom, separate dining area and custom-made grill. A screen door a few feet behind the pool led across a half-acre of sturdy sawgrass to a beautiful handcrafted dock and boat slip; the Intracoastal Waterway glistened in the distance.

"Wow! It's magnificent," she marveled. "Although I loved it from the moment we pulled up in the driveway."

She recalled the impressive arches, Roman columns and fairytale turrets that graced the front of the two-story, five-bedroom home, capped off with an S-tile roof and three-car garage. Professional landscaping utilizing bougainvilleas, hibiscus and palm trees of differing varieties added a warm, finishing touch to this shining example of renowned Florida architecture.

"Thank you. I'm really excited about it."

"As you should be. You've worked really hard, Kenny. I can't think of anyone more deserving of a place like this. And I'm sure the kids are going to love living here, too."

"Well, with the market being the way it is, I figured now was the time to make my move. I've always wanted to live on the water, though if I could, I'd buy a place on the beach. But even in a down-market, I couldn't quite swing that. So, I settled for the Intracoastal." He sighed facetiously.

"Sheesh, you're really slummin'."

They both cracked up.

"C'mon, I want to show you upstairs."

He escorted her to a gorgeous, curving staircase reminiscent of the Von Trapp family mansion in The Sound of Music. Its marble steps were partially covered by a thick, mauve carpet while the wraparound balcony led to spacious bedrooms on either side. Once at the top, Ken opened the white double doors of the master bedroom, revealing an exquisite space that overlooked the dock and patio to the south and the front lawn to the north.

"Oh, I just love French doors," she enthused, running past the light oak, king-sized bed. She stepped out onto a large veranda, where a breathtaking view of sunlight dancing on the water and streaking through lush, tropical foliage greeted her. "Gosh, it's so private, too. No neighbors directly across; how nice."

He came up from behind and slipped his arms around her waist, igniting a firestorm within.

"Yes, I thought so too," he agreed, nuzzling her neck.

"What a great place to have your morning coffee," she noted, leaning her head to the side to allow him easier access.

"Yes," he murmured. With that, he turned her in his arms and drew her into another passionate kiss. When they finally came up for air, he brought their foreheads together and held his hands around her waist, eliciting infinite memories of similar interludes.

"Madeline, I've missed you so much," he whispered hoarsely.

"I've missed you, too," she barely choked out.

"I never once forgot about you, you know. I read your letter so many times I could probably recite it verbatim now from memory. God, you don't know what it did to me." He stopped for a moment, overcome with emotion.

"It was meant to make you feel good," she reminded him softly. "There were so many things I never said to you, so much I'd left unfinished. When I thought back to some of the hurtful things I did in the past, I—"

"Shh," he placed two fingers on her lips. "Listen to me. I hurt you, too, and I am just as sorry for that. For whatever reason, the timing just wasn't right for us back then."

"That's true in so many ways," she admitted. "You were ready, and I wasn't. I honestly wasn't prepared for someone like you to feel the way you did about me, and I definitely wasn't ready to be your bride. Ugh, when I think about how naïve, how frightened I was of life, it astonishes me. Sure, we could blame other people or outside circumstances, but the fact is, I still had so much growing up to do. I never would've made you happy then, no matter how much I might've tried."

"It's ok," he gently stroked her face as he spoke.

"Hey," he said when he noticed a tear trickle down her cheek, "This is all behind us now, right? I'm here, you're here, and it's a brand-new beginning." She nodded her head, unable to utter a sound.

That's when he scooped her into his arms and carried her back inside. He strode up to the bed and carefully laid her down on top of a fluffy forest green comforter. Then he picked up a remote control and clicked on the stereo before climbing in next to her. Soothing love songs filled the air, enhancing an already emotional exchange.

"Like old times, right?"

His voice was comforting as he took her in his arms and planted a kiss on her forehead. Maddy laid her head on his chest, unable to distinguish now between fantasy and reality. *Were they really lying here together or was this just another exquisite visualization exercise?* At this point, she didn't care; all she felt was an overwhelming mixture of gratitude and awe, along with an intense desire to freeze this moment forever.

Of course, the weighty burden of having to coming clean about all of the things that had transpired during her personal odyssey of mind, body and soul development hung over her like a black summer afternoon storm cloud. She kept thinking back to Ann's strict admonitions about absolute honesty.

"Maddy? You ok?"

"Yes, I'm just a little shell-shocked. I still can't believe we're both here like this. It's a miracle."

"I know the feeling. How long has it been since I held you like this? A lifetime, I think."

"And yet in some ways it feels like yesterday," she sighed. "Kenny?"

"Yes?"

"There's so much I have to tell you."

"Same here. A few things have happened over the last, oh, thirteen or so years," he chuckled.

"I'm serious."

"So am I." Then, feeling her tense up in his arms, he asked with genuine concern, "What's the matter?"

Like an unrestrained dam, the tears began to flow freely, try as she might to hold them back. Ken held her even tighter though his continuous efforts to coax an explanation out of her only seemed to provoke a fresh eruption of tortured emotion. Finally, he decided to simply remain silent and wait for her as they lay there in the stillness of a secluded tropical afternoon.

Chapter 30

The soulful sounds of the Spinners' ballad *Then Came You* roused Ken out of his late afternoon catnap. He awoke to find himself comfortably ensconced on his new bed with Madeline nestled against him, the picture of pure contentment in a deep, restful slumber. She was lying in the typical fashion he remembered, curled up on her side with her small hands tucked beneath her chin; her once neatly coiffed ponytail had transformed into a disheveled mass of auburn spread across a contrasting forest green pillow sham. He smiled at the endearing image.

A quick glance at the nightstand revealed the impending arrival of dusk; it was hard to believe that several hours had passed, but he was thankful to have had this time with her. She'd finally demonstrated something he'd never before seen and had immensely desired ever since meeting her—an unshakeable faith and trust in him. It had taken a tremendous amount of courage for Madeline to come clean regarding the events of her past—events for which he felt at least partially responsible, though none had directly involved him.

During the recounting of her narrative, she'd willingly, in fact, eagerly, qualified every incident as a necessary lesson on her path of personal growth, no matter how devastating. And as he fulfilled his promise to simply listen without commentary until she'd finished, he had been consumed by varying degrees of guilt, anger, and sorrow.

Recalling her horrific experience with Ray Smith—a vile, disgusting excuse for a human being—visions of pummeling the former New York police detective into oblivion flooded his brain. *What was it with some of these older jerks anyway?* Their arrogance seemed boundless in a geographic region rife with shallow, surgically enhanced women. *Why go after someone like Maddy? Had it been the thrill of the chase? But why? Although physically beautiful, anyone could plainly see the differences between her and the stereotypical South Florida female; why not choose a willing partner instead of preying on an innocent victim?*

Ken surmised correctly that an expansive ego had driven the scumbag to play a deceitful game where he tricked her by speaking of his attendance at weekly church services, initiating a couple of "safe" lunch dates and claiming a patently false adherence to the traditional values she cherished. Then, he moved in for the kill. And one bad decision, one lapse of judgment later, Maddy was forced to cope with the resulting physical and emotional upheaval of having trusted this despicable man enough to allow him into her home—as if having to deal with panic and anxiety disorder hadn't been enough of a challenge. Thank God for her good friend, Elyse.

Her panic and anxiety phase. Wow. Now that was an amazing tale.

While Ken had always enjoyed reading his daily Pisces horoscope, his knowledge of all things metaphysical basically ended on the Lifestyle and Entertainment section of the newspaper. It had been so cute when Maddy prefaced her story with the disclaimer that she was still a devout, practicing Catholic—as if he of all people would've held a defection from the Church against her.

After all, it was her influence sixteen years ago that had led to his recommitment to weekly Mass. More recently, though, in light of his messy divorce and the fallout from the clergy pedophilia scandal, he found himself grappling with issues of faith once more; not that he doubted the theology for a moment—just the flawed human mechanisms upon which some of the man-made rules were based.

Much as it pained him to admit it, he truly had played an active role in this particular hardship, though she vehemently denied it. But the heartbreak he'd wrought upon her, first by moving away and then by subsequently marrying another woman, had been severe. Both transgressions joined with other enormously significant occurrences in the deep recesses of her unconscious mind, where she'd thought they'd remain dead and buried. These erroneous beliefs eventually wreaked havoc later in the form of a five-year bout with concurrent depression, agoraphobia, panic attacks, oppressive headaches, a perpetually sour stomach and frightening physical sensations that made her doubt her own sanity.

And yet through it all her gutsy determination fueled an unwavering persistence to get to the root of the problem. When efforts to resolve the issue through traditionally acceptable channels— including behavioral and cognitive therapy, prescription medication, deep breathing and exercise— all failed her, Madeline stumbled upon an unlikely alternative. He could only imagine what it must've felt like to have a complete stranger recite the intimate contents of your soul out loud, as Ann had done in front of Maddy's peers at her monthly women's networking meeting.

How that woman, psychic or not, could have possibly known about Louis being Madeline's "handicapped middle brother" and the fact that she'd still been in mourning for a grandmother who'd passed away when she was six was beyond Ken's comprehension. *Was the psychic gifted by God to help other people? Or was there something more sinister at work?*

Given the undeniable results of Maddy's one private hour-long session with Ann, a conversation that had yielded a successful recovery that was still going strong nearly ten years later, it seemed only logical that Ann's abilities sprung from a good—if not traditionally acceptable—source.

Whatever the case, Ken was incredibly grateful for her triumph; the thought of her suffering through something like that to begin with made his heart ache. He glanced over at her sleeping figure again, noting the peacefulness of her expression. Funny, she had often joked about the Rose family's ability to fall asleep at the drop of a hat—a genetic trait she'd most definitely inherited.

He chuckled softly remembering that very early morning long ago in Somers Point when he'd been unexpectedly called into work at the power plant and spent almost 30 minutes trying to wake her up to say goodbye. Gazing at her now with a newfound respect, he felt an even more deeply abiding love and pride that—unbelievably, exceeded anything he'd felt before. Then again, she always did rock his world.

She stirred in her sleep as if his silent thoughts had somehow managed to find their way into her physical hearing mechanisms and transport her back to the land of the living.

"Mmm," she sighed, stretching her arms over her head as she shifted onto her back. "Oh my gosh, how long have I been out?" she inquired of a smiling Ken, who promptly encircled her with his arm.

"Hey sunshine, not long. Don't worry, I fell asleep too—just woke up a few minutes ago." Maddy giggled.

"Is this what happens on a date after 40? You end up taking naps together in the middle of the afternoon?"

He cracked up.

"Well as I recall, we both did this a lot at 25, so I'm not sure if age is a factor here."

She settled her head on his chest and wrapped her arm around his waist.

"That is true," she agreed. "Ok, I feel better now."

Then suddenly becoming serious, she asked, "Ken? I hope I didn't scare you with my tales of horror. I mean, if you wanted to walk away right now I wouldn't blame you. I just couldn't live with myself if I hadn't been completely honest and aboveboard with you about all of this. No matter what you decide—"

"Is that what you think, that I'm so easily scared away?

That's about enough of that kind of talk. Honey, the only thing I'm feeling right now is anger at myself for not being there for you through this any of this crap. There's nothing you could ever say to me that would make me walk away from you—not after finally being free to love you again."

She shivered with excitement. Lifting her head to stare directly into his eyes, she repeated, "Love? Kenny, are you telling me you still love me?"

"No sweetheart. I'm telling you I never stopped." Still in a state of disbelief, she sought further confirmation.

"Even after everything I just shared with you?"

"Especially after everything you just shared with me. Don't you get it? Madeline, I want to protect you forever, for the rest of my life. I love you. That will never change. And there is nothing you could ever say or do to make me stop loving you. Nothing."

He held her face in his hands as he spoke. For a while, they just lay in the stillness of the semi-darkened room, each trying to absorb the reality of this long anticipated reunion.

"I-I'm blown away," she finally admitted. "I've desperately wanted to hear those words from you for as long as I can remember. Longer than I even realized. And I love you, too—I never stopped either."

"Hey, you like your burgers well done, right?" He called out to her from the screened-in porch, where he was busily getting their main course together while she tended to side dishes in his showroom perfect kitchen. They'd taken the opportunity to "christen" Ken's new grill together since the balmy, clear evening had proven conducive to an impromptu cookout. With the rainy season around the corner, it was wise to take advantage of nice weather while they could.

"You remember! I'm very impressed," she replied, lining up condiments including ketchup, relish, mustard and dill pickles on the granite countertop.

She laughed when she heard him retort, "Still doubting me after all these years. Ok, then you'll be forced to make it up to me later when we discuss a proper punishment." It felt so incredibly good to joke around again; she'd sorely missed all of the fun they'd shared together.

"How 'bout if I finally teach you how to ballroom dance properly?" she offered, awaiting the sounds of his faraway voice to drift into the room from his slightly distant location. Instead, she was treated to a mild shock when a playful Ken snuck up behind her and boisterously lifted her into the air.

"Kenny!" she scolded playfully. "I'm gonna kill you for scaring me like that!" But her uncontrollable laughter gave away her levity as he spun her around a few times amid the ultramodern, stainless steel appliances.

Placing her back on her feet, he whispered softly, "Not if I have anything to say about it," and then proceeded to smother her neck in soft, wet kisses.

"God, you feel and smell so good," he declared rapturously. "Maybe we should skip dinner and head right to dessert." And though she laughed again, he felt her tense up a bit in his arms.

"Hey," he said softly, turning her around to face him. "I'm only teasing. Well...not about how much you turn me on, but the part about doing something about it immediately. You know, I would never push you to do anything you're not ready for, right? I may be older now, but I am still the same patient guy you remember. I mean it, Madeline. Especially after everything you've been through, the last thing I would ever do is put more pressure on you."

"It's ok," she soothed. "Believe me; I know you're decent, honorable and dependable—at least, I do now, even if I didn't get it back then. And I want you to realize, I'm over what happened with Ray. It took a while, but I overcame.

"The hardest part was forgiving myself, believe it or not. Somehow I managed to forgive him for what he did but held a grudge against me for a long time. *Why didn't I throw him out? Why didn't I call a friend for help?* All sorts of self-recriminations. But I worked on it until I got there."

"You are persistent," he stated. "It's one of the many reasons why I am so crazy about you." With that, he pulled her into his arms for another spellbinding kiss.

"Thanks for agreeing to come back here, Kenny," she said, unlocking the front door of her place. "I know you probably would have preferred to stay in your new house tonight."

"As long as I'm with you, I don't care where we are," he replied truthfully, following her back to the pale peach leather sofas of the living area, where they snuggled up together on the love seat. They'd spent a beautiful evening out on the lanai, sharing meaningful conversation, along with a good, casual meal.

Released from the burden of worry concerning his reaction to the truth, she could, at last, relax and savor every second of their joyous reunion. And with luminous moonlight shining on the Intracoastal Waterway and romantic music filtering through wall-mounted speakers, it rivaled any five-star dining experience.

Feeling emboldened as they sat side-by-side on the patio dining table, she sought the answers she'd once thought unattainable. "Kenny," she asked, after swallowing a perfectly grilled piece of hamburger meat. "Can I ask you something? It doesn't really matter now, but I have to satisfy my curiosity. I never did get around to mentioning it to you before."

"What is it?" He braced for the worst, realizing that he owed her nothing less than complete honesty; after all, she'd laid all her cards on the table for him. He just prayed she'd be receptive to the real story, no matter how painful.

"Remember the ski date we had planned? You were supposed to drive up to my house from Somers Point, and we were going to head to Big Boulder in the Poconos?" His heart sank with the remembrance of that miserable time.

"Yes, I do," he replied quietly, staring down at his plate. Well, best to get it over with. Besides, wasn't it ancient history anyway?

"I waited for you for hours; took a day off from work and you never showed up. Then you didn't return my calls for weeks afterwards. Not even Kathy, your roommate, would tell my anything. It was so upsetting, but it felt like payback for everything I'd done to hurt you before we got back together. And after we'd spent such a wonderful Christmas and New Year's with my family, I just didn't get it. Why would you do that to me? I was devastated."

"I know. I am so sorry," he acknowledged, looking her directly in the eye.

She continued, "Then when you finally called—like months later, you told me you'd moved to Florida and that you missed me. You practically begged me to move here and promised to be my date for Greg's wedding. Then after you didn't get back to me about that I called to confirm with you, and you blew me off, saying you couldn't get the time off from work. For months after that, you'd call and cry about how much you loved me. And when I was finally ready to make the move, you started pushing me away—"

"Oh, Madeline, I am truly sorry about all of that." He felt genuine remorse as he took her hands in his and turned to face her.

"That time period? That was the darkest point in my life, just as your anxiety problem was for you. It was the absolute lowest period I can ever remember. I got fired from my job, but I was too embarrassed to tell you. I'd fallen behind on my mortgage payments and ended up selling my townhouse to a high school friend's father. It was debilitating—like I'd just taken a huge, gigantic step backwards after working so hard to accomplish something. I felt like a total failure."

"What happened at the plant?" Her voice was soft and low.

"Well one of the supervisors—this guy I used to have a good relationship with until I met you—had been picking fights with me for a long time. I did my best to ignore it, but he was such an instigator. And one day, I guess I'd had enough and I clocked him. Broke his arm, bruised his ribs—"

"Oh my God, Kenny. He must've really asked for it."

"You have no idea," he laughed ironically, remembering Quentin's snide, nasty insults.

"But what did any of it have to do with me? I never even met those guys."

"True, but you were all I talked about at work from the night we met. Remember all of our phone calls? I'd dial your number just to hear your voice every chance I got. Most of those guys couldn't tolerate the fact that a classy, nice girl like you actually wanted to be with me—you know—a blue-collar, ex-Navy sailor without an education."

She was suddenly filled with remorse for having proven his cruel co-workers right, thanks to her fear and unwillingness to fight for him...for their relationship. Instead, she'd allowed her own insecurities to form an impenetrable barrier between them. Letting go of him had seemed to be the best option; it freed her from having to deal with grown-up emotions and conflicts.

"Oh Kenny, I am so sorry. You know, I always considered you my equal in every way. In fact, in some ways I felt inferior to you—this brave man of the world who'd served his country honorably and had earned everything he had through hard work and perseverance. You were amazing to me—this larger than life personality, always laughing and upbeat, and so very patient where I was concerned. You never once pressured me to do anything I wasn't ready to do.

"I guess in many ways that was the problem—I was such a little girl. I felt like I wasn't being fair to you, expecting you to be happy with kissing and holding my hand, even though you were great about it. And whenever you would talk of marriage, I would absolutely panic, thinking of—you know, our wedding night. I was scared to death of sex back then."

"Wow, I wish I'd known. I mean, I kind of knew you were apprehensive about it but I just never realized the extent of it. Why didn't you tell me? All I remember is thinking how beautiful you were and how much I hated it when you would put yourself down. You had no idea how attracted I was to you, but I was head- over-heels. I would've waited for you for as long as it took, and if we had gotten married, I would've done everything in my power to make our wedding night beautiful for you. You gotta know I would have been so careful and considerate—my God, you were everything to me."

"Yes, I get that now," she sighed. "But back then, I was a wreck, trying to cope with all of these conflicting emotions. But as it turns out, I am kinda glad things evolved the way they did...even the experience with Ray."

"I'm so sorry you had to go through that," he said. "I better not ever run into the guy, or he's toast.

"But it's all behind you now and I'm here." She smiled as a lone tear trickled down her face; he gently brushed it away.

"Ken, please finish the rest of the story."

"Well, right around the time I sold my townhouse, my parents had bought a small condo in Pompano Beach for a steal. By then, my father and I had sort of reached an understanding, and they both thought it might be good for me to get away and start over. I think he really felt bad about what happened at work. And by then, I'd had enough of the Jersey Shore and was more than ready to get away—except for one thing."

"Erin," Maddy completed his thought.

"Yes," he sighed sheepishly. "Ok, I might as well tell the truth; I met her through a mutual friend some time after you'd sent me your rejection letter." She winced as she remembered.

"Go on," she urged.

"Look Madeline, at first, I didn't want to be bothered, but when I figured there was no chance for us, I thought, what the hell. I wanted to settle down and get married. So I agreed to go on the date. And while she wasn't you, I did develop strong feelings for her. Then you shocked the hell out of me by inviting me to the Eagles-Vikings game, and before I knew it, I was spending Christmas week and New Year's with you and your family."

"That was the best New Year's Eve I've ever had in my entire life," she confessed softly, thinking back to all of the fun they'd had dancing and joking around with her siblings and their dates at The Media Inn.

"It was for me, too," he admitted. "And then of course, after that my whole world fell apart, and Erin was there for me. I know it's probably hard to hear this, but she was willing to move; she had a career that was easily transferable and even though she was an only child, her parents were completely onboard with it. They really liked me. Look, I am sorry for hurting you Madeline. I was wrong, and I admit that. I hurt you deeply. And after listening to you tonight, I feel even worse about it. But if it makes you feel any better, I've paid the price for going through with a marriage I had second-thoughts about."

"Why?"

"I loved her; don't get me wrong. I truly did. And in the beginning, it was very exciting. Then things started to fizzle, but my mom kept telling me that real love wasn't just about intense physical attraction. And I thought that made a lot of sense. So, Erin eventually joined me in Florida, once she found a great job in Miami. The excitement came back, and it was fun again for a while. That is—until you threw a wrench into everything by moving down. And I bear a huge responsibility for that; like you said, I begged you to join me for almost a full year. That was when Erin and I had parted company, and I realized I still loved you.

"But when you kept refusing my offer over and over again, I eventually gave up. Then Erin and I got back together and moved into our own apartment in Aventura. And one day you showed up at my real estate office. God, I was so torn apart, especially when seeing you brought back all of those same incredible feelings. But I just couldn't dump Erin; not after she'd uprooted her whole life for me."

"That's understandable," she sighed, recognizing her own role in this tumultuous drama. "Do you remember that one time when you showed up at my first apartment in Boca Del Mar to tell me you'd gotten engaged?" He nodded his head. "By the way, it took a lot of guts for you to do that; you could've taken the easy way out by just calling me on the phone, but you didn't.

"Anyway, sometime after that, I had a dream that you'd broken off your engagement. It was real enough that I actually woke up believing it to be true. And then, oddly enough, you showed up again on my doorstep a few days later unannounced, and we ended up talking by the pool for what? Four hours or so?

"I specifically remember you saying something about how you hoped the excitement would come back after you were married. I just sat there wondering why you would share all of that with me, as if I were going to give you advice—or worse, come between the two of you and your solemn commitment. Yes, it killed me inside to think of you marrying another woman, but being a home-wrecker had never been my style. I wouldn't have dared to talk you out of it, no matter how badly I was hurting."

He remained silent for a moment, pushing his salad around on his dish with his fork. He well remembered those days and their accompanying torment.

"Madeline, I have a confession to make. The truth is I was really a coward; I was having second thoughts about marrying Erin because deep down, I still loved you. Didn't you get that? That's why I came by to tell you about the engagement in person. And the more we talked, the more I realized what a terrible mistake I was making. But I couldn't figure out where you stood because you seemed as if you'd happily moved on—to the point of telling me about all the dates you'd had. If I'd known you still had any ounce of feeling left for me, I might not have ever gone through with the wedding."

"Really?" she asked softly.

"*Really*," he confirmed. "God, as we sat in that apartment, talking like old times, it hit me like a ton of bricks that you were the girl I wanted to marry. The one who appreciated simple gestures and genuine tokens; the one whose face would light up over a beautiful view of the ocean from several stories high; and the one who would always listen to me with such interest and compassion. Even when it came to less important things, like watching Eagles games together or throwing a football on the beach, it was obvious you were the one for me, not Erin. We were so compatible. And just being in the same room with you excited me."

"Same here," she whispered. "But I couldn't show that to you then. I was just so angry, upset and overwhelmed about everything. I didn't even know Erin; it didn't seem right to hurt a woman I'd never met, just because you and I couldn't get our act together. I truly believed that the honorable thing was to step aside; if you came back to me, great. If not, then you and I weren't meant to be.

"But I wanted you to come back to me on your own, not because of anything I did or said. And I'm ashamed to admit this, but I was just too proud to give you the satisfaction of knowing I still loved you. I was determined to succeed without you, to prove to you and me that I didn't need you."

"Well, you definitely did. I am proud of you; it's just another quality that distinguishes you from every other woman I've ever known. If I had half your courage, I would never have gone through with the marriage. I think a huge part of it was guilt over potentially hurting her, disappointing both sets of parents and wanting to have a family."

"And you have two beautiful children," she reminded him. "They are the best things to come out of all of this."

"Yes, they are; I wouldn't trade them for anything." He gazed out at the dock as he spoke.

"It is interesting to look back, though," she noted. "I also remember that you called her on your cell from my place, but didn't tell her where you were. And then you told me about how she'd given you a hard time about buying her rollerblades for Valentine's Day, even though it was something she really wanted. Let's see; there was something else—ah yes, she was also mad because the two of you hadn't been spending enough time together."

"God, how do you remember all this?"

"You forget I am also a lifelong keeper of personal journals. Once most of my memories of you flooded back to me earlier this year, I finally found the courage to pull them out and read them—quite a revelation, let me tell you."

"Ok, well let me just make you a promise right here and now, from this moment on, I am going to give you nothing but uplifting material to write in your diary. We're starting over for real this time. And someday when you're an old lady reading your journals, all you'll do is smile and laugh—and maybe even blush—remembering all the crazy, fun times we had. Got that?"

Returning his high-five with gusto, she cracked up.

"Got it!" she confirmed.

"Do you mind if we go to sleep now?" After close to an hour spent trying to adjust his big frame to a tiny, leather loveseat, Ken was ready to call it a night. Besides, nothing was more appealing than the thought of curling up with her under the covers.

"Sure," she agreed, giving him a quick kiss on the lips.

"Hey, I'll meet you in there in a minute, ok? I just want to use the guest bathroom first." He picked up his duffle bag from the floor and left her to change in privacy.

Walking into her bedroom accented with angels, roses and mauve-colored verticals, she smiled to herself. Here they were, grown adults and in some ways, it felt like 1992 all over again. True, it was a blissful miracle that everything still felt so vibrant, fresh and exhilarating between them; it was just ironic that now that no one was watching—now that the rules no longer applied, they were still tentative about certain intimacies.

Maddy pulled open the bottom drawer in search of coordinating pajamas. Unfortunately, her most desired choices had been relegated to the bottom of her laundry pile. But when she spotted her green Eagles sleepwear—long bottoms with matching logo tank top, she realized she had a winner. If nothing else, it would make him laugh. And, truth be told, her chest was looking more—well—robust, thanks to functional training, which had built up her pec muscles. Yes, it was an illusion, but who cared? Ken loved her anyway and this time she was trusting in that.

"Comfortable?" He settled in next to her and pulled her close to him in the darkness, noting how the contours of her body exquisitely aligned with his. She felt safe and secure as she rested her head on a fluffy pillow and savored the feel of his strong arms around her.

"Mm-hm," she whispered dramatically. "Maddy?"

"Yes?"

"Will you come with me to my parents' house for dinner tomorrow? It's Mothers Day, and I promised to go over and cook for her. I was going to have them over to my new house, but not being sure if I'd actually move in on time we decided to just have it there."

"Wow, I finally get to meet the parents!" she exclaimed. Then a panicked thought occurred to her. "Your mother doesn't hate me, does she?"

"Huh?"

"Oh my God, what does she know about me, besides the awful facts that I stood you up for your cousin's wedding and a work party, and wrote you a Dear John letter—ugh."

"Are you crazy? Don't you think I've shared the whole story with her? She knows everything, especially the part about me still loving you." With that, he planted a few kisses on her neck.

"But still—"

"All is forgiven, remember? We were both wrong, and we admitted it. We've forgiven each other. It's over; the past is the past. So let's not waste any more time, ok?"

"Ok. Kenny?"

"Yes?"

"Thank you for forgiving me. And for being so understanding about all the other stuff. I love you so much."

"And I love you, Maddy. Please, don't ever forget that." They drifted off to a contented sleep, home at last.

Chapter 31

Madeline soothed the knots in her stomach as best she could as she adjusted the hem of her navy eyelet sundress. She and Ken had just attended Noon Mass at St. Ambrose and were now headed to his parents' house for Mothers' Day dinner. Standing in the pew with him again, reciting familiar prayers and singing timeless Church hymns had been such a powerfully emotional experience—and yet another example of having come "full circle." There were several moments during the service when she found herself dabbing at her eyes with a tissue, thoroughly overwhelmed in the best sense of the word. It was during those times that Ken would look over and smile, or squeeze her hand reassuringly.

She'd called her own mom, of course, earlier that morning, though time constraints had prevented a meaningful conversation regarding the life-altering events of the past few weeks. Maddy couldn't wait to share her incredible news with the whole family, but she knew her mother would be especially exultant; all she wanted now for her youngest child was to know that she was happily settled down with the right guy. While she'd suspected Kenny had been the real reason for her daughter's relocation and often wondered about his continued absence in her life, she'd respected Madeline's privacy. And putting Ken aside, Madeline had grown into a mature, self-adjusted woman over these past fourteen years.

While she missed her terribly, she also felt tremendous respect and admiration.

After all, hadn't it been Monica's stellar example of independence and determination that had provided the blueprint? Mrs. Rose had admirably handled formidable hardships of her own—the death of her beloved older brother Anthony during World War II, Bell's Palsy at age 13, and—in one of the biggest tests of her adult life—the birth of a Down syndrome baby when she was 28, at a time when conventional medicine dismissed such children as "stigmas" to be shipped off to nightmarish institutions, never to be seen or heard from again.

Then again, Monica herself descended from a long line of "tough" women, beginning with her paternal grandmother Rosaria, who as a young widow, uprooted her three small boys and relocated with them to America in search of a better life—a particularly gutsy move considering she didn't know a soul in the New World, nor did she speak the language.

But unshakeable faith and stalwart desire had spurred her on in spite of fear. And thanks to her abundance of courage, each of her sons had achieved remarkable success in their adoptive homeland as pharmacists, graduating from prestigious Philadelphia universities when such accomplishments were unheard of for immigrants. Raffaele, Monica's father—a consummate entrepreneur—had even owned a thriving corner drugstore in their Germantown neighborhood.

For over 25 years, it had been a beacon of comfort, where residents of all ethnic backgrounds could congregate for some good medicine, not just in the traditional form of pills or liquid, but also in the presence of Ralph's sparkling personality, boundless generosity and genuine concern for their wellbeing.

Monica had often regaled her children with stories of her father translating letters from English into Italian for the old folks who struggled with linguistic comprehension; playing the piano and singing songs with Monica, Maria, and their friends; bartering prescription medication for a simple, good meal when someone couldn't afford to pay; and hosting weekly "mystery nights" wherein he'd hold the elderly men spellbound with his recitation of suspenseful novels.

Having shared a special bond with her father, his life had always been an intense source of pride for Monica. When he passed away suddenly from a heart attack, his grief-stricken daughter nearly lost the unplanned life that had taken root within her. Madeline's conception could not have occurred at a more inopportune time for her parents, who were already struggling to keep a roof over the heads of their four young children. Joseph had just completed his residency and was knee-deep in debt; yet neither he nor his wife would've ever entertained the notion of terminating Monica's pregnancy. True, abortion hadn't been legal in 1966, although in states like New York, the procedure was certainly attainable.

However, faith, optimism and a clear-cut sense of right and wrong had conquered anxiety and fear—more for the baby's health than for financial matters. After all, they knew Joseph was destined for a brilliant career that would soon yield its own rewards; but this new child's fate would remain an unknown right up until the moment he or she successfully navigated out of the birth canal and into the material plane of existence.

While Louis had proven a source of indescribable joy to the family, Monica and Joseph had sweated out each of her three subsequent pregnancies, praying that God would bless each new child with the priceless gift of full physical, mental and emotional capabilities. Yet no matter the outcome, love would have prevailed.

But eight months after Raffaele's death, bouncing baby Madeline—who'd inherited her great-grandmother Rosaria's auburn hair as well as perfect health, had quickly fulfilled one of her many purposes by immediately replacing the void of sorrow in her widowed grandmother's life with happiness. As a further boon to the older woman's spirits, Monica and Joseph decided to give the infant her name, Madeline. And for Maddy's loving grandmother, there was absolutely nothing like the sweet, smiling face of a baby to make an adult forget all about her own problems.

Monica often joked with her youngest offspring that she sometimes wondered who'd actually given birth, as Nanny spent her days constantly doting over her namesake. And though young

Madeline was forced to say goodbye to her beloved grandmother in the most traumatic fashion six years later—an event that would unknowingly have significant repercussions over 20 years down the road—she never once forgot about her.

In a brief span of time, they created indelible memories that became an integral part of Maddy's psychic tapestry. From cuddling up in bed with Nanny to read her favorite fairytales to going to lunch at Strawbridge's department store, the older woman's positive influence had been expansive.

One of Maddy's favorite memories involved fetching her grandmother's medicine as a three-year-old "ward" who'd gone to live with her temporarily after her mother had contracted pneumonia— thanks to shivering through an Eagles game in sub-zero temperatures. Nanny had lovingly referred to her then as her "nurse," a title the little girl had assumed with pride. It was just one of several uplifting details that were forever etched in her memory.

Gazing now at the passing scenery, she couldn't help but feel her grandmother's presence, along with Aunt Maria's and every other loved one who'd gone before her. No doubt they were all celebrating right now, too.

"Hey," Ken piped up, noticing her faraway expression, "You ok? You seem a million miles away." He picked up her hand and kissed it.

"Oh sorry, Kenny," she laughed, "I was just thinking of how lucky we are—and how nervous I am about meeting your parents."

"There is absolutely nothing to be nervous about. They're going to love you as much as I do—well, maybe not quite as much as I do, but pretty damn close." He'd hoped a little lightheartedness would ease her mind.

"You sure?"

"Do you remember that New Year's Day when you encouraged me to call my father? I'd been staying at your parents' house, and I was really nervous about talking to him?"

"Uh, *coerced* would be a better word," she raised an eyebrow as she smiled at him; she clearly remembered how torn up he'd been about making that simple gesture.

"Ok, coerced is probably more accurate, but the point is, you helped me do the right thing. And while that one phone call didn't salvage our relationship, I firmly believe it had been the first important step. And I owe that to you."

"I never knew that," she replied, deeply touched. "You're not just trying to make me feel better are you?"

"No—I am telling you the truth, I swear. My mom and dad know all sorts of wonderful things about you, including how much you've inspired me, how much your whole family has inspired me. Hell, you still inspire me."

He kissed her hand again as they headed west on Camino Real.

Quintessentially middle-class Royal Oak Hills was one of Maddy's favorite Boca neighborhoods; a charming, well-maintained area devoid of the pretensions that characterized other city communities. With its ample lawns, meticulously landscaped tropical hedges and plethora of swing sets, bicycles and skateboards, it rivaled any Southern California counterpart as a classically American, warm-weather residence.

Ken pulled into a neatly paved circular driveway framed by rows of colorful croton and vivid pentas. The home itself was constructed of pale yellow stucco with a flat, white roof and matching plantation shutters; a polished wooden door accented with etched-glass windows greeted them at the entrance. Maddy took a deep breath as Ken rang the doorbell. Normally he'd barge right in but today was different.

Paula Lockhart radiated warmth and sincerity as she welcomed them with an affectionate hug and a bright, beautiful smile. As they exchanged pleasantries, it was evident to Maddy where Ken's good nature and impeccable character had come from.

"Madeline, it's so wonderful to finally meet you; Ken has told us so much about you and your family."

"Likewise, Mrs. Lockhart," she smiled, "Happy Mothers Day!"

"Well, thank you; come on in."

Maddy felt Ken's protective hand on her back as she followed their hostess through the formal dining and living room, and then across a terrazzo-floor kitchen, before reaching their final destination—a fully furnished, ceramic-tiled screen porch, where Carl Lockhart was intently watching the Marlins game on a big-screen Plasma TV.

Though his brown hair had long ago transitioned into salt-and-pepper, his six-foot frame retained a broadness and strength that were remarkable for a man of nearly seventy. It was as if Maddy had been given a glimpse of the future as she shook Carl's hand. While Ken's Colgate smile and winning personality had definitely been gifts from his mother, his father had also wielded his own noticeable influence in the realm of physical characteristics.

"Madeline, very nice to meet you," he said in a gruff voice, sizing her up with blue eyes that mirrored his son's yet lacked their effervescent sparkle. "So I hear you and Ken here have reconnected after a number of years. Good for you."

"Yes it has been pretty amazing," Maddy beamed.

"Uh Dad, how are you liking the TV?" Ken asked. "It's fantastic son. Thank you!"

"The television was sort of a combined Mothers and Fathers Day present," Paula explained. "Our son is really something else."

"Aw, Mom," Ken's naturally sanguine cheeks took on a deeper shade of crimson.

"Now don't be embarrassed honey. It was incredibly generous of you to buy this for us, especially since so much of your hard-earned money goes to support an ungrateful ex. We really appreciate how good you are to us."

"He's the best," Maddy offered, squeezing his hand. But before anyone could respond, some loud voices called out from the front of the house.

"Hello! Anybody home?"

"Your brother Patrick's here," Paula noted, excusing herself. A moment later she reappeared with her arm around another tall gentleman. Unlike Ken, Patrick had dark, straight hair and hazel eyes. Though nice looking, he bore no resemblance to his younger brother at all, save for his similar build. And whereas Ken possessed a naturally gregarious nature, Patrick tended toward reticence; however, he shook Maddy's hand politely when properly introduced.

"Ah Danielle, there you are; now we can start the party," Paula laughed, as she greeted her bubbly daughter-in-law with a peck on the cheek. The union of Patrick and Danielle was a classic case of opposites attracting, but her lively personality acted as a nice contrast to his laid- back disposition.

"Actually Mom, it's funny you said that because I brought along something that'll help make this a real fun celebration!" Danielle handed her a huge gift-wrapped box. "Pat thinks I'm crazy, but I think you're gonna love it."

"Well, it sure is heavy," Paula noted, just as Ken escorted Maddy over to meet another family member.

"Oh, you're the girl from the Jersey Shore with the beautiful voice!" Danielle exclaimed. She stood at about average height, with a slender build and an attractive, if not beautiful face. Her frosted hair fell in a blunt-cut that perfectly framed her angular cheekbones.

"Well, close enough. I grew up in Media, just outside of Philly, but I did meet Ken in Somers Point about a million years ago," Maddy explained. "And it appears he's filled all of you in on me," she added with slight embarrassment.

"Oh my gosh, Danielle this is great," Paula gasped, tearing away the wrapping paper to reveal a karaoke machine. "You know, I have always wanted to try this, but my husband would never go with me to any of those clubs. There are so many good ones around, too."

"Well, now you can sing in the comfort of your own home," Danielle proclaimed. Then she commented, "And since we have a professional singer in our midst, perhaps she can treat us all to a performance?"

"Oh, uh—I don't know," Maddy laughed. "I haven't sung in quite a while."

"C'mon, sweetheart, will you consider doing it for me?" Ken hugged her from behind as he pleaded.

"Oh, I'll deal with you later, Mr. Lockhart," she teased under her breath, "but yes, I'll be happy to sing for everyone—after you've prepared us all a good meal, of course."

"My pleasure as always, Madeline Rose." With that he disappeared into the kitchen, leaving her to bond with her future in-laws.

Amid the casual comfort of the sunny Florida Room, Maddy

socialized easily with the Lockhart family, chatting about her work, family, friends and hobbies—including, of course, ballroom dancing and singing. Sitting beside Ken at the table, she felt right at home entertaining the group with funny stories of how they met that distant summer night at the Key Largo club, and the ensuing comedy of errors: Madeline refusing to go back to his place for coffee; Ken trying unsuccessfully to get their waitress' attention at the Point Diner; and the mix-up later on that morning that ultimately resulted in Ken joining her family for breakfast.

"It was so cute," she explained, her enthusiasm lighting up her expression, "Ken kept saying 'I can't meet your family in my bathing suit!' and I was like 'What's the big deal? They're gonna see you in it anyway on the beach!' I'd felt so bad about him waiting for me all that time I was at church, but I never expected him to actually show up!"

"See, she's been doubting me from way back when," he interjected, sighing dramatically before pecking her on the cheek.

"Hey!" she played along, "You had a nice buzz going! How was I supposed to know you'd even remember my name? We'd had nothing to write with in the car, it was nearly 3 a.m.—all I was thinking was 'Thank God this adorable guy salvaged my evening!' I had such a great time."

Everyone around them was struck by their undeniable chemistry as they bantered back and forth; Paula and Carl were particularly delighted, given their son's recent tribulations. If nothing else, Maddy's presence here today proved he never should've married Erin in the first place; however, none of them would trade Bonnie and Brian for all of the money in the world. They'd been the only silver lining of an otherwise misguided and tumultuous union.

"So, then what happened?" Paula asked excitedly. Though familiar with this amusing tale, it was riveting to hear it told simultaneously from both perspectives.

"Well, he finally agreed to come over for breakfast, on the condition that I answer the door when he got to the house, which I did."

"And it was amazing," Ken continued, "When I walked in, there was her whole family seated around the dining room table, just laughing and talking over breakfast. I'd never seen anything like it—

they were so friendly and warm. When I sat down, I felt at ease right away. They welcomed me in like they'd known me for a long time and we talked about all kinds of stuff—mostly Eagles football since the season was about to start."

"That's right!" Maddy chimed in, remembering the specifics. "And later on that season, we ended up freezing our butts off at the Eagles- Vikings game with my sister, Lori. Funny how that worked out since the Vikings are your second-favorite team, Kenny. Remember how you got to my house sometime around 2 a.m.? I ran out to the driveway to greet you, so happy to see you again, after—after we were apart for a while."

Her tone became soft and serious as she recalled the awful letter she'd written prior to that occurrence, effectively ending things between them, at least temporarily.

Then came his phone call some time after saying he understood; Maddy had figured on that being their last conversation until her guilty mother had suggested inviting him to the game.

"Hey, it's ancient history, remember?" Ken consoled her.

"Let's concentrate on all the good stuff, like the first time you sang for me. Oh my God, when I heard your voice, I was blown away. And you were the one who taught me how to properly Jitterbug. Remember that, out on the Key Largo patio and then later at my house?" He put his arm around her and squeezed her shoulder.

"He is such a good dancer," Maddy exclaimed with renewed gusto. "I never saw anyone his size break-dance or moonwalk like that; he entertained all of us that New Year's Eve when we went to a party. That was the first time any of my siblings had seen him move. They were highly impressed—what a great night that was."

She thought back to his arrival at her former home on Martins Run that evening, and how he'd been running late, thanks to a terrible snowstorm, but had called to inform her he'd be there soon. Having been in the shower, Maddy hadn't actually spoken with him; her mom had conveyed the message. His cousin had just given birth, and he'd stopped by to see the baby before heading out of South Jersey. Funny, that child would be celebrating his 16th birthday this year. She made a mental note to inquire about him and his parents, whom she well remembered meeting on that dreary January day in Somers Point.

Madeline could still picture Ken's face when he'd finally arrived, beaming up at her from behind a gorgeous bouquet of white roses as she stood at the banister in her strapless black dress. Just imagining the entire scene now—with as much clarity as if it had happened yesterday—was making her heart beat fast.

"Sounds like you two have quite a history," Danielle remarked, smiling. She recognized the *real deal* when she saw it. Besides, this girl was a refreshing change from Erin; she could definitely understand why Ken was still so attracted to her.

"Oh and I forgot to mention the most interesting thing of all—God, how could I forget this. Madeline and I share the same birthday, right down to the year," Ken announced. "I think I told you that before, Mom."

"You're kidding; now that's really an odd coincidence," Danielle commented.

"I used to think that, too," Maddy agreed. "But now it just makes perfect sense."

Ken and Maddy shared a knowing smile before turning their attention back to the wonderful meal of pesto-encrusted salmon, rice pilaf, sautéed spinach and Caesar salad that Ken had expertly prepared.

"*Leather and Lace*?" Paula asked as she scrutinized one of the karaoke CDs that Danielle had given her with the unit.

"Stevie Nicks and Don Henley? It's a great duet from the 80's. Guess I wanted to relive my high school days," Danielle laughed. "But it's a really good song, Mom. In fact, everything on this CD is fantastic."

"I told her to go with Sinatra, but my wife wouldn't listen to me," Patrick joked. "But there's another one with various ballads. You might like something on that better, Mom."

"Your mother likes everything," Carl commented. "And I'm sure whatever Madeline performs will be wonderful."

"Uh-oh, I did agree to that didn't I? Maddy teased. Then with a revelation, she poked Kenny playfully in the ribs and said, "You know, *Leather and Lace* is a duet!"

"Yeah, so?" he joked, pretending to miss her meaning.

"So I think you and I should do a little entertaining together," she winked.

"Ah, no! I don't think so," he protested. "My job today was cooking dinner, Miss Rose. Your job is entertainment."

"Ok, I'll make you a deal," she bargained. "I will sing a solo first if you promise to sing a duet with me afterwards. Please, Kenny?" She implored him with her big, brown eyes and he found it impossible to refuse.

"Oh, ok," he promised, stroking her cheek. "Just don't expect me to sound good."

"Don't worry, I'll back you up," she said softly.

"Maddy," Danielle interrupted. "Can you sing this one?" She pointed to a beautiful Chantal Kreviazuk ballad that had been featured in a romantic comedy.

"Oh yes! That's one of my favorites, too," Madeline remarked. And a few minutes later, she found herself on a makeshift stage, performing *Feels Like Home to Me* for a captive audience.

Afterwards, the entire group sat in utter silence for a moment, completely spellbound by Madeline's powerful rendition of an already emotionally moving song. She sang with heartbreaking authenticity as if she herself had written and experienced the lyrics personally. And though she couldn't actually take credit for the words, they exquisitely portrayed her experience in the same profound way that only a handful of other ballads did.

Not surprisingly, the most affected audience member had been Ken, whose eyes teared up through the whole piece while they remained frozen upon her. Only the sound of robust clapping a minute later roused him from his reverie. Maddy blushed as she accepted their sincere compliments, feeling as if she was about to wake up to a blaring alarm clock to discover that this joyous occasion had simply been a product of her subconscious mind. That is, until Ken ran up and threw his strong arms around her. All of the sudden the rest of the room disappeared—at least until Mrs. Lockhart spoke up.

"Madeline, that was absolutely breathtaking."

"Aw, thanks," she repeated. As much as she appreciated the positive feedback, she'd never quite gotten comfortable with being the object of attention; it certainly defied the stereotype of "youngest child syndrome" with its need to be the center of the Universe.

"Ok, then," she added brightly, "I think it's time for Ken to entertain us."

"Whoa, you expect me to follow that?" he   protested.

"Hey, a deal's a deal," she teased.

Though he frowned at her in mock exasperation, he gladly took the microphone and joined her in a duet—a phenomenon that would soon define their lives in more ways than one.

Chapter 32

It felt like déjà vu as Maddy stood in the middle of her walk-in closet, contemplating her choice of attire for the special evening ahead—that is, with one notable exception. Sixteen years after her first date with Kenny, she'd finally achieved the figure she'd always dreamed of, thanks to functional training, a year-round outdoor lifestyle, natural therapies and, perhaps the most influential factor of all, her newfound ability to harness the power of her God-given imagination.

Unlike that faraway evening in Ocean City, her only problem tonight was making an ultimate decision between equally flattering styles, ranging from halter dresses with A-line skirts to sexy, strapless sheaths with accompanying bolero jackets. Fresh from a hot shower, she'd blow-dried her hair, and it fell in gradual waves far beyond her shoulders, barely reaching the strap of her ivory lace bra. Madeline patted her tummy now in admiration of its hard-earned muscle tone, which was evident from beneath her matching lace panties.

From the mysterious nature of Ken's earlier conversation, she sensed that this night had significant implications for their future. But it hadn't been that long since they'd reunited. Would he really ask her to marry him so soon? After all, she hardly even knew his children, though they certainly appeared to be well-adjusted, judging from the little bit of time she'd spent with them. And now that she was—gasp!—41 years old, it wasn't as if she felt compelled to wait for too much longer. If she and Ken had been strangers who'd just met, suddenly rushing to the altar based on nothing more than pure physical attraction that would be one thing; knowing each other for most of their adult lives was quite another.

"C'mon, Maddy, you've got a closet full of beautiful dresses that all fit you perfectly. Pick something already!" she admonished herself out loud. Just then the phone rang.

"Hello?"

"Please tell me you're wearing something sexy that I would approve of," Elyse ordered in a playful, yet serious tone.

"Ugh; I haven't decided, and he's going to be here any minute."

"Get it together girlfriend! I say you go with the gorgeous aquamarine halter dress with the rhinestone clasp and the short, flouncy hem. The gathers in the top make you look bigger where you need it, and the skirt shows off your nice legs. It's vixen-ish in a tasteful sort of way."

"You really think so?"

"Yes. Now, what are you doing with your hair?"

"Um, I was planning to wear it down. Debbie shaped it up a few days ago, so the layers are falling in perfectly."

"Sounds good. Oh and Maddy? Wear those strappy silver sandals and use your rhinestone clutch." Maddy cracked up.

"Why don't you just come over and dress me, Mom?"

"Hey, just tryin' to help; you know how excited I am for ya!" The effervescence in her tone validated the truth of her statement.

"I know, Elyse. You're an awesome friend, and I really appreciate you."

"You just make sure you call me if something interesting takes place."

"Like what? You know something I don't?"

"No, just a feelin' I have. You know me, I'm clairvoyant! Remember our night in Savannah?"

"How could I forget?" Maddy laughed at the memory of their "haunted" vacation a few years back.

"Ok, Mads, well hurry up and get dressed. This is going to be a huge night for you and Ken. I feel it in the air."

Ken buttoned his crisp, white shirt as he stared at his reflection in the mirror. It had been such a long time since he'd experienced this welcome mix of internal sensations: nervousness, excitement, arousal, and of course, authentic love and affection. As a much younger man about to pop the question to another woman, he couldn't quite recall the same energetic rush, though at the time, Erin had occupied a very special place in his heart. But now with Madeline, things were dramatically different—more mature, yet somehow more exuberant and fresh than they'd been back in their Jersey Shore days. The passage of time had only fueled greater desire and appreciation. Apparently, life really did begin after 40.

He studied his reflection for a moment, briefly entertaining the worrisome notion of Madeline somehow rejecting him this evening. Although older and wiser, Ken's natural ebullience had only grown stronger, recent trauma notwithstanding. There were still too many things that merited his gratitude, particularly being presented now with a second chance to get it right with her.

And as he checked himself out in his navy suit, perhaps a few pounds heavier than in his post-military stage, he was more than satisfied with his overall appearance. Besides, he noticed the smoldering look in Madeline's eyes when they first saw each other at the Samba Room on Las Olas that afternoon—it was the very same one that used to drive him mad back in Ocean City. Only this time she seemed much more relaxed and at-ease.

Striding over to the dresser, he picked up the blue velvet box containing the sparkling symbol of the next beautiful phase of their relationship. Lifting its lid, he stared at the breathtaking platinum, emerald-cut diamond ring with its braided design and complementing smaller stones. He couldn't exactly explain why he knew this was the ring for her, but when the jeweler presented it to him, something inside just spurred him on to make the purchase right then and there. As he gazed at it, he visualized the perfect scenario in which he'd proclaim his undying love and fidelity, prompting Madeline to jump into his arms and respond with a resounding "yes."

Slipping the box carefully into the inside pocket of his suit jacket, Ken grabbed his car keys and headed for the front door. He was halfway through the foyer when the phone rang. After a quick glance at the Caller ID, he decided to pick up.

"Hey, Mom."

"Hi, honey. I know you must be on your way out, but I just wanted to call and wish you luck—not that I think you'll need it."

He laughed.

"I hope not, but thanks for the good wishes."

"Ken, Madeline really is an amazing girl. Your dad and I liked her right away."

"I knew you would."

"Are you nervous?"

"A little, I guess."

"Don't worry, honey. She'll say yes—a woman knows these sorts of things. Besides, I saw the way she looks at you. She loves you truly. And from what I can tell, Bonnie and Brian are crazy about her, too."

"Well, she feels the same way about them. I just hope she can handle having to deal with Erin. You know what that's like."

"Ken, as long as you remember your priorities, you have nothing to worry about. Not even Erin will be able to ruin your happiness. Besides, she's too preoccupied with her millionaire sugar daddy to cause too many problems."

"I hope you're right, Mom," he said with resignation.

"Hey! You just focus this evening on you and Madeline. Don't worry about the kids; we're taking them to Guppy's for dinner and then over to Boomers to play miniature golf. And after Mass tomorrow, we'll take them out for breakfast. They love that. Just don't forget about the barbeque tomorrow afternoon."

"Oh, Maddy and I will be there, Mom. Hopefully as a newly engaged couple."

"Hello handsome," Maddy enthused, opening her front door to find her beloved outfitted in his Sunday best. But it was her favorite accessory—his signature, radiant smile—that took her breath away, in spite of the huge arrangement of fresh roses he held in his arms.

"Hey, beautiful." As soon as she closed the door behind him, he gathered her into his big, strong embrace. How was it possible that every time he saw her, she was even more desirable?

"Mm, those flowers smell wonderful!" she exclaimed as she accepted the bouquet.

"You look gorgeous, sweetheart," he remarked joyfully, taking in her appearance. Her sexy dancer's legs were set off nicely by the filmy, ethereal hem of her halter dress, which also showcased her porcelain smooth back and elegant neck.

"Thank you," she whispered, before reaching up to join his lips in a sweet kiss. As always, time seemed to stand still.

"Uh, Ken," she giggled, extricating herself long enough to speak, "I'd better get these into some water."

She took him by the hand and led him into the kitchen where she quickly searched for just the right vase. A moment later, the crimson blooms stood proudly on her glass dining room table, adding a contrasting splash of color to the French vanilla walls and pastel décor.

"Perfect," she declared with satisfaction.

"Like you," he added softly, taking her hands in his. Gazing up at him, she saw an extra twinkle in his eye.

"What's going on? I'm getting the distinct feeling there's something you're not telling me."

"Who me?" His tone was playful as he silently looked forward to the moment they'd both been anticipating for what felt like an eternity.

"You're not even going to give me a hint are you?" She teasingly poked him in the chest until pulled her close to him. Kissing the top of her head, he promised, "All things in good time. Trust me."

They settled into their private corner table in Arturo's Tuscan Room. The award-winning restaurant had long been on her list of South Florida places to experience someday, though she hadn't dreamed she'd ever share her first meal here with Ken. The romantic sounds of distinctively Italian music filled the air, along with the mouthwatering aromas of familiar cuisine. Glancing around the room, Maddy noticed some of the city's most well- known citizens sampling everything from flavorful veal scaloppini to creamy tiramisu, dressed in their finest designer duds.

While she relished the opportunity to dabble in some rare decadence, she couldn't help but suspect this was no ordinary evening. And when Ken asked their server to bring them a bottle of Asti Spumante, her curiosity was further piqued.

"So what are we celebrating? I mean, beside you and me." A slow smile spread across her face.

"Sweetheart, isn't that enough?" He pretended to be insulted.

"C'mon, you know it is Kenny. But there's something else going on that you're not telling me. I can feel it."

"You're right, I'm not telling you—yet." He winked at her.

"Ugh; you are such a tease." He just smiled before shifting his attention to the establishment's impressive menu.

"Well, that was delicious. Now I know what all the fuss is about," Maddy commented as they waited arm-in-arm for the valet under the canopy of the building's entrance. "My gosh, I am so full."

"You are? You hardly ate anything," he replied. "I practically finished your entire meal. You're not still worrying about food, are you?" He squeezed her shoulder as he spoke.

"Oh, no. I don't know why, but I just
had butterflies in my stomach tonight for some reason. Possibly because you're keeping me in suspense?"

She looked up at him with a hopeful expression, but he refused to take the bait.

"Nice try," he laughed. "But I'm not budging 'til it's time." With that, he took her hand and led her to the waiting white Lexus.

They cruised over the Spanish River drawbridge, heading east towards the beach. The blue velvet box rested against his chest, still snug and secure in its hiding place. He smiled to himself, imagining what was about to occur; from the speakers, the classic dance and love songs he'd recently burned onto a CD enhanced the scenery unfolding before them. And as they passed by hedges of tropical foliage, city parks, and quintessential condos, his heart began to race. Seemingly oblivious, she softly sang along to *The One*, remembering fondly their first slow dance as she rested her hand on top of his, which was occupying its usual place on her thigh.

"Hey," he said with sudden urgency, prompting her to turn her head to look at him. "I love you," he reminded her.

"I love you, too," she replied as he lifted her hand to his lips. "Are you ok?"

"Never better. Why?"

"You just seem so nervous. That used to be my role if you recall. Now I'm the calm one? That's quite a turnaround!" They both laughed hysterically.

"I guess I'm just seriously thankful to have another chance with you," he stated with sober conviction.

"Me too, Kenny," she reminded him. "I'd say we both have plenty of reasons to be grateful, starting with this beautiful night."

"The best is yet to come," he promised, pulling the car into a waiting space at the South Beach Pavilion on Palmetto Park Road and A1A—his chosen location for fulfilling a long ago promise.

The luminous full moon cast its shimmering beams on the calm, expansive sea as Ken and Madeline sat down on the wooden ledge that wrapped around the entire beachside structure. Though normally a densely crowded spot, given the late hour on a Saturday night—when most of the area's young adult population was busy bar-hopping either on Atlantic Avenue in Delray Beach or in downtown Fort Lauderdale—

they found themselves blissfully alone.

A light, balmy wind enveloped them as she rested her head in the crook of his arm and delighted in the warmth of his body. "I could stay here like this all night," she sighed.

"Me too," he agreed, holding her even closer. Beneath the fabric of his shirt, she felt the intense pounding of his heart.

Sitting up to face him, she asked, "Are you sure you're ok?" She took his face lightly in her hands as she spoke. "You're so preoccupied; is something wrong?"

"No, sweetheart," he whispered huskily. "That's just it—for the first time in forever, everything's right and I don't want to blow it. I guess I was waiting for the perfect moment, but I think it's here." With that, he abruptly stood up and, turning to face her, knelt down on one knee as shivers of excitement ran up and down her spine.

Taking her hands in his, he stared at her adoringly as he began. "Madeline, from the moment I first saw you sixteen years ago, I knew you were the one for me. Actually, from that night in the Key Largo parking lot when you absolutely refused to come back to my place three times—that was when I knew I wanted to marry you."

She smiled at the memory. He stroked her hair as he continued. "No other woman comes close to you—no one else has your innate sweetness, your incredible intelligence, and your stubborn determination. Over all of these years we spent apart, I thought of you so much. Oh, I tried to forget you, but I just couldn't. I've never known anyone as beautiful as you, Madeline, inside and out. And I know I don't really deserve a chance to make it up to you, but I'm hoping you'll let me anyway. Because if you agree to be my wife, I promise I will spend the rest of my days making sure you are happy, safe and loved."

He pulled the velvet box out of his jacket and opened its lid to reveal the identical ring from her treasure map, in all of its timeless, platinum glory; she gasped in awe at the sight of it.

"Madeline Rose, will you marry me?"

Completely at a loss for words, her brown eyes glistened with joyful tears as she watched this fervently desired miracle take place before her. There he was at last—her perfect match, her one, true love, pledging his eternal commitment with all of his heart and soul, along with the engagement ring she'd always wanted. Not something like it, but the actual one whose photo was glued to a montage of images on her bathroom mirror! How could this be? Yes, she believed in the principles she'd learned, but to have created everything exactly to her specifications? God sure was good.

And no matter how many times she'd envisioned this moment in her mind during regular intervals of tranquil meditation, the real thing far exceeded every detail of her highly advanced prayer time. Ken softly interrupted her internal reverie.

"Madeline?" he whispered, bringing his face close to hers. "Will you marry me?"

"H-how? How did you know that is the exact ring I've always wanted?"

"I know you," he replied simply. "But if you want to keep it you have to agree to marry me. Will you?" His blue eyes searched hers for an answer. Brought back to reality, she threw her arms around him.

"Yes! Yes, I'll marry you, Kenny!" She felt like heaven in his embrace as he buried his head in her hair. "I love you so much," she added.

"I love you, too, Madeline Rose."

Then remembering himself, he broke away to face her again. "So why don't we make it official?" He slid the dazzling stone onto her slender left finger, where it rested comfortably.

"Perfect," she marveled, unable to stop staring at it until he stood up and lifted her off the ground. He twirled her around boisterously for a few seconds before they melted into a passionate kiss—the first of many they'd share as a blissfully engaged and soon-to-be married, couple.

Chapter 33

Madeline smoothed her dress as she slid into the passenger side of Ken's white Lexus, still in a state of euphoria. Had she really just accepted his marriage proposal? With the glowing moon shining down on the ocean and the balmy breeze gently caressing them, it had felt like a dream. Despite her devotion to the principles of the prosperity course she'd taken, as evidenced by her countless hours spent   on treasure maps, meditation, journaling, and praying for her most desired manifestations, it still didn't feel quite real.

Still, it had taken her a long time to understand that the "perfect soulmate" she'd consistently visualized waiting for her in front of the altar had actually been Ken all along. And when the pieces began to come together at the beginning of this year, it felt like an answered prayer. Given their history, it was only appropriate that he'd chosen a seaside setting to pop the question.

But how could he have possibly known that the gorgeous platinum engagement ring on her left hand was the exact one from her treasure map? Other than Ann's crucial assistance with her panic and anxiety disorder, she'd never once delved into her metaphysical studies with him.

"You ok?" He kissed her hand as he settled into his seat.

"I'm just a little shocked—in a really good way."

"I told you a long time ago I was coming back to marry you, remember?"

"Yes, I remember," she assured him, thinking back to that cold winter night in Ocean City, and the two of them snuggled up in her twin bed. So much had transpired between then and now. "It's just—I still can't believe this is real. That all this time, it was you."

"Hey," he whispered, bringing their foreheads together. "I promise, I am going to spend the rest of my life making up for lost time; making it up to you for everything. I can't believe you still love me, Madeline. I am the luckiest man alive."

His eyes filled up as he gazed at her, tugging at her heart; she felt the warmth emanating from his chest as she laid her hands upon him. And while his words echoed with genuine emotion, Maddy knew beyond a doubt that their romance had evolved perfectly, if not according to what either of them had originally anticipated.

"I like the sound of that," she teased, earnestly studying his face before taking both of his hands in hers. "But there's nothing you have to make up for. Whatever you might think of this interesting road we've been traveling, it was exactly what we needed to get us to this point. We're both ready for this, now. The girl I was back then wouldn't have made you happy, not in the long run, even though she would've given it her very best. She was so unsettled, so unsure of herself..." her voice trailed off.

"And how is she now?" he asked softly.

"She's never been surer of anything in her entire life," Maddy smiled.

"Good," he replied, "She is definitely as beautiful as ever."

He traced the curve of her face as he spoke. "And if she thought this was the highlight of her evening, she should know that there's much more still to come—and a whole lifetime of happy memories ahead."

"Hmm, that's sounds promising," she teased. "But I don't know how anything can top a romantic marriage proposal by the sea."

"Well, you just settle in for the ride sweetheart. You'll find out soon enough."

He turned south on A1A, in the direction of the Camino Real drawbridge. The familiar sounds of Martina McBride serenaded them as they drove past the palatial homes, towering condos and ubiquitous palm trees that lined this lovely stretch of road. Not being much of a country music fan, he had grudgingly taken a liking to her favorite singer, in spite of his preconceived notions.

"Martina?" she inquired with a raised eyebrow.

"Yeah, well, she's pretty much the only country star I like, thanks to you. Besides, this is your night, and I want everything to be special."

"It's *our* night," she corrected him. He picked up her hand and kissed it as they approached the inlet; *There You Are* began to play, reminding

Maddy of yet another prosperity journal entry and visualization.

From the moment she'd first heard this beautiful ballad, she'd fantasized about it being her wedding song—the first dance shared between her and her future husband at their elegant evening reception. A celebration of an honorable, dependable man who loves his woman unconditionally, it resonated with Maddy, in the same way, Chicago's ballad, *Song for You*, always had. Whenever anyone would ask her about her ideal mate, she'd invariably tell them to play the famous rock band's classic song: it summed up her sentiments perfectly with an accompanying beautiful melody.

Ken headed west over the drawbridge; but instead of continuing halfway around the traffic circle and back onto Camino Real to Federal Highway, he made a right turn, much to Maddy's astonishment.

"The Boca Resort and Hotel? What are we doing here?"

"You'll find out in a minute." He hoped that the staff had arranged everything according to his instructions. A second later, he pulled up to the valet station, where a smiling, uniformed young man quickly appeared to open Maddy's door. As he assisted her, Ken came around and thanked him, slipping a few bills into his hands.

"Thank you, sir," the valet said appreciatively before driving the car to its designated space.

Giddy, ebullient and somewhat dazed, Madeline stared at her sparkling, emerald-cut ring with awe and gratitude while she held onto his arm with her other hand.

"Look at you, checking out that diamond," he laughed as they proceeded to the lobby.

"I still can't believe this is happening," she giggled, mostly out sheer joy, but also because of heightened anticipation of what was at last about to transpire between them.

Suddenly, she had a panicked thought. "I don't have anything with me!"

"Don't worry, you won't need anything." His tone was lighthearted and playful.

"Ken, it's not just that—what about my toiletries, my make-up and everything?"

"Relax, I have it's all taken care of."

The magnificent lobby greeted them with a medley of Spanish-style arches, Roman columns, marble floors, ornate chandeliers and strategically placed rows of lush, tropical plants. And though she had been here many times over the years for various charitable fundraisers, she'd never actually set foot in the main building of Boca Raton's most famous landmark. Never in a million years had she expected to walk through this celebrated space as Ken's fiancée, though this too, had been a visualization exercise.

As he checked them in, she stood nearby waiting. In spite of the late hour, she rummaged through her evening bag in search of her cell phone, realizing she hadn't yet shared her incredible news with her family. But just as she was about to dial, Ken took it out of her hands. Leaning in close, he whispered firmly in her ear.

"No, no. Tonight is all about us. We have plenty of time to make calls tomorrow, and I can't wait to tell everybody our wonderful news. But for now, I just want to focus on you and me. Please?"

She nodded her head in agreement and slipped the phone back into her purse as they walked arm-in-arm to the elevator. When the golden doors opened, he guided her inside and hit the PH button. As if supporting them in their desire to be completely alone, the doors immediately closed again, initiating a private journey to the top.

Pulling her into his arms, he assured her, "Don't worry about a thing. I've got it all covered, I promise!"

In between sweet kisses, she had a sudden flashback. "Doesn't this seem very familiar—you and me, riding a golden car all the way to the highest floor of a resort hotel?"

"Kind of like our first date at the Taj?" He smiled down at her.

"Exactly; it's that full-circle thing again."

"Except, this time, it's gonna be even better," he vowed.

When their ride came to an end, he ushered her into a small foyer, illuminated by an overhead crystal light fixture and defined by intricately carved cherry wood walls on either side. Beneath their feet, ceramic Italian tile created an appealing mosaic of muted floral design. Removing the key card from his pocket, Ken slipped it in and out of a brass slot located on the Penthouse's double doors. Turning the handle, he peeked into the room first. Satisfied with what he saw, he then took her by the hand and led her in.

She gasped at the breathtaking sight before her. The elegant suite was aglow in candlelight, thanks to a multitude of thoughtfully arrayed crimson and pink pillars of varying sizes. All around, her favorite flowers—red roses—decorated the space in sculpted glass vases, while the romantic melodies of an assortment of music, from popular love songs to soft rock and jazz, emanated subtly. Directly ahead, panoramic windows showcased a bright, full moon and a magnificent, tranquil ocean.

Clearly, he had spent many hours and hard-earned dollars to put an exquisite finishing touch on the happiest day of her life. Overwhelmed, Maddy hugged him tightly to her as her eyes filled with joyful tears.

"Y-you did all of this for me?"

Pressed closely against his body, she luxuriated in the irresistible warmth and unmistakable strength of his physique; the rhythm of his rapid heartbeat reverberated in her ear. It felt simultaneously safe, comforting, sensual and erotic.

"Madeline, you deserve all of this and so much more," he responded, raining kisses upon her forehead and neck. "I love you."

Raising herself on her toes to meet his gaze, she told him again how much she truly loved him, too, that she might have kicked him out of her mind for a good portion of her life, but never her heart.

And as they melted into another passionate kiss, his hands roamed her body, from her porcelain shoulders to her deliciously curvy hips. She massaged his back, neck and finally his chest, before starting to unbutton his shirt.

The heat radiated from his skin while his toned muscles rippled at her touch. At last in their "safe place," they couldn't seem to get enough of each other as their lips and tongues continued their joyful exploration.

Bonded together spiritually, mentally, emotionally and physically, the pain of the past melted away as she slid the white sleeves off of his shoulders and down his arms until the shirt fell to the floor. Staring at him in all of his glorious masculinity, Maddy was relieved to have been so incredibly disciplined about training.

But when Ken reached for the zipper of her dress, she was suddenly nervous. Sensing her anxiety, he stopped and, holding her face in his hands, gently asked if she felt ready to consummate their relationship.

"I want to be with you so much, Ken," she whispered. "It's just that I haven't since that awful experience with—ok, I won't mention the name, but I am a little nervous. It's not my first time, but it's my first time with you."

He chuckled, amused by her admission. "Well, the same is true for me. Do you have any idea how beautiful you are?"

She smiled. He always knew exactly what to say when she most needed to hear it.

"Come on," he whispered, lifting her into his arms. "I want to show you something."

He carried her into a gorgeous bedroom, where the cream-colored sheets of the queen-sized bed had been sprinkled with red and pink rose petals. On one nightstand sat a gift-wrapped box, adorned with hot pink ribbons and bows. Still holding her in his arms, he adjusted her on his lap as he sat down on the mattress and reached for the present.

"For you," he told her, with another smooch on the forehead.

"Something else? You are too good to me," she *protested* happily as she unwrapped the box and lifted the lid to reveal an exquisite pale-pink satin and lace short nightgown with matching robe.

"Oh my gosh, it's beautiful!" she exclaimed. "Thank you so much."

She buried her head in his neck as she hugged him.

"Madeline," he explained seriously, "Even if you are not ready to make love tonight, I just wanted you to sleep in something almost as beautiful as you."

"You are the most thoughtful man I've ever met."

"Why don't you go put it on," he suggested. Nodding her head, she reluctantly left his embrace. When she entered the spacious marble and tile bathroom, she was amazed to discover all of her favorite skincare and body products waiting for her. He hadn't been kidding when he said he'd remembered everything.

Stepping out of her flirty, feminine dress, she admired her hard-won body in the full-length mirror. Feeling fit and at-ease, Maddy took delight in her toned muscles, tiny waist, and hourglass shape, though she knew no matter what, Ken loved her for her. Good thing, because there was no way she would ever put anything artificial in her body like so many women in this town.

She pulled the flirty nighty over her petite frame and smiled as it draped stunningly over her figure; then she carefully stepped into the lacy briefs and added the robe to complete the ensemble, though she knew it probably wouldn't stay on for long. She brushed her windswept hair into soft, shiny waves, removed all traces of smeared mascara and lightly touched up her face. Once she'd cleaned her teeth, she felt more than ready to rejoin her love in the next room.

When she emerged, she found him by a bistro table, wearing sexy burgundy boxer's shorts and pouring two glasses of Asti. At the sight of her, his breath caught in his throat for a moment, just before he gave her an approving whistle.

"God, you are so beautiful," he enthused, handing her a flute of bubbly.

"You're pretty hot too," she replied, grinning.

"To second chances," he toasted, "and the road ahead of us."

"I'll drink to that," she laughed. Yet as she took in the sight of his muscles, she felt something more akin to an explosion of fireworks than good-natured humor.

"Kenny?"

"Yes?"

"I want you to make love to me tonight." His blue eyes sparkled at her.

"Are you absolutely sure?"

"Yes, I-I'm ready. I'm finally ready to be with you in every way. I want to show you how much I really do love you."

"I love you more than you'll ever know."

With that, he pulled her close to him, smothering her in kisses as he began to free her from the nightgown she'd just slipped into. Consumed by passion, she returned his advances with equal veracity, relishing the touch of his hands on her body and the subtle moves of his tongue in her mouth.

But when her silky negligee slid down her body and pooled around her feet, she suddenly buried her head in his chest and wrapped her arms tightly around him.

"What's the matter?" he whispered huskily, kissing the top of her head. Her skin felt like satin as he ran his hands up and down her bare back. Gently gathering her hair, he moved it to one side while his lips pursued her neck.

"Is this really happening?" Her voice was barely audible, though he could feel the intense pounding of her heart and the exquisite touch of her firm breasts against him. "I mean, if I'm dreaming, please don't wake me up."

He certainly understood how she felt, though his own obvious physical reaction to simply kissing and holding her eliminated all doubt as to the wonderful reality of the situation. In this long-awaited moment, the only thought occupying Ken's mind was how badly he wanted to show her what it truly meant to be loved and cherished.

While he looked forward to a lifetime of making love to her, he recognized the significance of their very first union and wanted this night to be worthy of every fantasy either one of them had ever envisioned. And as they stood there, surrounded by glowing candles and red roses, it appeared that promise was well on its way to fulfillment.

"Hey," he whispered, taking her face in his hands and gently compelling her to look up at him. Even in the subdued light, she noticed the moisture in his sparkling azure eyes and the sincerity of his expression.

"Madeline, I love you so much. I've always loved you. This is as real as it gets, sweetheart. I can't erase the past, but I'm here now, and I'm not going anywhere. Besides, you accepted my proposal, so that means you're stuck with me forever. And that's all I've ever wanted."

As they stood there holding each other in this present moment, she wished she could somehow freeze time as she rested her hands on his broad chest and admired the sparkling diamond ring that now adorned her left finger. Every hardship she'd overcome had led to this exquisite place.

There was absolutely nothing she would change about a past that had prepared her to be his devoted wife, lover, friend, and companion. She'd battled her demons and won; God's timing could not have been more perfect. She realized now, that if they had gotten married back then, their union might very well have ended in divorce—or worse, transformed into a cauldron of simmering resentment with each of them feeling shortchanged by the other's unwillingness to support a dream.

Would she have cheerfully relocated with him to Florida at age 25? The odds were highly unlikely. And yet, without him, she never would have embarked upon a path of spiritual growth that would eventually yield a satisfying career, excellent health, an amazing network of friends and a comprehensive soul-healing.

Whether he'd known what he was doing or not, Ken had acted as her ideal catalyst, forcing her to confront the darkest places inside and conquer her most menacing fears.

"Kenny, I love you, too. I've loved you ever since the night we met. And now...now that we're finally here, just the two of us, committed to a new life together, I am just thankful to have a second chance."

"Me too, Madeline," he confessed. She raised

herself up on her toes as he leaned down to meet her lips, igniting both of their passions. Their kiss began gently and slowly at first, before taking on a heated rhythm as his tongue hungrily sought out hers. She responded with matching fervor, feeling the familiar sensations flood her body.

His hands traveled down her back to her waist and back up through her long, satiny hair. Then they moved around to her sculpted torso, inching ever closer to breasts that ached to be touched, yet still caused her slight embarrassment. And though her reaction was subtle, he felt her tense up in his arms. That's when he moved away slightly to look at her— all of her, in the soft glow of candlelight. Maddy turned her gaze downward.

"Hey," He spoke in a comforting, yet firm tone. When she still didn't look up, he cupped her chin in his hands and brought them face to face again. "You are the most beautiful woman in the entire world to me. Everything about you is exquisite. Don't you see that? Don't you see what you do to me?"

Before she could answer, he placed her hand on his heart, which was beating rapidly. Slowly, he guided her down his body, all the while maintaining eye contact.

She felt electricity pulsating within her as his tangible muscle tone and hypnotic warmth were revealed beneath her touch. He stopped once he'd lead her to the essence of his manhood—hard and throbbing now with pure desire. She sensually stroked him through the soft fabric of his boxer's shorts as he continued to caress her back.

"That feels so good," he began to moan softly. "I want you so much."

"I want you too. Please make love to me."

With that, he lifted her up in his arms and carried her to the plush queen-sized bed covered in rose petals. He'd done everything in his power to ensure that this night was absolutely perfect for Madeline, a woman for whom his enduring love was matched only by his immeasurable pride.

He gently placed her back on her feet while he continued to taste the sweetness of her mouth and the softness of her skin. His hands roamed over the pale pink lace of her lingerie panties, delighting in every curve of her body. Consumed by desire, he slowly inched closer and closer to her, until all she could do was lay back on the bed.

Staring at this vision of Madeline—auburn hair fanned out against the opulent Egyptian sheets, warm brown eyes that seemed to penetrate his own and enticing hourglass figure displaying firm, beautiful breasts and alluring, shapely legs—it took every bit of self-control to slowly savor every facet of their long-awaited conjugal union.

He eased himself carefully on top of her as she welcomed him into her arms, immersing herself in the seductive scent of his spicy aftershave. And though there was no moonbeam shining down on them from an overhead skylight, through the floor-to-ceiling windows just beyond the foot of the bed, the stars twinkled brightly over the ocean and the Intracoastal Waterway.

"Hi beautiful," he whispered, smiling at her in his inimitable fashion. After all these years, it still sent shivers down her spine. "I can't believe we're actually here." He traced her cheek with his fingers as he spoke.

"Me, either," she softly sighed. "Or that you asked me to marry you after all this time."

"But I did," he smiled again. "And thank God, you accepted."

"Did you honestly think I wouldn't?"

"I don't know; I just didn't want to take anything for granted, so I prayed hard for you to say 'yes.' And lucky for me—and my children, you did."

"We're going to do it right this go-around, I promise. And I promise I will love Bonnie and Brian as if they were my own—but I won't step on any toes." Thoughts of Erin briefly clouded her mind.

"Hey," he gently chided her. "Tonight is about you and me. I think we deserve an evening to ourselves to properly celebrate our reunion. In every way," he added sexily, nibbling her neck while his hands sensually roamed her body. Still, she spared a moment for humor.

"You know, Kenny, I'm pretty sure this is the longest run to home plate in history."

He laughed softly, bringing his face close to hers again. "You really are something else, you know that?"

"Yeah, well, don't you forget it," she teased, before passion took over again.

As the sultry sounds of their favorite music mingled with the glowing illuminations of burning candles and the enticing scent of fresh roses, Ken and Madeline were swept away in a powerful tide of lust and longing. Yet even as their bodies passionately sought the satisfaction that could only be found in each other's arms, neither one could dismiss the miracle of this eagerly anticipated moment—the welcome fruition of their individual spiritual journeys.

"I'd say this song is appropriate," she whispered in his ear as Vanessa Williams' *Save the Best for Last* began to play. He'd been slowly savoring every inch of her, kissing and licking his way down from her forehead to her lips to her neck, while she caressed his chest and shoulders.

Pausing to look her deeply in the eye, he promised, "You haven't seen anything yet, sweetheart."

"Please remember what we talked about before," she reminded softly. "If it doesn't happen, if I don't have one, please know that I am completely happy just being this close to you. Nothing else matters."

"I know, I know. But I won't stop until you're totally fulfilled." His words were a firm and sexy promise.

"But I am right now," she protested.

"Madeline," he whispered, placing his fingers on her lips. "I think it's about time we both stopped talking. We can discuss an encore performance later."

Chapter 34

With Eric Clapton's *Wonderful Tonight* playing unobtrusively in the background, Ken and Madeline at last discovered the indescribable joy of becoming one in every sense of the word. Infused with a timeless energy borne of genuine love and affection at the deepest level, it was as if neither one of them had aged—though both had certainly matured since their star-crossed meeting at the Key Largo club sixteen years prior.

And when the precise moment for their union arrived—sometime after Ken had accomplished what no other man had, exhilarating them both—he paused first to look deeply into her amber eyes. Carefully adjusting his weight as he lay on top of her, he placed his hands on either side of her face; flush with color now from the excitement of what had just transpired. She felt as if she'd been lifted to the heavens, still floating around on a cloud of pure enchantment.

"Hey," he whispered, smiling down at her. "Feel good?"

"If I felt any better, I don't think I could stand it." She stroked his hair and the back of his neck as she spoke. "You're amazing, you know that?" her voice was soft. "I always knew you were the only man for me, and this just proves it. You're the only one I feel completely comfortable with; the only one who's ever loved me unconditionally." A single tear began to trickle down her rosy cheek.

Wiping it away gently, he comforted her. "Well, this is only the beginning of a lifetime of happiness. I plan to spend the rest of my days being the kind of man and husband you deserve. I love you, sweetheart."

"I love you." They exchanged a sweet kiss on the lips.

"Kenny?"

"Yes?"

"I want to do something for you, too," she smiled mischievously as she guided him onto his back.

"Really?" He played along, as thoughts of Madeline pleasuring him nearly drove him over the edge. Now settled comfortably on top of his chest, she whispered closely in his ear.

"Really," she repeated seductively, before smothering him with kisses, beginning on his forehead and working her way down to his lips and neck. He moaned softly as he ran his hands through her hair, relishing the feel of her against him as she slid further and further down his body.

As wave after wave of electrifying sensations rushed through his body, he suddenly grabbed her by the shoulders and pulled her back up to his face, feeling every part of her skim over his being as he did so.

"Was that ok?" Her voice was barely audible while her brown eyes searched his for an answer.

Placing a hand behind her head to bring her even closer, he whispered, "Madeline, you are absolutely incredible," before placing his lips on hers again.

A bold, orange sun began its ascent above the horizon, its luminous rays dancing on the turquoise ocean and warming up the endless stretch of beige-colored sand that defined Florida's Gold Coast. Nearby, the landmark pink tower came alive as resident speedboats, yachts and sailboats smoothly transitioned out of their slips and into the Intracoastal waters, initiating their journey to the crystalline sea. For those fortunate enough to live such a lifestyle, it was simply another day in Paradise.

But as the golden beams flooded through the panoramic windows and gauzy curtains of the Penthouse, gently rousing them from the sweetest of dreams, Ken and Madeline awoke with a sense of overwhelming gratitude and awe for the miracle of this brand new morning. She'd drifted off with her head resting on his chest, his corded arms wrapped protectively around her. Warmed by the heat emanating from his body, she'd hardly noticed that the Egyptian sheets had been relegated to the end of the bed, scattering rose petals all over the thick, Berber carpet.

She blinked open her sleepy eyes and smiled when she caught sight of her sparkling ring decorating the hand that rested comfortably on top of her fiancés.

Fiancé.

Ken, a man who up until a short time ago hadn't even been physically present in her life, was now her fiancé. *Wow.* That took some getting used to, but what a wonderful adjustment to have to make. As she silently thanked God for this incredible gift of a second chance, she felt his stimulating caresses up and down her shoulder.

"Mm, good morning sunshine," he murmured in his gravelly, early-morning voice.

"Good morning," she replied softly as he began to stroke her hair.

"Sleep well?"

"Mm-hm," she replied emphatically. Then in a teasing tone asked, "I wonder why?"

"Yes, I wonder," he played along. With that, he pulled her close to him, shifting her so that they were now lying torso-to-torso, their faces inches apart. He smiled at her dotingly as he recalled the previous night's wondrous events.

"You know, you are an incredibly beautiful, loving woman," he remarked.

"And you are an unbelievably considerate, affectionate man." Then after a brief pause, she went on.

"Kenny?"

"Yes?"

"I never dreamed I could be this happy. I mean—yeah, I dreamed about it, about this, the two of us—a lot. I guess I just never imagined that the real thing would far exceed anything I could conjure up."

"Well, you know what they say, baby. Ain't nothin' like the real thing!" They laughed before passion took over once again.

"Yaki! Tootsie!" Elyse called out to the couple she'd come to regard as her adoptive parents, addressing them by their pet names. She was standing in the baggage claim area of Terminal Four at the Fort Lauderdale International Airport. As usual, she'd been running late, but thankfully, the Sunday morning traffic had been fairly light. She'd no sooner consulted the airport's monitors to confirm their flight's on-time arrival when she caught sight of them coming down the escalator.

"Hey-hey, Elyse how are ya?" Joseph Rose replied with his trademark enthusiasm as he stepped off of the moving stairs, his wife closely behind. They all exchanged an affectionate greeting, during which Elyse inquired about their flight as well as the whereabouts of the rest of their group.

"Oh, the boys had to stop off in the men's room," Monica laughed. "Little Greg couldn't wait any longer, so Uncle Louis took him. Big Greg and Lori are with them."

"Is everybody excited?" Elyse asked, grinning from ear to ear.

"Oh my God, we're all so happy. This is like a miracle. Have you spoken to Maddy at all? I thought for sure she'd call me with the good news, but she probably figured it was too late last night. Then, of course, we left at the crack of dawn to catch our plane."

"Uh no, not yet, but I assume she had a late evening and was too busy celebrating to call me." She smiled, purposely omitting the part of the agenda involving the Boca Resort.

"Well, thanks for coming to get us, sweetie," Monica said, placing an arm around her as they strolled over to the luggage carousel.

"Get out, it's my pleasure," Elyse enthused. "I'm just so thrilled for Maddy and of you."

"Who would've thought after all this time, it was Ken," Joseph remarked. "I always did like that young man from way back in Ocean

City. I never quite understood what happened, since he's the   reason my daughter moved away in the first place. Guess the timing wasn't right until now."

"Well, I'm just relieved to see her finally settling down with the right guy," Monica added. "As a parent, you want to leave this world knowing your kids are taken care of." Then remembering Elyse's recent tragedy, "Oh honey, I'm so sorry." She patted Maddy's beautiful blonde friend on the shoulder.

"No worries, Tootsie. Today is all about Madeline and Kenny. I want to celebrate them."

"Sounds good to me!" Joseph laughed, eager to change the subject. Now a retired neurosurgeon, it still pained him deeply that modern medical science had been unable to save Elyse's nephew from the ravages of brain cancer. He couldn't even fathom his reaction had it been—God forbid—one of his grandchildren. As if on cue, little Greg came running up from behind, throwing his arms around his "Pop."

"Hey big guy, where's your father, uncle, and aunt?"

"Right here, Dad," Lori replied. "Hey Elyse, how are you?" The two women exchanged a hug before Greg and Louis followed suit.

"Ok, looks like the gang's all here," Elyse proclaimed before Lori pulled her aside and asked if she'd heard from her little sister.

"Not yet, so I'm assuming it was a good night," she whispered with a wink and a nod. "Ken would've called me if something had gone wrong. Besides, does anyone here actually believe she'd turn down his proposal anyway?" They both giggled.

"Nah, I don't think so," Lori concurred.

"So, weren't Lyle and Daphne supposed to be on this flight originally?" Elyse inquired.

"Yes, but you know them—always a story," Monica responded with a slight trace of sarcasm. "Let's just say they are on the Noon departure out of Philly now. They should land by three, but they're going to take a cab to the Lockhart's place." Elyse's face clouded over.

"Oh no! Surely someone can pick them up. I'll be happy to do it if you need me to."

"Don't be silly," Monica admonished. "It was nice enough of you to come down here early on a Sunday morning to get all of us. You're Maddy's closest friend, and I don't want you missing out on any of the festivities, especially when you've already done so much for her."

"Well, I talked to Paula yesterday, and she was pretty excited. We've had a ball putting this together—it was, even more, fun than planning your surprise arrival at her birthday party last year. Wait until you meet her, she's such a sweet lady."

"I can't wait to see the look on Maddy's face when she sees all of us," Louis giggled as a loud buzzer alerted them to the impending arrival of their bags on the rotating carousel.

"So, when are we going to tell the kids?" Maddy asked, raising a fresh cup of aromatic coffee to her lips. They were seated at a table for two in the Cathedral restaurant of the resort's Cloister building, amid vaulted ceilings, picture windows, and Roman columns.

"Well," he began, covering one of her hands with his, "to be honest, I kind of already did. I mean, when you came back into my life—when I knew you were still a free woman, there was no way I was ever going to let you go again. Even before we laid eyes on each other, I knew from just hearing your voice, I was going to do everything in my power to make you mine, forever.

"But, now as a father, I realized I also had two other very important people to consider. So, once I felt secure in your feelings for me, I began to prepare Bonnie and Brian."

"Prepare them how?" Her voice was soft as she contemplated the changes ahead for his two innocent children. While she reveled in her newfound happiness, Madeline wished it didn't have to come at the expense of their parents' marriage, though its failure rested squarely on Erin and Ken. She'd long ago done the honorable thing by staying as far away as possible, once apprised of their legal commitment; it was only very recently that Ken had even come to mind, thanks to Ann, and by then, the damage had already been done. Still, at ages 10 and five, Bonnie and Brian could hardly be expected to understand the intricacies of an adult world.

Maddy listened with undivided attention as he relayed the countless hours prior to the divorce spent talking with them about first and foremost, his unending love and continued devotion to their needs. Rather than criticize their mother, he gently explained that while both parents would always be there for them, it had become impossible for either one to live together as husband and wife. When an astute Bonnie had inquired if it had anything to do with "Mommy's surgery," it basically broke his heart.

"Maddy, you know the kind of man I am. None of that superficial stuff matters to me. Look, I did love Erin, and I just wanted her to be happy. That's why I never stood in her way—not that I would've been successful at talking her out of it in the first place. She'd gotten so caught up the scene around here, hanging out with women who undergo plastic surgery practically as a hobby; there was no reasoning with her." She noted the wistfulness in his voice, along with the sad truthfulness of that statement.

"And then one day I woke up and realized I didn't even know her anymore." They both paused while their waiter presented them with their entrées—a Greek omelet for her and Eggs Benedict for him, each served with a side of fresh, ripe berries and old-fashioned oatmeal.

"Looks great, huh?" he enthused, relieved to shift his attention to something much more uplifting.

"Sure does," she agreed, although she also acknowledged it was quite a bit more than she could handle in one sitting.

"You just enjoy it, sweetheart," he urged her, before adding seductively, "You did work up an appetite, you know." She blushed.

"Uh, you too," she shot back, coyly. Then after noticing that their waiter was safely out of earshot, she focused back on their serious discussion.

"Well, I have to admit, Bonnie and Brian seem remarkably adjusted to the divorce, as far as I can tell. I'm sure that has a lot to do with the fact that you continued to live there for so long. And, don't get me wrong, I am really excited about being a part of their lives. But I am a little nervous about it, too. I mean, it is one thing for them to accept the divorce; it's entirely another to accept me as their father's new wife."

"You worry too much, you know that?" His tone was gentle, though his words caused a somewhat defensive reaction.

"I'm serious."

"So am I," he replied soberly. "I've had many discussions with them about my intention to ask you to marry me, and they were absolutely thrilled about it. They think you're awesome, just as I do."

"Really?"

He reached across the table and laid his hand on top of hers. "Really," he repeated, holding her gaze. "Everything is going to be fine, you'll see. I am not going to promise you it will always be easy. I'm not saying it won't be a big adjustment because it definitely will. And I know on paper, this is not what you would've preferred—a divorced guy with two young kids. Maybe it's not fair for me, after all of these years, to ask you to take us on. But I swear to you, I will stand beside you the entire way; you will always have my support. No one and nothing will ever come between us again; I won't allow it. Not after having the incredibly good fortune of finding you again. I love you, Maddy. Don't ever doubt that."

His earnest plea melted her heart even as she silently admitted to some lingering insecurities where Erin was concerned. "Kenny," she began, "I know now how much you love me, how much you've always loved me. And I also trust that you will stand by me, no matter what. I would never have accepted your proposal if I thought otherwise. It's just that—well, how does Erin feel about all this, do you know? As their mother, I am sure she has an opinion. And if I recall, she didn't like me very much way back when, although I can hardly hold that against her. Had I been in the same position, I probably would have reacted the same way."

"You still remember that barbeque? Oh God, that feels like a lifetime ago. You're right, I can honestly tell you now she was less than thrilled by your presence, but it wasn't a personal thing. I guess that should've been my first clue to call off the wedding; even Erin could plainly see the unresolved energy between us."

"I remember she excused herself and went to bed early. After I left that night, I vowed never to call or see you again. I don't why I thought I was strong enough to just—poof!—transition into being friends, while watching you give your love and devotion to another woman. I was so overwhelmed by everything—adjusting to a different state, making new friends, trying to get my bearings—I guess my judgment was all screwed up."

"I never should have expected you to just segue into being my buddy. And to actually hope that you and Erin could be friends, so she could have a social life outside of me. That really wasn't fair to you. I'm sorry."

"Hey, it's all behind us, now. And we've both forgiven each other for the mistakes of the past. All I'm concerned about now is how to create some kind of civil relationship with her for the sake of our marriage and your children."

"Oh, she'll be civil to you if I have anything to say about it. Besides, she's all caught up in her romance with a retired CEO, an older guy with lots of cash. They're the typical Boca couple—he buys her everything she wants, and she provides him with the eye candy he needs to satisfy his ego."

"I can't think of anything more unsatisfying," Maddy sighed.

"That's 'cause you're one in a million. Now stop worrying and finish your breakfast. Today is all about celebrating, and there's a lot more ahead."

They toasted coffee cups to their new life together, before digging into the fabulous meal spread out before them.

Chapter 35

Surprise!" A chorus of loud, jubilant voices greeted Madeline as she walked into the sunlit expanse of Ken's ceramic-tiled living room, which was decorated festively with hot pink and red balloons, vivid arrangements of exotic, tropical flowers and a massive, professionally made banner bearing the words, "Congratulations, Ken, and Madeline."

An awestruck Maddy nearly collapsed into his arms as he instinctively wrapped them around her waist and kissed her temple. Scanning the gathered crowd, she noted some familiar faces, including her beloved nieces and nephews, just before her parents rushed over to welcome her.

"Oh my God, Mom! Dad! When did you guys get here?" She kissed and hugged each of them tightly before her three youngest nieces squealed for her attention. "My girls!" Maddy exclaimed. "It's so good to see you!"

She knelt down to embrace three-year-old Sofia, six-year-old Julianna, and eight-year-old Alexa. As usual, they looked absolutely adorable in matching white eyelet dresses with pink sashes and coordinating sandals.

"We got in this morning," Joseph replied excitedly, "Your good friend Elyse picked us up at the airport."

"Let me see your ring, honey!" Mom requested happily before Maddy held out her left hand. Taking it in her own, Monica gasped with admiration. "Oh my God, Ken that is magnificent. I've never seen anything like it before," she complimented.

"Well, nothing but the best for my girl," Ken replied smiling as he and Maddy exchanged a knowing wink.

"By the way, Mr. Lockhart, I take it you were in on this?" she teased him.

"Damn right," he laughed, just as his parents came over to embrace both of them.

"Congratulations," Paula said. "Madeline, it's a pleasure to welcome you to the family," she added, pecking her future daughter-in-law on the cheek before Carl did the same.

"Oh my gosh, the pleasure is all mine," she assured them.

"And we feel the same about you, Ken," Mrs. Rose stated affirmatively, reaching up to hug him. "It's been a long, long road, but we're so pleased that you and Maddy have found your way back to each other. We're so proud of both of you."

"Thank you, Mrs. Rose," Ken responded genuinely.

"Hey uh Ken, pretty soon you'll have to get used to calling us Mom and Dad," Joseph teased.

"That's great with me," he laughed, just as Bonnie and Brian ran up and threw their arms around him.

"Daddy!" Their unbridled excitement was evident for all to see as their father knelt down to talk with them. It warmed Maddy's heart to witness such a joyful reaction to the news.

And as the moments unfolded, so did endless surprises as Maddy encountered one beloved family member and friend after the other while she happily maneuvered through the assembled crowd. Even Elyse had been stunned by the presence of Lyle and Daphne, who'd rented a mini-van, along with Cassie, her husband, David, and son, Matthew. Though the seasoned small aircraft pilots would've preferred to have taken a commercial flight, they'd generously agreed to share the drive and the cost of the vehicle with the aerophobia sufferers.

The group had arrived on Ken's doorstep late Friday evening, where they'd hung out unobtrusively, enjoying the pool and easy access to the beach, while Ken kept Maddy away with tales of work obligations and a parent-teacher conference at Bonnie's elementary school. Though she'd thought it strange that such an event would take place on a Friday night, a trusting Maddy had gone to Baja Café for dinner with an unsuspecting Elyse and Billy followed by a movie at the Premier Theater at Muvico Palace.

Monica had perpetuated the charade as late as that morning, brushing off Elyse's inquiries with feigned condescension as she fabricated a story about Lyle and Daphne having to take a Noon flight. Likewise, she'd kept Maddy's good friend in the dark about Vanessa and the girls, and Vince and the two boys—all of whom had taken the Noon flight from Philly to Fort Lauderdale, where Ken had graciously arranged limo pick-up back to his home. Determined to execute the surprise flawlessly, Mrs. Rose believed that the fewer people who knew, the better; judging from her daughter's reaction, her decision had been vindicated. It thrilled her to witness an elated Maddy interact with her cherished siblings, cousins, nieces, and nephews.

Most importantly, she was overcome with genuine relief and gratitude for her youngest child's long-awaited engagement and subsequent marriage to her Prince Charming. As a concerned mother, she'd spent infinite hours in quiet contemplation in the Church sacristy, praying earnestly for God to grant Madeline her heart's desire, to send the absolute right one into her life—a man who would love her unconditionally, faithfully and eternally.

And God willing, Monica would always add a special plea for her own health and ability to witness the blessed event before ever joining her dearly missed sister in the next world. While it saddened her that Maria wasn't physically present to partake in the festivities for her favorite niece, she knew beyond a doubt that her presence—along with their mother, Madeline, and the rest of their departed loved ones, was filling the room with an undeniable peace and welcome reconciliation.

"Excuse me, everyone," Ken suddenly piped up, clearing his throat.

"Does everybody have a glass of champagne or Asti? I know this is technically a barbeque but it's still a celebration, and I want to make a proper toast."

As Maddy walked up beside him, he placed an arm about her. Looking around the room, she saw a multitude of happy faces beaming back at them, including Carolyn, Robin, Elyse and Billy, Audrey and her husband José, Damian and Laura, Greg and Vanessa, Vince and Lori, Louis and everyone who'd supported, loved and guided her over the years.

It was especially gratifying to watch all of the kids interact so easily, welcoming Bonnie and Brian as if they'd always been a part of the family. The teenaged twins, Tommy, and Ava, were immensely enjoying their roles as unofficial babysitters, happily tending to their two younger siblings as well as their cousins, both new and familiar.

"A long time ago," Ken began, "I agreed to hang out with a beautiful woman in a nightclub in Somers Point when she refused to be a fifth wheel and tag along with two other couples to Atlantic City."

Everyone laughed as Ken kissed her on the forehead. Just prior to the toast, Mom had relayed Carmen's good wishes; now happily married to her college sweetheart, she was living in Colorado and unable to join them, though she planned to come to the wedding. Maddy had noted how strange and wonderful it was that the most seemingly inconsequential decisions could have such a dramatic impact; little did she know back then that one weekend getaway to Ocean City, New Jersey would lead to such an amazing spiritual journey and the realization of an eternal love.

"Well you all know Madeline," Ken went on, "Nobody makes her do anything. But lucky for me, she wanted to stay at Key Largo and dance with me. In fact, if I remember correctly, she basically threatened to leave if I didn't shut up and dance." His tone was playful; the appreciative crowd lapped up the story as they listened with genuine interest.

"That's very true!" she confirmed, smiling.

"But within minutes I realized just how fortunate I'd been to run into such an incredible woman," he continued seriously, turning to gaze into her eyes for a moment. "And before the night was over, I knew I was going to marry her eventually, though I have to admit, I didn't think it would be sixteen years later!"

The room erupted into laughter again as he planted a quick kiss on her lips. "But I'd do it all again in a heartbeat if it meant arriving at the same outcome," he added.

"Me, too," she whispered.

He smiled at her as he raised his glass.

"So," he stated exuberantly, "Here's to the priceless gift of second chances, the power of forgiveness and the grace of God that can conquer even the most stubborn of human flaws. I am incredibly thankful and humbled that He's brought Madeline back into my life and given us an opportunity to begin anew, surrounded by the love of our family and friends. And I promise all of you right now, I plan to spend the rest of my days making her happy. For some reason, even though I was unbelievably dumb in the past, God saw fit to lead us to this place, to bring us back together. And I will never, never take this precious gift for granted."

Every face in the room was misty as they witnessed a miracle unfold before their eyes, renewing their faith and filling them with indescribable joy.

Epilogue

The Amalfi Coast, Italy

From an ornate, rounded balcony, Madeline gazed out at the azure blue sea, framed by lush, verdant mountains and steep, rocky crags. Behind her, white, gauzy curtains billowed in the breeze through the open French doors. She closed her eyes for a moment, luxuriating in this exquisite natural beauty while her mind recalled the miraculous events of the past year that had culminated in a blissful, eternal union. Lost in a prayer of thanksgiving, she was slightly startled for a second when she felt Ken's arms wrap around her waist.

Fresh from a revitalizing hot shower, he'd covered himself with a thick, thirsty towel, his blond waves still slightly damp. And as he walked back into the expansive bedroom suite, he caught sight of his beloved, dressed in a flowing, lacy nightgown, accented with pale pink satin ribbons. He smiled remembering how beautiful ocean vistas had always captivated her, since their very first date in Atlantic City; no doubt she was lost in her own world as she contemplated the personal journeys that had led them to this magnificent point in time.

"Good morning," she cooed, as a flood of sensation engulfed

her. Ken placed one hand on her shoulder while the other gathered her hair to one side. Leaning in close, he whispered sexily in her ear, "Are you happy?"

She turned around to gaze up at him and affirmed, "I didn't even know it was possible to be this happy." Around her neck, the diamond-cut Pisces pendant shimmered against her skin. "I'm just so grateful to God for this second chance, for bringing you back to me. It's nothing short of a miracle. And no matter where we are or what we're doing, as long as I'm with you, I will always be happy. I love you so much."

He gently brushed away a lone tear that had trickled down her sunburned cheek. "I love you, Madeline Lockhart. And it is a miracle; I am thankful to God, too, first for creating you and then giving you back to me, in spite of everything."

"Divine timing is always perfect," she replied softly as she stroked his face.

"Yes it is," he concurred, before scooping her up in his arms and carrying her back inside, while the sunlight glistened on the water and the fish swam joyfully, immersed in the depths below.

About The Author

Author, ghostwriter, blogger, editor, and social media professional Daria Anne DiGiovanni released the first edition of her novel *Water Signs: A Story of Love and Renewal* in 2008 to a receptive audience. Since then, she's consulted with a variety of clients on ghostwriting, editing, and independent publishing projects ranging from historical fiction to memoirs, utilizing her many years of marketing, recruiting, and communications in the corporate world. From 2009 – 2013, she co-hosted *Conservative Republican Forum* on Blog Talk Radio and in March of 2013 created the *Writestream Radio Network* with Lisa Tarves, where she hosts *Writestream Tuesday*. Daria Anne and Lisa launched their independent publishing company, *Writestream Publishing LLC* in June of 2015 and have released nine titles under the *Writestream* imprint to date. When not working, Daria Anne enjoys spending time with family and friends — preferably on the sunny Florida Space Coast where she makes her home.

Visit her at:
www.dariadigiovanni.com,
www.writestreampublishing.com
www.writestreamradio.com.

www.ingramcontent.com/pod-product-compliance
Lightning Source LLC
Chambersburg PA
CBHW051431260626
47162CB00001B/48